"Hi Cooper."

I stiffened and turned. The voice was that of a man I recognized as soon as I saw him: Lou Chieppa, the greaseball hood who had held a knife to my throat in Philly and told me the big man was Napolitano, Ice Cream, not the Chef. This morning he was dressed in cutoff shorts and a blue Izod shirt.

He stood, legs apart, menacing me with that ugly switchblade I had seen before.

"Careful Lou. He's no pushover," muttered Filly.

"Heh-heh, heh-heh. Pushover. Yeah, push him over is exactly what I'm going to do. Just stand clear, Fil."

Filly. She'd set me up. My God, how long had they been planning this?

I looked at her and shook my head. I'd been *stupid*!

The bitch smirked.

Chieppa moved forward, cautiously, on the balls of his feet.

They'd made a fatal mistake. . . .

Forge Books by Harold Robbins

The Predators
The Secret
*Never Enough**

*forthcoming

HAROLD ROBBINS

THE
SECRET

A TOM DOHERTY ASSOCIATES BOOK
NEW YORK

This is a work of fiction. All the characters and events portrayed in this book are either products of the author's imagination or are used fictitiously.

THE SECRET

Copyright © 2000 by the Estate of Harold Robbins

A Forge Book
Published by Tom Doherty Associates, LLC
175 Fifth Avenue
New York, NY 10010

www.tor.com

Forge® is a registered trademark of Tom Doherty Associates, LLC.

ISBN: 0-812-57179-7

First edition: April 2000
First mass market edition: June 2001

Printed in the United States of America

0 9 8 7 6 5 4 3 2

THE
SECRET

1

LEN

We were not supposed to play cards for money in our dorm rooms. We were not supposed to drink or smoke. We were not supposed to have copies of *Playboy* or *Penthouse*. We were not supposed to jerk off. We were not supposed to sit around in our underwear, without robes.

In fact, we were not supposed to gather in groups of more than three.

When the loud knock sounded on the door, this is how we were—

—I was playing poker with Joe and Lou and Bill, which was not allowed, even if we had almost no money on the table, and we sat in our T-shirts and shorts, without robes.

—Gus and Ted had their cocks in their hands while staring at a copy of *Hustler.* They were talking about how far they had gotten with girls the last time they were home—lying, of course, but making it sound very exciting, how they had touched this one's bare tit and that one's curly crotch hair. Ted claimed he had some pussy hair in an envelope at home but had not brought it to school. When they heard that awful knock, Ted had just come and had to jam his spurting cock down in his underpants.

—A bottle of gin sat on the poker table.

Knock! The gin went out the window. *Hustler* went under the mattress. Robes were tossed in all directions, one in mine, fortunately.

Bill opened the door, confronting Brad, the dorm monitor for our floor.

"Cooper. Headmaster's office, on the double. Get your goddamn clothes on."

Called so abruptly to the office of the headmaster, I knew something was terribly wrong. I went over in my mind what I might have done this time but couldn't think of anything so bad as to have me called from the dorm to confront the headmaster.

I mean, having been reported for masturbating in a toilet stall would not have produced such a summons. Besides, I had put a dark blue lump on the forehead of the last boy who had pretended he had seen me doing that. The word had gone around—beware of your back if you make bad words about Len Cooper; don't bend over the faucet when brushing your teeth; you may find your forehead slammed hard against the plumbing.

I was in my final year at Lodge. It was a boarding school, good enough I guess, but not in a class with schools like Choate, Groton, and Andover—the famed New England prep schools that my father held in contempt. Some Lodge graduates claimed the title "preppie." Most didn't. I didn't and wouldn't.

Anyway, the headmaster liked to be called Dr. Billings. He also liked to appear in academic regalia for chapel and assemblies—gaudy hood and mortarboard with gold tassel.

Chapel. That I was a Jew didn't excuse me from compulsory chapel. It was an excuse, though, for reading during the prayers. I had made peace with Episcopal

Christianity, and Episcopal Christianity had made peace with me. So long as I read textbooks and not novels. *Catcher in the Rye* was okay classroom reading but not chapel reading.

I arrived at the walnut-paneled office of Dr. Billings, a big fellow with a square face and looming eyebrows. He tried to affect a mixed persona of kind and understanding, plus stern and disciplining. He did not entirely succeed in affecting either, much less the difficult mixture.

He wasn't wearing his academic gown now but only a dark gray suit spattered with cigarette ash. He came out from behind his desk and shook my hand: also an ominous sign.

"My dear boy," he said. "I am afraid I have the most terrible news for you." That oversized old man was on the verge of tears. He handed me a telegram:

PLEASE ADVISE MY SON THAT HIS MOTHER PASSED AWAY THIS AFTERNOON IN LYON STOP ADVISE HIM ALSO THAT I WILL FLY TO NEW YORK ON THE EARLIEST AVAILABLE FLIGHT AND THENCE ON TO VERMONT TO BE WITH HIM STOP COMFORT THE BOY AS BEST YOU CAN UNTIL I CAN BE THERE STOP
JEROME COOPER

Lodge School kept a VIP suite on the second floor above the commons. Officially it was for the bishop when he made his occasional visit. Mostly it was for distinguished commencement speakers and for generous contributors. But it had a more ominous use. When a boy suffered the death of a parent, or both parents, he would be moved into the VIP suite, where he could cry alone, absent his roommates. We called it the funeral parlor.

I was moved into the funeral parlor. My masters came. My friends came. The boy whose head I'd banged on the bathroom faucet came. I had to hold back my tears, which was no easy thing to do; I was genuinely devastated by the death of my mother, which would force me to live with just one parent: my forbidding father.

I was in shock. My mother *couldn't* be dead! I was young. I should have been more sensitive. I should have understood the symptoms that had been there for me to see.

I should have read them more in my formidable father than I read them in her. Formidable. Yes, he was. She weakened before my eyes, but she was brave and did not let it occur to me that I was about to lose her. He was brave, but this required more than courage. When they went off to France on that final visit, I had no idea it was a final visit to her homeland and her family.

I suppose it was something my mother and father meant to spare me. I would learn of it soon enough, and it would be bad enough when it came; no need for me to suffer until it was necessary.

"Got somethin' for ya, Len."

He had something for me, all right. His name was— God help him!—Beauregard, of course called Bo. He was not one of my roommates, but he was the only boy I ever mutually jerked off with. You know what I mean? Boarding-school ha-ha. Boys thinking they were being bad.

Anyway, Bo had brought me something. It looked like a bottle of hair tonic. It wasn't. It was a little bottle of *Scotch!* And, God, did I need that!

Old Dr. Latrobe came. The school chaplain. He was an Episcopal divine and offered to pray with me—and took no offense when I said thank you, no. He was well meaning but I couldn't take him right now. His doctorate, as I learned later, was phony. He was a D.D., doctor of divinity.

He had brought a tray with a pot of tea, cups and saucers, sugar and cream. I hadn't drunk my Scotch, but I was compelled to sit there and listen to that old man talk about life and death. I shouldn't be too hard on him. He was inoffensive.

"Death, you see, is only a part of life. It awaits us all. Mourning is painful. Sometimes it seems more than we can bear. But think of this—there is a certain way that we can avoid the agony of mourning, and that is never to love. Because we don't mourn because our loved one is dead; we mourn because we loved that person. So, if you would never mourn, you can escape it easily. All you have to do is never love. But, you know, we will go on loving and go on mourning, and we wouldn't have it any other way."

I thanked him when he left. It was the only decent thing to do.

2

I know something about funeral customs, now. They are designed to keep people from being alone in their grief. You can't very well cry in the company of others. So . . . wakes and all the rest of it. The religions know something.

They brought me dinner in the suite—pot roast and mashed potatoes, string beans, tossed salad, and chocolate cake. With milk. They did not suppose I drank coffee.

What the hell? I'd tossed off half the Scotch in the hair-tonic bottle as soon as the chaplain left—saving the rest for later when it would help me sleep.

The headmaster came, and two masters—so called. My roommates came and sat uncomfortably.

The headmaster encouraged me to talk about my mother. It would be good for me to talk, he said. I did talk, if only to get rid of these intrusive men.

I could tell them this much—

She was French, from Lyon. Her name was Giselle. My father was her second husband, and I have half-siblings in France named Martin—pronounced Mar-*teen* in the French manner, not Mar-tun, à l'Americain. The French Martins were quite wealthy. They were, in fact, the orig-inal bottlers and exporters of Plescassier Water, which rivaled Perrier and Evian and was sworn to by many, as a benefit to the skin and overall good health, not just when drank but when poured over the face and body. I have tried it. In my experience, Plescassier Water has a mildly laxative effect, and if that is what you need for your overall good health, God bless you.

At one point in his life, my father had been the American importer of Plescassier Water. That is how he came to know my mother's first husband, Jean Pierre Martin, and how he came to know her and marry her after M. Martin died. They never really told me much about it, and there was a great deal more to the story that I didn't know.

"I loved my mother," I said tearfully. "She was a *saint!* My mother was a saint."

When all of them had gone and I was at last alone and free to sob, I tossed down the remainder of the Scotch from the hair-tonic bottle. It did little good. More might have done better.

A saint . . . Yes. She was, really. My mother had been a saint. But how little I knew!

I would rather have been on my own cot, with my roommates, in the dormitory. But that choice was not open to me. Bereaved boys were condemned to the VIP suite.

I undressed. All my life I have slept nude, except in those dreary pajama days in dormitories.

I lay down.

Knock, knock. A knock so quiet and discreet I decided to answer it.

It was Brad. I never did know Brad's last name, though I could have learned it easily enough from the school catalog. He was a master—which is to say an instructor without academic standing, which he could not have attained in a boarding school—in history and political science. His ambition, I knew, was to achieve academic status in a college, any college—to be, in time, a professor.

Fat chance!

He was what he thought a boarding-school academic should be: tweedy, toady, and chummy.

He was also a fairy, as we then called them—something the naively straight Dr. Billings did not suspect.

Brad was nervous. He glanced up and down the hall before he entered my room.

Brad was a handsome blond guy. If I saw him today I'd write him off in an instant. Not because he was a fag. Because he was a professional failure.

He was wearing a robe and slippers and pajamas. He was the proctor on my floor in the dorm.

As a proctor he was entitled to administer minor punishment—meaning he could paddle us. Which he did, often. He was proud of the fraternity paddle he had brought from college. I remember it well. It bore the Greek letters—

$$\Delta Y$$

—of which he was, for some unfathomable reason, proud.

Anyway, he loved to use it, and he never used it on anything but a bare ass.

He'd take us to his room, order us to take down our pants and underpants, and have us grasp our knees with our hands. With our cheeks in the air and our balls and pricks in view, he would walk around us and lecture us on the advantages of upright conduct and the penalties that awaited the unrighteous. Three or four whacks followed. He never hit hard. We would dutifully sob and whimper. Then we had to stand and face him with hangdog expressions, with our clothes around our ankles, and promise to be better boys in future.

Not one of us above the age of ten failed to understand the true meaning of these sessions. That he did it to boys as young as eight told us something.

"My poor boy!" he whispered hoarsely as soon as he was inside the VIP suite and I had closed the door.

I knew what was coming. The only question for me was would I resist it?

"I brought you something," he said. "You must never tell anyone about it."

From the pocket of his robe he took a flask of brandy. He screwed off the cap, and I took the first swig of brandy I had ever tasted. I think he was surprised. In the past I'd swigged Scotch and bourbon and gin, and the brandy did not make me choke or turn red in the face.

"Feel better?" he asked.

I surprised him again. I tipped back the flask and slugged down about half of what he'd brought.

Well . . . what then? What to be expected?

As I said, he was tweedy, toady, and chummy. He explained to me he was going to do something for me because he was my friend and wanted to comfort me. He was bigger than I was and led me rather firmly to my bed. He shoved down my pajama pants, shoved me back on the bed, and took my half-erect dick into his mouth.

I was fourteen. His educated tongue ran around and around my eager glans, he sucked, and he needed only minutes to bring me to raging spasms of ejaculation. I filled his mouth, apparently, because my come ran down his chin.

Oh, more ignorant than that. He wiped his chin on his pajama shirt and said, "Now you do it for me, Len. That's how it goes. Two guys. One does it for one, then the other does it—I mean, that's the way it goes: total friendship, one man for another."

"Forget that," I interrupted.

"You can't say that to me! I've already done it for you. You *can't* refuse me!"

"The hell I can't. How do you think Dr. Billings would—?"

"He wouldn't believe you! You little piece of shit, you think you can—?"

"My father will be here tomorrow or the next day," I said. "You want to argue it out with Jerry Cooper?"

He ran the back of his hand over his mouth, wiping off more of my come; or maybe not, maybe he imagined it was there. His eyes bugged. He shook his head.

"You don't need me to make you come, Brad," I said. "You get it off pounding some poor kid's bare ass. Well . . . you can forget that with me. Never again. I may want you to suck me off once in a while, now that I know you do it. When I want you, I'll let you know. But don't expect me to take your cock in *my* mouth."

I got away with it. I didn't know what my father would have said or done. Neither did Brad. But he would take no chances.

That's the way it is, always. Some have got guts. Most don't.

3

JERRY

When Uncle Harry handed me the cashier's check for two million dollars, he was a happy man. He figured he'd fucked me. Again.

It was nothing personal. Uncle Harry fucked everybody. Everybody he did business with. People he worked for, people who worked for him especially; Uncle Harry fucked them all. He might have been a bigger man if he hadn't been so blatant about it.

That I was family gave him more satisfaction, not less.

To start with, he fucked me out of what my father had left me. He even fucked me out of the life insurance. When my Aunt Lila died, Uncle Harry married my girl— whom he'd been fucking in the other sense for some time—and encouraged her to screw me out of the little bit of money I'd let her deposit into her account for me.

He fucked the Kastenbergs, Fat Rita and her brother, out of their seltzer-water bottling business. In the process he fucked me out of a little money I'd invested with them.

Hey, I was no innocent, always getting fucked. My father had been a numbers runner, and Uncle Harry ran a numbers store and a bookie besides. I was a hustler from the word go. What else could I be? I worked for Harry. I fucked him a little. He fucked me big-time.

While I was away in the army, first in Detroit, then in Paris, he got himself affiliated with the Carlino family. He was not a Sicilian, though, and to the Honored Society that fucked him. He was a condemned small-timer.

I'm a veteran, I was in the war, but I never saw or heard a shot fired in anger. In Paris in '44 and '45 I co-operated with a hustler colonel in a small-time racket that made both of us good money. It was then that I met Paul Renard, who introduced me to the great love of my life: the beautiful, then-seventeen-year-old Giselle. She was a nude dancer, but she was not a hooker, not a bar girl. It seems odd to say, maybe, but a nude dancer can remain entirely innocent.

I stayed in France after the war with my darling Giselle, and spent months and years learning the ins and outs of the French spring-water business.

Hey! There was a day, once, when if you wanted a bucket of Plescassier water, you just walked over to the spring and dipped it out. I suppose it was the same with Perrier and Evian.

Promotion was what made spring water as pricey as wine. I saw the opportunity to import it into the States. Perrier and Evian would, and Plescassier could.

We tried twice. Once in New York. Once in L.A. Each time we were screwed by . . . oh, all kinds of things, chiefly union problems, dock theft, and once by straight muscle applied to our vendors, threatening death if they continued to sell Plescassier water.

It took me a little time to figure this out, but the problem was, once more, Uncle Harry. He'd stolen the Kastenbergs' seltzer-water business, and knew something about selling designer water.

Finally I had a chance to fuck Uncle Harry—and fuck him good. I sold him my company, Plescassier America, for two million dollars. Plescassier America had just one valuable asset: its contract with the Martin family to sell the water to us. I assigned that contract to him.

Only Uncle Harry didn't understand one thing. Under French law that contract bound the Martins only, not their successors if they sold the company. And they were selling the company. The buyer would not be in the least bound by the Martins' contract.

Uncle Harry paid me two million dollars for nothing. Worse for him, it wasn't his money. It was the Carlinos' money. When the Carlinos figured it out that Uncle Harry had been screwed out of *their* two mill, they put muscle on him for the money, out of his own pocket. He had it and paid it, but it ruined him.

Uncle Harry never recovered. The Five Families scorned him more than ever after that. They never trusted him again. He was a small-time punk once more, just like he'd been when he stole my inheritance. There is something like justice in this world.

I'd got him good. And the best part of it was, Uncle Harry knew it.

Actually, that was the second-best part. I was not yet forty and had two million dollars. What could I buy with two million dollars? I would have a little problem with that.

I got a summons, one I had expected. I was to meet Frank Costello for lunch, again in the Norse Room at the Waldorf, again at twelve-thirty. People who never met Frank Costello personally remember a raspy-voiced witness taking the Fifth before the Kefauver Committee and think of him as a menacing mafioso, like Lucky Luciano. In fact, Costello disliked violence and was known to Cosa Nostra as a conciliator. He was a rather good-looking man, black hair, a tan.

"Sit down, Jerry," he said. He was always one who went straight to the point. "Somebody tried to do us dirt," he said.

"I know. They were gonna do me dirt. I didn't know it, but they had it all figured. They knew when they sold Plescassier, its contract to sell water to Plescassier America would be null and void. But I swear to you, Mr. Costello, I didn't know that."

I'd never lied so skillfully in my life. I'd never had so much at stake in a lie. I didn't have to wait to hear what he said to know he believed me. I could see he believed me.

"I've got a cashier's check for the two million, made out to you," I said to him.

Costello shook his head. "We got the two mill off your uncle." Then he shrugged. "You wanta hand the money to Harry, that's your business. *We* don't need to double up."

I smiled. "I don't think I'll offer it to Uncle Harry. He owes me that much, all things considered."

Costello laughed. "Didn't figure you would. Harry's a small-time grifter from the word go."

"Exactly."

"Which you're not," said Costello. "That two million ought to set you up in something good. I have an idea you'll come up with something. When you do, let me know. Partners can do a lot better than a guy working alone."

There was the problem I'd figured would come. Partners. An affiliation, whether I wanted it or not.

"Uhh . . . this French guy . . . Jean Pierre Martin. Was he giving us a screwing all along?"

"Hard to say," I lied.

Costello fastened on me a look of amused skepticism. "I hear he married your girl."

I nodded. "He did that."

"I hear he's a fairy."

Again, I nodded.

"A Frog fairy mixed up in a scheme to screw us, who's already screwed you. I'll have to pass the word along."

I didn't really guess the significance of that. I should have. I was still naive.

4

Having the two million dollars was fine. But it was nothing compared to what I wanted much, much more. Giselle. My darling Giselle. I had to endure for a long time, and then . . .

Giselle was the mother of my son, Len.

But almost wasn't.

I arrived in Paris shortly after it was liberated and immediately became involved in the kind of racket that hustlers like me always found. Briefly said, because this is history, the army had scores of thousands of Jeeps in Europe. When a vehicle became too badly damaged to be repaired, the army would authorize its destruction. But if you had enough of these Jeeps, plus skilled mechanics, you could salvage parts from them and build a few serviceable Jeeps. Which you could sell for good money. The French automobile industry was down and would be a long time recovering, and the French wanted cars. Jeeps were perfect for them. They were rugged, dependable, and burned little gas. Europeans thought they were the greatest thing since sliced bread. Well, no, since that was a cliché that Europeans didn't know and didn't use.

Because I'd lost an eardrum somewhere along my way,

I was disqualified for combat service. That's why the army made a mechanic out of a dumb New York kid who'd known nothing about machinery. And I, with some others, built a profitable business out of scrounging parts from damaged Jeeps and making condemned Jeeps run. The business involved little risk and very respectable profit.

Of course, it did involve certain problems, chiefly officers. I learned a new level of corruption. Officers, when they found out about this illegal racket, did not want to prosecute; what they wanted was a share. Pretty soon I was sharing too much, but it kept me in business. I made less and less but still did all right.

I learned, too, that the Corsicans were the most dangerous mob in the world. Even the Mafia was afraid of them. And still is.

Other guys ran crap games, smuggled, forged orders, and did a whole lot of other things. Some guys actually fought the war.

In connection with my business I met a man named Paul Renard, a Corsican hustler, who was the proprietor of a sex club on Montmartre. Giselle was a stripper there. She was not involved in the S-M things that went on in that club, and she was not for sale. She just stripped and danced nude.

As an American I was naive about these things. When I say Giselle danced nude, I mean she danced *naked,* one hundred percent, stark, staring naked, without even shoes. It was not so much a strip—she came out wearing a little but soon rid herself of that little—as it was simply a nude dance. Not under dim lights. Not under colored lights. Her dance was so completely naked and so completely bold that it was innocent.

And she was an *angel!* She was beautiful! *God,* I had never seen such beauty. And—I had never before been, and would never again be, so fascinated with a woman, so drawn to her.

Well . . . My good fortune. I was working with Renard

in the Jeeps business. He owned the club. He introduced me to Giselle. More than introduced. He suggested we should become a pair. He owned an apartment we could share, for rent a little high for either of us but not high at all for us together.

We shared that homey apartment, simply as a practical matter at first; then, shortly, we were in love. I couldn't help myself about that. The French are an eminently practical people, and maybe she could have stayed out of love. But she didn't.

Through Renard I also met the Martin family, whose fortune was the mineral-water spring that produced Plescassier water. Generation after generation, the Martin men were homosexual. They married women only as much as needed to generate the heirs that were necessary to keep the family going. Otherwise, they were strictly homo. The Martins loved their boyfriends and made babies with their women. It was a practical arrangement, typically French.

What happened is difficult to understand. It was difficult for me to understand, and I lived it. The French are different from us. They have their ways.

Under the French law of inheritance, seventy-five percent of the stock in Plescassier would go to the government if Jean Pierre Martin did not father an heir. When his father died, that made the matter absolutely urgent.

Jean Pierre solved his problem in a very direct, very French style. He married Giselle. That I loved her made no great difference. That she loved me made no difference at all. It was business. We would enter into a highly practicable, reasonable arrangement that would satisfy everybody.

It would all be very cozy. She would continue to love me. Jean Pierre would continue to love his boyfriend, Jack. And we would be four good friends.

It was okay if you were French, I suppose. It was not okay with me. We didn't have a screaming confrontation. I was not so much angry as sad. I left France, settled in the United States, and tried to introduce Plescassier water on the American market—with the difficulties I have already mentioned.

Which is where things stood when the Carlinos funded dear Uncle Harry in buying Plescassier America.

About a month passed after Frank Costello's comment that he'd have to pass along the word about the Frog fairy, during which time I didn't think about it much. Then word came from Paul Renard in Paris. Jean Pierre Martin was dead!

The news came in the form of a wire from Turin. It read—

JPM EST MORT. IMPORTANTE! NE VENISSEZ PAS VOUS À FRANCE. J'APPORTEREZ G ET LES ENFANTS À NEW YORK. RESTEZ VOUS LÀ. PAUL.

It meant: Jean Pierre Martin is dead. Important! Do not come to France. I will bring Giselle and the children to New York. Stay there. Paul.

I didn't see that I had any alternative.

5

LEN

I went from the Lodge School to Amherst, remaining always a dormitory student. I met more than a few guys who didn't know who their fathers were. I was odd, in that I always knew full well who my father was—indeed, as in the matter of Brad, well enough to use his name as a threat—but I never had the remotest idea what my father did for a living.

I did not press the question. My father was to me too formidable a figure to be questioned. When I had asked my mother, she told me my father was an honest man in an honest business—and when he wanted me to know more, he'd tell me.

My first memory of a home was a brick house in Scarsdale, in Westchester County, some fifteen miles out of New York City. Five of us lived there—father and mother, my half-sister Jacqueline, and half-sister Jeanne. The girls were three and two years older than I was. They were the daughters of Jean Pierre Martin, mother's first husband. When he died suddenly, not having reached his sixtieth year, my mother and father married, and my birth followed a year or so later.

I was not easy for my mother. She was nearly forty

when I was born. The ordeal was so dangerous that she and my father decided I would be their only child.

I remember her as a stunning beauty. Everyone who knew her remembered her as a stunning beauty. In spite of the sudden, tragic death of her first husband, she was a bright, optimistic personality. And a loving mother.

She loved me, and I never doubted it for an instant. But she loved Jacqueline and Jeanne, too. Embraces and caresses were a big part of our lives. People wondered about us, always embracing and kissing one another. I don't know if that was a French characteristic or just a family characteristic. My father probably would have called it French, since to him "the French they are a funny race."

He had grown up in a Jewish family in New York City, but their ways of expressing their love were not as exuberant as my mother's.

My father never spoke much about his parents. They were killed in an automobile accident when he was in high school. He talked a little about his Uncle Harry, who was apparently a cheap little crook who stole everything he could lay hands on, including my father's modest inheritance.

"One thing I learned from Uncle Harry," he said more than once. "It's always better to be the fuck*er* than the fuck*ee*."

He struggled not to show me more affection than he showed M. Martin's daughters, but he not could help favoring me. Even with me, though, something was always held in reserve. He was more likely to shake hands than hug, and remains that way to this day. I had to study him for a while before I came to understand that he had loved me as much as my mother did but had a different way of expressing it. I suppose I was in college, or maybe out of college, before I got that straight in my head.

French was my first language. The Martin girls spoke French almost exclusively. They had begun their English studies, but they struggled to say anything more than "No, thank you," or "Well, maybe a bit more."

When they were eight and seven, the decision was made to send them back to France for their education. The extended Martin family accepted that with enthusiasm. I have to wonder if the two girls did not leave the States with a sense of relief. I have rarely seen them since.

Mother wanted me to continue to speak French. I worked with her on it. I do speak French.

With only three of us now, my father sold the house in Scarsdale and we moved into an apartment on East Seventy-second Street. The apartment was comfortable. It was, in fact, luxurious.

Seet down here, Lennie, on the edge of the bed." She took my hand in hers. "Now your daddy is going to go on with what he was doing. You will see it does not hurt me. It is how your father shows me he loves me."

When I was old enough, I was enrolled in The Friends School, which was a distinguished secondary school, one of the best in New York, if not *the* best.

I was an urban child. I knew the streets, though they were very different streets from the ones my father had known. There was another lesson I had to learn. When I was at Friends, I didn't know the meaning of the term "mean streets," and I never guessed that my father had grown up on them.

My father—Let's start with this: When the time came to send me to a boarding school, my father adamantly rejected the New England prep schools, though my mother thought they would be good for me. He consented to a boarding school, not to a prep school. Why? He grew up on the streets. To him, preppies were nauseating snobs. I think if he'd had his way absolutely, he would have wanted me to serve an apprenticeship with him and learn life as he had learned it. He had a sense that he knew more of life than one could ever learn in any school.

My mother said *school.* And a good school.

Hey! I don't speak of my father in the past tense. He's very much alive. He's one shrewd, tough son of a . . .

The more I know of him, the more I respect him.

It's been my ambition to be a son he can respect.

I wonder if my mother would not have demanded of me a better ambition.

6

I could write memoirs about the people I saw in our apartment in those all-too-few years before I went off to boarding school. They were lessons in life.

To begin with, there was a black guy named Buddy. If he has a last name, I never heard it. His wife was named Ulla, and she was Norwegian.

Buddy may be my father's best friend. They go back a long way. Buddy's weapon of choice was a razor, and he taught my father to use one, though I don't believe my father ever did. Buddy might have done a lot of things with his life, but he chose to stay close to his roots in Harlem, where he was a bookmaker, a numbers book, and so on. He was a skilled player of the main chance who knew the streets as well as any man ever did. He was also smoothly handsome and appealing to women. In certain senses he was my father's mentor.

I was wholly unable to understand the relationship between my father and Buddy. Two men could hardly have been more different. But something between them drew them close. Some secret I would work to penetrate for a long time.

I remember being introduced to other visitors, the

meaning of whose names I would learn later.

"Len, say hello to the Prime Minister." It was, of course, Frank Costello. In Cosa Nostra he was known as "the prime minister," meaning he used brains, not muscle and smoothly accomplished what others failed to accomplish. Remembering him later, I was surprised to know that my father had a friend in Frank Costello.

"Len, say hello to the Little Man." Meyer Lansky, known as "Little Man" and "Chairman of the Board," was the mob's banker and strategist. I remember an appealing, even charismatic man who always had time to say a cordial hello to a little boy and sometimes produced a paper bag of candies from his overcoat pocket.

"Len, say hello to Mr. Hoffa." Costello and Lansky had manners and pretended for a moment to take an interest in a little boy. But even as a child I detected in Jimmy Hoffa a crude bully, a menacing man I hoped I would not meet again.

I knew nothing of these men but those impressions I gathered. It would be years before I identified them and began to wonder what connection they had with my father.

I didn't worry about it much. I relied on my mother's assurance that my father was an honest man in an honest business. Her word was all I needed to settle any unease I later felt about my father's association with these men. And I must say, even now, that not everyone who befriended men like Costello and Lansky were criminals.

When I was nine and home from school for summer vacation, my mother's family came to visit. Her father was old, fragile, and very French. When he sat down, his suit only reluctantly sat down with him. It was of stiff fabric and seemed to have been built around him like a cardboard box, to pack him in.

He was my grandfather. I have almost no memory of my French grandmother. I do remember my Aunt Thérèse, because my father confided in me about her.

"You're old enough to know this," he said. "But don't

tell your mother I told you. Thèrése, who is your mother's elder sister, lived with a German officer during the war. She was what we call a collaborator. When the Germans were driven out of Lyon, the people of the *Résistance* stripped her naked, shaved her head, and marched her through the streets—she and half a dozen or so others. And . . . well, let me tell you for sure, your mother never did anything of the kind and was never treated that way. Your mother had no relationship whatever with any German, of any kind. She did not betray her country. I don't judge Thèrése. But that's in her history."

Whenever I looked at Aunt Thèrése during the remaining few days the family visited, the image came to my mind of her bald and naked, and that image made my little dick stiffen and stand. Aunt Thèrése gave me the first erections I ever had.

I would see Thèrése again. One evening over chocolate and cognac she talked to me about her punishment—

"Eet ees *relief,* you must understand. We are afraid they are going to *shoot* us. We are afraid they are going to flog us. In some town, like in Corsica, they streeped girls naked, shaved them, and drove them out of the town, throwing rocks at them as they ran along the road. We feared *zees,* and when all they did was march us through the street and let us go home, we shook and cried because we have *escape* such thing."

"And how did you live in Lyon after that?" I asked.

"Weeth *scorn.* Weeth some hate. But alive and let to leef in our house."

"My mother . . ."

"She has nothing to do with thees. She never deed what I deed. But . . . she ate the sugar and drank the coffee my *Boche* brought. And so deed my family. I performed a service for zem."

7

When my father arrived at the Lodge School, I was still in the VIP suite being cosseted as the poor boy who had lost his mother. I was, in fact, a poor boy. I was in shock. I couldn't imagine what life would be like without my mother. She had been my stabilizing influence, and I had loved her deeply.

I loved my father, too. But that had been different. He was a giant figure, to be respected—actually even to be feared—and he had been absent much of the time. When he talked to me, usually it was to give me words of advice, which he expected me to remember. I respected him, but my mother had stood as a buffer between us, and I had to wonder how it would go between us without her.

He had begun to treat me like a man before I was old enough to be treated like a man. He did it because he didn't know how to deal with a little boy. When he told me about Aunt Thérèse, for example, he told me something a boy of nine didn't need to know.

He had the good sense not to tell me certain other things I definitely didn't need to know.

He told me a funeral was a burdensome thing, and that my mother had left specific instructions that she was not to have one. He'd had her buried in France according to Jewish custom, though she wasn't a Jew, so by the time he arrived at Lodge she was in the ground. That was how he operated—decisively, abruptly. He decided I did not need to see my mother's body—in which he was absolutely right.

He took me to dinner and saw to it that I drank wine. He talked to me about women.

"Do you understand why I loved your mother so very much?" he asked me.

"I loved her, too."

"Yes, but . . . the love between a man and woman, a husband and wife . . . is not the same. How much do you know about what men and women do?"

"I know what they do."

"I'll arrange for you to have an experience," he said. "What you boys do in dorms is not the kind of experience I want you to have. I want you to have the kind of experience your mother and I shared, though for the first time you may have to share it without the love she and I felt for each other."

"Then is it any good?" I asked him. "If it's just . . . physical, is it any good? Have you done it with a woman you didn't love?"

"Yes. And so will you."

I nodded and said nothing.

"I don't want you to imagine that what boys do in dorms in boarding schools is—"

"I haven't had that kind of experience either—except once."

"Tell me."

I told him about Brad.

In a minute he was on the phone. He summoned Brad, gave him twenty minutes to be at our room in the inn. I could hear only our end of the conversation, but I understood that Brad's protest only made my father angry.

A timid knock on the door. Brad. Flushed. Afraid.

"I swear before God Almighty, Mr. Cooper, that I—"

"Strip down, fag," my father said coldly. "I don't talk to faggots with their clothes on."

"Mr. Cooper, I swear to you, nothing improper happened between me and Len. The boy was and is distraught—"

"We can discuss it when you're naked."

"Mr. Cooper, *please!*"

My father had a bottle of Scotch on the desk. He went to it and poured himself a drink, standing with his back to Brad.

I'd threatened Brad with my father, but I'd had no idea what fear the name Jerry Cooper could invoke. In the next few minutes I learned to know my father in a very different way.

Brad hurried to strip out of his somewhat shabby, tweedy clothes and in a moment stood stark naked.

My father poured a stiff drink and handed it to him.

Brad accepted the glass and, hands shaking, drank the Scotch.

"I wanted my son to have his first experience with a nice little girl, a nice little girl showing pink knees at the hem of her plaid skirt, with a navy blue cashmere sweater and a single strand of pearls. Who gets his virginity instead? *You!*"

"I gave it to him," Brad muttered tearfully. "I didn't take anything from him."

"Oh, perfect," my father said with the most complete scorn I have ever heard come from anyone's mouth.

"Mr. Cooper . . ."

"Not much of a cock, you got there. Hold it up. Pull on it. Let's see the best you can show."

Brad tried. It was true he wasn't well hung, and being terrified didn't help.

"Let's see you make it come, queer. Jerk off. Here. Have another drink. Then let's see you jerk off."

My father poured me a splash of Scotch, too, and another drink for himself. Then we sat on the couch and watched Brad struggle to masturbate.

He did not manage to come. Instead he began to sob. I had not expected to feel sorry for Brad, not anytime, for any reason, but I felt sorry for him then.

I spoke to my father. "Let him go," I said.

My father shrugged. "Okay, fairy. Get your clothes on and get out of here. And don't you ever come anywhere near my son again. Don't even say hello to him."

When Brad was gone, my father looked down at me and said, "Sympathy is a fine sentiment. But it's like money. Be hesitant about spending money and also about extending sympathy. When that fag gets to thinking about it, he'll conclude you were weak. Count on it. But I don't think he'll bother you again."

8

JERRY

Paul brought Giselle and her two girls to New York. He told me why he had urged me to stay put and not fly to France.

"In France we put a suspect in jail and keep him there until the authorities can figure out whether there is enough evidence to bring him to trial."

"Do you mean to tell me that I am a suspect in the death of Jean Pierre?"

Paul nodded. "The Martins accuse you. And you may not be surprised to hear that Jack accuses you."

Jack had been Jean Pierre's lover for many years. "I suppose I need not be surprised at that," I said dryly.

Paul went on. "They think, of course, that you hired someone to do it."

I hadn't, of course, but Frank Costello's words sprang to my mind—"A Frog fairy mixed up in a scheme to screw us, who's already screwed you. I'll have to pass the word along."

"I sent the telegram from Turin," Paul continued, "because I knew any telegram sent to you from France would almost certainly be intercepted and read by GIGN—"

"GIGN?"

"*Groupe d'Intervention de la Gendarmerie Nationale.* A tough police organization."

"It's their goddamned counter-terrorist organization!" I said. "What the hell . . . ?"

"Just police nastiness," Paul said with a Gallic shrug. "Their suspicion was all the more aroused because I'd driven Giselle and her girls across the Italian frontier almost before J. P.'s body was discovered. I thought that a wise precaution. They thought it was something other than a precaution."

"You're a resourceful man."

"I'm Corsican. Anyway, I hope you don't forget that Giselle is my niece."

"So you told me, finally, after letting me believe for years that you were just a friend of the family."

"Anyway, *l'affaire J. P.* is over. He left heirs, and you'll have to send them back to France sooner or later."

Giselle and I slept together her first night in New York. Things were the way they'd been before. Almost. She remained a delicately beautiful woman, adroit at love-making and filled with enthusiasm to be in *my* bed once more. It was a memorable night, maybe the most memorable of my life.

Giselle was not a typical Frenchwoman. In the first place, she was blond. There was no way to tell if that was natural or not, since she kept her pussy shaved, always had. When she was dancing naked in Paris, her pussy was naked. Also, in my observation, Frenchwomen tend to be flat-chested, or at least have small, firm breasts. Giselle's were not huge, but they were more than the typical Frenchwoman had. They were pendulous, too—which is to say, they hung rather loose from her chest and swung a little, this way and that, as she moved. She had a flat belly, broad hips, and gorgeous legs. Her face was perfect: perky nose, luscious lips, a strong chin. She was an acknowledged beauty. Everyone thought she was beautiful.

We took no precautions against pregnancy because we

had already agreed that we would marry and start a family as soon as possible. We both wanted that.

After her two girls were asleep that night, we put on records, and Giselle did an erotic strip for me. She had not forgotten how to do it. She was thirty-four years old. My God, she'd been only seventeen when I first saw her dancing nude in Paris!

Later she told me my cock tasted good. "Jerr-ee . . . I never have taste a cock that taste like yours. You should have come to me in France. When we had two daughter, no son, J. P. lost interest. It could have been that I would have been licking your balls many time. Like this."

I couldn't honestly tell her that her cunt felt better to my cock than any other cunt I'd ever put it in. I couldn't even tell her it felt different, or that it felt familiar. They say all cats are gray in the dark, but that is not so. They say it's not how much cock a man has but how he uses it that makes the difference, and that is so. Well, it's true with a woman, too. The equipment is the same, but how they handle it is not. She knew how to welcome me in, then to tighten her muscles and grip me. I don't think I could have pulled out if I wanted to, sometimes.

She was a vocal lover. Frenchwomen often are. I don't mean she heaved and panted and shrieked like those bimbos who fake orgasms on porno tapes. I mean, she moaned softly and purred and let me know what pleasure she was taking. I always knew when I was doing what she liked most.

There was another way in which she was no Frenchwoman. She was clean. She showered at least once a day. On the other hand, she had lived in this country several years before she began to experiment with deodorants. And she, who shaved her pussy at least once a week, didn't shave her armpits. Her pungent, musty odor was part of her attraction. I think she knew it.

I thought I'd settled into the love and marriage that would last the rest of my life. We'd have two or three kids. I bought a house in Scarsdale. We'd need it for the family. We would need more than a city apartment, Giselle and I.

After some discussion, we invited Uncle Harry and Lila to our wedding. They didn't come. Not long after that, Harry was found with his throat cut. They found him, sprawled half on the sidewalk, half in the gutter on the street outside a small-time book-and-crap game he was running. The police didn't press the investigation very hard. Too many people wanted him dead.

I went to his funeral. Somebody said to me that he'd been a broken man, anguished by disappointment and frustration, having seen everything he'd built during his life come crashing down. The man who said it knew part of the story. I told him not to waste his sympathy. Harry had fucked everybody, and finally life fucked him.

9

So there I was, sitting with two million dollars spread out in six banks and with no sure idea what I was going to do with it.

Buddy had ideas. I could fund the biggest numbers operation in town. The biggest bookie.

"C'mon, Buddy. The Families got all that. Even if I invest in partnership with the Carlinos, the other Families are going to come after me. What I need is a business the Families haven't thought of and don't want."

In fact, the Families hadn't forgotten me. I had a call summoning me to another meeting with Frank Costello at the Waldorf, in the same room at the same time. But when I sat down with him this time, I had a real surprise coming.

Sitting at the table with Costello was a pallid, wizened little man with bushy black eyebrows, deep lines around his eyes and mouth, and a wide mouth with a fleshy lower lip.

Direct as always, Costello opened the conversation by saying, "Here's the man who can tell you how to invest that two mill wisely. Meet Meyer Lansky."

It was big-time to sit down over lunch with Meyer Lansky. Costello was big, but Lansky, who was sometimes called the Chairman of the Board, was bigger. A Russian or Polish Jew, he could not be a member of the Honored Society, exactly, but he was acknowledged to be the brains behind a wide variety of highly profitable businesses. A story was told of him that he was once overheard saying in an FBI-bugged room, "My God, we're bigger than United States Steel!"

Big. Not physically. He was also called the Little Man. Reputed nearly all his life to be a major gangster, he had never spent any major time in any pen. His personal specialty for a long time had been what were called "carpet joints"—that is, illegal gambling houses fancy enough to have carpets on the floors, in towns all the way from Florida to upstate New York. He had achieved his ambition in Cuba, where he had established a plush casino hotel. Gamblers flew into Havana on flying boats from Miami and played at the high-stakes tables of Lansky's Riviera Hotel.

I knew he had just been expelled from Cuba and his casino hotel had been confiscated by the new Communist regime of Fidel Castro. I assumed, wrongly as it turned out, that he had plenty of other assets stashed here, there, or somewhere.

Lansky looked tired, exhausted in fact. He would suffer a near-fatal heart attack not long after. The sudden loss of the Riviera had damaged him.

He did propose an investment, but in a half-hearted way that inspired no confidence. The term was not yet in use, but what he suggested was that I buy into a money-laundering scheme. I didn't understand it at the time, and I don't understand it now. I said as much, and Frank Costello said, "Hey, that's just the point, Jerry. Meyer does understand these things. I figured, you being a Jew like him, the two of you would get along just great."

"There's heavy risk in this kind of thing, isn't there, Mr. Lansky?" I asked.

"All profitable enterprises involve risk," said Lansky.

"The man who is not ready to take a risk condemns himself to being a small-timer all his life."

"My problem is that I've worked all my life to get this two million dollars, and if I'm going to risk it, I think I'd rather risk it in something I understand."

"Put in a hundred thousand, Jerry," Costello suggested. "You can afford that."

I did. Then Lansky had his heart attack and nearly died, and I wrote off my hundred thousand. But after almost a year there came a knock on the door one evening at my place in Scarsdale. A young man handed me a package.

"That's from Mr. Lansky," he said. "You should count it. It's $165,000, what you got coming from your investment. Mr. Lansky suggests you take the $65,000 and reinvest the $100,000."

I handed the package back. "Tell Mr. Lansky I'll reinvest the whole schmear," I said.

I got another payoff a year later. It didn't come to $272,250, as it would have if my investment had done as well the second time as the first, but it came to $205,000, which still wasn't bad at all.

I figured this couldn't go on forever, and I was right, it couldn't. But I stuck with Lansky, and the next time I got a payout I sent $100,000 to Frank Costello.

All well and good, but I wasn't in a business of my own, and I damn well had to have a business of my own.

10

Buddy was a smart fellow. "The way to make money in business," he said, "is to sell people something they want."

What he meant was sell them opportunities to gamble, sell them prostitutes, sell them protection, or—the coming business in the 1960s—sell them narcotics.

Fine. Except that the Five Families had gambling and prostitution tied up in New York, and other families of Cosa Nostra had it tied up in other cities. I think Frank Costello could have arranged to let me buy into a piece of the gambling action in Manhattan, but the Families were fighting turf wars, which meant a chance of losing everything, including your life, in one hellish night.

So far as prostitution was concerned, I didn't want anything to do with it. Exploiting girls was not my idea of a way of turning a profit. I had scruples. You could never be sure if a girl came to the life because she wanted to, or because necessity pushed her, or—worse—because some guy forced her. I didn't want to have to worry about that. Besides, more and more, girls were entering the life because of addiction. It was the worst of all possible combinations.

Narcotics? No way. The problem there was that dope had been sold to the dregs of the community for years, and as long as that was where it was sold nobody much cared, but in the sixties, the trade was expanding into the good neighborhoods and the suburbs, which meant that the law was going to turn fanatical. Ohio, for example, had already made it law that a guy would go up for life for selling just one hit. Imagine that! Life in the slammer for selling just one hit of heroin! And I'm not saying that was wrong. Bad chemicals make people into animals. Worse, it makes them into walking corpses.

Buddy suggested a chop shop—that is, a garage where stolen cars were modified, numbers filed off, repainted, and so on. Sure. Okay. A small profit. A small-time operation.

I wanted a legit business.

Okay. Sell people something they want. Better than that, make them want something they didn't know they wanted, and then sell them that. A thousand billion-dollar businesses had been built on selling people what they didn't know they would ever want—what, in fact, they didn't want when they bought it, and had no need for.

My idea came to me when I wanted to buy Giselle a present, as much for me as for her, something very sexy to wear on her gorgeous body. Remember the fifties? Where would you have bought a really brief bikini or a G-string or a pair of crotchless panties? Department stores did not carry much in the way of intimate apparel. Neither did women's shops. White rayon panties and white cotton bras from Woolworth's or Penney's were standard underwear. I remember a nylon panty-and-bra set based on a leopard-skin print. It was considered daring, even though the waistband covered the navel.

You might try a sex shop, almost all of which were so sleazy a man or woman would be embarrassed to be seen coming out of one. You could order something by mail from Frederick's of Hollywood, but that was about it.

It's unbelievable, when you think about it. In those

years young women still wore girdles! Also panty-girdles. And rigid bras of nylon and rubber that forced their breasts into unnatural pointy shapes that were ogled on television. Nothing was too hideous for women to force their suffering flesh into in those years. Giselle wore no bras most of the time, and seeing her breasts moving naturally under a blouse or sweater caused some men to ogle and some women to cluck.

The fifties ended, the sixties began, and it didn't get much better. We were on the verge of the so-called Sexual Revolution, but—okay, I've made my point.

It occurred to me that here was a business: selling sexy scanties in respectable shops in silk-stocking neighborhoods. Men would buy to please their wives and girlfriends. Women would buy to please their husbands and boyfriends. We could go into that business on the basis of a cautious investment, and who could guess what would follow?—utter failure, modest success, or a big business all our own that the Families had not thought of and didn't want.

Giselle thought a fine name for the shops would be *Presque Nu*—almost naked. I liked her idea of using French words. In those years, "French" still connoted something naughty. I liked the idea but knew Americans wouldn't understand its meaning. Finally, we came up with a name. It was simple, yet carried a suggestive double entendre. We would call our shops Cheeks. The fashion was chic, a woman might need cheek to wear it, and she might show something of her nether cheeks to anyone who saw her from behind.

Buddy thought the idea was insane. "Oh, man! You want to open a buttons-and-ribbons store? What kind of man sells ladies' undies? What kind of business is that?"

It is a business that last year had almost eleven billion dollars in gross sales, through almost seven hundred stores, plus catalog sales.

Not bad. But it didn't come easy.

Giselle and I talked about it. She would be my partner

in Cheeks, in every sense of the word. I talked to Frank
Costello. All he could do was shrug. "It's an original idea,
I gotta say."

"Nobody's gonna object?"

"Nobody's gonna object. You could go into other lines
and nobody would object. You got friends, Jerry."

Giselle heard him say that. She had no idea what he
meant. In Paris, I had learned, there was an organization
vaguely referred to as *les Messieurs,* and she'd had contact with it through Paul and still knew nothing of it.

Anyway, we had to define what we would sell. We
ordered a substantial shipment from Frederick's of Hollywood and decided, essentially, that what Frederick's offered was not what we would offer.

Remember, it was still the era of nylon and rubber. By
no means everything offered by Frederick's was like that,
but some of it was; and we were firm in our commitment
to offer something different.

Giselle and I made some of the signature items of our
early line. When I say made, I mean we sewed together
and dyed items that we could show to makers and suppliers. It seemed the best way to give them the idea.

Giselle bought one of the leopard-print panty-and-bra
sets that seemed so bold. At home we snipped holes in
the bra so as to expose the nipples. Then we dyed the
thing black. Then we photographed it, on Giselle. When
we showed that to prospective suppliers, they understood
what we wanted.

We didn't cut down the panties, just dyed them black
and folded them to make a bikini style.

Giselle put on the black bra with her nipples bared, the
panties, a black garter belt, and dark sheer stockings, and
she posed for my camera. That outfit became one of the
pilot styles for Cheeks.

Nighties were not so difficult. The only problem was
that most of them included modesty panels. A woman in
those days might wear a nightgown that displayed her
legs, her hips, even her butt through sheer nylon but ex-

pected a modest covering over her pubes and her breasts. We could easily induce manufacturers to omit the modesty panels. Our sheer nightgowns were sheer all over.

Those became another one of our pilot styles.

We couldn't know yet how the public would receive our merchandise, but we had a philosophy—if it can be dignified by that name—and meant to venture on the market with it.

11

Apart from merchandise, the first problem was real estate. No point in opening one shop. I opted for three, one on the Upper West Side, one on the Upper East Side, and one in Midtown.

Merchandise. I knew we would have to design and manufacture our own. For the moment, I hoped to import from France, where women no longer walked around in hip-length panty-girdles and bras of . . . well, there was something called a "whirlpool bra," a contraption so horrid it was almost beyond imagination.

I called on Paul Renard. Lingerie was not one of his many interests, but he had contacts in every business in France. Shortly, crates of "unmentionables" were aboard cargo planes destined for Cheeks, U.S.A. I also asked him to find me a supply of the briefest possible bikinis. Nothing flimsy. Only high-quality merchandise.

We rented a ballroom in the Lexington Hotel and arranged a style show to introduce our line. The hotel was accustomed to fashion shows and set up a catwalk for our models. The hotel supplied the bright, dramatic lighting. I hired a rock band.

Most of the guests for the show were people from the

news media: fashion writers, commentators on city life. We made them comfortable with generous drinks, and then started our show.

I employed six models. To my surprise, Giselle decided that she wanted to model, so she made seven.

Immediately I had a decision to make.

The bikinis were brief. So were the panties. In those days it was unusual for a girl to trim or shave her pubic hair. Few of the bikinis of the fifties required it. When the first model came out of the dressing room in an iridescent white bikini, she was grinning and pointing down. At least a quarter of an inch of her thick, dark bush overhung her bikini.

Her name was Melissa Lamb. "Do you want me to trim it, Mr. Cooper?" she asked in mock innocence, giggling. She was a charming girl. I would know her for many years and would never forget that day when she offered to trim her dark pubic hair.

For a moment I could not answer. My attention was focused on her luscious breasts, which were spilling out of her bikini top.

"I don't know," I said. "How do *you* feel about it?"

"I don't care. I've posed nude a lot. My pussy doesn't embarrass me."

I may have been influenced by Giselle. I will never forget the first time I saw her nude on the stage. She'd been shaved, and her fleshy nether lips showed. She spread her legs without hesitation or embarrassment, showing her dark slit and the shiny pink parts outside it. Strippers today are close-trimmed, if not shaved, and *flaunt* their pink and glossy parts. The mere suggestion of it was shocking when we opened our stores. So has the world changed.

"No, Melissa," I said. "If it doesn't bother you, it doesn't bother me."

I had to see the reaction. If it had been negative, I would have sent the girls scurrying back to the dressing room to shave.

But it was not negative. The style columnists and suchlike people gasped when Melissa appeared with that generous blossom of dark hair showing above her bikini bottom, plus strands showing around the sides. But then . . . then they applauded!

As model after model appeared, each showing more or less, interest grew. The musicians, who had been blasé about this gig, became spirited, as did their playing. Their beat dominated the room. I had a microphone, but I didn't have to say anything.

Each model showed a bikini. Then they began to show lingerie. When Giselle appeared in the black bra-and-panty set, with her shiny nipples peeking out through the holes in the bra, some in the audience actually stood— though whether it was to pay tribute or to see better, I couldn't say.

The next day the models gathered in a photographer's studio and were photographed in the things they had modeled.

I had invited Buddy to stop by during the shoot. He was no innocent, but he was rattled when he found himself sitting in a huge room, sipping Scotch, and watching naked girls running around, changing in and out of things and having body makeup patted on their skin. He had, of course, seen Giselle nude in Paris, but she was thirty-five now, and my wife, and I think it made him a little uncomfortable.

I ordered big color prints made of the photographs. They would become the basis of the décor in our first shops. Notice I say they were the basis of the décor *in* our first shops. We did not put them in the windows, and in fact they were not visible from the streets.

My wife's photo appeared in each of our shops.

We were demure. We kept drapes closed over our show windows and displayed nothing in them but walnut plaques with carved, gilded lettering. It said:

CHEEKS
LINGERIE FRANÇAISE

Anyway . . . there are problems with starting a business in New York City.

My first confrontation came in the Upper East Side shop. I was paid a visit by a tall, slender, coffee-with-cream complexioned man sharply dressed in a camel overcoat over a natty black suit. He strolled around the shop, taking an interest in the merchandise and in the big color photographs of models.

"Nice new business you got here," he said.

I nodded. I guessed what he wanted, but I played it cool. "I figured there'd be a market for this kind of stuff."

"I'm sure there is. I'm sure there is. Uh . . . you got the place well insured?"

"Oh, sure," I said. I'd expected this visit and knew what was coming. "Fire, theft, the works."

He nodded, then walked around the store again, pretending to take an interest in some sheer and skimpy black panties. "Tough town, don't you think?" he asked.

"I've lived here all my life," I said.

"Really, now? Then you know the score. Who's insuring you against accidents?"

"What's your name?" I asked.

"I don't give that information out very readily."

"Then when somebody else comes in to sell me insurance, who am I gonna tell them insures me against accidents? I mean, I can't just say, 'I got insurance.' I gotta say 'I got insurance with Doug or Mike or somebody.' Otherwise, your insurance isn't going to do me any good, is it?"

"Okay. You tell 'em you're insured with Leroy."

"And what does your insurance cost, Leroy?"

"Oh, let's say a C and a half a week. If your business goes real good, the insurance might be worth more. But we can start that way. Okay?"

"Okay." I reached in my pocket, pulled out a wad, and peeled off three fifties. "Tuesday," I said. "This covers me till next Tuesday. Figure I'll see you then. Right?"

I called Buddy. He'd heard of Leroy.

Leroy did not return for another $150 on Tuesday. He did not return any other Tuesday.

A body that washed up on a Jersey beach a couple of months later might have been Leroy, but it was hard to say; too many fish had nibbled on it. The camel coat and black suit suggested Leroy.

"Anybody else tries to sell you protection, you tell them you're covered by Buddy."

Which I did. For some reason all his own, Buddy had become a sort of big brother to me. I thought I knew the city. He knew it better.

12

LEN

My father said to Brad that he had wanted me to give my virginity to some nice little girl with pink knees showing under a pleated plaid skirt. I did, if my virginity could be said to be intact after I was sucked off by Brad.

Sue Ellen did not want to be called Sue or Ellen. She was Sue Ellen. I met her at Amherst, of course. We met at a dance and at first didn't much care for each other. I don't know why, exactly. She was all too ready to tell anyone who would listen that her father was a senior partner in Hale & Dorr, in Boston, and was a friend of Joseph Welch. I didn't tell her exactly what my father did for a living—I honestly didn't know—which made her think I was either standoffish or was the son of someone in a dishonest racket. She didn't find this attractive, and so didn't find me attractive.

It is odd to say this about a young woman, but I am going to say it because it was true. Sue Ellen was defined by her boobs. They were beautiful but so extraordinarily large that she was almost a freak. Her mother hired a woman in Boston to make bras especially for Sue Ellen. The things were expensive, and their purpose was not to thrust her up and out but to contain and support her. More than that, they were made to relieve her of the discomfort she experienced with off-the-shelf brassieres, whose straps cut into her shoulders and left red marks.

There were cruel jokes about Sue Ellen. She didn't pick the lint from her navel because she didn't know it was there. She couldn't play the piano or type because she couldn't see the keyboard. She couldn't drive because her tits would get caught in the steering wheel. She couldn't play basketball because someone would confuse her boobs for the ball. And so on. I say cruel. I mean cruel. And I know she heard some of these jokes.

Naturally, every boy who dated her tried to grope her. They couldn't wait to get their hands on those enormous jugs. They were a disadvantage for her—though I must add that she never considered having them surgically reduced. In fact, she was proud of them.

As for the rest of her, she was simply an attractive, appealing girl, no raving beauty, maybe, but regular in her features and taut in the remaining elements of her figure. I well remember watching her walk away, her tight little butt twitching. I supposed she was unconscious of that. She wasn't. Sue Ellen was not unconscious of anything about herself.

She was bright and personable and warm. I liked her. I persisted in asking her for dates, and she began to accept.

When I graduated from Lodge, my father bought me an automobile for a graduation present. It was a brand-new black Oldsmobile Cutlass with a real leather interior. Maybe one of the reasons Sue Ellen accepted me was that I could drive her to Boston, or to Hartford, or other places she might want to go.

Anyway, inevitably we began to park and kiss. And so, one night—

"Len, I have to ask you a question."

"Sure."

"You're the only boy I've ever gone out with who didn't try to feel me up. Why?"

"Because I figure you've had to put up with enough of

that. Sometime, when we . . . respect each other enough, then I'd like to—Sue Ellen. I don't want to just feel you up. I want to kiss you there."

It was the right thing to say. In a minute she had pulled off her sweater, unhooked the corsetiere's masterwork, and bared those magnificent hooters.

I kissed them, believe it. I sucked her nipples into my mouth, caressed them with my tongue, and felt them harden. She had been the victim of too much crude groping and was eagerly waiting for a guy to treat her right. Sue Ellen moaned with exhilarated pleasure.

So did I.

I kept licking and sucking. She kept thrusting her big, soft knockers against my face until she all but smothered me with them. I was painfully hard. She fumbled with my erection. I rubbed her panties. They were wet. Still, we didn't do it that night. We knew we would another night. Unless something awful happens between two people, you don't go that far and decide to go no farther.

Well . . . inevitably, she got pregnant. Inevitably because we were a pair of stupid kids. We knew what would happen, but when you are that age you think you are invincible, that nothing bad can happen to you. Besides, it didn't feel as good through condoms, not to either one of us.

We couldn't tell her parents in Boston. One Saturday morning we drove to New York and faced my father. He was at home. Nonreligious though he was, he usually took a day's rest on the Sabbath.

"Well, for Christ's sake, kids," he said.

He was living at the time with a former model named Melissa Lamb. It was interesting. They were friends. He'd met her some years before my mother died. She was not just a romp in the sack—though for damn sure she must have been one: a brunette with a body that would have given Cardinal O'Connor an erection. She was a little vacant in the brains department, but she was good-hearted, as they say, and devoted to my father. I could tell by the way they looked at each other that they made each other happy.

"How far are you gone?" my father asked, using an expression Sue Ellen had never heard before.

She understood him, all the same. "Two months, two and a half," she said.

She was painfully embarrassed. Besides the two of us and her doctor, my father was the only person who knew.

"Well, it looks to me like you got a decision to make, Sue Ellen," he said. "It's a decision nobody else can make for you. Len can't make it. I can't make it. Your parents can't make it. The church can't make it. You'll have to make the decision all by yourself. Other people can advise you, but it's the woman's decision."

"What would you *advise,* Mr. Cooper?"

"Have the baby and put it up for adoption," my father said without so much as an instant of hesitation.

"I can't do that," she said tearfully. "People would see I was pregnant. My parents would find out."

Things like that just came out of him now and then. I am sure it genuinely surprised him when Sue Ellen began to shake with sobs.

"There are places where you can go," he said. He didn't apologize but he tried to relieve the situation by being rational. "Places where you can—I mean in total confidence."

She shook her head. "My father and mother would have to know," she wept.

"Well then . . ."

Well then was what happened. He called her dormitory and spoke to the house mother. He introduced himself and told the woman that he had managed to get tickets for *Amadeus*—a very difficult ticket to get—and would like for Sue Ellen to stay so he could take her and me to the show. It was not the house mother's responsibility and she suggested he should call her parents.

"Oh, of course. I haven't reached her parents yet, but I'll keep trying until I get them."

Sue Ellen pondered for three hours, then made her decision. The abortion—at that stage in a pregnancy a very simple procedure—was performed Saturday evening. She had all day Sunday and Monday to rest, before we drove back to Massachusetts on Tuesday morning.

She wept softly for hours on end. During the drive she was silent. I wasn't sure she wouldn't break it off with me and never let me see her again. It was during that weekend and that drive that I decided I loved her. I had hurt her, after all, and there is some perverse instinct in a man that drives him to love a woman he has injured.

13

It is difficult to believe there was a time when a woman could not get a prescription for the Pill unless she showed the doctor proof that she was married. Naturally, that sort of thing continued in Massachusetts when it had died elsewhere. At the very least, the doctor might insist on notifying the girl's parents. My father saw to it that Sue Ellen got a prescription in New York and had it filled in a New York pharmacy before we went back to Amherst.

"You can make her your woman, if that's what you want to do," he said to me. "But don't worry about her. She can take care of herself. With knockers like that, she can have any man she wants. And she knows it."

I was the man she wanted. She was the woman I wanted. Our shared experience of the abortion drew us closer together, rather than alienating us as we had been warned. My feeling for her was not just the old ache in the crotch but tenderness. She saw that and was drawn to me.

I don't mean to say that we weren't horny anymore. We were, for damn sure, and the Pill made it possible for us to be carefree in our lovemaking. It was a great time to be alive, what with the ardor of kids and the prescription protecting us.

When we left Amherst, we married and moved to New Haven where I would study law and she would study Chinese.

Why Chinese, for God's sake? Because, she said, it would be an intellectual challenge.

That was Sue Ellen. She could think up the most hairshirt things to do. For example, she played a musical instrument. An accordion maybe? The piano? No. She played the violin. Never very well. I thought she could have played the piano very well, but to her the violin was the most challenging instrument, so that was what she wanted to play, and she struggled with it until she did manage to generate tunes that were at least recognizable.

By now I knew what my father's business was. He'd told me and shown me the summer after I graduated from Lodge. The partner at Hale & Dorr was damn well not going to allow his daughter to marry the son of a man who sold women's undies for a living—and not only that but sold erotic undies that a respectable woman would not wear, in his judgment. He changed his mind when he found out what a big business Cheeks was.

By the time I married Sue Ellen, there were forty-seven Cheeks stores, all in cities on the Atlantic seaboard. Her father scowled and harrumphed but had to concede that my father ran an immensely successful business and was a wealthy man.

One Sunday evening in New York my father took Sue Ellen and me to a Cheeks shop on Madison Avenue. It was, of course, closed, and we explored it privately.

As always, the façade of the shop was discreet. The show window was dominated by a small cast-metal sign that stood on a pedestal and was lighted by low-wattage spotlights:

CHEEKS
LINGERIE FRANÇAISE

Behind the little sign, a dark blue curtain hid the interior of the store, as did a matching curtain on the door. From the street you knew this was a shop that sold intimate apparel, and did so discreetly. In the daytime passers-by could not glance in and see someone they knew shopping for scanties.

Otherwise the window displayed a few—a very few—posters advertising concerts and art exhibits and the like, all nonprofit and for the benefit of various causes. The posters were not enough to clutter the window but did suggest the store management's commitment to culture and good works.

Inside, Sue Ellen was astonished to find a marble floor, subdued lighting, gilded showcases, and racks and hangers of negligees, nightgowns, corselets, teddies, bra-and-panty sets, bikini bathing suits, and so on, all conspicuously high-quality merchandise offered for high prices. Displayed in the showcases were G-strings, crotchless panties, and bras with holes cut to display the nipples. One showcase was given to leather goods: leather corselets with no bras, leather pants, and leather collars that could be fastened with little padlocks.

" 'Supermarket Sweep,' " my father laughed. "Take anything you want. You'll find something very different for your wedding present—that is, different from what will be on display at the wedding as your gift from me."

Sue Ellen was not bashful. She chose a sheer black shorty nightgown and a pair of black crotchless panties. But she grinned. "Great bras and . . ." she said. She cupped her hands over her bosom. "I only wish . . ."

"Let me show you something, then," my father said. He pulled a tray from under a counter and displayed an assortment of nipple clips, most of them in pairs attached by fine chains. "I guess you can figure out how they work."

Sue Ellen was fascinated with the nipple clips and chose a pair of wire loops that would fit over erect nipples and be fastened in place by slide rings that tightened the loops. My father nodded his approval of her choice, then disappeared into a back room for a moment and returned with the identical item in platinum, with a square-cut emerald hanging from the chain.

"Slip back there and try them," my father said. "You get them on right, it takes a pretty good tug to pull one off. Try them."

We did. I used my tongue to bring her right nipple erect, then helped her slip the loop over the rigid, wrinkled bud. She pulled the slide ring up until the platinum loop was snug. She tugged experimentally and found that my father had been right: The loop would not easily slip off.

I helped her put the loop on her left nipple.

I pulled down on the emerald. Her nipples stretched but did not yield the loops.

"Oh . . . Len!"

"Feel good?"

"Like you can't believe. Pull more. And so *sexy!*"

I never knew the price, but I guessed that my young wife would be wearing two thousand dollars worth of platinum and emerald on her nipples. She took great pride in her clips and wore them often. She showed them to her girlfriends.

14

JERRY

We didn't discuss our business with our neighbors in Scarsdale. I suppose it was Buddy who discouraged me from identifying myself as the owner of Cheeks. He persisted in sneering that I'd gone into "the ladies' undergarments business." He actually made me reluctant to talk about it. It was difficult to live with the self-image of a merchant of women's underwear.

Even Giselle didn't broadcast the definition of our line of business. Our son didn't really learn what it was until long after his mother was gone—and he was surprised and I think a little distressed at first to know what his father's business was. He'd thought of me as a tough guy, and selling erotic lingerie contradicted that image.

Anyway . . . I remember a cocktail party in Scarsdale. It was the first to which we were invited. Giselle always attracted invitations. Her beauty attracted attention. Her accent charmed. Besides, our country had not yet matured enough to have ceased assuming a Frenchwoman was especially erotic. We all remember President Kennedy saying in Paris, "I am the man who brought Jacqueline Kennedy to France." Well, at parties in Scarsdale I was usually the man who brought Giselle Cooper.

She drank well, she ate well, she talked well. She didn't smoke. She was elegant in simple black dresses and single strands of pearls. She was admired.

"And what business is your husband in?" a woman asked her that evening of our first Scarsdale cocktail party.

It was a small-town question. People in the city were less likely to ask what you did for a living or what was your religion. Scarsdale was a Jewish town, and maybe that had something to do with it. People there had a sense of community and imagined they had a right to know just who their neighbors were and what they did. Around their swimming pools, everybody knew all about everybody— or thought they did.

"My husband is in a business we don't very much talk about," Giselle said.

The woman who had asked her was shocked and offended. She was offended because she took herself as having just been emphatically put down. She was shocked because to her Giselle's answer meant that I was in a criminal business. Visions of Mafia danced in her head— visions of guns and blood.

Giselle understood instantly. "He is in a completely lawful business," she said. "But it is one involving confidentiality. I am sorry."

That exchange gave us cachet in Scarsdale. In a community of suits—stockbrokers, bankers, lawyers, and a variety of corporate hacks—I was in some mysterious business we would not discuss.

No one went to any great effort to find out what that business was. Okay, not the Mafia. But a few people actually suspected I worked for the CIA. Or something like it.

Oddly, though Frank Costello and Meyer Lansky were in our house from time to time, as was once or twice Jimmy Hoffa, no one ever seemed to recognize them. We were damn lucky about that.

Today I am proud of the business Giselle and I built. Why I wasn't proud from the beginning, I don't know. It is something from our past, that is from the culture of our past. When I was growing up in America, a photographer was prosecuted for pornography after he showed photographs that displayed a model's *underarm* hair. When the first bikinis appeared on public beaches, girls were arrested. In television studios, silk handkerchiefs or silk flowers were fastened to the necklines of dresses, lest the audience should see on those black-and-white sets the shadow in the cleft between a woman's breasts. Faye Emerson was condemned for refusing to tolerate this and so showing a modest little suggestion of cleavage. Audiences ogled—supposedly—a blonde called Dagmar because her breasts were big. Operators of carnivals attracted crowds by arranging for jets of air to blow up women's skirts, and in many towns the law closed shows down for that—this, of course, before Marilyn Monroe laughed before the cameras while air from a grating blew up her skirt and showed her panties.

I could go on. We were an uptight society. By the time we opened the first Cheeks store the country was well on its way out of that, but remnants of old attitudes hung on—and, though diminishing, *would* hold on—and sometimes cause us worry.

I've said before that launching Cheeks wasn't easy. Worry about anal-retentives was the least of our problems.

Acquiring merchandise to stock the stores was a far bigger problem. For the most part, the kind of stuff we wanted just wasn't manufactured in America. Not in any quantity. Not so that you could place an order and expect delivery.

For the first year or so, almost everything we sold came from France. The merchandise came in through Idlewild Airport, as it was then named. That is to say, 90 percent or so of what we bought in France arrived at our stores in Manhattan. Some 10 percent was pilfered at the airport. Not just ours. Everybody's.

If you didn't like the cost of air freight, you could use

ocean freight—and pay the cost in pilferage off the Jersey docks.

For decades, maybe for a century, the longshoremen had lifted what they regarded as their share of every shipment they handled. They took a relatively modest percentage and heard few complaints. When freight shifted to the airports, the freight handlers there mimicked the old dock custom.

It was a "tax" for doing business in New York, just as protection was another tax, and every business understood it. You paid more for having your trash hauled than a business in, say, Scarsdale paid—and in Scarsdale you paid more than someone in, say, Springfield, Illinois.

If you wanted to do a little remodeling or have part of your store repainted, the contractors ripped you off for inflated labor costs, plus a little extra profit on the side for the contractor himself.

How many times did I hear something like this?— "That'll come to twenty thou, even. 'Course, if you could give me fifteen by check and, say, three in cash, the eighteen thou will cover it." That meant he was going to pay income tax on fifteen. It also meant that I was going to pay eighteen and be able to claim only fifteen as a business expense. Another tax on doing business in New York.

All you could do was raise your prices to cover this element of the cost of doing business.

But my losses on air freight rose and got out of hand.

I talked with Buddy. I always talked with Buddy. Since the day not long after my parents' death when he had mysteriously appeared and made himself my friend and mentor in street smarts, I had always talked with Buddy.

"Your problem is like this," he said. "Stock of *your* merchandise shows up in a shop in, say, Philly, how's anybody, including the cops, going to lay an identification on that an' say, 'Hey, these here scanties belong t'Cooper!' Y'follow me?"

"I follow you," I said bitterly.

" 'Nother thing. You ain' got no *affiliation*. I'd like to affiliate with you, but affiliation with me is gonna bust no balls at Idlewild or on the Jersey docks. You got two ways of doin' business, Jerry. One is straight, an' you gonna get ripped off good. The other is affiliation."

I knew what he meant. All I wanted from Buddy was confirmation of what I already understood.

I had two options, just like he said. I could work straight and take my lumps, be ripped off by every two-bit racketeer that preyed on business in the city, or I could—as Buddy put it—affiliate.

Well, what the hell? Tens of thousands of businesses survived without affiliating. Some, actually, were pressured into affiliating. Most were not. They paid their tribute and raised their prices and made a profit.

But I was just hard-nosed enough to prefer *having* muscle to *being* muscled. I have never been content to be a victim. It had taken me time to settle with Uncle Harry, but I had, eventually—and found great satisfaction in it.

I called Frank Costello, naturally. We met again in the Norse Room, in the Waldorf. I was not entirely surprised to find Meyer Lansky with him.

"A neat little business," Lansky said quietly, with that sly small smile that characterized him. "A lot of potential."

"If I'm not nickeled-and-dimed to death," I said.

"That can happen," said Costello.

Understand that I'm sitting here with two *statesmen* of Cosa Nostra. Albert Anastasia, whom I had met once, was called the Executioner, for good reason. I'd met Crazy Joey Gallo and Tony Pro Provenzano. When you're a hustler around New York, you do meet these characters. But Frank Costello, so far as I know, never killed anyone and never arranged a hit—and neither did Meyer Lansky. These two men were *peacemakers,* conciliators. They understood there was more money in the insidious invasion of businesses than there had ever been in violence, particularly in gang wars.

On the other hand, they represented *muscle*. It was not wise to get crosswise with men like them. They might not kill you, but they could break you, for damn sure.

"You're looking for a partner," Lansky suggested. "That's how I figure."

"You think so? Well . . . I suppose I am. I don't *want* a partner, but I suppose I should have one."

Lansky stubbed out his cigarette in the heavy glass ashtray on the lunch table. "It damages a man's pride to have to take a partner he doesn't want," he said in a soft, sympathetic voice. "But pride is not all that important, Jerry. I've been arrested, handcuffed, made to stand in a lineup." He shrugged. "None of that hurt me. I did a few months in jail, once. It didn't hurt me. A man who puts too much emphasis on his pride is looking for a sure fall."

"I'd like to keep control of my business, Mr. Lansky. I built it and . . ."

"Understood," said Costello. "And that's how it'll be. But like you said, they nickel-and-dime you, nickel-and-dime you. Suppose you were to turn over, let's say twenty-five percent of Cheeks to a partner with connections. And the nickel-and-diming stops. Not only that. This partner can help you expand your business. I have a man in mind who can also help you solve a problem you're going to have sooner or later."

"Which is?" I asked.

"You can't always import all your merchandise. You're going to have to start manufacturing it here. So, what do you know about the garment district, Jerry?"

"Nothing," I admitted.

"The boys that rip you off at the airports and on the waterfront are nothing compared to what you'll meet up with in the garment district," said Lansky. "It's a special culture, all its own. They have their ways that have been goin' on for all of this century and even before. It's more subtle, but it's more effective."

15

So it happened that I met Sal Nero: Salamon Nero.

I won't play around with this the way he did with me. His name, really, was Solomon Schwartz. He was a nephew of Arnold Rothstein, one-time kingpin of New York rackets who was whacked out in the late twenties. He was also a cousin of Bugsy Siegel, who is credited with having opened up Las Vegas. Violence was part of his background. Rothstein was murdered in 1928, Siegel in 1947. They—and Lansky—were relics of the day when Jews controlled the rackets that came to be controlled by Cosa Nostra.

Sal was a sort of Lansky writ small. Well . . . Lansky was only five feet four and a half, so of course I don't mean physically small. What Sal had was a trigger mind and a photographic memory. Some people compared him to Abbadabba Berman, the mathematical genius behind some of Dutch Schultz's most profitable scams. Writ small? No, he wasn't. He was writ large, a tall, muscular, handsome man who was irresistible to women. A flashy dresser.

I'll add one more fact. He was hung like a horse. Like a friggin' horse! It was amazing. I remember standing at a urinal and glancing over at Sal's cock. Men are not supposed to do that and will deny they do, but I've yet to meet a man who didn't, sometimes anyway. Sal was absolutely unbelievable!

What is more, he was connected. Officially—if there could be such a thing as *officially*—he was with the Carlino family. But he had always been careful to avoid doing things that would offend the other families, and no one despised him.

He was one year older than I was, and he had—to use words everybody will recognize but I never in my life heard seriously used—made his bones.

In 1947, when I was learning the Plescassier Water business, Sal found out that a Carlino underboss was messing with his wife. He went to Joseph Carlino, as the story is told, and complained that the underboss was screwing his wife, the mother of his children. He humbly asked Carlino's permission to whack the guy out. Sicilians are sensitive about that sort of thing: family relations. They have very little tolerance for guys who mess around with other guys' marriages. It's like the way Masons pledge on their souls never to fuck the wife or daughter of another Mason.

"Very well, my friend," Carlino said, as the story is told. "I will take no offense. But you must know that Vince has friends and will be well protected."

"I am only concerned that I do not offend you, Don Carlino," said Sal—as the story is told; I am always skeptical of things like this.

Carlino thought little more of it, apparently. But within a week the underboss was dead.

As the story is told, he got out of his car one night at his home on Staten Island. Two men were with him: his protection. As the three of them walked toward his front porch, huge blasts erupted from the shrubbery near the steps.

Vince went down first, nearly cut in two by the blast from a twelve-gauge shotgun. As the story is told, red and

yellow bits of his gaudy silk necktie were found between
his vertebrae. At short range, a twelve-gauge can do that.

The second blast took off the head of the first bodyguard, and the third blast cut through the knees of the
second bodyguard, leaving him crippled for life but alive
to tell a cautionary tale.

Sal had bought an automatic shotgun and cut down the
barrel and the stock. He drilled a hole in the remaining
wood of the stock and put in a leather strap. That way he
could carry the shotgun hanging under his left arm and
hidden by his raincoat. It was as dangerous as any weapon
ever used.

What was more, it was used once. No trace of it was
ever found. The New York cops know how to find guns
tossed in the saltwater, but they didn't find this one.

Nothing happened. If the cops suspected who whacked
out Vince, they didn't care. But after that Sal Nero was
known as a man who could be crossed a little but not big-
time.

My partner.

16

The advantages of having Sal Nero for a partner made themselves apparent quickly.

Pilferage at Idlewild did not stop, but it went down to the standard take. Nobody said a word, but the pilferage diminished. That was just one thing. What was more, the cost of having trash hauled went down a little, as did the cost of minor repairs and major remodeling.

Things like this happened—

A wise guy came into my West Side store one morning. "Figured you'd want to send flowers as a tribute," he said to Giselle. "Everybody else is."

"Flowers?" she asked. "For what?"

"Well . . . You know Paulie died. Paulie C. All the neighbors are sending floral tributes. Figured you'd want to send—What you want to send? I mean, like five hundred. Five buys a real nice tribute. Everybody'll notice. Everybody'll appreciate the way you're making your business a part of the neighborhood. Be good for your business. Be very good."

People who didn't know Giselle took her for an innocent because of her French accent. Giselle was as innocent as Sal. "Five hundred dollars," she mused, frowning. "I don't know. . . . Man like Paulie ought to get at least a thousand."

She said it, though she had not the remotest idea who Paulie C. might have been—if indeed there had been a Paulie C., and if indeed he had passed to his great reward.

"Oh, yeah, well . . ."

Giselle nodded solemnly. "All this kind of thing is handled by my husband's partner. Yes. You speak to him, and I am sure he will do what is right."

"Well, lady, who *is* your husband's partner, and where do I find him?"

"My husband's partner is Sal Nero."

"Uh . . . right. Okay. I'll talk to Sal. Right. I'll take it up with Sal."

Of course, that was the last we ever heard about sending money to buy flowers for Paulie's funeral.

Sal had a formidable reputation among the small-timers. They were afraid of him. They had heard the story of the twelve-gauge. He had a respectable reputation among the bigger fry, but his reputation among the small-timers served us well.

He was like Meyer Lansky. He wasn't a capo, and he didn't have any soldiers. He didn't work that way. So far as I have ever been able to find out, he never killed anyone or had anyone killed after the incident with the Carlino capo in 1947—with one very big exception. But the word on him was that he *had* done it, so he might do it again. He was a smart man, a wheeler and dealer who made things happen by brains and not muscle—but don't get seriously crosswise with him.

He drank nothing stronger than wine, and of wine he drank only the best. He cared nothing for champagne or, in fact, for any white wine, but he knew French and Italian reds and could order them by year.

I was amused at how wise he was to the specialty waters. If he wanted fizz water, he ordered Canada Dry or Adirondack water that was just as good but even cheaper.

He laughed at the people who made it a point of honor to have little green bottles on their tables.

"Shows what you can do with the right advertising," he said. "With the right kind of promotion we could bottle and sell horse piss."

His taste in women was entertaining.

He liked heavyset women. He explained why:

"Y'know, when y'got a whang like mine, y'gotta do it with a *big* gal; I mean, one with plenty of flesh around her pussy. Hell, with a little thin woman I'd go through her and come out the backside."

I was already curious about his whang, of which I'd had a glimpse as we'd stood side by side at two urinals. One day we were in my office. He stepped to the door and latched it. "Go ahead and have a look," he said, and he pulled on his penis to bring it all out of his pants.

As God is my witness, the man had a ten-inch penis! It was formidable.

"I'm a friggin' freak," he said. "But what can I do? I can't have it cut down."

When I met him, his current girlfriend was a chubby twenty-five-year-old named Truda. She was not obese, but she was oversized in all dimensions. She was fascinated with the line of merchandise we stocked in our Cheeks shops, but we had almost nothing she could wear, which caused Sal to offer his first idea about our business.

"Y'know," he said, "there's a lot of girls like Truda. We oughta offer a bigger choice of sizes."

He was right, and our next shipment from Paris included merchandise in larger sizes.

His next idea had to do with advertising that we carried the larger sizes. We couldn't put up signs saying "SCANTIES FOR *BIG* GIRLS, TOO!" We could, though, Sal suggested, feature bigger girls in some of our color photos. That would get the message across. All we needed was one or two fat models.

"Hell," he said, "why not my Truda? She'd be flattered. I mean flattered."

So we took Truda to the photographer and had her pose in bra-and-panty sets; also in skimpy nighties and bikinis. Sal bought her a blond wig, which was so conspicuously a wig that there could be no doubt that was what it was—which made her even cuter. Within two weeks at least one photo poster in each of our shops was a picture of Truda showing a lot of skin.

This inspired her to think she could become a model. Her hair was red, so she took to calling herself Ginger. She had a portfolio of pictures taken and began to offer herself as a model. Sal and I thought it was strange, but a number of photographers hired her. She never became the fashion model she had dreamed of being, but her picture appeared from time to time in magazines given to photo art. One caption suggested a fat girl like her had to have a lot of courage to pose in the nude. That showed how much the caption writer understood about a woman like Truda. She wasn't ashamed of herself. She was proud.

17

Frank Costello had suggested that Sal's chief value to Cheeks would be his contacts in the garment district. And so it turned out. He knew his way around in that business.

When we went to the district, I expected to meet a bald, cigar-chewing man in a soiled shirt and vest, sitting at a scarred old desk, probably with his feet up—an Uncle Harry come back to life.

What I met instead was an emaciated Chinese named Charlie Han, dressed in fashionable faded blue jeans and a light blue flannel shirt with white buttons. Charlie was a chain smoker of unfiltered Camels, and a pack of them always stood in his shirt pocket. He did not put his feet on a desk. If he had a desk. If he had a desk, I never saw it. In fact, I never saw any room that might have been his office. If you didn't find him in one of his shops, walking around, supervising, you would find him sitting in a booth in a coffee shop on Thirty-eighth Street. As I would learn, Charlie did business in cash and kept no records, so the tax authorities could find no way to audit him. Well . . . actually, they could have, but he also made it his business to be inconspicuous, and I doubt that the agencies who might have wanted to look into his operations were even aware he existed.

Everyone has heard the word *sweatshop*. Few have ever seen one. Charlie's employees were almost all Hispanic women, from a variety of Latin-American nations. Few of them were legal immigrants. They worked at sewing machines on the upper floors of district buildings, in conditions that even I—who thought of myself as reasonably knowledgeable about how things were on the streets—found unbelievable.

For example, there was just one toilet for as many as fifty women. They had one ten-minute toilet break in the morning and one in the afternoon, at which time a line naturally formed and most of them did not return to their machines by the end of the break. When they didn't—or if they went to the toilet at another time—they were docked an hour's wages. *An hour!*

These women were young, most of them, and many of them were conspicuously pregnant. Abused by the sweatshop all day, they went home to some hovel at night to be abused by the man who had gotten them into this country, and who took their money from them. They were slaves; there was no other way to put it.

Charlie paid his people cash. That way there was no record of how much he paid to whom, so he paid no social security, no workers' compensation premiums, no unemployment compensation tax. God knows what other taxes or charges he did not pay. Of course he paid nothing like the minimum wage. Very few of the women who worked for him knew there was such a thing.

Once in a while a union organizer came around and tried to organize the women. Those fellows were in a risky business. They had a way of . . . disappearing. Various kinds of reformers came around from time to time, representing organizations as lofty as the United Nations. An operator like Charlie could move his sweatshop in a matter of hours, so that when inspectors came in response to a reformer complaint all they found was a bunch of empty floors.

"That's the garment industry," Sal told me. "Forget you ever saw this shop. The most upscale stores in the country sell name brands that come from sweatshops like Charlie Han's. Their buyers have no idea—or can pretend they have no idea—about the conditions in which the clothes they buy for their stores are made. Charlie is a contractor. He gets a contract—an *oral* contract, nothing in writing—to make a thousand dozen skirts, let's say, for Big Store chain. That contract comes from a middleman who may have got it from another middleman, and only the middlemen deal directly with Big Store. Big Store defines design and fabric, Charlie buys the fabric and thread and zipper for, say, a dollar seventy-five per skirt, has the sewing done in his sweatshop at a cost of a dollar twenty-five per skirt, and sells the skirt to Middleman One for seven-fifty. Middleman One sells it to Middleman Two for eleven twenty-five, and Middleman Two sells wholesale to Big Store Corporation for, say twenty-one dollars—"

"Why two middlemen?" I asked.

"Levels of insulation," Sal explained. "It's illegal to sell sweatshop merchandise, so they build a barrier between Charlie and Big Store. Now, Middleman Two sells the skirt to Big Store for twenty-one dollars, and Big Store sells it to the public for seventy-five fifty. Sometimes Big Store has a sale and sells the Leigh skirt for fifty-six fifty. Customer thinks she's got a great deal!"

"So we . . . ?"

"We make a deal with Charlie Han to make stuff for us. We don't want to get in trouble with the law, so we deal with Charlie through a guy I know by the name of Murray. That way we don't sell stuff we know is sweatshop-made. Murray insulates us from Charlie. That's his business. He's an insurance broker, so to speak. He takes the risk of getting in trouble with the law for dealing in sweatshop merchandise. He takes the fall if shit happens, and we're protected."

"Jesus!"

"Hey, don't think you can reform the garment industry. That's the way it is. That's the way it's always been— hell, for a century at least, and more than that I imagine. And let me tell you something else: Charlie will deliver quality merchandise. Forget how it gets made. From the standpoint of quality and cleanliness, it's made *right*."

Okay. If I didn't take a profit out of this way of doing business, somebody else would. And, of course, if Herr Standartenführer Schultz hadn't had his squads shoot all those Jews down there in the woods, somebody else would have. It's a common rationalization, one that covers a multitude of sins. The unsubtle don't even realize they are rationalizing and soldier on with clear consciences.

But Charlie Han would only do the sewing. We had to provide the designs, and as it turned out we would have to provide the fabrics.

For Cheeks, design would be everything.

In this, Sal was not at all helpful. Giselle tried to be helpful. But she knew little about American designers. Help came from an unexpected source.

Melissa Lamb, whose hair had shown above the top of her bikini when we took the first photographs for the shops, was a professional model and modeled for many sales campaigns for my lines. I had kept in touch with her. When I mentioned to her that I was looking for a designer, she named a name. He was good, she said, and he specialized in the sort of thing I wanted.

So, with some reservations, I contacted the designer she recommended: Larkin Albert.

I took him for a flaming fag, a swish. God knows I'd had my fill of fairies, having had to work with a whole family of them and their cutie-boys for almost two decades. But Larkin was something else. And I was wrong about him. He was not homosexual. He was a cross-dresser. What's more, he was damn good at it.

Often he went on the streets as a woman, wearing a wig, falsies, and high-heeled shoes, carefully limited makeup, and a miniskirt. I hardly need say that men tried to pick him up. They could experience not just one but sometimes two most unpleasant surprises. Discovering that the woman they had the hots for was in fact a man was only the first surprise. Occasionally one of them would turn aggressive, which generated the second surprise: Larkin Albert held a black belt in karate. He had made for himself an interesting life.

In his studio, he wore one of his many wigs, skin-tight leggings, high heels, and stuffed-bra T-shirts. He smoked cigarettes in a holder, which he brandished effeminately, even with people who knew full well that he was a man.

But he was a genius designer, as Melissa had promised. I was soon to learn how much a genius.

I talked to him about a design for a swimsuit.

"You know, Jerry," he said. "We've gone about as far as we can go with the bikini. Some beaches girls can go with tits bare. But not with pussy bare. I . . . a lot of women are uncomfortable with the bikini, anyway. On the other hand, the maillot looks like an old maid's suit, like something a candidate for Miss America would wear. So—I've been thinking. I have an idea in mind."

What he was thinking of was a one-piece, form-fitting nylon swimsuit cut out all the way to the waist, exposing all of the thighs and a broad expanse of the backside. Being one-piece and covering the navel, it seemed modest. One had to look a second time to see that on each side it bared what no bikini designer had ever yet exposed: everything from knee to waist. The crotch was covered by a narrow strip of fabric, just enough to cover the pubes themselves, while in the rear only the actual cleft was covered, leaving the fleshy butt bare.

I told him to go ahead, make me a prototype. And make it to fit Melissa.

A week later I went back to his studio to see Melissa model the first Cheeks original design. Larkin had chosen international orange for the first suit, the color of a traffic cone. He pronounced it stunning. That was a word I didn't use, but I agreed that it was stunning. I judged it would make a real splash in the market. Giselle agreed.

Whether or not stunning was the word for it, it was an instant success. I hardly have to say that newspapers and magazines made much of the inevitable play on words— that Cheeks was putting female cheeks on show. At first the cut of the suit was dramatized by the fact that the skin newly exposed was white, showing the boundaries of the bikini the woman had been wearing before.

Newsweek ran a quarter-page color photo showing the tan, the white, the orange.

Of course the white skin, too, tanned in a little while, but while the contrast lasted it was to our advantage. It sold suits.

It didn't hurt either that a crew of Florida beach cops arrested three spring-weekend beachgoers for appearing on the sand in "indecent" swimsuits.

The orange Cheeks suit became an international symbol. They began to appear on beaches from Florida to Maine, at country-club pools from New York to Ohio. Because of the distinctive orange, they were identified at a distance.

The quality didn't hurt us. As Sal had promised, Charlie had things sewn right. There were no incidents of seams opening. The suits did not fade in saltwater and chlorine water, plus sunlight.

We couldn't make the things fast enough. When the word got around that if you wanted a Cheeks suit you had better buy it while you could, that didn't hurt us either. We got calls from Big Store Corporation, wanting to know if they could stock our suits. In cities where we had a store, we let no one else sell the suit. When we did let other stores handle our swimsuits, they were sporting-goods stores, not Big Store department stores. If you wanted a Cheeks suit, you had to go where they were sold.

Naturally, that meant a new flow of traffic through our stores. People came in and discovered our line of merchandise. I can't say that many people who came in for swimsuits left with packages of scanties, but their visits did help our reputation. Some bought other things. Many came back and bought something else later.

We were on our way.

18

LEN

During the years when my father was turning his little string of shops into the major chain that would be selling scores of millions of dollars worth of Cheeks products by the time I was old enough even to know what his business was, I was blissfully living in the care of my mother, then in good schools, having no idea what kind of struggles were going on. Those were my years of oblivion. I have memories, but the highlights are rare, and the rest is foggy.

——I remember that one summer we rented a house in Greenwich, Connecticut, so that we—that is, my mother and I—could go to the beach every day. I remember that the house was grand but the floors were deeply scarred. Last summer's tenants had roller-skated over the parquet.

——I remember that Aunt Thérèse came to Greenwich and stayed with us for two or three weeks that summer— Thérése, the collaborator who had been stripped and shaved. By the time she wore her Cheeks international-orange maillot on the beach in Greenwich, it was no longer scandalous, though she turned heads. I had no idea my father manufactured and sold it.

——I am too young to remember the assassination of

President Kennedy. I do remember the election of Richard Nixon and what my mother said about it. She said, "Well, that's the end of optimism in America. The country has been taken over by the pancake eaters."

—I remember Nixon's resignation. I remember with what quiet, tearful horror the event was noted in the halls of Lodge, in contrast with the amused satisfaction I saw in my father and mother when I went home.

—I remember a lot of dumb things, like my fascination with the first color television set in our home; my pride in learning that my father went to business meetings in his own corporate airplane, a twin-engine Beechcraft Baron—named Cheeks, of course; understanding that my father and mother could, well, *do it* at eight thousand feet over some obscure town in Pennsylvania, and did, behind a curtain that hid them from the pilot.

It dawned on me, slowly, that my father was *somebody*.

—I remember trips to Europe—to Paris, chiefly, but also to Lyon and to Nice and St. Tropez, where for the first time I saw topless girls on the beach. I remember eating *hamburger au cheval* without realizing it was horsemeat. (And why not? If we slaughter a steer to eat as flesh, why not a gelding?) I remember Paul Renard and visits to the Lido and Folies Bergère. I would learn only much later that my mother had once danced on the stage of a Paris nightclub as naked as those girls who gave me erections.

I should remember the symptoms of my mother's fatal illness. I loved her, and I was not insensitive to her, but I suppose I thought—like many children—that my parents were invincible. You are so dependent on them when you are young that you cannot imagine what it might be like to have to try to live without them.

My father lost both his parents at once, in a car crash, when he was about the same age I was when I lost my mother. *Both!* I shuddered. I couldn't even think about it.

Anyway, if I had been a more realistic boy I might have realized that it was not natural for my mother to be losing weight so fast. She turned into a pallid wraith within a few months. Suddenly she was delicate and vulnerable. I saw that, but still I had no idea that when my parents left for Europe that fall that it was for her last visit to her native land, her sister, and her friends. I guess they knew she would not return alive from that last visit.

Before I went to Amherst my father educated me a little.

"Len," he told me, "we are Jews. Some people are proud of that. Some are ashamed of it. I am neither. It is a part of life. I am a Jew just as I am a male. Nobody asked me if I wanted to be. I am. Your mother was a Catholic. Same thing. She just was. There are some things you can't change, and I would be disappointed in you if you tried. You can renounce Judaism, and you don't need to practice it, but you are a Jew. Look at your pecker. The God of Israel commanded us to cut off our foreskins, which we do because we were so commanded. Many Christians do it, too, but they don't have our excuse."

Then he handed me a slender book: the annual report of Cheeks, a Partnership. I had no idea how to read a balance sheet or a profit-and-loss statement, but even to me it was apparent that I was scanning the report of a highly profitable business.

He left me alone with it for half an hour, then came to me and asked, "Have you ever heard of Cheeks stores? Your mother and I built the business together. We don't compete, exactly, with Victoria's Secret or with Frederick's of Hollywood, but we sell a daring line of merchandise to daring customers."

"Can I ask you a question?"

"Of course."

"Do Frank Costello and Meyer Lansky have anything to do with your business?"

"I take your point," my father said. "The answer is no. Those two men have helped me, mostly by giving me valuable advice. If you are asking me if I am involved in

Cosa Nostra, the Mafia, that sort of thing, the answer is definitely no."

I nodded—skeptically, I am afraid.

"I've known gangsters, Len," my father said soberly. "Albert Anastasia, called The Executioner, who was murdered. Crazy Joey Gallo, who was murdered. When you start a new business in this city, you meet these people. You have to come to terms with them. I've come to terms with them. I might have been found floating facedown under a dock, otherwise. But I never joined them."

I nodded. I glanced at the numbers he had shown me. I remembered the private plane named Cheeks. I had to say something. I didn't know my father very well yet. But I was unable to believe my mother could have been involved in anything that involved the men my father said he wasn't involved with.

I'd met Sal Nero, but knew nothing about him.

To me, he was Uncle Sal—though my father told me he was really Solomon Schwartz and as much a Jew as we were. He had a wife and children, but he was divorced as I recall, and his children were grown and saw him seldom.

I would hear many stories about Sal Nero as the years passed by, but I did doubt and do doubt that many of them were true.

He took an interest in his partner's son—me—and when I was at home he would take me to baseball games. I suppose I went to half a dozen Yankees games with Uncle Sal. Usually his girlfriend, Truda, went with us. Always, we had box seats on the first-base line.

One evening I will never forget. Sal wrote a note and handed it to an usher with a twenty-dollar bill. In a few minutes a baseball player appeared just outside our box and greeted Sal with a hearty hello.

"Hey, ol' buddy," said Sal. "Meet Len Cooper, son of my business partner."

I stretched out over the fence and shook hands with the

player, Number 15, whom I could not identify. I had no idea who he was.

"Thought you might sign a ball for my little buddy," said Sal.

"Sure thing," said the baseball player. He summoned a bat boy and got from him a brand-new baseball. He scribbled on it and handed it to me.

The player saluted and returned to the field.

I read what he had written on the ball:

> *To Len with best wishes—*
> *Thurman Munson*

I still didn't know who Thurman Munson was, and had to look it up when I got home. He was the catcher for the New York Yankees—and a very big baseball star. He had less than twelve months to live when he signed the baseball I now display inside a Lucite box. He was killed in the crash of an airplane he was flying, in Canton, Ohio, the next year.

So . . . that's the kind of guy Uncle Sal was. He was a guy who could walk into Yankee Stadium and call one of its all-time great players to come to his box and sign a baseball for a kid who didn't know who he was.

19

When I was at Amherst and Yale I was conscious of my father's fortune and how he had earned it. It was while I was at Friends School in New York and then at Lodge that I was ignorant of all he'd gone through, and my mother, to build their small chain of lingerie shops into a big business.

The problem was, there was no one to tell me. My mother would have, I am sure, if she had lived. My mother was open and honest. She told me what she wanted to tell me when she thought I was old enough to know it.

So has my father, though he has a very different idea of what I should know and when I should know it. My father has been honest with me—but in a different way, his own way.

I've had to pick up bits and pieces from here and there. From wherever I could get it.

I have never liked Buddy. He knows it. Still, when my father met my mother, Buddy had already been his best friend for many years, since my dad was a kid. Why Buddy so closely befriended my father was a mystery to me—and to my father, really. Inevitably I am thrown into

Buddy's company, and when that happens I encourage him to talk about the years when they were not just friends, but partners. Buddy knows more about my father than even my mother knew.

The sudden death of both his parents was a defining event in my father's life. How could it not have been? Then he discovered that his Uncle Harry had snookered him out of what little inheritance he might have had. Though he had reason to hate Uncle Harry, he had to work for him. In 1941 jobs were not easy to come by for a kid just leaving high school. He was forced to work for a pittance and watch his uncle cheat everyone who came near him.

My father became a hustler. Buddy was a hustler. A certain bitterness lay behind it—Buddy's probably because he was a victim of racism, my father's because he was a victim of his Uncle Harry and also, in a far larger sense, because he was a victim of the way too many people had to live in New York City in those years. I know about poor people. But poor people today don't live the way poor people did when my father was a boy—with no so-called "safety net" offered by welfare, and no hope.

Why Buddy chose to befriend my father is a complete mystery to me—and I wonder if it's not a mystery to my father.

But then came Pearl Harbor Day. There was something irregular about the way the two friends went into the service. I am not sure what happened. It was even a scam when my father was given noncombat status and somehow managed to get the same for Buddy, though Buddy didn't deserve it. The two of them had all kinds of resources and knew how to use them. They were hustlers. Not only that, they were hustlers who were willing to take risks.

They wound up in Paris, which is where my father met Paul Renard and Giselle, my mother.

* * *

My father liked to eat at the Palm. I went there to meet him one day and found Buddy waiting for me. He said my father would be a little late, but we would have a glass of wine and wait for him.

As we sat I made a few comments about Sal Nero, specifically that I found him an bad character. "In fact," I said, "I'd think he was Mafia connected, except for one thing."

"What thing is that, Lenny?"

"Well . . . when he joined my father in the business, my mother was still alive and active. My mother would never have consented to be associated with—"

"Lenny, for Christ's sake! What do you think your mother was, some kind of plaster saint?"

"She was a good woman," I said truculently. "She was a *good* woman."

"Damn right she was," said Buddy. "A good woman. Brave. Smart. But you want to know what she was the first time I saw her?"

"What?"

"Stark staring mother naked. She was a stripper in a Paris club called the Blue Note, which was run by Paul Renard. A stripper. No funny business. She didn't hustle. But she danced in the nude. I don't mean in a G-string and bra: I mean in the *nude,* showing her . . . well, she didn't have any. She shaved."

I knew he was telling the truth. Why not? What motive could he have had for lying to me about that? And that's how I found out that my mother had been a nude dancer.

It made no difference. I have never thought less of her. And I have never told my father that I know about the Blue Note. I have never mentioned either that I also know that my mother modeled skimpy lingerie in Cheeks stores during the early years. The truth is, I respect her and regret her death even more, now that I know she was a whole person. I'm glad she was not a saint. I'm glad Buddy didn't tell me until I was old enough not to be judgmental any longer. But I am glad he told me.

20
JERRY

We were almost wiped out by one colossal foul-up.

To start with, Sal wondered just what American women would wear. At the beginning we sold *lingerie française*—meaning that we imported our merchandise from France where, supposedly, the most daring lingerie in the world was produced and worn. It *was* bold and brief, when most American women were still wearing white panties with waistbands at their navels, with legs cut so that nothing of their hips or hinder cheeks showed. Most American women were still wearing bras that were *contraptions*: gizmos of nylon and rubber designed to shove the breasts into unnatural pointy shapes. French women had liberated themselves from this sort of thing. They wore bikini panties and soft, sheer bras—if, in fact, any bras at all. Even so, what was sold in French lingerie shops was timid compared to what was about to be offered in America.

The time was passing when France was the naughty nation. When we went into business, to suggest your lingerie was from France generated a sexy image. Today in France you can generate a similar image by suggesting you sell lingerie imported from the States. The picture keeps getting better.

Larkin Albert designed, and Charlie Han sewed up, thousands of dozens of sheer bikini-style panties, opaque only in little triangles in the crotch—until we eliminated even the little triangles. Giselle modeled for me—and me alone—one without the triangle. With her shaved pussy, the panties were exciting. One of the most popular models of those was studded with rhinestones.

We decided to introduce a new line, holding a style show: this one at the Hilton. Here again we had a runway for the models, dramatic lighting, and music that would be anything but subdued. Again, most of the invited guests were from the news media. We did not allow cameras.

Of the models, only one, Melissa Lamb, had appeared in our first show. Giselle decided not to appear. The girls were eighteen and nineteen years old, every one of them stunning, with generous figures. I had specified: no Twiggy.

The first item we showed was what we called a bridal nightgown. It was white and sheer and had a long pleated skirt. As the bride's legs moved inside the pleats her legs were exposed, then hidden, then exposed, then hidden, erotically. Depending on how the bride walked, she might even give brief blurred glimpses of her pubic hair. Nearly all of the nightgowns sold in America at the time had an opaque panel across the upper chest, so that even if the legs and hips and tummy could be seen, the breasts would remain discreetly hidden. We showed two versions of that nightgown, one with a sheer panel across the breasts, one with nothing there at all, showing the breasts bare.

One of the young models blushed and said she just couldn't wear the version with the breasts bared. She did consent to modeling the one with her breasts almost as fully displayed under the sheer panel. Melissa volunteered to wear the bare model.

As I now anticipated they would, the assembled writers applauded the two nightgowns, the bare version more than the other. They published reviews of our show, and we sold tens of thousands of that nightgown, about half-and-half divided between sheer panels and bare breasts.

Melissa and another girl modeled a sheer black baby-doll nightie. The other girl wore skimpy black panties under it. Melissa wore nothing and showed her hair.

When we were ready to show a red version of the same nightgown, the girl who had worn panties asked to be allowed to model this one without panties. "On second thought," she said, "it's more honest. Why fool around?"

We showed bikini panties that were nothing but triangles of fabric fore and aft, attached by strings over the hips.

We showed bras with circles cut out to expose the nipples. Things like that are common enough now, but they were once brazenly lewd.

The hit of the show was the first crotchless panties I ever saw. Albert Larkin had designed them. They were slit from just below the waistband, and the model's most private parts were exposed. It had been our plan that the show's finale would be a parade of all our models, wearing bras that displayed the nipples and crotchless panties.

Two of our models refused. One of them wept. "Oh, Mr. Cooper, I just can't! I just *can't!* I'm engaged to be married, and—" I excused her without reproach. The other girl offered no excuse, and I didn't ask for one.

Four girls appeared: one in black, one in white, one in red, and one in green. The writers loved them.

Giselle and I took the models out for drinks after the show. "I never thought I'd ever—" one of them said. "Well, hell," said another, "we knew what kind of show it was. It's something for my diary!" And another said, "So long as it's anonymous and my name isn't mentioned, I'd walk out there in the altogethers, for the money. My mother doesn't see me, but if I appear in an underwear ad for Macy's, she sees me in the paper."

* * *

We sold a lot of cutout bras and crotchless panties, and it brought a question to Sal's mind. "Okay, they aren't going to wear that stuff under their clothes all day. This kind of stuff is what you might call boudoir lingerie, to wear only in the privacy of the bedroom. So, okay, I wonder if they'd buy G-strings and like that. Maybe not, but their boyfriends and husbands might buy them, hoping the gals would wear them. It might be worth a try, to see."

Larkin Albert would not design a G-string. There was no challenge in it, he said. Giselle and I designed our first ones ourselves. We bought black nylon and cut a variety of triangles, ranging from large enough really to cover the pubic region to small enough barely to cover the trench. Giselle was no seamstress, but she could sew well enough to put G-strings together.

We settled on one sample—not the one that covered most or the one that covered least—and I took it to Charlie Han and asked him if he could run me up a hundred dozen of them. He laughed and said of course he could, but that G-strings would hardly sell except as part of a set that would have to include a totally sheer bra. Even women who did not wear bras would want sheer ones if they were pretending to be strippers. He didn't need a design for that from us; he would make it up from his own idea.

We decided not to make big posters to advertise the strip sets in the stores. Instead we bought Lucite frames and put eight-by-ten black-and-white prints on the counters.

Giselle wanted to pose for those photos. She was forty-one years old that year. She didn't look like a woman in her forties, but she didn't look like a girl in her twenties, either. She thought we should make the point—and she was right!—that Cheeks merchandise was not just for chicks, but for *women*. So she did pose, and her pictures were displayed: a mature woman dressed to please her husband in the privacy of their bedroom.

That simple strip set—strip *panels* they were called,

believe it or not—became the basis of a complete new line of merchandise for Cheeks stores.

And there is where the trouble began.

Giselle and I had opened three initial stores in New York. By the time Sal came in, we had eleven. We had five in Manhattan, one in Brooklyn, two on Long Island, one in White Plains, one in Greenwich, Connecticut, and one in Ridgefield, New Jersey.

I spent a hell of a lot of my time traveling from one of these stores to another, trying to be sure they operated the way we wanted them.

When we tried to open a store in SoNo, a restored waterfront area of pricey shops and restaurants in South Norwalk, Connecticut, the town fathers found all kinds of ways to discourage us—zoning problems to start with, then expensive renovations to the building that would be required by fire laws, sanitary laws. The truth was, they simply didn't want scandalous undies being sold on the main drag in SoNo, no matter that our store would show nothing to the street and would generally be a good municipal citizen.

We almost had to close the Ridgefield store when our manager put some of our photo posters in the window. That brought pickets from the religious community. We fired that manager and cleared that window just in time to avoid irate regulators coming in, thinking up all kinds of problems, and shutting us down.

When we tried to open a store in Rye, New York, we came under fire from a local Bible-banger who declared that "this kind of filth" had no place in a Christian town.

"Well, there's more than one way to skin a cat," Sal said to me when we were talking about the problem in my Manhattan office. "I've done a little checking. And guess what? The Reverend Mr. Wright is not so cool and clean as he makes out. Lemme show you something."

Sal rarely carried a briefcase, but he was carrying one that morning, and he took from it a bundle of papers. The first thing he showed me was a Denver newspaper. With his hand he covered everything of a certain story except a picture.

"Know 'im?"

The photo was of the Reverend Mr. Wright, beyond question.

He uncovered the rest of the story. It read:

JR. HI CAGE COACH CHARGED WITH SEXUAL ASSAULT, STATUTORY RAPE

A junior-high school basketball coach has been charged with assault and statutory rape after three cheerleaders charged that he had improper intimate relations with them. The girls, two of them fourteen and one fifteen, whose names are being withheld because of their ages, allege that the coach groped one of them, partially undressed another, and sexually entered the third. Arrested last night and held without bail is Theodore "Ted" Bligh, 29, a teacher and coach at Blair Junior High School.

The story went on to say that Bligh had been arrested on the complaint of three fathers. And so on.

Later issues of the newspaper reported that Bligh had been found guilty of the charge and sentenced to five years in the penitentiary.

Sal also had a copy of Bligh's—Wright's—FBI record, including mug shots and fingerprints.

"Where do you come up with stuff like this, Sal?" I asked. I was genuinely surprised.

"There are ways of doin' things, and there are ways of doin' things," he said. "I laid a little dough around. I'll give you an expense account."

A week later Sal met with the Reverend Mr. "Wright" in his pastoral study. We showed him photocopies of the newspapers.

He grinned almost insanely. "You can't stick this filth

to me," he said with a brittle laugh. "Sure, the picture looks like me, but—"

"Maybe your fingerprints look like or don't look like," said Sal with grim calm.

"I know what you're trying to do! And why!"

"You're licensed to marry people," said Sal. "Your application for that license is a public record. When a man has a church, the state doesn't ask questions particularly; it just issues the license. Well, you got a church, buster, but you don't got a degree, and you were never ordained."

"The board of my church—"

"Is a little gang of ignoramus boobs," Sal interrupted harshly.

"I know what you're trying to do!"

"And we know what *you're* trying to do. I got an idea the Rye police are going to find your FBI sheet very, very interesting. Not to mention the newspapers."

In this episode, Sal showed how effective he could be. It was also evidence of a problem we would have with him. After he left, two enforcers arrived. They gave the Bible-banger forty-eight hours to get out of the State of New York. Forty-eight hours! Or they would hand over to the local police and newspapers their evidence of his Colorado crimes. To place emphasis on their demands, they thumped him a little.

After he was gone—within his forty-eight hours—they gave the police and newspapers the whole story, anyway.

Sal believed in direct action. And he took no prisoners. But that wouldn't help us in what was coming up.

21

The big problem came in New Haven.

It seemed like a good town for us. We figured Yale students might buy some of our stuff, and faculty people would have open minds and might be receptive to Cheeks merchandise. Besides, New Haven was a good-sized town, and prosperous. It had a certain cachet, also, that we figured would be good for us. Greenwich was like that. Ridgefield was like that, too. Prestige locations.

The way we opened a store in a new town was to hold a preview evening for invited guests, and that is what we did in New Haven.

We invited the mayor, members of the council, people from the chamber of commerce, newspaper editors and writers, the president of the university, and a few senior faculty members—all with their wives, of course. Obviously, not all these people came. But half an hour after the announced time of opening, we had twenty-five or so people in the store.

On four tables covered with white linen, set up in the middle of the sales floor, we had bottles of red and white wine and platters of assorted yellow and white cheeses, with crackers, melba toast, and bread sticks. Our caterer had been told to supply glasses and real plates, no paper cups or plates. Candles burned on each table.

At these parties we didn't display our more daring items, such as crotchless panties, and focused on high-quality lingerie and bathing suits. The identity we wanted was one that would allow people to be seen coming out of our store and not be embarrassed. We wanted it understood that we were not a sleaze operation.

We offered no speeches. I circulated among the guests and tried to get my message across conversationally.

"We like your show window, Mr. Cooper," one man said. The "we" he referred to was himself and his wife. A heavyset man, he was a member of the city council. "Will it stay that way?"

"Absolutely. We never display underthings to the passersby on the street. The window will always be just as it is—with the exception that civic organizations can bring in a limited number of posters announcing concerts, plays, and the like, and we will display those in the window. Otherwise—"

The show window had only our signature cast-metal sign that said nothing but—

CHEEKS
INTIMATE APPAREL

When just about all the guests we could expect were in the store and it seemed unlikely that more would come, we had girls model a few of our more modest items, especially our orange maillot swimsuits. Giselle modeled negligées and nightgowns. I would always introduce her as my wife. Melissa, who continued to work with us from time to time, modeled panty-and-bra sets, with garter belts and stockings.

We got our point across, as we almost always did. The people we shocked were amused-shocked. Clearly we were no threat to the town's morals.

As the guests left, each woman was presented a

wrapped gift box. They opened them in their cars, we knew. They expected to find . . . God knows what. What they found in each box was a handsome silk scarf.

We had employed a woman from Hartford to manage the store. Betty Logan. She was a woman in her fifties, with graying hair and eyeglasses she wore hanging from a chain around her neck. She was widowed, and had managed a boutique in Hartford to put her son through the University of Connecticut.

"I've hired two girls to model for the party," she said. "They are Yale coeds, and that will make a good impression."

"Ordinarily we bring along our own models."

Betty shrugged. "I can cancel them."

"No. Maybe you got an idea. Two Yale girls *will* make an impression."

The two Yale girls had glorious figures, but were not otherwise outstanding beauties. One of them modeled our international-orange maillot and the other a couple of our bikinis. I had still brought along Giselle and Melissa, who modeled the lingerie.

I should have figured it out when—

Giselle suggested we go down to the hotel bar and have a nightcap. I said okay, and I said I'd stop by Sal's room and ask him to join us. Giselle told me to go ahead; she needed to use the bathroom and would catch up with us in five minutes.

I went to Sal's room on the floor below and knocked.

"Who's it?"

"Me, Jerry."

"C'mon in. It's not locked."

He was right; the door was ajar, so I walked into the parlor of his suite.

"In here, Jer'," he said from the bedroom. "C'mon in."

He was lying on his back on the bed, with his pants down around his ankles, and one of the Yale girls, the one who had modeled the maillot, was naked and lay with her face in his lap, her head vigorously pumping up and down as she worked on that ten-inch cock of his. She couldn't get much more than half of it in, but she obviously wanted all of it.

"Siddown," said Sal. "You can watch her finish me, and then I'll watch her do you."

"Giselle is waiting for me in the bar. I came to ask you to join us for a drink."

"Oh. . . . Well, okay. Gimme five minutes. Will five minutes do it, Val?"

"Oom-hoom. Better had."

When he came down to the bar, he brought her with him. Her name was Valerie, and she was in fact a Yale student, majoring in economics. She had a gorgeous figure, as I've said, but otherwise she was no raving beauty. She had absolutely no sense of embarrassment or shame. She saw that I was sitting with Giselle and could guess that I'd told Giselle about her, but that didn't bother her either. She accepted a Scotch and soda and sat glancing around the room, as if judging her chances of finding another cock to suck, another hundred dollars to pocket.

When we got back to the room, I called Betty Logan and told her she was not to hire Valerie as a model again.

"What's the problem?"

"She's a hooker."

"*That little girl?* My God!"

The fact was, Betty knew full well that Valerie was a hooker. So was the other girl who had modeled at the preview. Betty was a panderer. Her specialty was college girls, and New England colleges supplied her plenty of inventory for her trade. There were always college girls who were short of money or who longed for adventure. There were plenty of men, most of them well educated, secure, and prosperous, who were not interested in bar hookers but entertained fantasies of bedding a college girl. That she was not flashy-beautiful made her all the more attractive to these men. Betty had found a market. It was like Buddy said: sell something people want, maybe something they didn't know they wanted.

Betty had a stable of four or five girls she could call on anytime, plus a list of maybe ten others she could call for occasions. They had to show up dressed like college girls: skirts, sweaters, subdued makeup; and they had to be able to talk like college girls, whether they really were or not.

When I hired her to manage my store, Betty was in the process of renewing her stable. If she was going to be in New Haven, Yale could be her prime source. Her clientele would be intrigued by the idea of bedding down with a coed. But there were other schools. I discovered eventually that she had two girls from Fairfield, two from Quinnipiac, one from Bridgeport, and one from the University of Connecticut—among others.

Except for the Yale ones, these girls had to have cars! Well . . . they charged a hundred dollars a visit. Betty took twenty. Sal had handed Valerie a hundred dollars. If I had let her suck me off while he watched, that would have cost *me* a hundred. This was no small-time trade. It was, as the old story went, the carriage trade. Like Buddy said, sell people what they want. . . .

The New Haven Cheeks store was to be Betty's showroom. Her girls came to the store and hung around there, ostensibly as clerks. Sometimes they stimulated interest by modeling pieces of our merchandise.

Betty damn near ran us out of business.

22

She used our store as a showroom for her hookers. Then she did something more.

Generally, we didn't go for this kind of thing, but in a few towns we did cooperate with a local restaurant to put on a weekly lunchtime lingerie show for businessmen. The restaurant had to be respectable, not just a bar, and it could not be a joint that offered strippers in the evening. We preferred a restaurant that had a separate room for our show, like the room where the local Rotarians or Kiwanians met for lunch or dinner. That way, only people who wanted to see a lingerie show with their lunch saw a lingerie show. And, finally, we allowed only our less daring merchandise to be shown.

It wasn't a bad deal in the towns where it worked. The nighties, bikinis, and lingerie they modeled were for sale, and typically we sold several hundred dollars worth each show. Better yet, it was a perfect form of advertising for us.

It was also a perfect form of advertising for Betty's business. She brought her hookers—some of them college girls—to model lingerie. With something less than subtlety, she let it be known that her models might be receptive to a profitable proposition.

"You like that nightie? Laura would be glad to model it for you at your office. There's a scantier version, too, that we don't show in these public appearances. In fact, we have a lot of merchandise that we don't show publicly, that might interest a gentleman like you. Of course, the model doesn't have to be Laura. We have several other models who'll be glad to come to your office, or your home for that matter, to model for you."

Pimping was not our business. "Hell," said Sal. "If we wanted to do that, we could organize it a whole lot better and make a hell of a lot more money."

It also had its hazards.

Sal didn't like to meet in the office. He preferred to sit down over a nice lunch or dinner to talk business. We met at Sparks. We had thick steaks and plenty of rich red wine.

"That bitch in New Haven is giving us a problem," he said when our steaks were in front of us.

"I figured she would."

"Gonna have to do something about it," he said.

"Gimme the problem."

"Okay. Remember the little gal you saw blowin' me? Valerie? You told Betty to get rid of her, but she didn't. Valerie has been working for Betty right along. I mean, hey, you have to figure the little bitch is too good to just shove out the door."

"Well, Betty is not that good. Maybe we gotta shove *her* out the door."

"You don't know what the problem is."

"Okay. What's the problem?"

"Well . . . Valerie specializes in . . . you know what she specializes in. So, okay, one night she's givin' it to a guy named Earhart, who's president of one of the New Haven Rotary clubs. For some reason she starts to *bite* the guy. I don't know what he did or said, but he swears she started bitin' him. He couldn't stand that, so he slugged her hard and broke her nose."

"It could happen," I said. "A long time ago, in the thirties, I think, a professor at Ohio State University, by the name of Dr. Snook, had beaten coed Theora Hix to death with a ball-peen hammer, with the same justification, that she was biting him. Years later Robert Chambers claimed he killed Jennifer Chambers for the same reason, that she was causing him unbearable pain."

"Well, everybody in New Haven knows about it and attaches it to our store. It's a great big joke in New Haven, and we're part of it."

"So what do we do about it?" I asked.

"Lemme finish telling you the problem. Valerie's parents haven't seen her yet. But they will, and when they do they're gonna wanta know why the busted nose. Valerie's threatening to sue Earhart. Betty is in a tizzy. Only thing I can think of to do is go up there and visit the parties."

"I'll go," I said. I was concerned about just what Sal might do.

"We'll both go."

I called Betty and had her arrange a meeting with Earhart and Valerie. Sal and I rented a hotel suite, had a bar stocked in it, and ordered a display of hors d'oeuvres to be displayed.

Earhart arrived first. I had called him after Betty spoke with him and asked him to meet us earlier than she had specified. I wanted to talk with him before Betty and Valerie arrived.

He was a small man, maybe fifty years old, afflicted with male-pattern baldness, so much that his head was shiny. He was a realtor. I think he had a sense that he was in the presence of the Mafia. He accepted a Scotch and soda and chose a few nibbles from the table.

"Have you recovered, Mr. Earhart?" I asked.

"Not entirely," he said wryly. He sat on the couch, looked down at his lap, and frowned. "Painful . . ."

"I can imagine," I said. "How did you make the connection with Valerie?"

"It was the third time. Betty had brought her to the restaurant where our Rotary Club meets. They were sitting at the bar when our meeting broke up, and I came out, and Betty introduced her, said she was majoring in economics at Yale. We talked awhile and—"

"And Betty offered her for—"

"We talked awhile, and Betty said Valerie knew how to make men feel good. She'd make *me* feel good for a hundred dollars. And that's how it got started."

Sal, who was standing at the window looking down on the street, grinned.

"I want you to understand something, Mr. Earhart," I said. "Valerie doesn't work for us. She doesn't work for Cheeks."

"She's around the store a lot."

"I know. She works for Betty Logan."

"And Betty Logan works for you."

"Not after today she doesn't."

Betty arrived a few minutes later, with Valerie in tow. The girl had been no great beauty before, but now, with her nose flattened, she was anything but. She took a Scotch, drank it, and poured herself another.

"What we have here is a nasty incident, followed by a nasty scandal," I said. "It's in everybody's interest to settle it."

"I want my plastic surgery paid for," said Valerie.

"By *me*, you mean?" Earhart asked. "Forget it."

"Did you bite him, Valerie?" I asked.

"Damn right I did."

"Why?"

"He started to complain I wasn't doing it right, wasn't making him feel good the way I'd done before. That was his imagination. I was doing exactly what I'd done before."

"No, you weren't."

"So he grabbed me by the hair, pulled my face up, and

slapped me. Then he shoved my face down again. And I bit him. What'd he expect?"

Now Sal intervened. "Would you want the details of this thing, which still is just a rumor, covered in the newspapers?" he asked.

"Who are you?"

"I'm Sal Nero."

"Who's Sal Nero?"

"Ask Al Patrioto."

Earhart drew a deep breath. "Uh . . . okay." He turned to me. "You used the word 'settle.' What's it take to settle this thing?"

"Five thousand," said Sal.

Valerie shook her head. "*Five thousand!* No way!"

"It'll buy your new nose," said Sal coldly. "With some left over for bent feelings. That's the deal, Valerie. You wanta deal with *me* instead?"

"*I* might have something to say about this," Betty interjected.

"You don't have anything to say about anything," Sal told her roughly. "You're fired."

So that's how it worked out. Earhart paid Valerie five thousand dollars in cash. Valerie's parents accepted the story that she had broken her nose playing touch football, and the authorities heard nothing of the whole deal.

Or did they? Of course they did. They just stood aside and waited to see how it would turn out.

Firing Betty didn't solve our problem. The word was around New Haven and Connecticut that the Cheeks store was where you went to arrange for a first-class piece of tail.

An element of the problem was that Betty's girls *were* first-class. Think of it. You're a Bridgeport lawyer, a Hartford doctor, a New Haven realtor, a Groton engineer . . . you've got a failed marriage, or no marriage, and you've got the hots. What you might pick up in a bar risks mugging, to start with, and a multitude of other complications besides. So how about a cute little girl working her way through college? No great beauty maybe, but ready to earn her money and able to carry on an intelligent conversation, too, if that's what you want. She doesn't look like a hooker. She shows up in a pleated plaid skirt, a cardigan sweater, a single strand of pearls, wearing undies she didn't get at Cheeks . . . and she does a job of play-acting that she enjoys what you do to her as much as you enjoy it yourself.

But—hey!—how long can the cops and the district attorney let this go on in a town that prides itself on a *degree* of propriety?

Which, in the end, was still not the problem.

I'm sitting in my office in Manhattan, only half aware of what was going on in New Haven, now absent Betty Logan, when I'm visited by a guy who introduces himself as Alberto Patrioto.

I'd heard the name. The Five Families ran New York. The Patriotos ran New England.

Oh, he was a caricature! Camel coat. Gray hat. Black suit. Paisley handkerchief carefully folded in his breast pocket. Cigar.

He was direct. "I supposed," he said, "that we did not intrude on each other's territory."

"I am agreeable to that," I said, though I had no idea what he might think *my* territory might be.

"You agree that New Haven is not in your territory?"

"It is not in my territory, Mr. Patrioto."

"Then why the hell you runnin' a first-class whorehouse in my family's territory?"

I remember that I closed my eyes and nodded. I should have known. "Mr. Patrioto . . . All I'm trying to run in New Haven is a lingerie shop. Betty Logan turned it into a whorehouse entirely against my wishes and my instructions. When I found out about it, I fired her."

He stared at me for a moment, then nodded, to my relief. "I can believe it. The woman has always been a bitch. But she makes money. She's always done that. What I got in mind is a little deal. You take her back and let her run her little business on the side. You hand us, say, twenty-five percent of the take from your store—and we'll make sure that includes twenty-five percent of what Betty's takin' in. We'll excuse you for hornin' in on our territory. We'll take care of a couple little problems that might be comin' your way, like with the cops. And everybody'll be happy."

"Everybody but me," I said. "All I want to do is run a chain of lingerie shops. I didn't check with you before I opened my store in New Haven because I didn't think you would be interested in selling women's underwear. If word gets around that my Cheeks store in New Haven is a whorehouse, that could ruin my whole chain. So, let me suggest a different deal. I'll turn the store over to you, one hundred percent, the whole schmear. You can run it any way you want, with Betty and her girls or without. I'll supply you with merchandise at my cost. And all I ask is that you take the name Cheeks off the store."

I didn't tell him but would let him discover that the Cheeks label wouldn't be in the merchandise I supplied him and that the international-orange maillot, which was the only item distinctly identified with our name, would not be supplied.

Patrioto shook his head. "What my family has in mind is that we work together."

"Well . . . I'll have to check it out with my partner and my business advisers."

"Okay. Who's them?"

"My partner is Sal Nero."

"Sal . . . ?" He pinched up his face. "Of the Carlino family?"

I nodded. "Right."

"And who're your advisers?"

"Frank Costello and Meyer Lansky."

"You're shittin' me," he said, turning uglier than he already was.

I shrugged. "Call 'em."

I did not advise my twenty-five-percent partner why I had sold the store in New Haven. I told him the town had become unfriendly and that we'd be lucky to get out of there without taking a beating. I mean, literally a beating.

And we were.

23

LEN

I realize that what I am telling of this story is set in a very different time frame from what my father is telling. I was as unconscious of the trials he and my mother endured to get their business going and expand it as I was of their experiences in World War II—until at last I prodded someone to tell me.

Sue Ellen and I were married and moved to New Haven. We rented an apartment and enrolled at Yale. I was a law student. She studied Chinese. We lived comfortably but not luxuriously in a furnished apartment. Sue Ellen was confident in my father's generosity and was never surprised when his monthly check arrived. Her family were generous with gifts that arrived irregularly, but we lived on my father's subsidy.

I was curious as to why there was no Cheeks store in New Haven. There was one in Hartford, one in Providence, three in Boston, but none in New Haven, which I would have thought an ideal market. I asked my father why, and he told me.

I went to the location where the store had been. It was occupied by a pool hall. I made a few casual inquiries and learned that—

—The store had changed its name and operated under new management for about a year, at which time it closed—which pleased me because it demonstrated that my father and mother had not just achieved something anyone could achieve but had used their brains and built a business others could not build.

—Betty Logan, now a woman of sixty-five or so, was still a procuress. She worked under the dominion of the Patrioto family, which appreciated her expertise and took half her earnings. She made her living in a way that afforded her no Social Security, no medical insurance, no retirement benefits, and no future but to do what she could as best as she could as long as she could. Her girls were not terribly pretty, but they were skilled at what they did and were happy with the money. What was more, she had taught them her specialty: making a john believe he had a Yale or Quinnipiac girl in the sack and glad to do anything he might want of her. Betty Logan was a merchandising genius. If she had chosen to sell some other line, God knows what she could have been. I never met her, though later I would have a most indirect contact with her. I have not ceased to be curious about her and regret that my father so airily dismissed her when he was telling his story. She must have been a smart, brave woman.

—Since his contact with my father, Alberto Patrioto had served a four-year term in the federal prison in Danbury, for tax evasion, but was now the Patrioto godfather, with authority over all New England. His term in prison had not diminished his authority. If anything, it had augmented it, and no one questioned him.

I didn't press my father on why he didn't open a *new* store in New Haven. He had a personal distaste for the town. He disliked New Haven for reasons beyond his Betty Logan experience. I never have learned what they were.

* * *

I had to warn Sue Ellen about Betty. My wife's conspicuous boobs and taut, bouncy butt, plus the fact that she was genuinely a Yale graduate student and could talk about what she was studying, made her a prime target for Betty Logan. She would fetch a premium price.

I didn't have to worry about Sue Ellen going into the trade. She had firm ideas about that. Happy to give and receive much and varied sex herself, she obsessively condemned merchandising it. In fact, she reserved—but I knew it was there—a nagging doubt about the Cheeks merchandising operation. Clearly Sue Ellen would never go into the trade. And I mean never.

On the other hand . . .

Betty Logan paid her girls to recruit others. "I've always got more trade than I can serve," she assured them, "so earn the pay for a trick you didn't turn by bringing me a new girl."

When Sue Ellen first told me she had been talked to very solemnly by a girl who suggested she think about making a whole lot of money by doing something that was not difficult at all, she laughed about it. Then suddenly the crusader in her reared its head.

"How *could* she?"

She meant, how could her new friend—like herself, a student of Chinese—sell her body? It was unthinkable! The whole idea was abhorrent to Sue Ellen.

She decided to save Mollie from Mollie—actually, from Betty Logan, though she had not yet heard of her.

When I met Mollie, I judged that what she looked for from the men who bought her was not so much the money but acceptance and approval, even admiration. She was a graduate student, as was Sue Ellen, and she had come to Yale from Mount Holyoke, to there from Sacred Heart in Greenwich. You could see when you looked at her that she had never attracted dates.

If two words could describe Mollie, those words would have to be *small* and *square*. Her little face was square, framed by carelessly cut, dishwater-blond hair. Her eyes behind her little, round steel-rimmed spectacles were blue, her nose short and flat, her mouth wide and thin. She wore blue jeans stretched tight over her broad hips and generous ass, with sweatshirts draped over her round breasts.

She had a pleasant personality. That she was anxious to please came across from the moment you met her. It was an appealing anxiety, and it would have been difficult not to like her. It was difficult to think that this innocent-looking, small, square girl turned tricks. That it *was* difficult to imagine was part of her appeal. A john could fantasize that he was seducing a horny, adventuresome virgin.

Sue Ellen and I had our apartment. So did Mollie, sharing hers with another woman graduate student. Sue Ellen took to inviting Mollie for dinner one evening a week, usually Friday. Mollie would bring wine and a dessert, and Sue Ellen, typically, would prepare a platter of one or another type of pasta. Sue Ellen had made herself a close friend to Mollie and was trying with some degree of subtlety to lure her out of prostitution.

Mollie was no fool. She knew what Sue Ellen was trying to do and was amused by it.

I came in from the law library early one Friday evening to find my wife and her new best friend bare-breasted. Sue Ellen's nipple clips were on Mollie's nipples, and her emerald pendant hung between Mollie's melonlike boobs.

"When I told her about them, she asked if she could try them."

Mollie was not embarrassed. She had no sense of modesty whatever. We were friends, and she knew that I knew she played for pay. If she was flustered, it was not because I was staring at her naked tits but because she was wearing Sue Ellen's clips, chain, and pendant, which she knew were a gift from my father.

For myself, I was dumbfounded, not just to see my wife's jeweled clips hanging between another woman's tits but to see both of them with their hooters naked.

She started to take one of the clips off, but I shook my

head and said, "No. Leave them on awhile. It looks almost as good on you as it does on Sue Ellen."

I reached down and gave a short, gentle tug on the chain. Her nipple stretched, but the clip did not come off, as I had known it wouldn't.

"They're *nice,* Len. I'd give anything to have a pair of my own."

I called my father and asked him to send me another set of nipple clips and chain. I told him why. A package arrived a couple of days later. These clips were not like the loops of platinum wire, tightened by little slide rings, that Sue Ellen wore. These were *clamps,* spring-loaded. They did not loop around the erect nipple the way the wire clips did. No. They were alligator clips with soft rubber sheathing over the teeth, and they pinched. The chain between them was not fine jewelry chain but stainless steel chain with links almost a quarter of an inch in diameter.

Mollie took off her sweater and bra, squeezed the clamps to open them, and let them close, pinching her nipples and distorting them. Sue Ellen winced, but Mollie threw back her shoulders and shoved her boobs forward. Mollie was game. These clips hurt—though not very much—and I wonder if in fact the pain didn't arouse Mollie.

That evening at dinner my wife and her new best friend sat at the table with tits out, chains swinging between their nipples. What was coming was obvious.

I had mixed feelings. It was some kind of privilege to have two bare-titted young women at dinner. I can't deny it gave me a hard-on. But it was going to change the nature of my marriage. That was unavoidable, and I had to wonder what was coming and what I should do.

24

I came home one afternoon and found Sue Ellen wearing a dog collar. It was a heavy leather collar, suitable maybe for a Great Dane or some such breed: a dog big and strong and heavy. The prong of the buckle ended in a little loop, through which passed the shackle of a tiny laminated padlock. The collar could not be removed except by opening the lock—or cutting the leather. She smiled coyly and handed me a key.

"There y'are, lover."

It was Mollie's idea. Whenever Mollie went out to meet a john she wore a dog collar. It turned them on. It would turn me on, she had promised Sue Ellen—

"Hey! Every guy dreams of making a slave of his girl. So . . . let 'em think so! I guarantee it'll turn him on."

Well . . . I have to admit it did. And after that Sue Ellen wore the collar whenever we were at home alone. She even wore it outside the apartment sometimes—under a turtleneck. It turned her on more than it did me.

The simple truth was, Sue Ellen's erotic tastes were more varied than mine.

Sue Ellen was determined to exert an influence over Mollie, to get her to quit turning tricks. Mollie didn't need the money. She did it for her personal satisfaction. She mistook the passion men showed her for affection.

Well . . . they had their fantasies about Mollie, that they were seducing an innocent college girl and so on. Why should she not have hers—that some of them, at least, really cared for her and were not just using her as a receptacle?

Mollie admitted that she worked for Betty Logan.

"She'd get very upset if I quit," said Mollie. "She doesn't like to lose her girls, particularly the ones who make real money—and *I* make real money."

"Who the hell cares what she likes?" asked Sue Ellen. "Piss on the old bag. Anyway, what's she gonna do about it?"

There we sat at another Friday-evening dinner: angel hair pasta with a cream sauce of shrimp and peppers and onions, laid out on a red-and-white checkered tablecloth on our scarred maple table. We ate by candlelight, the candles in two Chianti bottles we had emptied sometime earlier. Both girls were bare-titted, with chains swinging between their nipples.

Sue Ellen could not endure Mollie's clamps for more than an hour, but Mollie took grim pride in enduring them, even though they pinched as Sue Ellen's loops did not. I had become hesitant about expressing sympathy, knowing it would make no difference.

"Mollie says I don't give you a good blow job," said Sue Ellen abruptly.

"I haven't complained," I said. The fact was, she didn't much like to do it and didn't do it often. "I . . . have no complaint."

"You might have a complaint, if you'd ever had head from a real pro," said Mollie.

"Okay, I might, but I'm married to Sue Ellen, and she—"

"Listen to her, Len!" Sue Ellen protested. "Don't talk so much. Just listen."

"Well . . ." said Mollie. She shrugged. "I can teach her,

but I can't teach her by sucking my thumb. I need a cock."

In my life I have been surprised. I have never been more surprised than when Sue Ellen agreed to take a cock-sucking lesson from Mollie—I supplying the cock. Imagine, for God's sake!

"It's all I do, just about," said Mollie. "Hey, I turn two, three tricks a week, once in a while four. I don't spread my legs once a month. Which is okay with me. Giving head . . . no sweaty weight bearing down on my body, no pounding into me, no sore afterwards. I've suggested to Betty she tell guys I give blow jobs only."

"Jesus, Mollie . . ." Sue Ellen murmured. "I mean—"

"You mean it's *humiliating* to put your face down in a guy's crotch and suck and lick his cock. Well—okay, you better believe it is. It's demeaning. But if you're gonna sell yourself for money you're better off sucking than fucking, believe me. Put your goddamned pride away. There isn't any in what I do."

"But with my husband?"

"Why not make him happy? You can make him happier this way than by spreading yourself and letting him pound it into you."

"Well . . ."

"C'mon."

They guided me down to the floor, pulled my pants and underpants down below my knees, and Mollie solemnly lectured Sue Ellen as she worked.

"First thing to do is suck it in, as much of it as you can. But don't gag yourself. Use your tongue and your lips. They're your tools, and every skilled worker has to know how to use the tools of the trade."

I didn't know how my wife, Sue Ellen, would react when she realized that the square little Mollie could lift me to heights I hadn't realized were there.

The lecture went on.

"Now lick down here. No man I ever knew came from having his balls licked, but it does get 'em ready. And up and down the shaft. It's licking, not sucking, that does the job."

She gently lifted my scrotum and licked it vigorously. She was right. I wouldn't have come from that, but it did raise me to a height of readiness.

Then—

"Okay, Sue Ellen, he's all yours. When he comes, make sure it's inside your mouth. And don't go spitting when he's squirting. Swallow it! Swallow it!"

Sue Ellen was reluctant. She was an adventurous lover, but she did this hesitantly at first, her face flushed, tears glistening around her eyes. Once she gagged. But she made a rhythm and was soon working at least as well as Mollie.

She was wetter than Mollie. My parts were wet with her saliva.

Mollie might be her teacher, and Sue Ellen might work with less skill, but she was for me a far more satisfying oral lover. That she was doing what she didn't really want to do made it more exciting. As I approached my climax, I felt that I might actually rupture. Also, Sue Ellen warmed to it and shortly was at me with actual zest— whether to get it over with sooner or because she was learning to like it, I couldn't be sure.

Mollie taught Sue Ellen to give a professional blow job. Sue Ellen gradually weaned Mollie off prostitution. At first Mollie would just make excuses to Betty Logan— she was having her period, she didn't feel well, she had to go home to Greenwich to visit her sick mother, her confessor was giving her a hard time. . . .

The last was absolutely true. Mollie was Catholic and confessed regularly to a New Haven priest. Sue Ellen asked for the name of that priest and went to see him. The priest would not discuss anything Mollie had told him—the sanctity of the confessional—but he agreed to cooperate with Sue Ellen to do what was appropriate for the good of Mollie's soul. Between the pressure applied by the priest and that from Sue Ellen, Mollie determined to abandon the life and live straight.

She so told Betty Logan, who went into a screeching, foot-stamping hysteria.

A week or so later, I got a telephone call. It was from a wise guy. He said his boss would like to buy me lunch and named an Italian restaurant and a day. I agreed to the lunch and immediately called my father. He said he would come to New Haven and join me for the lunch.

The wise guy's boss was Alberto Patrioto. The don joined us after a few minutes.

Fifteen years had passed since my father and Patrioto had met and disagreed about the New Haven Cheeks store, and Patrioto—as my father told me after the meeting—had aged more than fifteen years. Maybe his years in prison had done it. Even so, he had the style of a *capo de tutti capi:* still the camel coat, still the gray homburg, still the paisley handkerchief carefully folded in his jacket pocket, still the cigar.

"It's a real pleasure to meet you again, Don Patrioto," my father said.

I have to say, my father and Patrioto were of an age, a passing age. My father was sixty-one that year. He showed little gray. He was a trim, muscular man who dressed well but did not wear clothes conspicuously well tailored.

Patrioto grinned. " 'Don' Patrioto," he chuckled. "You do me more honor than I own, Mr. Cooper. I am just a struggling businessman, as you are."

The conversation went on for some time, with nothing in particular being said. Patrioto recommended the veal, which he said was the best available in New Haven. We ordered it. He ordered the wine, a heavy, dark red of a type I had never tasted before.

Finally, we got down to business.

"Mr. Cooper, Junior," said Patrioto, "is it your plan to reform all Mrs. Logan's girls, or just this one?"

I glanced at my father, whose face was bland and seemed just as interested as was Patrioto in hearing what I would say.

"Mr. Patrioto," I said cautiously, "this girl has become my wife's best friend. They are students together—students of Chinese. My wife has, in fact, discouraged this one girl from—"

"From earning a tidy profit for my friends."

"She is a devout Catholic. Her priest—"

"What priest?"

"Father Benedict. At Holy Mother."

Patrioto turned down the corners of his mouth and nodded thoughtfully. "Ahh . . ."

"How much was she earning for you?" my father asked.

Patrioto shook his head. "No, Mr. Cooper. That will not be necessary. I would like your son's assurance that he and his wife do not mean to become moral crusaders here in New Haven."

"You have it," said my father quickly.

"From *him.*"

"I so assure you, Mr. Patrioto," I said.

"Well, then . . ." said Patrioto with a faint smile, lifting his wine glass to toast the assurance. "I know your father, so I know your assurance is good."

That night at home I had to grab Sue Ellen by her dog collar and demand she join my assurance. That may have been the beginning of the end of our marriage. Two principles clashed: hers of high morals and pride, mine of being practical as I knew my father was, of fighting battles worth winning when I believed I could win them.

She was the daughter of Hale & Dorr. I was the son of Jerry Cooper. Like oil and water, we could never mix.

25

JERRY

Giselle and I rarely disagreed, but when she decided our son should be educated in a prep school, I balked. She had even chosen the school, a place in Connecticut called Choate Rosemary Hall.

Now, this was not about to happen. Rosemary Hall, for Christ's sake! *My son* would go to a school called *Rosemary Hall?* What kind of guy would he turn out to be, going to a school called—I said no, emphatically. I believe in education. I wish I'd had a whole lot more than I've got. But I also believe in street smarts. I wanted my boy to have both, an education and street smarts. He sure wasn't going to get any of the latter at a school called Rosemary Hall.

The years when we had to choose a school for Len were years when the schools of New York City, and a lot of other places, were being torn apart by racial hate. I myself—me, a Jew with a black best friend—was called "honky" on the street one day. I was waiting for a light, and this coffee-with-cream-colored smart-ass sneered at me and hissed. "Honky!" I felt like decking him, but it would only have caused him to go back to his street and tell everybody that a honky had busted his nose, for no reason at all.

Anyway, Giselle set her foot down flat against his going into the city's public schools. "Okay," I said, "we move back to Scarsdale or some place like that. I mean, we can live in the suburbs, where things are peaceful—and boring."

"I will not risk his being cut with a knife, or beaten senseless, over something he has nothing to do with."

I talked to Buddy.

"You're askin' for what the world ain't got, man," he said. "You move out to Westchester or up in Connecticut, who's he goin' to be in school with? Sons and daughters of real-estate guys, insurance guys, stockbrokers who commute . . . and so on. You send him to P.S. Whatever here in town, who's he goin' to be in school with? Not the sons and daughters of those guys I just mentioned, 'cause they all got sent to private schools some place or other."

"I want the kid to be smart, Buddy. Educated, sure. That's one thing. But also smart."

"Educated you can get to be. Smart has got to be born in ya. The kids I've had with Ulla are smart. They better be—half nigger, half Norwegian. Len's got smarts from both sides. He'll do okay. Send him to a prep school, if that's what Giselle wants."

In France I had learned the British word "toff." I didn't want my son to become a toff. I didn't want him to become a white version of Buddy, either. Buddy had taught me to cut, and I always carried a folded straight razor in my right-hand pants pocket, usually inside a roll of bills. I didn't want Len to learn that.

I couldn't send my son into a nest of pretty little boys from pretty little families in pretty little towns—which is what I thought a prep school was. So we compromised on a boarding school. We *thought* we'd compromised. Giselle looked at several. I guess we were taken in by some bullshit in the Lodge catalog that said, "Boys from every walk of life live together, work together, and share the values they bring from disparate backgrounds." I had to look up the word "disparate."

I never met any of the fathers of Len's Lodge friends. Maybe I figured they'd sneer at me—behind my back. When he went away to Lodge, I lost him, lost a lot of him, that is. Hell, I lost something of him when we sent him to Friends. From *that* point he was going to be different from me. Which is what I wanted, up to a point. He turned into someone I didn't know.

Temporarily.

I suppose I must admit I wasn't the world's greatest father. I rationalized the way too many other fathers do, by saying that the demands of building my business and earning the living that would allow my family to live the way I wanted them to live were too great and left me too little time.

Besides that, I had problems. Among them was that I had to face threats.

I despised Jimmy Hoffa. If he had not gone to prison in 1971, he might have been a big problem for us.

Anyone whose business involved a lot of shipping sooner or later came into a confrontation with the Teamsters. Anyone who came into confrontation with the Teamsters sooner or later was confronted with their swaggering arrogance. They cared nothing about the law. They did things their way, with muscle or the threat of muscle.

I knew a man who went into a business I knew something about: selling seltzer and soda. He did well and soon was running about a hundred trucks. One day two guys from Teamsters came in his office and told him that from then on their union would represent his drivers. The man said, okay, get your signatures on the NLRA cards, and we'll have a sanctioned election. Their answer?

"Don't talk to us about bullshit NLRA elections. *We represent your drivers.* You'll take our dues from their paychecks, and we'll write their contracts. That's how it is, buddy. You wanta argue? We don't usually argue. We get our way, sooner or later."

Hoffa took pride in being a scrappy little man who would bounce around on the balls of his feet and shoot punches at people. He had been a playground bully, I imagine. Usually he was just playing juvenile games, but sometimes he hit. He broke noses, knocked out teeth, fractured ribs.

Some of the men he hit could have cold-cocked him, easily, but he always had a thug or two with him to protect him. Like all bullies, he was also a coward.

He called a meeting. To put the matter more accurately, he *summoned* a group of us to meet with him. All of us were in businesses more or less dependent on truck transportation. We met in a suite in the Waldorf.

I was there. A man was there from a laundry company, one from a magazine distributor, and so on. Hoffa was blunt. He was going to represent our drivers—in my case, it was the drivers for the express company we chiefly used—and he would give us our terms. He hadn't called us to negotiate; he had called us to tell us how things were going to be—that is, the way he wanted them to be.

Knowing Hoffa would be backed by thugs, I had asked Buddy to come with me. Buddy loved to be menacing. And he was not easily intimidated.

Hoffa, in an out-of-style double-breasted black suit with a bow tie, bounced around the room, grinning, swaggering, dictating terms to our half a dozen companies.

"Okay, fellas," he said. "That's it. That's how it's gonna be. Anybody got any questions?"

"I have one," I said.

"Oh, yeah? Which is . . . ?"

"Which is . . . who the hell do you think you are?"

He didn't offer to answer. He lurched toward me and shot out a left jab that would have hurt had it landed. But he never had a chance of landing it. I was as much a street tough as he was, and I was bigger. I sidestepped his punch and caught it on my right fist. I could have slugged him with no trouble and flattened his nose—which had already been flattened more than once.

But Buddy didn't like what Jimmy Hoffa had done. He moved between me and Hoffa with the sleek grace of the born street fighter, and he slammed a hard punch into Hoffa's solar plexus.

Hoffa bent over and began to vomit.

His thugs pulled guns.

Buddy had expected that. By the time their guns were in their hands, he had a left arm around Hoffa's upper body, and his right hand pressed the gleaming blade of a razor against his throat.

"Tell your boys to wait in the lobby," Buddy said.

Hoffa grunted and pointed.

It could have been an interesting battle, I always thought—the cocky little union gangster with his thousand thugs against the slick, black, street-smart slasher whose guys could come out of a thousand doorways on any street, from between the cars in any parking lot.

The battle was never fought. Hoffa went to the slammer to wait for his close friend President Nixon to give him executive clemency. For a while the world had things other than Jimmy Hoffa to think about.

26

When his good friend the President commuted his sentence, Jimmy Hoffa showed up again. It was a condition of his commutation that he could not try to recover the presidency of the Teamsters. He expected Nixon to cancel the ban in time. Even after Nixon resigned, Jimmy confidently expected President Ford would remove the condition.

In the meantime, he drew a pension from the union of one and a half million dollars a year. The money was burning holes in his pockets, and he set out to look for investments.

Coal mining was one of his ideas, and he did ultimately manage to buy into a mining operation. But he was looking around, looking for something to raid, and to our bad fortune his cold, snakelike eyes fell on Cheeks.

I don't know if it was because he remembered and resented what Buddy had done to defend me—which, incidentally, Buddy remembered very well—or if someone had pointed us out to him as a growing company that could be raided without an immense amount of capital. All I know is that Jimmy Hoffa began looking for ways to acquire my company.

He couldn't buy stock. The sole stockholders were myself, Giselle, and Sal Nero. He couldn't push us through our creditors. We were by no means overextended. His connections were no better than ours. Through Sal we had a good relationship with the Carlinos.

So, being Jimmy Hoffa, he decided to muscle us. He was no longer the head of the Teamsters, but old Teamster tactics came into play against us.

Merchandise began to disappear off our trucks. Our drivers had more accidents than they'd ever had before. They got cut off in traffic and were forced off the road. Rocks fell down from overpasses and smashed their windshields. Their tires were slashed.

Sal was furious. He put wise guys on me and Giselle as bodyguards. They were unable to be inconspicuous. I guess he didn't want them to be.

Buddy put bodyguards on Len. They *were* inconspicuous. Len never knew they were there.

Hoffa was in the process of making horrible mistakes. The reason was that he was not smart. He was a thug. He had bullied his way to the top of his union. He had supposed he could bully his way past Bobby Kennedy, who was as tough as he was, only ten times smarter. He had actually cocked a fist at Bobby one day in a Senate hearing room. If he had thrown that punch, there where his thugs couldn't help him, Bobby would have broken his nose or jaw, maybe both. I'm a little sorry it didn't happen.

Trying to bully Cheeks, he enraged Sal Nero, which was not a good idea.

But that was not the only bullying he was trying to do.

I was with Sal when we sat down with a few men to talk over what to do about Jimmy Hoffa. They introduced themselves by their nicknames. Sal was the Fireman because his huge penis reminded men of a firehose. Why Frankie Shots was so called I do not know. The Fat Man had his name for obvious reasons. Tony Pro was so called because his name was Anthony Provenzano.

Tony Pro presided over the meeting. He was a member of the Genovese family. Sal was of the Carlino family, but that didn't make any difference because—as I have said—Sal had always been careful not to make enemies in any family.

"He wants what you got, Tony," said the Fat Man. That meant control of the Teamsters, since Tony Pro was a big man in the union, with his power based in the New Jersey Teamsters.

"Soon as he gets the Bum to lift the condition," said Tony Pro. The Bum was Gerald Ford—the Stumblebum in their lingo.

"That'll take a big envelope," said Frankie Shots. He meant it would take a major payoff.

"The question is—" Tony Pro started to say.

"The question is," Sal interrupted him, "what are we gonna do about Jimmy? I mean, he's tryin' to muscle my partner here into sellin' his business. I don't like that, and I'm not going to stand for it. He's not going to muscle *my* friends."

That gave me a clue as to why I was sitting there in that meeting of capos. I was a right guy who was being muscled by Hoffa, and Sal wanted his pals to see I was a right guy and a victim. I never thought of myself as a man who generated sympathy, but that, apparently, was why I was there.

"It's not just Jerry here," said the Fat Man. "Jimmy's musclin' an' musclin'. Nobody's business is safe from that son of a bitch."

"He's threatenin' to talk about what he knows," said Tony Pro. "So, I guess we know what has to be done. I mean, does anybody have any doubt about what has to be done?"

They weren't unanimous—Frankie Shots dissented—but I sat there that evening and heard Jimmy Hoffa sentenced to death.

27

Before he died, Sal told me how it was done. I believe what he told me. Other people have other ideas about what happened to James Riddle Hoffa, but I think Sal told me the truth.

For one reason, I had heard the sentence pronounced. I can think of no reason whatever why Sal would have lied to me. He wasn't bragging. He wasn't a man given to bragging, and telling his part in the death of Hoffa was not something he would brag about. He might brag about the size of his cock but not about killing a man.

"The big point, y'understand, was that Jimmy had to back away from union politics. He wanted to be president of the Teamsters again, and apart from the money he could throw around, he knew too much. Like, he knew about how the pension fund had been used, and stuff like that. He knew where everybody's skeletons were. He was—What's the words they use? He was a loose cannon. He had to be whacked out. Dammit, he *had* to be! Nobody had no choice. Too many guys were at risk with him runnin' around loose."

"I was there when you decided," I reminded him. "Don't you remember? I was there with you and Tony

Provenzano and Frankie Shots and the Fat Man."

"Oh . . . yeah, well, sure." Sal frowned. By now there were some holes in his memory. "Okay. The job fell to Tony Pro and me. Tony Provenzano was the kind of guy you could trust with a job like that. Some guys had tough names but couldn't be trusted when the shit was happenin'. I trusted Tony Pro, and he trusted me. Can you guess how surprised I was when he called on me to help him? I mean, Jerry, I'd made my bones, like you know, but I was no hit man. Well . . . neither was Tony. But this job needed top-notch guys. 'Hey, Fireman,' he said, 'let's you and me settle this thing. We don't need any help. We don't want any help. A couple guys like us can solve our problem. Deal? So we didn't ask anybody's by-your-leave. We just set out to do it. He called Jimmy Hoffa and set up a meeting in Detroit, and off to Detroit we went—just the two of us with nobody's okay."

"Could you have gotten the okay?" I asked.

"Yeah. But it would have taken too long, and too many guys would have had to know about it. We got us a car, a titty-pink Cadillac, a pimpmobile. We taped our biscuits up in the chassis, where they wouldn't be found if we got stopped for speedin' or somethin'. Mine was a forty-four magnum, a goddam *cannon*. Tony's was a what they called a street-sweeper, a mini-Uzi. We were equipped like a goddamn *army*."

This was years later, remember, when he was telling me this. Sal died in bed. He was not the first guy who ever wanted to get something off his chest when he knew he was going. That's another reason why I believe him.

"We took our time driving to Detroit. We stayed overnight in Youngstown, Ohio, where I got laid but good. I used to play a game with waitresses. I'd say, 'I'll show you my cock. If you can honestly tell me you ever saw a bigger one and will name the guy who's got it, I'll give you a hundred bucks. If you never saw a bigger one, you still get the hundred, but you got to put out for me.' Some of them were so fascinated with the damn thing, they'd have paid *me* a hundred. It hasn't always been an advantage, Jerry. To be honest, I guess it's more often been a disadvantage. But what could I do? You can't get an inch or three cut off.

"Anyway, besides gettin' laid, we planned how we'd do the job. The fact that Hoffa was so damn cocky was gonna help. He was so cocky he was careless.

"We got to Detroit. Jimmy'd known Tony was comin'—though he didn't know I was comin'; I doubt he knew who I was—and suggested they meet at a steakhouse called Machus Red Fox, just outside Detroit, on the road to the airport. Tony told him he was drivin' a titty-pink Caddy and would meet him in the parking lot. He said they'd talk in the car and then go in for lunch. Which suited Jimmy just fine. It was one of his favorite eateries, and he had friends there—in case Tony had any bad ideas.

"Tony let me out up the road, and I walked to the Red Fox and went in to check it out. Guys there were expectin' somebody. Hey, I got patted down by a couple of wise guys, just for comin' through the door. They could tell I didn't have a biscuit, so I sat at the bar and had a beer. Then I went out, walked around to where I couldn't be seen, and got in the back seat of the Cadillac.

"I got down on the floor, out of sight. Tony told me he was comin', so I was ready when Jimmy Hoffa opens the door and climbs in on the passenger side.

"He got just one thing said. 'I'm not backin' down, Tony. I'm gonna do it, and you're gonna help me. You know why. You're gonna help me or I'm gonna put you where I was: in a federal slammer. Any doubt about that?'

"At that point I blasted him, right through the seat of the car. The slug from that cannon went through the seat back, through Jimmy, and wound up in the dashboard of the Caddy—along with some small parts of Jimmy. Hey! Jimmy Hoffa never knew what hit him. We made it easy for him, truth be known.

"He had two thugs with him, bodyguards. They came runnin' up just in time to face Tony's Uzi and my forty-four mag. They stopped and looked at each other, and then they shrugged and walked back to their car and drove off. It was a blue Buick, I remember. They could see their boss had been whacked out. It had been their job to *prevent* that happenin', not to shoot it out with the guys that did it. There was no percentage for them in tryin' to take some kinda revenge. They knew exactly who they were and what they'd been hired for, and revenge was no part of it—any more than loyalty had been a part of it. Nobody was loyal to Jimmy. Nobody was sorry he was gone. Hell, I'd probably left readable fingerprints on my beer bottle, but nobody said a word to the cops about it—so far as I know, anyway."

Sal chuckled weakly. "Y'know, all we had to do was prop him up in the seat and fasten the seat belt and shoulder harness. He had a hole in him big enough to drive a truck through, but I covered that with an old raincoat we'd brought along for the purpose. I pulled on his hair to make him sit up and look alive, and we drove out of Michigan with Jimmy sitting there looking natural, almost smiling. We drove all the way across Ohio with that body sitting there. Sometimes I had to wonder if he wouldn't open his mouth and say something. I'll tell ya something, Jerry. It was spooky."

Sal turned grim.

"You want to know what we did with him? Well, he ain't in the Meadowlands, and he ain't under the goalpost in Giants Stadium. We drove him to Youngstown, where Sal had made arrangements. He handed some guys a pretty big envelope, and we watched while they dumped Jimmy into an open-hearth furnace just before a big pour of molten pig iron. Hell, we didn't even take off his wristwatch. It melted in two seconds."

Sal grinned. "You wanta know where Jimmy Hoffa is? Well, he might have been in the fender of your 'seventy-six Chevy. He was just a tiny little bit of excess carbon in that open-hearth steel.

"The same envelope paid for gettin' rid of the biscuits

and the titty-pink Caddy. The mag and the Uzi went in the furnace with Jimmy. The Caddy was smashed flat and wound up in a furnace itself. The steel industry don't waste nothin'."

28
LEN

I am damn lucky Sue Ellen and I did not have a child. She wanted to, but by the time we were in a position to think about it—that is to say, by the time I graduated from law school—I knew I did not want to have a child by her and be committed to living with her for the rest of my life.

Blinded by the sex we shared, blinded also by the sympathy and guilt I felt for getting her pregnant, I had overlooked our differences and had failed to realize how difficult marriage was going to be for us. She was a very different person from me, in fact entirely different from the woman I had supposed she was when I fell in love with her.

She was shallow in many ways—though it is difficult to think of someone as shallow who elected so challenging a study as Chinese. Still, she was shallow. She bought fads as if they were eternal truths.

For example, she got interested in Eastern religions. For a while I thought she was going to shave her head and become a Krishna. She went around the house humming, "Hare, hare, krishna, krishna"—until I told her she was driving me nuts and she didn't believe in it anyway, so cool it. I was a little surprised that she did cool it, which told me that what I had suspected had been right: Like many other things in Sue Ellen's life, Hare Krishna was a fad, a little game.

For a brief time she decided that, not only would she become a vegetarian, she would not wear shoes or belts made of leather. Somebody promoted this idea to her, and she bought it. I unsold her pretty damn quick. She began to make us meals with meat again, and shortly she took to wearing the dog collar I mentioned before—and it was sure as hell made of leather.

She was a sexpot. I for damn sure had no complaint about her in that respect. But that, too, was a little game. I'm not sure where she found boundaries between reality and fantasies—or *if* she found any. I am not sure if she thought my hard-on was evidence, not just of arousal, but of love.

In truth, I had a hard time making that distinction myself.

She got into S-M. She would bare her butt, stretch out across my lap, and tell me to spank her. If I didn't turn her cheeks red, she'd be petulant, like a child denied candy. I can't say I liked that. I guess I can't say I disliked it, either.

I have to say of myself that I was confused. On the one hand, I was kept aroused and sometimes was lifted to heights of passion, which would have been damn difficult to give up. On the other hand, I sensed there was something mechanical, artificial about it, that it did not represent as strong or deep a relationship as its surface appearance suggested.

Mollie had taught her to give head like a pro, which she did, happily and vigorously and repeatedly, volunteering to do it even when I had something else in mind, even when I would rather have gone to sleep. I suppose guys think life will be heaven if they can just find a woman willing to suck them off whenever they want it. Believe me, it isn't so. Fantasy and reality.

When I met her she had been uncomfortably self-conscious about her outsized breasts, which were not all she had; she had long legs and a tight, twitchy butt. Now—under Mollie's tutelage—she had become exorbitantly proud of her boobs. One night we drove to a beer joint near the Bridgeport Airport in Stratford, where—though I hadn't been told what to expect—they were having a wet T-shirt contest. Sue Ellen happily entered the competition, went backstage to take off her sweater and bra, and came out in a white T-shirt, as did Mollie; and when the master of ceremonies exuberantly sprayed Sue Ellen's T-shirt with warm water, the room went wild. She took the applause that won the contest, and when the man suggested she strip off the T-shirt, she did. She strutted around the stage, laughing and flaunting, making those outsized hooters bounce up and down, while guys stood on chairs to cheer.

That got her arrested. She and Mollie thought it immensely funny. She even thought it funny when she was handcuffed and driven to the justice court in a paddy wagon. I posted a hundred-dollar bond for her in Stratford and drove her home.

Her comment? "Why shouldn't a woman be allowed to show her boobs? I'd appeal the damn case if it wouldn't drive my daddy up the wall."

Fancy that. Fancy Hale & Dorr defending a partner's daughter on a charge of indecent exposure! I can just see it now. Joseph Welch's law firm defending—Defending someone else, maybe. Defending Sue Ellen . . .

Right. I don't want to say anything negative about Hale & Dorr. I graduated high in my class, not at the top, and Sue Ellen expected me to be welcomed into her father's distinguished firm. The firm might have welcomed me. But her father had, in effect, a veto; and he didn't want a son of Jerry Cooper in his firm. He was subtle about it and imagined I would not understand how he had worked it, vetoing me while expressing the warmest sympathy. I got the message.

He had done his homework on my father. His problem was not so much that my father was in the business of selling lingerie, some of it boldly erotic. It was that he didn't like some of my father's history and associates. He had learned who my great-uncle Harry was. He knew about the Plescassier Martins. He knew the name Paul Renard and the name Charlie Han. He associated my father with the name Betty Logan. He did not know, I guess, that I myself had one day sat down to lunch with Don Alberto Patrioto.

What he most disliked was the name Sal Nero. My father has since told me that Sal was the man who pulled the trigger that killed Jimmy Hoffa. Sue Ellen's father obviously did not know that. In point of fact, no one knew that. It was the subject of endless television "unsolved mysteries" shows.

Her father spoke in a stilted, fancy language. "You will perhaps not mind my saying that your father does seem to have some . . . how shall I say? Some *remarkable* friends. You do not mind?"

"Not at all," I said, facing him where he sat by his enormous fireplace sharing Napoleon brandy with me. "My father had to struggle for everything he has achieved. He had no advantages. Family . . . education . . . whatever he's done, he simply did it. On his own."

"Yes. I quite understand."

But of course he didn't understand that my father made his own opportunities.

To have become an associate in the firm of Hale & Dorr was the fondest hope of every man or woman who ever graduated from any law school. There were better-known firms, but none with the quiet dignity of Hale & Dorr. There were more flamboyant law firms and more flamboyant lawyers. There were no more *lawyers' lawyers* than the partners at Hale & Dorr.

I would gladly have taken an associateship there if it had been offered me. Realistically, I knew it wouldn't be offered.

And it wasn't.

I took the bar examinations and got myself admitted to the practice of law in the states of New York and Connecticut. That made me a lawyer—in theory, at least.

The question then was, what should I do? My father immediately suggested that Cheeks needed full-time counsel. I hope I convinced him I was grateful but that I had valid reasons not to become counsel to his company.

I hope I don't need to explain that. By then I had complete respect for my father. But I lived a cliché. I didn't want to remain dependent on him. I wanted to demonstrate—or to find out, anyway—that I could make it on my own.

My father arranged for me to meet for lunches with several Manhattan lawyers. After two or three weeks one of them offered me a job. I suspected my father had placed me with that firm as surely as he could have placed me as general counsel to Cheeks. But I expected to have at least a degree of independence, and I accepted.

The firm was named Gottsman, Scheck & Shapiro. Besides the three partners, there were three associates. I became the fourth associate. Our offices were in the Empire State Building. My office was tiny, but it had a north-facing window, from which I could see all of northern Manhattan and in fact all the way out to Connecticut. I could see the planes landing and taking off from La Guardia and Kennedy.

When my father saw my office, he declared the furniture, left behind by an associate who had failed to make partner, inadequate; and he completely refitted that office with a Herman Miller desk and credenza made of zebra wood, with an ergonomically designed chair. When Sam Gottsman, the senior partner, looked at it, he remarked that furniture like that belonged in the offices of Deveboise, Plimpton, not at Gottsman, Scheck & Shapiro.

The old story is that a new young lawyer spends his first six months finding the men's rooms at the courthouses. In fact, he spends that time learning what paper is filed where and why and discovering which clerk will look over something offered for filing and kindly point out the minor defect that would render the filing ineffective. He totes a briefcase and rides the subways, carrying files here and there. In short, he learns what he did not learn in law school.

Sue Ellen did not want to live in New York City, so we leased a small house in Greenwich, Connecticut, and I became a commuter. I had a lawn to cut, trees to trim, leaves to rake, gutters to clean, snow to shovel, firewood to lay up, a fireplace that wouldn't draw, shrubs that wouldn't blossom, bulbs that wouldn't sprout, tomato plants that bore no tomatoes, brats who rode their motorbikes across my lawn or climbed my trees and broke off limbs . . .

I caught the 6:45 express each morning and was in my office before eight. I rarely reached home before seven and soon came to wonder if I should not have accepted the job my father offered, after all. Independence had its grim side.

29

My father is monogamous. That is, essentially he is, meaning he has one woman at a time. After my mother died, he established a relationship with the model Melissa Lamb. Melissa was absolutely devoted to him, and I could not object to a companion for him who so perfectly suited him as she did.

She was beautiful. She was ingenuous, the kind of woman who had given rise to the silly stereotype that a beautiful woman is likely dumb. You had to give her a chance, but given a chance she would establish that she was not as innocent as your first impression had suggested. In fact, I don't think my father would have lived with a dull woman.

He didn't feel comfortable living with her in the apartment that had been my mother's home, so they moved into a two-bedroom place on the forty-fifth floor of a building on Third Avenue.

The apartment was small, but it was luxurious. It had parquet floors and two marble baths—plus a powder room, also marble. Their view over the East River was spectacular. They hired a designer to choose furniture and art. I know for a certainty that my father had no idea what he had paid for—prints and mobiles and forty yards of books in cases—and that he regarded the art as effete and ostentatious. He was, in fact, embarrassed by what hung on his walls and from his ceilings. Since he had left Melissa to work with the designer, he supposed *she* liked it all, never guessing that she was neutral and had no better idea than he did of what the designer had imposed on them. He did read many of the books. At this point in life my father discovered a new source of pleasure—besides which he hugely increased his store of learning.

Sue Ellen loved it all. It changed her opinion of my father. I remember her breathlessly telling *her* father that *my* father had an *original* Calder mobile in his living room.

"Can you imagine? An original Calder mobile! Hanging in his living room."

Her father nodded gravely. "That's very impressive. It shows excellent taste."

My father didn't know Cald*er* from Cald*or*. He didn't know the artist from the discount chain.

He called me one afternoon at my office.

"I want you for dinner tonight. Be at our apartment. Seven."

"I'll call Sue Ellen."

"No, no. Don't tell Sue Ellen. Just tell her you'll be late. In fact, tell her you may be spending the night in our guest bedroom. I don't want her coming in to be with us on this particular night. This is a business matter."

"Well, I—"

"*Do it,* Len. See you at seven."

It was, in fact, a business matter. When I arrived, the business matter was already there. She was a tall, slender, black-haired woman of maybe forty or forty-five, wearing a clinging black dress and a simple strand of pearls. Her eyes were dark. Her lips were full, colored with red lipstick. She wore a perfume with a pronounced odor. She was drinking a martini up, with a twist.

"Let me introduce my son, Leonard. Len, this is Vittoria Lucchese. She is looking for a lawyer."

"Call me Vicky," she said. "Everyone does, and I much prefer it."

She offered her hand, not to be shaken, but high, to be kissed. I did it, and she nodded to the couch. We sat down. The woman was calm and completely self-possessed. Lucchese. I had heard the name, of course. I wondered if—

"Vicky lost her husband a few months ago," my father said as he poured me a Scotch on the rocks. "This left her the chief stockholder of Interboro Fruit, Incorporated. You may know the company. You buy a piece of fruit imported from overseas, likely it came into this country through Interboro."

"We don't deal in apples and pears," she said, cooly picking up the recital. "We deal in pineapples, Israeli oranges and strawberries, guava, kiwi fruit, mangos . . . We import from all over and distribute in the tri-state area. We have warehouses and a fleet of trucks, plus, of course, all the things that go with running a business: an office with all the personnel and equipment that takes. We actually just bought a computer, if you can imagine. I hope you know what *that* is good for. I haven't figured it out yet."

"I have heard the name Interboro Fruit," I said. "And the name Lucchese."

She nodded, still totally cool. "My late husband retained as counsel a firm I don't like. I am interested in finding someone to represent me. You are very young and inexperienced. I understand your firm includes some experienced lawyers, shrewd lawyers. If you brought me to your firm as a client, it would be to your distinct advantage in the firm, would it not?"

This was how she would always talk. Vicky was direct. She was never subtle.

I was no less direct. "That would be to my very definite advantage," I said.

My father beamed. "Then we can have dinner and talk about it some more."

We had dinner at Four Seasons. By then my father had a regular table there, at which no one else was ever seated either at noon or in the evening until it was plain that Mr. Cooper was not coming. A telephone was always placed at his table, though he never used it; I never saw him use it. People did know who he was, though, and he got a lot of greetings—not from celebrity types, beaming in their glow, but from people prominent in business and money.

Melissa was tolerant of the conversation, in which she could not participate at all, and pretended she found it all hugely absorbing. Melissa had a talent for that sort of thing.

"I offered Len the position of general counsel to my company," my father said to Vicky. "But he wanted to try his hand at what he calls the real practice of law."

"He wanted to be independent," she said dryly.

"I know," my father said, equally dryly.

"I can respect him for that."

Vicky sat beside and very close to me. Shortly I felt the heat of her hand on my leg, gently caressing. I looked at her. She fixed an ingenuous, coquettish gaze on me. I put my hand on hers. She seized my hand and moved it to *her* leg.

My father stared at me, mock-innocently. He knew what he had gotten me into.

He and I went to the men's room. "The two of you will sleep in the guest room tonight," he said. "She has a sixteen-year-old son at home in her apartment, and she doesn't want him to see her bringing home a man only ten years older than he is."

"Is this such a good idea?" I asked. "I mean, isn't a lot of complication implicit in this?"

"You better believe it's a good idea. I've known her for years, first by name only, then personally. I did some business with her father. Her maiden name was Castellano. I imagine she's a first-class piece of ass, to start with, and she likes you. Besides which, she makes you a rain-maker at Gottsman, Scheck and Shapiro and the way I understand it, that's what you've got to be if you expect to go anywhere. Suppose you bring in Interboro Fruit as a client. Doesn't that make you a rainmaker? They'll kiss your ass!"

"She's old enough to be my mother."

"Well, she's *not* your mother," he snapped impatiently. "You're a big boy. Act like one."

No one was subtle. I doubt that Vicky knew how to be. In fact, there was no way any of us could have been sub-tle. We chatted as we drank final brandies; then Vicky got up and went to the guest bedroom. I followed her.

The rooms in the apartment were not very large, but there was space in the guest bedroom for a double bed and for a love seat, which faced a coffee table. An Im-pressionist landscape hung above the love seat. The room seemed to have been designed for cozy shacking up. I went immediately to the window and pulled the drapes.

When I turned around, Vicky was on me, clasping me in her arms and kissing me fervently. She kissed with her tongue, using it to caress mine and thrusting all the way to my throat.

"Unzip my dress," she whispered huskily.

I did and helped her pull it over her head. Under her dress she wore nothing but goodies from Cheeks. Every-thing was black, of course: a bra cut to expose her nipples, crotchless panties over a shaved pussy, and a lacy black garter belt trimmed with red, holding up sheer dark stock-ings.

She paraded around the room to show me herself and her undies. Then she said, "Let's take a shower together. There's no better way in the world for two people to get to know each other than to take a shower together."

She helped me out of my clothes, shedding the intimate Cheeks things at the same time. Then she grabbed my hand and led me into the bathroom.

I needed to use the toilet and turned toward it. "Just a minute," I murmured.

"No, no!"

In a moment we were in the shower stall, under the stream of warm water. When we were wet she grabbed the soap, soaped her hands, and soaped my hard and rigid penis.

Then—"Pee on me, Lenny," she whispered hoarsely. "Pee all over me."

She stepped away from the stream and faced me. I accommodated her. I pissed on her belly, her cunt, and her hips, then on her legs—giving her a thick, hot, yellow stream. She laughed. She shoved me out of the shower water, tipped her hips back, and pissed on me.

"You got any left, honey?" she asked.

I nodded. I had a little. She dropped to her knees and offered her face. She held her eyes tightly closed while I pissed on her forehead and nose and cheeks and chin. Some of it went between her lips and into her mouth— and she was in no great hurry to open her mouth to the shower stream and rinse it out.

And that was just the beginning.

Before that night was over we had settled a great many things. I knew in the first place that this would be no ordinary relationship, that it was going to be a relationship with levels of complexity I don't think my father had guessed.

In the intervals between the things we did, Vicky told me a lot about herself. She was forty-four years old, and knew that I was twenty-six. She told me her maiden name was Castellano—which meant that she was *connected*. She talked frankly about that:

"It's not like *The Godfather*. It's not like—People are family; people are friends. They try to take care of each other. Look. If we didn't take care of each other, who would take care of us, in the face of other people who are taking care of *themselves?* That's the way of it. It's a *network*. It's not just Italians. The Jews did it, the Irish, and now the blacks—everybody who's scorned and put down."

"The Boston Brahmins," I said, "came to this country because they were scorned and put down in England."

Vicky nodded. As I was to learn, she had given a great deal of attention to this topic. "Well . . . sometimes mutual-protection societies make wrong turns. Sometimes—I don't have to name names. The most respectable of respectables do things they shouldn't do. People get killed? How many people were killed by the Robber Barons a century or so ago? So Arnold Rothstein gets whacked out. Dutch Schultz. Bugsy Siegel. How many men and women were whacked out on the orders of Andrew Carnegie? John D. Rockefeller?"

We coupled again. I plunged into her as deep and hard as I could. Then she sucked me. She was as good as Sue Ellen or Mollie. I returned the favor. That I did that was a measure of how enthusiastic I had already become about Vicky. I pushed my tongue as deeply as I could where my cock had been. She guided me to her clit, and I licked that until she stiffened and moaned.

She was obsessed with me, which was staggering. I was bewitched by her, drawn to her, irresistibly. We were very different people, but the differences got submerged. This was no one-night thing. It was not just passion. I knew that Vicky Lucchese was going to be an important part of the rest of my life.

Before morning we settled it also that Gottsman, Scheck would represent Interboro Fruit.

30

Bringing Interboro Fruit to my firm as a client made me a rainmaker. A rainmaker is a lawyer who brings business to his firm, and is more valued than one who does competent work. *Getting* business is more important than *doing* business.

Most of Interboro's work was assigned to other lawyers, specialists in the various legal problems such a company would have. We even assigned its problems with interstate truck licensing to another firm. Under Hugh Scheck's supervision, I handled the company's corporation problems. I should have spent another year toting briefcases, but having brought in a good client I got special consideration. Scheck took a liking to me and became my mentor.

Hugh Scheck was one hell of a lawyer. He was one hell of a man. He'd taken a spinal wound in Vietnam and lost 70 percent of the use of his legs. But the gutsy bastard would not sit in a wheelchair. He stumbled around on two canes, red-faced and huffing and determined. He took no crap from anybody and was a good enough lawyer that he didn't have to. He was one of the few men I've ever seen who could simply stare someone down. The power of his personality, plus the power of his intellect, were formidable.

"Y'know what this fruit company is, don't you?" he said to me one day within a month after I brought in the client. "I mean, I suppose you know its history."

"I've got my suspicions. Suppose you tell me."

"Okay. Selling high-quality fresh fruits and vegetables has been taken over by the Koreans. Oh, you can get the same in supermarkets but not like the quality the Koreans offer. Those bastards work their tails off to run their little stores. They drive downtown every morning before dawn to buy their kiwi and mangos and what all, plus the apples and tomatoes they get from New Jersey. They buy the very best. They buy the imported stuff from Interboro."

"So?"

Hugh sighed, as if he supposed I should know what he was about to say. "Louie Lucchese was a Carlino. There was a time when most grocers didn't buy from anybody else what they could buy from Louie. You can guess why. Then he got it through his head he didn't have to use muscle. Interboro is a respectable business now. I wouldn't have let it in here as a client if I didn't think so. But watch out for the widow, Len. Vicky's maiden name was Castellano—Vittoria Castellano. Do I have to introduce you to that name?"

I shook my head.

"One of the Five Families. Daughter of a capo. Vicky is connected like nobody is connected. Which . . . I don't know if she uses it or not. But she's *big*, man. Don't cross her."

I didn't tell him I slept with her, and I don't think he guessed.

I confronted my father. "What have you done to me? Vicky Castellano! Jesus Christ . . . !"

"The world has got two kinds of guys, Len," he said calmly. "You and I ain't Rockefellers or Vanderbilts. And we never will be, no matter what we do or don't do. Or uptown Jews, either. You're Uncle Harry's great-nephew. Your mother was a . . . I guess you know by now. A nude dancer. Not a hooker, by God, not anything like, but a nude dancer. Me, I'm—"

"You're not Mafia!"

He paused for a moment. "No. But I'm not holier than thou, either—like your father-in-law."

He'd hit me there. I had a failing marriage, and one reason it was failing was that my wife's family never ceased to look down on me. The son of Jerry Cooper would never be good enough—no matter what he achieved—to be Sue Ellen's husband.

"Vicky can do a hell of a lot for you," he went on. "Already has. Besides which . . . tell me she's not the sweetest piece of ass you've ever had."

"She's Sicilian," I grumbled sullenly.

"Hey! Whatsa matter with you? Arnold Rothstein was not Sicilian. Neither was Dutch Schultz. Neither was Bugsy Siegel. Neither was Meyer Lansky. And—ha!— neither is Sol Schwartz."

"There's a relationship," I said. "I mean—"

"Of *trust*," he interrupted me. "If I'd ever wanted to be connected, maybe I could have arranged it. I never wanted it. I *don't* want it. But Vicky Lucchese is a *source*. Your law firm understands that. And if it doesn't, fuck it. Vicky can do more for you than Gottsman, Scheck and Shapiro. And a hell of a lot more for you than Sue Ellen and her father."

I don't know how soon Sue Ellen began to suspect that I was seeing another woman. When I began to stay in town overnight three or four nights a week, I suppose. She called one night after midnight, checking up on me. I was in my father's guest room, as I'd told her I would be. I talked to her for ten minutes that night, while Vicky went in the bathroom, sat on the closed toilet seat, and read.

"How many nights a week you have to stay in town?" Sue Ellen asked peevishly.

"It's business, honey," I said.

"What kind of business? I've started to think it's funny business, lover. You don't come home like a guy who hasn't had any since night before last."

"Law business," I said. "I was with a client until just half an hour ago."

Vicky smirked.

"Your voice sounds funny."

"I was with people who smoked."

What was funny was my struggle to speak in a normal voice, since Vicky had come out of the bathroom and stood nude, hands on her hips, grinning at me.

"You'll come home some night and there won't be any for you." She hung up.

"We're gonna have to come to a conclusion," Vicky said as I put down the telephone.

"I know."

"I'm too old to commit myself to a relationship with no future."

"Yes."

"Well . . . we have to think about it."

Anyway, Sue Ellen was jealous without knowing why she should be. And I was playing with fire.

Sue Ellen continued to study Chinese and became fluent. So did Mollie. One day she announced that she and Mollie wanted to go to China for a month. Her father would put up part of the cost, and she wondered how much *we* could afford to pay. I was doing all right at the firm, but I was not doing well enough to fund an extended trip to China while meeting all the other obligations we had. Would *my* father contribute as her father was? He contributed enough, and one late-summer day Sue Ellen and Mollie boarded a plane at Kennedy and flew to Hong

Kong, from where they would make excursions into China.

Vicky was pleased. She rented a love nest for us—complete with a telephone that would ring in my father's apartment so that he or Melissa could switch the call as if only sending it to the extension in the guest bedroom.

It was an adventure to live with Vicky.

I was not an experienced lover. I had dated, but I had never had sex with any woman but Sue Ellen and Mollie until I met Vicky. Sue Ellen, still in her twenties, had gained a little weight. She was not heavy, but she was a little looser than she had been when I married her. Vicky, who was eighteen years older than Sue Ellen, had a perfect body. Vicky's body was no longer youthful, but it was taut and flawlessly proportioned. Sue Ellen, though the daughter of Boston Brahmins, had a slightly dusky complexion. Her skin was smooth but not glossy. It was as if road dust had been used to powder her all over. Vicky's skin was almost white, and her big, shiny, vivid-pink nipples were in distinct contrast to the white skin of her breasts. Because she shaved her crotch, the darker pink of her inner parts showed whenever her legs were more than a little apart.

Three words did not yet pass between Vicky and me. "I love you." We didn't say it. I wouldn't have dared say it unless she said it first, though I did, in fact, love her. I still could not guess exactly what she felt for me. I know she didn't want her sixteen-year-old son to meet her twenty-six-year-old lover. Beyond that . . . she was caring. She was generous. She was mysterious.

She was also the only woman I ever experienced who could suck my entire scrotum and testicles into her mouth—or ever wanted to.

31

JERRY

By early 1978 Giselle and I had to accept the fact that she was dying. Cancer. I had avoided the specific subject before because I was not sure I could handle it.

She was not afraid. Her chief worry was that I would not be able to rear Len properly, and she asked me for certain promises about that. I was to see to it that he got a fine education and entered a learned profession. He was not to become a street hustler. He was not to be like Buddy. What she meant, of course, was that he was not to be like me. We might have a fine, successful business, she and I, but I had started out a street hustler, and, whatever Len became, he was not to start that way.

The only question was, would we tell him she was dying? We agreed not to. The shock would be bad enough. Anticipation would be worse. It was worse for me. It nearly destroyed me. If not for the knowledge that I had a son to raise, I think it might have led me to suicide. I am honestly not at all sure I would be alive today if it had not been for my son. I couldn't abandon him. I could readily have abandoned everything and everyone else.

I suppose most people think there is nothing worse than dying. There is something worse: having to watch someone you love die, knowing you are going to have to live on. That, believe me, is much, much worse.

When the end was near, I took her to France. She wanted to see her daughters, the ones she'd had by Jean Pierre Martin. She also wanted to see her sister.

Her daughter Jacqueline was married and the mother of a little girl. Her daughter Jeanne was not married but was the mother of a son. Her sister Thérèse—the one who had collaborated with the Nazis and had been marched naked through the streets with a shaved head—lived quietly in Lyon in the family home, with a wine merchant her own age, and seemed to have been forgiven by the city. I suppose people remembered, but by then the whole French nation, not just its collaborators, knew it had something to be ashamed of.

Giselle died in Lyon. She was fifty-two years old.

Sometimes I called Sal by his real name, which was Sol. At first he didn't like it, but when he saw he couldn't bully me out of it, he accepted it.

He went through girlfriends like shit through a goose. Truda, the big fat girl who modeled for us, lasted a year or so. I remember a Jeannie and a Suzie. Most of the names I don't recall. I didn't even meet all of them.

He was very kind to me when I lost Giselle. He met me at the airport and drove me up to Lodge. He didn't even go in. He waited for me in the parking lot. He knew Len didn't like him and figured the boy was enduring enough pain without a visit from his Uncle Sal. I was touched by how sensitive Sal could be.

Sal knew our designer, Larkin Albert, of course. One day the three of us sat down over lunch at 21.

Albert had become a great deal more—how shall I say it? He had become more skilled, more artistic, more subtle, in his cross-dressing. He sat there in 21, smooth and

self-confident, assured that no one in the room guessed he
was a man. He wore an ivory jaquard suit: padded shoulders, button-front jacket, slim miniskirt. It was entirely
appropriate to 21. His makeup was understated. His wig
was styled to expose half his forehead and his ears and
earrings. I can't guess what he used to suppress his beard
and other hair, but his face and legs were as smooth as
any girl's.

Sal asked the question I would not have asked. "Tell
me, Lark, have you had the operation?"

"No, for Christ's sake," Larkin said in an amused, vel-
vety voice. "What would I do for fun, if I . . . ? Well . . .
Sal, I'm not one of *those* guys! So far as *doin' it* is concerned, I'm as straight as . . . well, as I suppose you two
are."

"I guess there are all kinds of guys," said Sal.

"You better believe it," said Larkin. He glanced across
the room. "See the suit with the big Bloody Mary?"

He had used the term "suit" aptly. Nixon vest. John
Dean haircut. Rep tie. Wing-tips. Smoking a cigarillo.
This . . . creature said *Wall Street*, said *broker*, said *law-
yer*. It could have worked in the Nixon White House.

"She's a broad," said Larkin. "She hasn't noticed me,
but I've noticed her, and I'm here to tell you she's a first-
class piece of tail."

"Explain this to me," I said.

Larkin smiled. "You're sitting here. Sal's sitting here.
Of the three of us, I'm the only one's who's *charged!*
Man, if one of you groped me, I'd come! And Mary Beth
over there—which is her name—is *wet*. I mean, she's
ready! We may be the only ones in the room who are
having a really good time."

"You don't wish you were a woman?" I asked.

"Are you kiddin'? Hell, no, I don't wish I were a
woman. And Mary Beth doesn't wish she were a man.
Guys . . . I get off by dippin' my wick—and I don't mean
by dippin' it between the teeth of some fag."

We changed the subject. Sort of. Larkin led off.

"Listen to me, guys. I'm wearing a pair of silicone boobs. I don't mean implants. I mean silicone boobs in my bra. If I took off my bra, they'd fall off. But if I let you see them through a sheer bra, you'd think you were looking at real boobs. You could feel me up, and you wouldn't immediately feel the difference. If one of you felt me right now, through my dress and all, you'd *swear* you had your hands on real tits. These little babies are imported from Germany, and they cost me five hundred bucks a pair. Well, shit, man, why doesn't Cheeks sell silicone tits?"

It was something Giselle would have objected to. She loved merchandise that showed off a woman at her best. Anything that dishonestly enhanced her, Giselle did not like.

"The krauts got a patent on these things?" Sal asked.

"Can you patent false tits?" Larkin asked. "I don't know, but I doubt it. If you can, it must be easy enough to put together a different chemical combination that would do the same thing in a different way. I can't think it would be too difficult."

It was a departure for Cheeks, the first of a series that would change the nature of the business.

The German company did not in fact have a patent on their silicone breast enhancers. What else to call them? But they manufactured them beautifully, and we signed a contract to import them at $186 a pop. We sold them for $400.

They came in a variety of sizes, ranging from rather thin ones that changed a girl from an A to a B, all the way to the kind that Larkin wore, to give a person with no tits at all a luscious bustline. They could not have changed, say, Larkin into a Dolly Parton. But they very convincingly changed him into a believable woman.

"Hell," Larkin had said. "When the word gets around that we sell these, we'll sell fifty to women for every one we sell to a man. I guarantee it."

The ratio was more like ten thousand to one. Millions

of women wanted bigger tits, but they didn't want two things: first, they didn't want to wear those hideous pads of rubber and kapok called falsies, and, second, they didn't want surgery.

What a business! But it was, as Giselle would have emphasized, a departure for us.

I put my foot down against one thing. Silicone boobs, maybe. Rubber cocks, no. Sal and Larkin couldn't see the difference, but I could and vetoed merchandising fake penises.

I consented to the sale of a device called an Arab strap. It was a contraption of straps and buckles that went around the penis and down under the balls, holding the penis up in an unnatural erection, caused chiefly by the constriction of the veins in the shaft. In point of fact, the thing was a little bit dangerous. Interfering with the circulation of the blood was not the world's greatest idea, and after a short time I banished the Arab strap from Cheeks stores.

32

We continued to import about half our merchandise, most of it from France but an increasing amount from places like Hong Kong and Manila and Singapore. What we didn't import came from contractors hired by Charlie Han. He was an important element of our success.

Charlie had become almost a partner in Cheeks. He was not just a small-time sweatshop manager anymore. He was an entrepreneur, running a score of sweatshops through layers of subcontractors. We hadn't made him that. He had many customers, and he sewed into his clothes the labels of some of the most prominent chains of stores in the nation. He also sewed in the labels of important designers.

What is more, he was not just the maker of underwear and swimsuits; his laborers assembled blouses and skirts, jeans and jackets, dresses and suits.

He didn't do business any longer from a table in a coffee shop. His office was in a building on Twenty-seventh Street—isolated and well insulated from the grimy lofts where his employees worked under the tyrannical supervision of his managers. He had the kind of smarts that Buddy admired, and he had used them to grow.

By now Charlie could have made a colorable case that he didn't know the working conditions in his shops—and in fact he would, when he had to.

And if he could make the case, we could make it. This was the deal. This was the way it worked. We could pretend innocence. In truth, I had visited Charlie's sweatshops once or twice, and that had been enough; I had not gone back anymore. I could testify, if need be, that we bought our merchandise from various makers, including Charlie Han, and had no idea what were the working conditions in the shops where our clothes were sewn. We were not obligated, under the law, to inspect the factories of our suppliers.

As Sal kept reminding me, this was the garment industry, and Cheeks wasn't big enough to change it. Other companies might be, but they had no interest in changing it.

Charlie did get in trouble once. Federal inspectors found a lot of violations of various laws in a loft on Thirty-fifth Street, and they traced the ownership to Charlie Han—that is, they thought they had traced the ownership.

Charlie was arrested, hustled out of his office in handcuffs, taken before a federal magistrate, jailed briefly, and then released on bond—protesting all the while that he did not own or manage the loft where they found all the violations.

He was indicted on six counts nevertheless, and in the fall of 1979 his case came to trial.

I was shaking. Among the merchandise found in the sweatshop were things we sold in Cheeks stores.

I sent a lawyer to observe the trial. He bought a copy of the transcript on the testimony I would be interested in.

MR. JULIUS: Mr. Han, I hand you an article of clothing. I suppose we must call it a pair of panties. What had you to do with the manufacture of that article?

JUDGE GRIFFITH: There will be no laughter or other noise from the spectators in the courtroom.

MR. HAN: Nothing.

MR. JULIUS: Please read the label in that article of clothing.

MR. HAN: It reads, "Cheeks. Intimate apparel."

MR. JULIUS: What is Cheeks?

MR. HAN: It is a seller of women's intimate apparel.

MR. JULIUS: Have you ever been involved in the manufacture of merchandise for Cheeks?

MR. HAN: I was at one time, briefly. Some years ago.

MR. JULIUS: How many years ago?

MR. HAN: To the best of my recollection, twelve or fifteen years ago. About that. Something like that.

MR. JULIUS: Do you do any business with Cheeks today?

MR. HAN: Yes.

MR. JULIUS: What kind of business?

MR. HAN: I am a manufacturers' representative; in other words, a salesman. When one of my manufacturers comes up with something I think might appeal to Cheeks, I show it to them.

MR. JULIUS: Obviously this pair of panties was manufactured for this Cheeks company. It has their label sewn in it.

MR. HAN: Cheeks bought the entire supply of that item. That's what it usually does, buys all of an item, together with the exclusive right to merchandise it.

MR. JULIUS: How many pairs of these panties did Cheeks buy?

MR. HAN: I think a thousand dozen.

MR. JULIUS: You have said you never saw the sweatshop in which these panties and a lot of other items were made. Is that your testimony?

MR. HAN: I deal with the executives of the companies I represent, in their offices or mine. I never go to their manufacturing facilities.

MR. JULIUS: With whom did you deal in securing a thousand dozen pairs of these panties for sale to Cheeks?

MR. HAN: I dealt with Mr. George Alexander, vice president for sales, Alexander and Company. It is a family business.

MR. JULIUS: Where is Mr. Alexander now?

MR. HAN: I haven't seen him for some time.

MR. JULIUS: A family business, you say. Where are the other members of the Alexander family?

MR. HAN: I never met any of them but George.

MR. JULIUS: They are all missing, disappeared.

MR. HAN: If they were running an illegal sweatshop, I am not surprised.

That was Charlie Han. He had covered his tracks extremely well. He always did. And he carefully kept my name out of the case. How could I be anything but grateful?

The crotchless panties handled by the prosecutor as if they were dirty and would soil his hands drew a lot of media attention. The publicity didn't hurt us.

George Alexander was like Murray. He was insulation between Charlie and his businesses. We would encounter him again later, in a surprising way.

Melissa waited two months after Giselle died before she made it plain to me that she would not mind doing what she could to relieve my horniness. My God! What a piece of luck! To have lost Giselle and then so soon to be able to form a relationship with a woman like Melissa. . . .

Melissa had been around in one capacity and another since that day when, as a twenty-year-old model, she had offered to trim her pubic hair so it wouldn't show over the top of one of our bikinis. She was the one who had recommended Larkin Albert as a designer. We had used her as a model often.

She had married. She had divorced. She had no children.

For a short time she was in tough circumstances, and we made work for her. One year I sent her to Paris to tour the shops that supplied what we imported, to identify what she thought would sell in the States. She turned out to be good at it. She had a very good sense of what American women would wear.

She was never a top model. There was too much of her for that. But she appeared in hundreds of department-store ads for bras and panties. Twice she appeared in ads in *The New York Times Magazine*, once in *Vanity Fair*, and then in catalogs, modeling very ordinary American-style white undies. Her name remained unknown. Her face and figure were familiar to people who had no idea who she might be.

Sal tried to put the make on her. She rejected him gently but emphatically.

Okay. I recognized her subtle suggestion for what it was and took her up on it, gladly. She spent the night in my apartment. Then some more nights.

Winter settled things for Melissa and me. One morning we left the apartment and went down to try for a cab. New York can be a terrible place when the weather is bad. Snow had fallen overnight, leaving the streets curb-full with slush and filthy water. Sleet was falling now. New Yorkers, taking their quirky, surly pride in the myth that they can't be defeated, were fighting each other for cabs and scrambling along the slippery sidewalks toward the subway entrances.

Melissa and I stood in the foyer of our building, looking at the challenge.

"What the hell are we doing?" I asked her.

She shook her head and shrugged. "Damned'f I know," she said. "I'm really damned if I know."

I remember how she looked. She was wearing a leopard hat and coat that had Dupont, not Africa, in their ancestry, plus vinyl boots against the slush. Her brown hair turned under her chin. Her skin already glowed from the harsh, cold wind. She was thirty-five years old.

"Let's go back upstairs," I said. "Make a pot of coffee. Scramble some eggs. Eat and go back to bed."

She shook her head. "I have to be at—"

"No, you don't."

"I do if I expect to make a living."

"You don't have to make a living, Melissa. Or you can make one in my business. And it's silly, isn't it, for you to keep a separate apartment?"

We went back upstairs. She called the photographer— who thought she was twenty-seven, not thirty-five—and said she could not come in to model underwear because of the weather. I called my office and said I was not coming in because of the weather. That was it. From that day, we lived together.

We slept in the guest bedroom. She understood why and one night suggested I should replace the furniture in the master bedroom. We did, together, and after that slept in a room that was ours—until we moved into a new apartment with decor done for us by a designer.

That place—Ha! I owned art done by guys I'd never heard of. Hey! By me an artist was Norman Rockwell. Him I knew. His stuff I liked. In the new place I lived with things that dangled from the ceiling and made no sense at all.

Melissa was thirty-five. Hell. I was fifty-six. I was robbing the cradle, and I was like the cat who swallowed the canary.

Melissa was not just an easy piece of ass. That had been Sal's mistake: to imagine she was. I mean, Melissa sometimes said no. She didn't lie back and spread her legs just because I said I wanted it, any more than Giselle had.

I never compared Melissa to Giselle. In my mind, they occupied two separate compartments. They were the ornaments and the comforts—no, more than that; they were my help and support—in two different times in my life.

If I have been a success in this life, I owe a lot of it to a pair of fine women: Giselle and Melissa.

33

By the time my son married Sue Ellen, I had forty-seven stores. Twelve of them were in the five boroughs. I had a store in Scarsdale and one in White Plains, one in Greenwich, Connecticut, and one in Stamford. I had one in Westport, one in Bridgeport, and two in Hartford. Two in Providence, one at Newport, four in Boston, and one in Springfield. We had stores on Martha's Vineyard and Nantucket that were open only in the summer. In New Jersey, I had two stores in Jersey City, and one each in Trenton, Camden, and Atlantic City. There were five Cheeks stores in Philadelphia and its suburbs. We had two stores in Baltimore, one in Wilmington, Delaware, and four stores in Washington.

Look at a map, and you will see that not one of our stores was more than a hundred miles from the Atlantic Ocean. None was as much as three hundred miles from New York. We weren't even regional. We were provincial.

The reason was that I insisted on dropping in on any one of the stores unannounced, anytime. I now know the term for the way I ran my business. It is called hands-on management. I did not choose to be a hands-on manager.

I simply didn't know any other way. Len would know a better way, but I didn't know it.

I've heard that managers of Howard Johnson's restaurants sometimes discovered that the inconspicuous old man sitting in a booth eating a platter of fried clams was Howard Johnson himself, who would afterward sit down with the manager and deliver a quiet appraisal of the franchise. I'm sure that was effective management, whether the Harvard MBAs thought it was or not.

The limits of our province were defined, essentially, by the range and speed of our Beech airplane. We kept it at Teterboro initially, then at Westchester County Airport. I would call the airport. One or more qualified pilots was always hanging around, waiting for a call, and he—occasionally she—would fly me where I wanted to go. While I was on my way to the airport, the pilot would plot the navigation and check out the airplane. Word got around that I would pay a pilot $50 just for discovering and telling me that the weather was not suitable for the flight. I accepted their word for that: the word of the pros. So I took no chances and had no trouble.

In the air.

"It can be a very different game in Philadelphia," Sal warned me. "They play by their own rules in Philly. Very different rules. Not what we're used to."

"Like?"

"Well . . . here in New York we sort of put the quiet on things. I know some guys have been whacked out, even recently, but you do that regularly here you're gonna come up against the Council. In Philly . . ." He shook his head. "They still do things the old way. Like—The chief family in Philadelphia is the Boiardo Family. Sicilians. Old-timey Sicilians, from a town called Partanna, where they were members of the Honored Society. They came over here in the 1890s, first to New York and then moved on to Philly."

"Right. I know the name."

"Don Enrico Boiardo is called the Chef, because the

name sounds like the name on Chef Boyardee Italian food packages. Don Enrico is an old Mustache Pete. He's a grandson of Don Vittorio Boiardo, the original one that came on the boat."

"So . . . ?"

"The problem is that the Boiardos don't have internal peace. The don's heir apparent was called Chef, Junior. He was killed by his uncle, Plato Boiardo, the Chef's brother, 'cause *he* wanted to be the heir. When the Chef found about that, he had Plato whacked out and also Plato's wife and two sons, plus the son's wives. I mean, that kinda stuff doesn't come down in New York. The old Sicilian tradition is that you can go after guys but you leave their wives and kids alone. Plato's whole family!"

"Jesus!"

"Jesus is right. That kind of stuff don't come down in New York. The Families respect wives and kids and never come after them. The only guys I know who do stuff like that are the Dominicans in Washington Heights. Man, they're vicious. When they go after a guy, they go after him and his whole family and anybody who's got a rep for bein' a friend of his."

"In Philadelphia—"

"It brought down a war. For a while it looked like all the Boiardos would die. It got so bad that the Boiardos of Partanna sent a don over here to settle things down. That was in the late 'twenties. There's supposed to be peace, but it's been a blood feud, and some Boiardos still hate other Boiardos, so who knows how long any peace is gonna last? A nephew of the Chef was whacked out only a couple of years ago. Somethin' about turf."

"Are you saying we should stay out of Philadelphia?" I asked him.

Sal shrugged. "Maybe. I'd think about it. Philly's a tough damned town."

"Then what other towns do we get scared out of? I hear they got a pretty rough gang in Cleveland. What about Chicago? L.A.? We gonna be toughed out? Hey! All we wanta do is sell scanties. The families haven't shown any interest in that in our other cities."

He shrugged again. "They show interest in who does our hauling," he said.

We were sitting over steaks at Sparks. Sal loved Sparks. He didn't like Four Seasons, for example. Sparks wasn't the very best steakhouse in the city, but it was close. Sal was a meat-and-potatoes man. And he loved red wine, lots of it—which was how Sparks served it: in eight-ounce water glasses.

"I guess I could talk to Jimmy Lead Eyes," he said. "He might have an idea or two."

Jimmy "Lead Eyes" Francione was now the head of the Carlino family. He told Sal we should make our peace with Don Enrico Boiardo, who wasn't going to take much interest in whether or not Cheeks opened stores in his city.

Quoting him—"Selling ladies' undies isn't exactly a business guys want to get into. You guys keep your noses clean, and nobody's gonna take any notice of you."

I met with Don Enrico Boiardo in an Italian restaurant in King of Prussia, where they served the best Italian food I have ever tasted.

He was an elderly man, attended by two thugs who served as bodyguards and personal servants. He was wearing a handsome gray overcoat, though it was not overcoat weather; they helped him out of it and took his hat and scarf. They sat down at a table nearby and glared at me for a full ten minutes before they decided I was not about to draw a gun.

Don Enrico did not have a mustache, but he had great, gray eyebrows. His hair was gray. His face was lined. His watery eyes were blue. His voice was thin and tended to crack. It was impossible to believe that this man had ordered the murder of his brother and his brother's sons and their wives.

"I hear from Jimmy Lead Eyes that you want to establish a new business in Philadelphia," he said.

"A *small* business, Don Enrico," I said. "I am honored that you would meet me on so small a matter."

He turned up the palms of his hands and turned down the corners of his mouth. "I like to know what is going on," he said. "It is a key to success in business."

I explained to him what Cheeks was and presented to him a box containing an assortment of Cheeks merchandise. Tucked among the panties and bras, nighties and corselets were hundred-dollar bills: a hundred of them.

"I am afraid my wife is beyond wearing these," he said with a wanful smile.

"Daughters, then, Don Enrico. Or—"

"Yes. Of course. I will find someone who will appreciate them. Oh, yes."

Over lunch and red wine we talked about all kinds of things. He expressed admiration for Ronald Reagan, particularly for how he had handled the air-controller strike.

"Do you have a wife and children, Jerry?" he asked. He had begun calling me Jerry.

"My wife died four years ago. I have a son. He's at Amherst and will start law school next year, at Yale."

"I am sorry about your wife. But you have a son who is going into an honorable profession. You must be very proud."

"I am, Don Enrico."

"I had a son many, many years ago, who was murdered by my brother. Can you imagine such a thing? How is a man supposed to forgive such a thing?"

He did not mention the revenge he had taken, though I suspect he knew I had heard about it.

"You brought me presents for my"— he paused to smile slyly —"daughters. I will send something nice for your son."

He did, in fact. He sent a gift certificate for $1,000, redeemable at Gucci. That is the origin of Len's habit, sustained ever since, of wearing Gucci loafers.

When we had finished our lunch, he nodded to his

thugs, who brought his coat and hat. We stood facing each other. I extended my hand to shake, and to my surprise the old man embraced me and kissed me on each cheek. I supposed the kiss was a quaint, old-world Italian custom and had no idea it had any great significance. I returned the kisses. I did not guess I had exchanged the ritual *abbraccio*, the kiss of peace with the don of the Boiardo family.

We opened two stores before the trouble began. Flying down from Westchester, we landed at a small airport outside Philadelphia—the name of which I don't remember. A car picked me up and drove me to whichever store I wanted to visit. Routine. I only flew in good weather. It was all routine. Sometimes Melissa went with me, and we pulled a curtain between us and the pilot and made out, sort of.

It was a joke between Melissa and me, as it had been between Giselle and me, to wonder what that pilot thought he was hearing. You know, you really can't do it in those small plane seats. Armrests are only a part of the problem. Seats don't recline all that much, either. Of course, you can find *some* fun things to do. You can vary the routine. Flying doesn't have to be boring.

This time it was not routine. I was alone, but my driver was not alone. He had with him an oily little man who looked vaguely like Michael Corleone's brother Fredo in *The Godfather*. "Fredo" waited until we were just outside the airport before he turned around and shoved the point of a switchblade knife to my throat.

"What the shit?"

"Lou Chieppa," he said. "We hear you traded the kiss of peace with the Chef."

"Don Enrico Boiardi," I agreed as calmly as I could.

"You think he runs this town? He don't."

I shook my head. "Okay. I'm from New York. I don't know from Philly."

"Well, you better learn before you come here. *We* run it here."

"'Kay," I said. I was in *their* car, with the point of Chieppa's knife within an inch of my throat. "So, how was I supposed to know who runs what?"

"Well, you knew enough to go see the Chef," said Chieppa with indignation that may have been genuine. "How'd you know enough to do that?"

"That's who I was told to see."

"Who told you?"

"Jimmy Lead Eyes."

The name effected a pause. Obviously, Chieppa had heard of Jimmy. "Well . . . Jimmy Lead Eyes ain't up to date. The Chef's days are over. You tell Jimmy that Ice Cream is the man now."

"Ice Cream . . . ?"

"Napolitano Boiardo. He's a cousin. You tell Jimmy Lead Eyes that Ice Cream is the man to see now. The Chef is history. Ice Cream has taken over."

"Okay. So what am I supposed to do? Does Ice Cream want me to get out of Philly?"

"You're gonna get out if you're the Chef's man."

"I'm not anybody's man."

"Then why'd you trade the kiss with the Chef?"

"I didn't know what it meant. I'm not a made guy."

"Then why'd you ask Jimmy Lead Eyes who to see?"

"My partner's a Carlino. Sal Nero. He's a made man. He's made his bones, too."

My oily little hood frowned. Here was another name he'd heard. "We'll want you to meet with Ice Cream," he said. "He's gotta be satisfied you ain't the Chef's man. If you're not, nobody cares who sells underwear in Philadelphia."

34

Sal was upset. "Goddamned Boiardos! Jesus Christ, man! Why'd you exchange the kiss of peace with the Chef? How goddamned stupid can you get?"

"In the first place, I didn't see what was coming. He shook my hand, pulled me close, and embraced me. Then he kissed me on each cheek. What was I supposed to do, pull away and offend him? How good a judgment would that have been?"

"You pledged your goddamned loyalty to him, is what you did. You pledged your loyalty to one don in a family that isn't loyal to just one don at a time."

"You didn't tell me that. You told me to go meet the Chef and take him a present."

"I shoulda gone with you."

"You should come with me to meet Ice Cream."

"That, my friend, I'm gonna do. For sure. I mean, you couldn't keep me away."

He explained to me the twisted logic behind the nickname Ice Cream. That man's name was *Napolitano* Boiardo. A popular ice cream flavor was Neapolitan. So . . . Ice Cream.

We met Ice Cream in a steakhouse on the outskirts of

Camden, New Jersey, which I should have found ominous. But Sal didn't—or if he did, he said nothing. The place was about as uninteresting a restaurant as I ever entered. The clientele were interesting. They seemed to be divided into two armies, each glaring at the other. I wondered if ordinary people ate there at all.

He shook Ice Cream's hand, bowed perfunctorily, and murmured, "Don Napolitano."

Ice Cream was a fleshy man, nattily dressed in a black cashmere overcoat and matching cashmere suit. His bald head glistened. His remaining hair was coal-black. He had a scar in his right eyebrow, as if someone had just missed blinding him. The handkerchief in his breast pocket matched his necktie. He wore a monogrammed white silk shirt. His pointy black shoes were mirror-shined.

"Mr. Nero. And Mr. Cooper. Sit down. The steaks are good here. Unfortunately, it's all they have that's good. Try the filet mignon. That's what I'm having. And they know how to broil them right, too: just rare enough and not too rare."

He had already made a heavy inroad on the basket of crusty French bread and the plate of butter, and on a bottle of red wine as well. He raised a finger and by gesture ordered replenishment of the bread and butter and a second bottle of wine. Obviously they knew him here. His bodyguards kept eyes like the eyes of snakes on Sal and me.

"Do you have a wife, Don Napolitano?" Sal asked.

"Yes, of course," said Ice Cream. "And five children, three boys and two girls. They are the pride of my life. I tell you, the pleasures of family life are not exceeded by anything else life can bring us. I accept no dinner invitations. I gather my little group around our table every evening, and we enjoy one of life's other great pleasures: first-class Italian cooking with first-class Italian wine."

"We have brought along a gift box of Cheeks merchandise. For your wife, or . . . for a friend, as you may choose."

He would find $10,000 in cash in the package, as the Chef had. We could figure he knew about that and maybe the Chef would hear about this, so the amount had to be the same.

"It is thoughtful of you," said Ice Cream. "It will go to someone who will appreciate such things."

We knew that meant they would go to a girlfriend. After he had enjoyed the incomparable pleasures of family life, he would slip out to know the pleasures of another life.

Over lunch the talk was about the difficulties of running a business: union problems, how hard it was to find trustworthy managers, taxes, regulations. . . . Ice Cream described himself as being in the produce business, supplying fruits and vegetables wholesale to local markets in Pennsylvania, southern New Jersey, Maryland, and Delaware. He said not a word that suggested he was a Mafia don. Until—

"Perhaps you understand why I was concerned that you might be affiliated with my dear friend Don Enrico. He is a great man, a very great man, but he and his group control too many things in our city. Of course, who sells what you sell is not a matter of concern for me. I was only worried that you might be something different from what you were represented to be."

"Jerry didn't understand the meaning of the *abbraccio,*" Sal explained. "He did not mean to pledge his allegiance."

"Of course. I understand entirely. You do not need my blessing to do business, but you have it, in any event. For whatever little it is worth, you have it."

"Thank you, Don Napolitano," I said. "It is our business to be friends with everyone and to intrude on no one else's business. We sought out a business we could enter without intruding on anyone else's business. I hope we have guessed right about that."

"I tell you, though," Don Napolitano said finally. "I got more truck capacity than I need. If sometime you need trucks to deliver your stuff to your stores, I'd appreciate your business. Whatever you can give me, you know. Anything."

"You got it," said Sal. "You understand, it's not a lot of stuff. But what we got, the business is yours."

"I might have people you could use. You know, store clerks. Like that. I mean, gals would love to move out of the produce business and into a fine, perfumed type of shop like you run. In my business I always have a surplus of young people looking for good jobs. Besides, it's hard to find people you can trust."

"You're too good to us, Don Napolitano," said Sal. Soapy as Sal could be, he could not conceal the sarcasm behind that statement. He didn't even try.

I interjected. "With an understanding, Don Napolitano," I said. "We had a problem in Connecticut with a few girls who were hustling on the side. We know you would never send us a girl who intended to hustle out of our stores. If you knew it. But if one happened to deceive you, we know you would expect us to send her back."

Ice Cream smiled. "Absolutely. I'd put her to work tearing the spoiled leaves off the outside of cabbage heads."

We shook hands. Significantly, we did not embrace or exchange the kiss. If we had, it would have been reported to Don Enrico within the hour.

"The shit piles deeper and deeper," Sal groused on our return flight to Westchester Airport. "Don Enrico thinks you're *his* man. Don Napolitano has us committed to using his trucks and taking his gals into our stores. Christ, Jerry! We better pull out of Philly."

And maybe we should have. Ice Cream's girls began to appear and apply for jobs. They were attractive, generally, and intelligent. They asked for more money than we were paying our other girls. It was only little more, and we decided to pay all our clerks what the don's girls asked, to keep peace.

It wasn't so simple. The manager of our downtown

store was a woman named Wanda, and one day Wanda asked me to go back to her little office for a talk.

"We got a problem," she said.

"Which is?"

"The Boiardos sent us a girl named Franny. Well . . . Franny calls herself a collector and is telling the non-Boiardo girls that they have to pay what she calls dues. It's just five dollars a week, and of course they all got that five-dollar raise when the Boiardo girls started coming in, so they're paying it. I've got eleven girls on the payroll, so the Boiardos are collecting fifty-five dollars a week."

"A hundred fifteen," I said. "If they're doing it here, they're doing it at the other store, where we've got twelve girls on the payroll."

"Nickel-and-dime business," Wanda said scornfully.

"Maybe. How many other businesses do you figure have got Boiardo people on their payroll and pay dues?"

Sal didn't like it. He said the dues would go up in time. "It's a classical extortion," he said. "It's just like paying protection. No difference at all."

"So what can we do about it?" I asked him.

"I don't know. Let me talk to Jimmy Lead Eyes."

I have no idea what he said to Jimmy Lead Eyes or what Jimmy Lead Eyes said to him. Whatever it was, it didn't do us any good. Ice Cream kept on collecting dues.

Even so, Philadelphia was a prime market for us. We did so well there that, after four months, I decided to open a third store.

So far we had not called on Ice Cream to provide us any trucking service. Furnishing and stocking a new store gave us the opportunity to call on Ice Cream. We did. I figured the shit would be in the fan if we didn't.

There was almost trouble when a Pennsylvania-licensed truck with the sign BOIARDI PRODUCE showed up in the garment district to pick up a load of merchandise. The New York teamsters didn't like that a little bit. But somehow the driver convinced their muscle man it was cool—

probably by handing over an envelope—and the truck left for Philly carrying an inventory of scanties and nighties.

It never made it. Between Exits 7a and 7 on the New Jersey Pike, the truck blew up. The driver, shielded by the steel between the cab and the cargo compartment, was not severely injured. Our merchandise was blown out of the torn-open truck and scattered along half a mile of highway. Much of it was burned, but much of it was intact. We did not recover a single carton. Hundreds of cars stopped, and delighted travelers looted everything in sight. Worse than that, we learned later that half a dozen state police cars left the scene with their backseats littered with panties and bras, garter belts, negligées, nightgowns, strip sets, and what have you.

I had no chance to ask Ice Cream what insurance he carried. Two days later his car blew up and scattered bits of Don Napolitano Boiardo along half a mile of Frankford Avenue.

Six weeks later, old Don Enrico Boiardo was literally cut in two by blasts from a twelve-gauge shotgun. I elected for the time being not to tell Len what had happened to the man who had bought his Gucci shoes for him.

The newspaper accounts of the gang war made something of the fact that the blown-up truck had been delivering merchandise to stock the city's third Cheeks store.

We were left orphans in Philadelphia, so to speak. What to do now? For example, did we tell our managers to stop the business of collecting dues from our employees? I decided to take a chance on that. I told them to stop it. We'd find out how badly demoralized the Boiardo family was. Or if it wasn't.

35

LEN

Sue Ellen and Mollie returned from China. I went to Kennedy Airport to pick them up. I had received cards and even a couple of calls from China and knew they were having the time of their lives. I had very realistic notions of just what kind of time that was—bedtime, lover time.

Well . . . I was living with Vicky. On the other hand, I was a man and Vicky was a woman, for Christ's sake! Sue Ellen and Mollie had become woman-woman lovers. I could guess why they were happy with their trip. They had discovered a new kind of experience, one that suited them very well.

Both of them had to submit to a strip search at customs. I think they raised suspicion by their dog collars, which they were wearing even on their long flight. A customs agent had me paged in the waiting hall, came to me, and showed me Sue Ellen's passport.

"That young woman says she's your wife, Sir. Is that young woman your wife?"

"Yes. What's the difficulty?"

"I'm afraid she fits a profile for people who enter the country carrying narcotics. That doesn't necessarily mean she really is, but we have to search her thoroughly. Also her companion."

I was pissed. "If she's carrying anything, she's in deep shit and on her own," I said. "If she's doing that—" I softened. "I'm pretty damn sure she's not doing that. Not her thing."

"May I ask what occupation you are in, sir, and where you live?"

"I am a lawyer in New York, with the firm of Gottsman, Scheck & Shapiro. I live in Greenwich, Connecticut."

"It's probably nothing, Mr. Cooper. It's just that they tend to *look* like the kind of people we have to worry about."

Ultimately, Sue Ellen and Mollie came out, pulling their wheeled suitcases and laughing.

"You won't believe this!" Sue Ellen chortled. "Naked. Nak-*ed*. The poor Hispanic woman who had to do it was embarrassed out of her skull."

"They didn't miss anything," Mollie laughed. "I all but *came*. Hell, I thought I was going to. To have a stranger's fingers up—"

"Enough!" I snapped. "I don't think it's funny. If they'd found anything, it would have hurt me as much as you. You two are . . . you're half sloshed."

"You're no fun," Sue Ellen protested. "You're more like my father every day. *Lawyer!*"

When I told Vicky, she was grim. "Your wife . . . It would have been up to you to prove you weren't . . . ."

Sue Ellen and Mollie got in the car. When we were out on the Van Wyck, I turned to Mollie in the backseat and asked, "Where do I drop you off?"

She smirked.

Sue Ellen answered my question. "She's going to bunk in with us for a while."

"Really?"

"We're family, aren't we? I mean, after all, what else can you call a girl who gave you the best blow job you ever had and taught me to do it, too?"

I knew what this meant. If not for the fact that I had been sleeping every night—and would continue to sleep as often as I could—with Vicky Lucchese, I would have said flat no. As it was, I simply shrugged.

"Tai-barng-le!" said Sue Ellen. This was something else I would have to put up with, that this pair would communicate with each other in Chinese, knowing I couldn't understand a word of it. They had it on me that they were fluently bilingual and I wasn't, and they amused themselves at my expense constantly.

They had no more surprises for me. I had expected that during their month of living together in hotel rooms they would not only share sex but would fall in love with each other. In fact, it had happened before they traveled to China.

I think of Mollie as my means of escape from my marriage to Sue Ellen.

Sex is an important part of my life. It always has been. It had become an overpowering obsession with Sue Ellen. I thought I had married a somewhat placid little girl who was embarrassed by her oversized breasts. Not gradually, but rather abruptly—since, after all, I'd been married to her only four years when she fell in love with Mollie— she turned into a lesbian.

But not a very clever one.

I don't know why she wanted to show me what she and Mollie did. All I know is that she was an exhibitionist, too. She wanted me to watch while she shoved her face into Mollie's crotch and vigorously licked Mollie's woolly pussy. Sometimes she would have to back off and pull a hair out of her mouth. When Mollie had come two or three times, they would change positions, and Mollie would lick Sue Ellen.

They giggled and joked while they did it.

—"Dammit, you need a haircut. I'm getting a mouthful of cunt hair."

—"So-o-o *wet!* It's dripping off my chin."

She wanted Mollie to watch when she and I coupled

and wanted to watch when Mollie gave me head.

Sue Ellen and Mollie were kinky and got kinkier.

They wore their dog collars pretty much all the time. I would come home from New York and find them naked and chained together by some four feet of chain that ran from one dog collar to another, locked on them with laminated padlocks, and they would give me the key. They thought it was sexy that they were chained together. I was supposed to think so, too. I might have if they had been a couple of hookers; but, dammit, Sue Ellen was my *wife*.

Then . . . I made some kind of excuse and stayed in the city with Vicky three nights. When I came home, I found that my wife had had both her nipples pierced—as, of course, had Mollie. Both of them were in a little pain, and I had to daub their tits with an antiseptic that stained and stung. They wore rather crude-looking steel rings, something like key-chain rings, which they called "training rings." Fortunately, no infection set in, and shortly they swore all pain was gone and the rings were comfortable.

After a couple of weeks they went back to the man who had pierced them and had him install permanent platinum rings, fastened with solder, that could not be removed except by cutting them. They were about the size of a nickel and as thick as the lead in a pencil. They hung in visible holes in their nipples.

After that they never wore their clips. They didn't have to. They hung tiny silver chains between their nipples and suspended ornaments from them. Sue Ellen wore her engagement ring hanging between her breasts. I am not sure if she was mocking me or not.

Of course, they went topless all the time. I never thought I would get tired of looking at women's boobs, but I got sick of looking at Sue Ellen's and Mollie's.

Then they began to talk about labial rings. The man who had pierced their nipples would pierce their inner labia, and they could wear rings there, as described in *The Story of O*. They had read the book, and the idea excited them. I did not bother to remind them that the rings installed on O's most private parts were installed by and for *a man.* There was no point in talking to them.

They even asked me to get the skin of my penis pierced and to wear a pearl stud.

I'd reached a point where I confided a lot in Vicky. I had to be careful about that. I had to avoid reminding her that she was eighteen years older than I was—old enough, as I had objected to my father, to be my mother. I had to be careful not to treat her as a trusted older adviser.

She shrugged. "I know a young woman who wears rings in her pussy," she said. *"Gross!"*

"The only thing worse, that I can think of, is piercing your tongue," I said.

"If this kid wants to have her cunt pierced, she's weird, Len."

I nodded.

Vicky smiled. "Hear what I've just said. I called your wife, who's your own age, I suppose, a kid."

She put her hands to her own shaved crotch and separated the fleshy lips. "To punch holes in there . . . Too painful for me."

"I've got to get rid of her, Vicky."

"Both of them," she said.

Suddenly it occurred to me that we'd just said something significant. If I got rid of Sue Ellen, did that mean . . . ? I think it occurred to Vicky, too. We dropped the subject.

My wife was not bright. Or maybe it was Mollie who was not bright. More likely, neither one of them was. They simply handed me my opportunity, carelessly. I imagine they thought I would never act against them.

Maybe I should have tried to evict Mollie and worked to save my marriage. Maybe I would have, if not for Vicky. Vicky had taken the place Sue Ellen had once had and could have had still.

I came home one night to find Sue Ellen and Mollie naked and making video tapes of each other. They had bought a camera.

They put a tape they had made on the VCR and pushed me down on the couch to watch it.

It was pretty tame. They had not yet figured out a way to photograph themselves together, so the tape showed only one of them at a time. Each one stripped. Then she posed, showing herself off. They had focused on their crotches, then on their anuses, each spread apart with fingers. Even they were disappointed in the results.

"What we need is a cameraman," said Mollie.

They made me the cameraman. While I aimed and focused, my wife shoved her face into Mollie's crotch and licked her labia and clitoris. The camera recorded sound, and they recorded talk as well as pictures:

"Oh, *God! Oh,* God!"

"You taste so *good!*"

"You gettin' this, Len? You *gettin'* this?"

"Don't care if he don't. We'll do it again."

"*Yeah!* Ha-ha-ha-ha! Yeah! Ten times more."

Sue Ellen pulled back, and Mollie set to work on her. Well . . . this kind of stuff has a certain sameness about it. If you've seen one of these, you've seen them all; and seeing the girls do it is no more a turn-on than the tape.

Hey! I'm not one of those guys that pretends nothing can turn him on. I've been with guys at strip shows, where an absolutely gorgeous gal is showing it all, and watched a guy pretend he was just so, so blasé. What's boring is not the show but him. Who the hell's he think he is?

Sue Ellen turned over, and Mollie ran her tongue up her ass. Sue Ellen moaned.

Am I gonna say I wasn't turned on? If I said that, who'd believe me?

The two girls loved it. They loved to watch their tapes. They commented on them as if they were drama critics:

"What we supposed to think you are there, Mollie? A virgin?"

"You know, you lick sloppy sometimes."

"I wondered when you were gonna come up for breath!"

They begged me, literally, to let one of them tape me taking sex from one of them. I refused. Flatly.

When we had a stack of tape cartridges, maybe a dozen of them, I began to take them, one at a time, into the city to a duplicating service. I knew what those bastards would do. They handed me back my original and my copy, and they sold the dozen or so other copies they had made. In a short time, Sue Ellen and Mollie were underground porn stars, their bodies and faces and voices known to thousands.

I waited a few weeks. Then I went into a tape-rental store on East Forty-third Street.

"Have you got the Sue Ellen and Mollie tapes?"

"Sue Ellen and . . . ?"

"Mollie. Two gals doing it to each other. I hear they're really something."

"Well . . . yeah, I think we got one or two of those. You wanta rent one?"

"I want to *buy* one."

"I'd have to have a hundred bucks."

"How many do you have?"

"I think I got three. Y'understand, they're not new. They been rented."

"I'll give you two hundred for the three."

"Uh . . . two-forty."

"Two twenty-five."

"Deal."

I went back to Connecticut and talked to a lawyer. I handed over the tapes and told him to view them. In a few days I talked with him again.

"What do you want, Mr. Cooper?"

"I want a divorce. Quick, easy, and cheap. I bought those tapes in a store on East Forty-third Street. My wife won't want her father to find out that she—"

"I get you. Quick, easy, and cheap."

I let Sue Ellen and Mollie live in the Greenwich house until the lease expired, that is, for a year and a half after I moved out. I paid the rent for that year and a half. That

was all she got from me. Her father at Hale & Dorr was
furious, mostly at her for letting me off so easy. He
guessed something was radically wrong, though, and
when Sue Ellen showed up in Boston with Mollie in tow,
he *knew* what was wrong.

How'd ya pull it off, for Christ's sake?" my father asked.
I told him, and he said, "Blood will tell. Uncle Harry
couldn't have screwed anybody better."

I grabbed his hand and shook it. "You think better of
me? I mean, seriously?"

He squeezed my hand. "Believe it or not, your mother
would think better of you, too. And I mean that seriously."

36

At twenty-seven, I guess I was smug. I thought I had some reason to be satisfied with myself. I had escaped from my marriage with little fuss and little cost. I was living with a forty-five-year-old mistress whose maiden name was Castellano. I was a rainmaker at Gottsman, Scheck & Shapiro. Only two years out of law school, I was well on my way to being made a partner in a law firm that was very respectable, though it was not one of the preeminent firms in New York City. No one else in my class had done any better.

Of course, I was reluctant to admit that contacts and luck had had a good deal to do with it.

Though we agreed that the firm would not become general counsel to Cheeks, my father sent me several clients. I did not get Charlie Han, but through Charlie I got two of his subcontractors: sweatshop operators. Vicky helped me bring in business besides Interboro Fruit. I need hardly say that she had a wide circle of acquaintances.

My relationship with Vicky broadened and deepened. We vacated the little love-nest apartment where we had been shacking up and rented—that is to say, *she* rented, chiefly—a much bigger place with a handsome view from the living-room windows of the East River and Roosevelt Island.

Her son was seventeen now and knew about me, which was a little awkward. His name was Anthony, and he was always so called, never Tony. Vicky's widowed sister moved into the apartment that had been Vicky's home, shared the rent, and Anthony lived there with her. He had dinner with us two or three times a week. Vicky went to his school functions and took him on his tour of colleges. The day they went to look at Yale, I drove them to New Haven.

The relationship between Vicky and me was anomalous, no getting around it. We had passionate sex together, but neither of us ever spoke the word *love*. Our living arrangements were as much like marriage as could be, but I never thought of marrying her and was certain she never thought of marrying me.

We were friends. Very good friends. I suppose we didn't realize how good friends we were.

Cheeks continued to expand. I said to my father that he had to learn to delegate authority, that he could never build the really big business he wanted until he abandoned his personal, hands-on management style. His response was to lease a Lear jet, so he could fly farther, faster—a typical Jerry Cooper reaction.

It was the first time I had any influence on the business. He opened stores in Pittsburgh, Cleveland, Columbus, Detroit, Louisville, Raleigh, Durham, Atlanta, Fort Lauderdale, and Miami—all within easy range of the little jet.

Then, shortly, he let me influence the business in a more important way.

Cheeks was a partnership, based on handshake agreements. When my mother was alive, she and my father had had a basic understanding that she owned half of his share of the business. But no document said so, and when she died her share was not listed as an asset of her estate. So, far as my father was concerned, Sal owned maybe twenty-five percent. He and Sal had drawing accounts and took money out regularly. So long as neither of them took so much as to alarm or offend the other, it was a good enough arrangement.

While he lived, everyone assumed Meyer Lansky had a small share, maybe five percent. He never demanded anything, but my father sent him a check from time to time, which he cashed without comment. When Lansky died and his estate proved almost insolvent, his heirs made no claim on Cheeks. My father sent a final large check to help with the funeral and other expenses.

Anyway, partnership, I explained to my father, was a dicey way to run a business. It involved too many uncertainties. I convinced him to form a corporation.

On January 18, 1989, Gazelle, Incorporated was chartered by the state of Delaware. The name was a play on *Giselle*.

It issued ten thousand shares of common stock. My father would own 5,500, which gave him clear control. Sal would own 2,500. I would own five hundred. Vicky bought five hundred. Unknown to my father, she endorsed her share certificates to me immediately—though we did not register the transfer on the records of the company. That left one thousand shares as treasury shares retained by the corporation.

My father was president and treasurer. Sal was vice president. Vicky was second vice president. I was secretary.

The board of directors was: Jerry Cooper, Sal Nero, Vicky Lucchese, Leonard Cooper, and Roger Middleton. Roger Middleton was a vice president of Allied Chemical Bank, where my father did his business and personal banking.

My father was not accustomed to reviewing his decisions with others, not since my mother died, anyway. Sal often interfered, but he did not try to take a regular part in running the business.

Now, I advised my father, he had to at least go through the motions of doing business as a corporation.

"Meaning I gotta do what?"

"It means you have to hold annual stockholders' meetings and monthly meetings of the board of directors. You report to the stockholders and directors, tell them what is going on. They can make motions, and votes are taken. Minutes have to be kept."

"Len . . . that's a lot of bullshit."

"I suppose it is. But it can make an important difference some ways, some times. Like . . . suppose sometime we wanted to borrow a lot of money—"

"Not likely."

"Suppose. A bank would run an audit, which would include a look at the company's minutes."

"Jesus!"

I remember one meeting in particular, which had to do with expanding our line of merchandise.

Although our signature line was daring, it did not include much that could be called fetishist merchandise. The nipple clips were about as close to that as Cheeks stores came. What was more important, the line did not include S-M items.

Sal raised the question in a directors meeting. "Hey, I think we're missin' out on a line of business that could bring in a bundle." He opened an attaché case he was carrying and took out a pair of shiny, nickel-plated handcuffs, then a pair of leg irons. "They also come in dull black," he said. "They sell cheap. For a little more money you can get leather ones that strap on, with little padlocks on the buckles. Hey, there's all kinds of stuff like this."

He withdrew more items from the attaché case— battery-powered vibrators, one of them shaped like an oversized cock, hard-rubber dildos, a red rubber ball with a strap running through it, to be fastened in a woman's mouth as a gag . . .

"Where'd you get those items?" my father asked.

"I picked this stuff up in a place on Forty-eighth Street. He does a *business* in it."

"Stocking that kind of stuff would change the whole

character of the business, wouldn't it, Sal?" I asked.

"The business of a business is makin' *money,*" he answered. "I'm sayin' that for a small investment we can add a line that will damn well definitely make money."

"There's lots of things we could do that would make money, Sal," my father said. "I'm not sure I want to get into any of them."

"It's related," Sal argued. "Guys that come in to buy scanties for their girlfriends will—Well, some of them will buy vibrators or handcuffs."

"There really is a brisk trade in this sort of thing," said Vicky. She picked up the pair of handcuffs and examined them intently, distastefully, wrinkling her nose. "But it is true that getting into it would change the character of the business."

Vicky did not keep silent in our meetings. She was a businesswoman in her own right, long accustomed to saying what she thought and to being heard. My father knew her character well and listened when she spoke. Sal, who was used to ignoring the judgments and opinions of women, had learned not to discount what she said.

I remember what she was wearing that day: a pale orange cashmere jacket over off-white linen slacks. Everything under those items was Cheeks merchandise. I had watched her dress that morning and could testify to that.

"It don't hafta change the character of the business," Sal argued. "Ya put this kind of stuff in a separate room. Some customers will be lookin' for that kinda merchandise, and they'll find it. They'll ask for it. Lotsa customers won't."

"Well, I'd like to suggest something," said Roger Middleton.

We had learned that Roger was a great deal more than a suit. He looked like a suit. He talked like a suit. But he was a shrewd businessman, with lots of useful ideas. And he was not unacquainted with our line of business.

"Shoot," my father said. "Let's hear your suggestion." He was bored with the discussion. He intended to make a decision very shortly, and he had patience for just so much talk.

"This is an expanding business," said Roger. "It has huge potential. But, Mr. Cooper, you run it like a country store, if you don't mind my telling you so."

"Even if I do mind, you just told me so."

"Here we have an example. Would offering—" he paused and pointed at the handcuffs lying on the table. "—*those* bring in more customers, or drive away some who would be offended? We shouldn't guess. We should find out."

"How we gonna find out?"

"Two ways. First, we offer that kind of merchandise in a few selected stores and see how it moves. Also, we should do a demographic study of our customer base. Who buys in Cheeks stores? Men mostly? Or women? Young or old? We interview a selected base of customers and see how they'd feel about finding handcuffs in a store."

To my surprise, my father agreed to Roger's suggestions. "Okay," he said. "We'll try it in ten stores, say. Then, how we gonna do these interviews?"

"We hire a consulting firm to do the demographic study," said Roger. "That's their business: interviewing customers. They can do it unobtrusively, and they will know how to evaluate the answers."

"I wouldn't be surprised you got in mind a firm to do this study," said my father.

"I do. Andersen, Brisk and Associates. There are other firms, but I have seen their work, and they are pros."

"What will they charge us?" my father asked.

"That will entirely depend on how thorough we tell them to be. I am sure it will be less than two-hundred thousand dollars."

"You think it will be worth it?" he asked Vicky.

"I'd do it, Jerry."

"You wanta call them for us?"

We would be surprised by the outcome of both these ventures.

37

Andersen, Brisk & Associates did the demographics study. They conducted discreet interviews with one thousand of our customers. Their interviewers were innocent-looking little girls for the most part, but they had been intensely trained. Every question they asked had been approved by my father, by Vicky, and by me. The phrasing was not accidental. Their tone of voice derived from their training. Gazelle, Inc. paid $175,000 for the survey.

Many of the interviews were taped—after advising the interviewee that it *would* be taped "for quality control." I listened to a good many, and they were very discreet.

"Let me assure you that, though I am audio-taping, you are not being photographed. I don't want to know your name or where you are from. At the end of the interview I will offer you a twenty-dollar gift certificate. I will not try to sell you anything."

The interviewer then established the age and sex of the interviewee and whether or not this was the person's first visit to a Cheeks store.

"When you visit a Cheeks store, do you usually come alone or with a friend?"

"With a friend. After all, *she's* the one who's gonna wear the stuff."

"Not in this store but in a few other Cheeks stores a new line of merchandise has been offered lately. It includes steel handcuffs and leather straps to restrain a person in various ways. Would the presence of such merchandise in a store make you less likely to go there?"

"How is it the French say? *Chacun à son goût?* Each to his own taste. What somebody else buys is none of my business."

"Then would you consider buying, say, a pair of handcuffs?"

"Ask the woman who's going to wear them."

"Would you wear them?"

"Might be interesting."

The results, ready in four months, were immensely interesting:

54 percent of our customers were men.

46 percent were women.

7 percent of our customers, men and women, were twenty-five years of age or younger, 24 percent were in the range twenty-six through thirty-five, 34 percent were in the range thirty-six through forty-five, 21 percent were in the range forty-six through fifty-five, 9 percent were in the range fifty-six through sixty-five, and 5 percent were over sixty-five.

In the stores where handcuffs and the like were offered, 11 percent of the customers bought them, and of the 89 percent who did not, only 8 percent said they wished we did not offer that kind of merchandise.

Of the customers who did not buy handcuffs, etc., 46 percent said they might buy them sometime. Those customers were about equally divided between men and women. They also tended toward the higher age groups.

Sal had insisted on a question: If they were offered, would you consider buying whips? Of men, 4 percent said they would consider it. Of women, 11 percent said they would consider it.

12 percent of our customers said they preferred not being seen at our stores.

38 percent sometimes, or even usually, came with a friend.

Of those who came to the store with a friend, it was the friend who was going to wear the merchandise and that friend took part in selecting what was purchased.

39 percent wished we would offer underclothes for men.

Well . . . a lot of it was surprising, particularly that 39 percent thought we should offer sexy things for men.

Larkin Albert was enthralled. To design erotic scanties for men! I had met him several times and now sat down over dinner with him and Vicky at Four Seasons. Albert was dressed as usual, as a woman. Vicky was there at my father's insistence. Albert, he insisted, was not above coming on to me.

Actually my father was kidding us, just to get Vicky to meet the man. Albert was not about to come on to any man. He might have tried to come on to Vicky, if she'd been alone.

I suspected at the time that Four Seasons knew who he was and what he was, and I wondered if he would have been made welcome there if he had not asked for my father's table. He was, anyway, among the most glamorous women in the room, and was maybe the very best dressed. I remember his "basic little black dress." I remember that I could not have guessed he was a man. She wouldn't admit it, but neither could Vicky—though later she insisted she had known all along that he was a man.

"My! You say thirty-nine percent? Well! What a challenge!"

"Challenge?" Vicky asked.

Albert grinned. "About seven percent of women—an unscientific guess, not based on a study like yours—think their boobs are too big. Maybe another ten percent think theirs are just right. Which leaves eighty-three percent who think theirs are too small. Men—I'd guess ninety-five percent of men wish their cocks were bigger, no matter what size they are." He shrugged. "The challenge of designing men's scanties is to make them think their undies make them look bigger. And that is *one hell* of a challenge."

He would solve the problem.

My father had chosen two stores in Manhattan—Midtown and the Upper East Side—and one in Stamford, Connecticut, one in Boston, one in Jersey City, one in Philadelphia, and one in Washington for our experiment in selling S-M merchandise.

He stocked them pretty much the way Sal suggested, with steel handcuffs and leg irons, leather versions of the same, and leather collars. He expanded each store's stock of nipple clips. The printed instructions that went with them suggested they could also be attached to the labia or the foreskin of an uncircumcised male.

One item he allowed surprised me. It was a gag, consisting of a soft rubber ball pierced with a narrow strap that could be buckled behind the neck, making it impossible to spit out the ball. Of course, the subject's hands would have to be cuffed behind the back.

We wondered if we would not run into trouble with local authorities, once we began selling this kind of stuff. It didn't happen.

Sal visited the stores and asked for volunteers to model these things. In every store, at least one young woman did volunteer.

Some of these girls were pretty good actors. I went to the Midtown store and watched a girl model. She stripped to Cheeks scanties, black of course, and then the woman manager cuffed her hands behind her back and locked on a pair of leg irons. Finally she shoved the bright red ball into the girl's mouth and tightened and buckled the strap. The girl took it for a few minutes, stumbling around the room and showing off. Then she began to struggle and shake her head and moan. When tears began to run down her cheeks, the manager unfastened the gag, and the girl hung her head and wept. Another clerk came in and led the "victim" out of the showroom. Five minutes later, out of sight of the customer of course, the girl was laughing and drinking a Coke.

The customer, embarrassed at having put an innocent kid through such discomfort, bought a set of cuffs, shackles, and gag. I wondered how he thought some other young woman was going to react at being restrained the same way.

Oddly, this line of merchandise generated curiosity in Vicky and Melissa. One evening when we were having dinner in my father's apartment, Melissa went in the bedroom and came out carrying handcuffs and leg irons, which my father locked on her. She blushed and grinned and muttered something to the effect, "Don't knock it if you haven't tried it."

Vicky volunteered that she would try it, just for a minute. My father took the things off Melissa and handed them to me. I fastened them on Vicky. She walked around the living room, lurching and awkward. The one minute was enough. She demanded I take them off, and I did.

In our own apartment, later, she told me she wanted to try them again. I picked up a set at one of the stores. That night after dinner she stripped to a pair of panties and a bra, and I locked the chains on her. She tugged at the cuffs, apparently pretending she really was a prisoner. She did not stumble in the shackles, quickly gauging the length of the chain and the length of the steps she could take. She walked around the apartment. When she sat down beside me I felt the crotch of her panties and found she had soaked them. I pulled them down, and we made love without removing the cuffs or shackles.

She liked them—within limits. Sometimes she wore the handcuffs and leg irons for a whole evening.

This kind of stuff sold. It was never a major profit center, but Cheeks sold handcuffs, leg irons, and gags. The nature of the business was changing.

Larkin Albert called us to his studio to see what he had designed. My father, Sal, and I went to his little show.

Larkin—I had begun to call him by his first name— had hired four models to show us the line he knew would sell. Charlie Han had worked the items up for him. It was all of ribbed combed cotton, a sort of knit with some stretch in it.

Okay. The four models came out wearing Larkin's designs. Each of them was a young man with a shaved and lightly oiled body. One of them was muscle-bound.

The underwear was striking. The big-line companies like Jockey had been selling slingshots for years. No one would be shocked by bikini styles in men's briefs. Larkin had designed thongs. Straps circled the hips to attach front to rear. One of the designs had no rear. A string ran from the back end of the pouch, up along the anus, and reached the string coming around from the corners of the pouch. Most of the styles, though, had a definite pouch in front and a stretched cover for the butt.

My father shrugged and spoke quietly to me. "Colored jockstraps."

"Maybe," I whispered. "But . . . I think there's something more to it."

There was.

Standing before us at this point was a handsome young man with an out-of-season tan and a hairless torso. His male parts filled the pouch of his thong. In fact, they stretched it.

"Ken," said Larkin. "Pull it down and let the gentlemen see how you are hung."

Ken smiled nervously, but he pulled the thong down to his knees.

His penis was nothing unusual. He didn't have a hard-on. He had a normal, circumcised penis.

Larkin gestured to him to pull the thong up again. With the cotton stretched over him again, he looked huge.

Larkin had solved his problem. And the solution was simple. The pouch was sewn to capture the scrotum as well as the penis. In other men's briefs, and in jockstraps, the scrotum and testicles were allowed to hang between the legs. In Larkin's designs, the scrotum was lifted like breasts in a bra. The pouch was filled, overfilled. And this shoved the penis forward and made it look twice its real size.

The other three models were told to shove their thongs down and let us see what they had. One was bigger than average. The others were average. But with their under-pants in place, they looked like they were hung like horses.

Cheeks had another line of merchandise. It would prove highly profitable.

38

JERRY

As my son Len became more and more involved in my business, I told him more and more of the history until he knew most of it. I did not tell him much about the Boiardo feud in Philadelphia. I told him that the man who paid for his first pair of Gucci loafers was a don. That was, of course, Don Enrico. I told him the old man was dead, but not exactly *how* he got dead.

That whole deal in Philadelphia was a pisser, an absolute pisser. Don Napolitano—Ice Cream—was whacked out. Don Enrico—the Chef—was whacked out. And we'd had, supposedly, a cozy relationship with both of them. Jimmy Lead Eyes told Sal we had to be nuts. Then Jimmy Lead Eyes got whacked out. He was found with a cigarillo between his teeth and a bullet hole between his eyes.

This kind of stuff wasn't supposed to happen anymore. The problem was that men like Meyer Lansky and Frank Costello, Cosa Nostra statesmen who had worked to keep the peace, were gone. A new breed of dons had come along, cowboys who wanted to make their mark fast—amateurs compared to the old guard. John Gotti was typical of them: reckless and flamboyant, impulsive and cruel, swaggering. Some of the older *capi* complained he was giving Cosa Nostra a bad name.

What was more, for the time being there was no *capo di tutti capi* and no commission. There was no one who could demand peace and enforce it. In a real sense, nobody was in charge. Nobody could make rules and make them stick.

In Philadelphia there was no one I could go to and say, "Look, I'm not a made guy and don't belong to nobody. I'll cooperate with anybody. Just tell me who."

If there had been anyone I could have talked to, I figure he might have said something like this to me: "Okay, Cooper. You exchanged the kiss of peace with the Chef. Then you turned around and let Ice Cream collect dues from your workers, plus you hired his truck to deliver your merchandise. You're right when you say you don't belong to nobody. You're fair game for anybody."

At least we would have known where we stood. As it was, we didn't know from what direction the knife might come. It was possible nobody gave a damn about us. The dons had plenty to worry about without giving much attention to four little stores selling women's undies. Both dons had been a little condescending, after all.

We had four stores in Philly. Sal and I talked about closing them. But to hell with that. We might *get* run out of town. We weren't going to *just* run.

"It may be dangerous," Sal warned me. "Those guys don't play fair."

"It may be," I agreed.

We weren't about to have other truckloads of merchandise blown up. I sent Sal over to Jersey City to talk to the heirs of Tony Provenzano. We arranged that our stuff would be driven from New York to Jersey in New York trucks driven by Teamsters. In Jersey the stuff was transferred to other trucks and driven to Philly in trucks driven by other Teamsters men who worked for the Provenzanos. I figured none of the Boiardos, one family or another of them, would want to provoke a gang war by attacking those trucks. And I was right. Our shipments went through without trouble. The off-loading and reloading ran up our costs, but it was worth it.

Okay, I was right. But I had fucked the Boiardos, both clans of them, the Enrico Boiardos and the Napolitano Boiardos—which were still active families in spite of the fact that their dons had been whacked out. One time the Enrico heirs highjacked a truck driven by a Jersey Teamster—to test the waters, I suppose. The heirs of Tony Pro took quick and effective revenge, killing a nephew of Don Enrico.

What the hell? It wasn't my fault. If these people were animals, they were animals. I didn't make them animals. They didn't get that way from anything I'd done. You can rationalize anything, anything at all, with thinking like that.

One evening I was sitting at a table in Bookbinder's. I was negotiating with a painting contractor about repainting the inside of two stores. He was supposed to meet me for dinner, and he was late.

"Excuse me. You're Jerry Cooper, aren't you?"

I looked up into the face of the most beautiful girl I had ever seen in my life, more beautiful even than Giselle, though I am reluctant ever to say that.

I'm not sure what it was about her that made her the most beautiful girl I had ever seen; all I knew was that she was. She had high, visible cheekbones, and her jawbone clearly defined her chin. Her face was long, her hairline high, giving her a tall forehead. Her shoulder-length glossy blond hair was simply styled to hang smooth, with no sharp lines. She wore no makeup. Her eyes were blue, light blue with little flecks of green. Her nose was straight and short. Her lips were full and sensuous.

Her face was, in fact, flawless.

She was wearing a pair of faded blue jeans that rode her hips and would have revealed her navel except for her tucked-in yellow Izod shirt. She was, in fact, not dressed for Bookbinder's, and was a little conspicuous there.

"I'm called Filly—Filly O'Reilly. My name is Philadelphia, actually, but everybody calls me Filly, like a little female horse. You wouldn't be aware of this, but I work for you."

"Really? Where?"

"Walnut Street. Can you spare me a minute? I hope I'm not interrupting or interfering, but can you spare me just a minute? You're waiting for someone. I'll get right up as soon as he—or she—comes in. Okay?"

"Sure. Sit down."

I was already fantasizing about her.

She sat down in the chair to my right. "I have a little problem," she said, "and—"

She was interrupted by a waiter who asked if she would like a drink. She hesitated. I said of course she would. She asked for a martini up, with an olive.

"A problem with your job?" I asked her.

"Sort of. It's embarrassing, Mr. Cooper. My problem is with Mr. Nero."

I nodded. I could imagine. I knew he banged the help, and I could understand he would never overlook Filly O'Reilly. "The problem is?" I asked, trying to sound sympathetic.

"When he comes to Philadelphia, he wants to . . . screw. Wants to? He insists! And he hurts me, Mr. Cooper. He's a monster. He's more than I can take. Did you know that? Did you know he's got . . ."

I knew what she meant.

"After he screws me, I'm sore for days," she went on. "The last time I was bleeding and had to see a doctor. The doctor said Mr. Nero had torn me. If he'd take it a little easy, it might not be so bad. But he won't. And he won't leave me alone, either. Honestly, Mr. Cooper, I'm afraid of him. I really am."

I believed her. This wasn't the first time a girl had

complained of Sal's size and vigor—though they usually didn't complain to *me*.

"What do you think I can do about it?" I asked.

"I figured you'd have more influence over him than I do. I've got none, almost."

"Why don't you just tell him no, you won't go out with him?"

"I'm afraid he'll fire me. Anyway, he knows where I live. He took me home one night, late. I'm afraid he'll come to my door. Mr. Nero is a scary guy. I don't think he'll take no for an answer."

The waiter brought her martini. She took a demure sip. She was a girl of great contrasts. She sipped her drink so modestly I wondered if she would not have drunk it through a straw if she had one.

"How'd you know where to find me?" I asked.

"I overheard Louise calling for your reservation."

"How come I didn't see you?"

"I was in the back room, where we model things. I was showing off some hard-on undies. You know . . . undies that give guys hard-ons. Like that. We don't come out in the main store when we're wearing undies and so on."

I frowned. I didn't know what to do about this, if anything. What *could* I do, for that matter?

"You ever see his schlong?" she asked, her eyes widening. "Did you ever see that thing?"

I nodded, quickly adding, "At a urinal," in case she might get another idea.

She sighed heavily and shook her head. "Hey, I'm not a virgin, Mr. Cooper. I've had 'em in me, plenty. And . . . if you say anything to him, he'll probably tell you he always gives me a nice present afterward. Which doesn't make me a hooker. I'm not that, goddamnit. If he just wasn't so fuckin' *big!* Or if he'd just take it a little easy. And he . . . he's *connected*, isn't he? He's—well, he's one of those guys. Isn't he?"

I had a dumb idea. "Tell you what," I said to Filly. "When you see him next, tell him you're my girl and I don't like it when you do it with anybody else."

She grinned. "Mr. Cooperrrr . . ." she purred.

The painting contractor never appeared. I had dinner with Filly, then took her to my room in the Rittenhouse.

When she was naked and I dropped my underpants, she reached for my cock and squeezed it lightly, gently. "Now there," she said, "is a schlong a girl could learn to love!"

I ran my fingertips over her boobs. They were big, but not awkwardly big; firm, yet soft. They seemed to welcome my hands, and when I squeezed them she arched her back and chuckled. She had a great bush of pubic hair that had never been trimmed, and when I ran a finger through it and into her moist, slippery crevice she grabbed my hand and led me to her clit. It was engorged. I mean, Filly had an *erection*, about like what I had.

"I want you to fuck me out of my mind," she said. "And I'm going to give it to you like you never had before."

Giselle and Melissa were by no means the only women I'd ever had, but generally I stayed faithful to the women who satisfied me. I had no formal obligation to Melissa. We were not married and had never talked about marrying. I cherished her, but I did not love her.

Before that night in the Rittenhouse Hotel was over, I had fantasies of settling a nice piece of money on Melissa and moving Filly into a new apartment in Manhattan.

I could smooth some of her rough edges . . . me, a rough-edged guy if ever there was one smoothing off a girl! But I could march her around New York, my twenty-two-year-old chick with the perfect, youthful face and the luscious body, dressed in style the way I could dress her. Hell, I was sixty years old that year. I could put aside my forty-year-old mistress and take a twenty-two-year-old.

Or maybe I could keep both of them! How about that? Melissa and Filly, both! It was the dumbest idea I ever had, but that was how much I wanted this girl. I thought of myself as a sort of worldly guy, who knew his way around. Filly needed no great skill to make a fool of me.

39

I had no great difficulty in getting Sal off Filly. To him, she was just another piece of ass. He could have cared less.

"Kiddo. When a cunt takes money, that makes her a whore. I was dropping a couple hundred on her every time. Not bangles and beads—cash."

"She claims you hurt her. And you know why, and how. She says her doctor told her you—"

"She never said any such thing to me. I've had gals say that. She never did."

I didn't know which of them to believe. I had never entirely trusted Sal. To tell the truth, I wasn't even sure he had really fired the shot that killed Jimmy Hoffa. At that point I was ready to believe the girl, and I forgot what Sal had said.

"Tell you something else," he said. "Some guy called me. Name of Spencer. He told me the broad was bad news. I told him to mind his own fuckin' business. What was I gonna do, be intimidated by a piece of tail? Anyway, I figured the guy had something in mind, so I brushed him off."

I guess I had a little smarts. I did not move Filly to

New York to take Melissa's place. I set her up in an apartment on the Jersey side of the Walt Whitman Bridge, and I made reasons to go down there often. In fact, when I was on my way to Washington or Baltimore I would pick her up and take her with me. I'd have the pilot land, take Filly on board, and we'd take off again.

When Len married Sue Ellen, Melissa sat in the church beside me, as if she was my wife. She went to the receptions and parties with me, as if she was my wife. Modestly and appropriately dressed for the occasion, she made a favorable impression even on the partners from Hale & Dorr. I know it surprised Sue Ellen's father to see how the woman with me was not a model from a Cheeks store—though I wish he could have known!—but a well spoken, dignified woman. I might have wished it were Giselle there beside me, but I could be proud of Melissa, and I was.

Even so . . . Filly was waiting in a motel room near the airport, and the day after the wedding and reception I sent Melissa back to New York on the Metroliner and flew Filly to Martha's Vineyard. So much for respectability.

There was on the Vineyard—and still is, for all I know—what was called a "free beach," meaning clothing optional. I had a camera with me, and I took the best photograph I've ever taken in my life. It was of Filly standing at the edge of the water on a foggy morning when there was no surf. The water is visible behind her but quickly vanishes in the fog so the background is gray-ish white, even though it is a color photograph. She was wearing only a pair of cutoff blue jeans that hung across her hips and left her navel exposed. Her bare breasts rested on her arms that were folded over her stomach. She had raised her chin and was staring with half a frown at something out of sight to the camera—maybe another photographer behind me.

I had a magnificent color print made from that slide and had it framed. It hangs in my apartment to this day.

I took Filly with me when I went out to Pittsburgh and

Cleveland. Giselle and I had had a heavy curtain installed behind the front seats of the Beech so we could have some privacy back in the passenger seats. In a Lear jet you don't need that curtain; the passenger compartment is separated from the cockpit by a wall. Anyone who has ever flown in a bizjet, though, knows you can't really screw, not comfortably—unless you reconfigure the passenger space for the purpose. In fact, we did it on the floor. That was some great sex, too, on that hard floor. The plane was almost always moving, up and down, side to side, or both—which added to the fun.

Well, there's something else a girl can do for a guy. Giselle did. It's said that Frenchwomen have an instinct for giving head. I don't know if Giselle had an instinct or not. I only know it was entirely natural to her, something she expected to do and did without hesitation. Melissa did it, too, though for her it was a concession. She didn't like it, especially not on her knees, which she thought was demeaning, though that was by far the best way to do it in an airplane. Filly . . . ? I don't think she could have faked the enthusiasm she brought to sucking cock. She loved it! She'd lick my balls for ten minutes before she ever moved her tongue up my shaft—until I was ready to beg her. Then she licked my shaft, all of it, especially the tip. Suck? It was only when she sensed that I was about to come that she took me inside her mouth and licked and sucked and swallowed.

In Pittsburgh, Cleveland, and other places I introduced her as my chief model, and she did model the Cheeks product line, especially to politicians who wondered if they should oppose the introduction of this kind of store into their cities.

Introducing the product line to a meeting of politicians and "community leaders" had become a routine. We held shows in hotel suites, all very much alike. Before Filly I had hired a local model or two. Now I used her and hired just one. They modeled a few of our more conservative lines—nightgowns and teddies, bra-and-panty sets. No crotchless panties, no strip panels, no nipple clips.

Then we ran a film or videotape showing our stores—showing how they were elegant and dignified. We showed our windows, with nothing on display but our signature cast-metal signs. We showed our counters and displays.

We presented each guest a small gift package.

The gifts were items that would fit any woman, unless the fellow had a hugely oversized woman at home, and we figured if he had that he would have a girlfriend somewhere who would get the gift.

We did run into a problem. Occasionally a pol or community leader was a woman. We gave her the same gift, and usually they were flattered. In Baltimore one evening we encountered a woman who must have weighed two hundred pounds. After that we were careful to take along a few gifts in our large-size line.

We encountered a different problem in Cincinnati. There, an organization of women decided a Cheeks store would be degrading to women, and they set up a picket line outside our store on the night when we meant to introduce it to the civic leaders. I went out on the sidewalk to talk to these women, expecting to find a group of hefty, blue-haired, bespectacled women. They were nothing of the kind. Some were students from the University of Cincinnati. Some were young wives. Most of them were attractive.

I spoke to them. "I would be very grateful if you would come inside," I said. "I'd like for you to see the line of merchandise we expect to sell. If you find it degrades women, I will be very sorry. I sell the same line in most of the major cities of the United States. I'm not going to tell you that nobody objects, but very few do. Please come in and let me show you."

For an opening like this we displayed no restraints, no whips, no crotchless panties. That was routine with us. The women came in, some of them reluctantly, and saw our line of lingerie and swimsuits.

"Maybe," I said, "you would like to come in the back

room and try on some of these items. I would like to tell you that my late wife, who died of cancer some years ago, wore Cheeks lingerie and wore it proudly."

A young woman—I have no idea who she was—spoke up and said, "I'll try it."

In ten minutes about half the women who had come to protest were walking around in our merchandise, posturing in front of mirrors, and asking the prices of what they had on. We sold them what they were wearing. We didn't give any of them anything, so it would not seem as if we were trying to buy them off. The young woman who had volunteered appeared before our civic leaders a little later, wearing one of our international-orange swimsuits. She turned out to be the wife of a city councilman.

A late-middle-aged woman I would not have thought to be interested in revealing lingerie bought a sheer black nightgown that exposed every square inch of her body. She was wearing it when she said to me, "I never thought—It's going to be like our wedding night, all over."

As we went around doing the shows, I had to restrain Filly from talking too much. Unrestrained, she would innocently say things like, "I guess it shows a lot of ass, but what it shows is what I'd want my boyfriend to see," or "Y'notice, it covers your twat okay."

One night in Cleveland a prominent Democrat and clubwoman laughed nervously and said to Filly, "I'm not sure I could show myself to my husband in that."

"He'll love it," said Filly.

"Well . . . I'm not sure. You see, my husband is a Presbyterian pastor."

"If he's not a priest, he'll love it," said Filly.

She had a talent for saying things that, coming from anyone else's mouth, could have been offensive. But she seemed the very embodiment of youthful innocence—with, even so, a vague suggestion of narrow-eyed sensuality. Her figure was exactly right: newly ripened and as nearly ideal as any I ever saw since the night in 1944 when I first saw Giselle on the stage.

She got propositions. She fended them off by saying she was *my* girl. Most of the people who saw us had figured that out anyway. Chief model. Anyone who believed that believed in the tooth fairy.

Some nights we never slept at all, not at all, and crawled out of bed in the morning exhausted. We learned to hate linen sheets. They were abrasive.

For six or seven months I maintained my balancing act between Filly and Melissa. I had fallen in love with Filly, but like any love affair, this one had matured. Cracks began to appear.

Her crude vocabulary, which had seemed so refreshing when I first heard it, turned boring, then actually offensive. Filly wanted to fuck. She wanted my dick in her cunt. She liked to suck me off, and she liked to swallow my come, but she also wanted me to eat her pussy, which I did, and I loved every minute. She wanted me to grease my schlong with Vaseline and ram it up her ass. She wanted to do everything imaginable—some of it really placing on me demands I could barely meet—and she used the grossest conceivable words to express it. She was Kitty all over again.

I don't know. I was sixty years old, then sixty-one. She was twenty-two, then twenty-three. Thirty-eight years was too much difference. Filly made me feel *old!* I couldn't maintain the pace.

I could wish that had been all the problem.

For some reason, I took her fishing. We rented a boat with crew on Cape Cod and went out to the end of the Cape, where the fish all but jumped into your boat.

Filly loved it, or said she did. Her enthusiasm was infectious. After that, whenever we traveled where a boat could be rented and we could go fishing, we went. Later that year I began to open stores in south Florida, and boating and fishing became a bigger part of our lives. After sessions where I sold the idea of a Cheeks store and Filly modeled, we chartered boats and went out into the Gulf Stream to fish. We soon learned enough about boats that in time we didn't charter anymore but just rented boats and ran them ourselves. Eventually I leased a boat. It was called the *Key Princess*.

At Key Largo. Yes, the same Key Largo as in the film with Bogart and Bacall and Robinson. The guy who leased to me kept the boat fueled and maintained. I had to provide the food and drink, the fishing rods and bait, and so on. Sometimes we got into Key Largo late and slept on the boat, so as to get out early in the morning.

Fishing out of Key Largo, you had to go out to sea some twenty-five miles so as to be outside the federal marine sanctuary. I was very much an amateur with boats and went out only when good weather was forecast, relying on my compass and my marine radio to make sure I was where I was supposed to be. If the radio advised us of deteriorating weather, we reeled in our lines and made for the Key.

I remember the morning of January 27.

We had arrived after ten the previous night and carried our food and gear aboard. Then we fucked. I remember that night as one of the few when Filly was easily satisfied. We fucked only once, and we went to sleep. She was edgy and restless. I might have taken note and been suspicious. Yeah. I might have.

At dawn we cranked up the diesels and set out to sea.

There was little wind and only gentle swells on the surface of the Atlantic as we headed eastward to get beyond the sanctuary. My thoughts were of tarpon and sailfish, though we had on one occasion hooked and lost an eight-foot shark.

Filly was happy, and to make things more interesting she tossed aside her white T-shirt and stood topless beside me at the wheel. After a little while she broke out the rods and reels. The drill was that I would lower the engine revolutions to trolling speed, lock the wheel, and we would sit in the fishing chairs and hope for a bite. It was a routine we had followed many times, and we had brought in bonito, typically, and redfish, and one decent-size sailfish.

I throttled back, locked the wheel, and walked into the stern. The bait was in a box there, and I opened the box and bent over, ready to bait both hooks.

"Hi, Cooper."

I stiffened and turned. The voice was that of a man I recognized as soon as I saw him: Lou Chieppa, the greaseball hood who had held a knife to my throat in Philly and told me the big man was Ice Cream, not the Chef. This morning he was dressed in cutoff shorts and a blue Izod shirt.

He stood, legs apart, menacing me with that ugly switchblade I had seen before.

"Careful, Lou. He's no pushover," muttered Filly.

"Heh-heh, heh-heh. Pushover. Yeah. Push him over is exactly what I'm gonna do. Just stand clear, Fil."

Filly. She'd set me up. My God, how long had they been planning this?

Not from the beginning. I couldn't believe it had been from the beginning. On the other hand, why had the painting contractor not shown up at Bookbinder's? I knew why *she'd* shown up: the overheard phone call and so on. But the contractor . . . ?

I looked at her and shook my head. I'd been *stupid!*

The bitch smirked.

Chieppa moved forward, cautiously, on the balls of his feet.

They'd made a fatal mistake. Buddy had taught me to fight with a razor, and over all these years I had always carried a folded straight razor in my right pocket, the way some men carry a penknife or a Swiss Army knife. Buddy had rehearsed me a thousand times in the movement I now had to make. It was like riding a bicycle—once you've learned, you can always do it.

Chieppa struck. Or he meant to. But I stepped aside. And in one quick, well-learned, long-practiced movement, taught me years ago by Buddy and practiced a thousand times, I ran the razor across his throat, slitting it deep, cutting off his breath as he choked on his own gushing blood.

He staggered against the gunwale, where he was unbalanced and half over the side. I grabbed him by the seat of his shorts and heaved him overboard.

Filly screamed. Chieppa couldn't swim. He floundered, splashing and throwing water—and, of course, gushing blood in great black-red gouts. The boat, though moving only at trolling speed, had opened ten or fifteen yards distance from him. Filly threw herself into the ocean and swam toward him as fast as she could.

I ran into the cabin and reversed the engines. I backed toward them cautiously, aware that the propellers were as great a danger as drowning. I was already wondering how I was going to explain, back on the dock at Key Largo.

Filly shrieked. Chieppa was gone. He had disappeared below the surface. Then *she* disappeared.

My God! One moment she was there, searching frantically, and in the next moment she was gone!

Chieppa's blood and his thrashing had attracted sharks. They were in a feeding frenzy. I didn't see what was happening underwater. I am glad I didn't.

I, too, screamed. I stopped the propellers and slumped over the wheel, sobbing.

I had to think. Nobody had seen us come aboard last night. No one had been stirring when we eased away from the dock. The owner of the boat would see that it was out. He had no way to know if Filly was with me or not.

Chieppa? I guess he had been hidden somewhere all night. Or maybe Filly had gotten up while I was asleep and signaled him to come aboard. He couldn't make his move until we were well out at sea. He could kill me then and throw me overboard.

So far as anyone knew, I had taken the *Key Princess* out alone. No one could know.

Still sobbing, I tossed Filly's fishing tackle overboard. And her shirt. And her handbag. Finally, her clothes and brush and cosmetics, which were in my bag. I dragged up buckets of seawater and sluiced Chieppa's blood off the gunwale.

I stayed at sea for eight more hours, crying and drinking beer.

Then I went in.

My friend, the owner of the boat, took charge of the *Key Princess* at the dock.

"The young lady not with you this time, Mr. Cooper?"

"Naah. You know how it is. She's off someplace with her new boyfriend."

"I thought she really enjoyed fishing."

"I got another gal in mind who'll enjoy it even more."

Just to be sure of the appearance of things, I flew Melissa to Florida a week later, and we went fishing off Key Largo.

"Oh, this is marvelous, Jerry. Why did we never do it before? You've got to take time off for fishing. I *love* this place and this boat!"

She caught a respectable sailfish, and the owner saluted me meaningfully when he saw Melissa and her fish. We returned to fish three more times before I let the lease on the boat expire.

I felt guilt. For Melissa. I'd betrayed her, and I couldn't imagine she didn't know it. I resolved to make it up to her, somehow.

40

All of which," Sal said when I told him, "doesn't tell us who in Philadelphia was all that interested in having you whacked out—*that* is the fuckin' question."

"Or why."

"Or why," he agreed.

"The guy who tried it—Chieppa—was with Don Napolitano, Ice Cream," I said.

"Ice Cream has been dead so long that God knows who Chieppa was with. Maybe he was just trying to make his bones. Maybe he was just trying to make himself a big guy. Incidentally, I've heard that he'd worked his way up some. Not everybody gave him any respect. For a lot of guys he was still the cheap little hustler. Some people called him Don Cheap."

"Well, Don Cheap sleeps with the fishes," I said, nodding. "*Inside* the fishes."

"Too bad about the piece of tail."

"I couldn't save her, Sal. No way. I couldn't. I *couldn't*. I thought too much of her, and who knows what dumb thing I might have done if I'd had a chance? But I didn't! She was just . . . gone."

Sal put a gentle hand on my shoulder and offered comfort. "Hey. She was *something*. But . . . me . . . I'd have slashed her, too." Then he grinned. "Any time I get it in mind to whack out somebody, I'll come to you. You did it great! Nobody's ever going to figure out what happened to Don Cheap."

"He set himself up for it," I said glumly. "And she did, too."

"They worked hard to set *you* up for it."

"What's next?" I asked.

"We gotta find out who and why," said Sal.

I went back down to Philadelphia and discovered that my store managers regarded me with awe. That was a strange and unexpected development.

Maybe they hadn't known that Chieppa had gone to Florida to kill me, but they knew he had not come back from Florida. His rented car was found in a parking lot not far from the docks at Key Largo. In his one small bag was an airline ticket from Miami to Philadelphia.

Maybe they hadn't known that Filly was supposed to set me up for a hit, but they did know she had disappeared just as Chieppa had disappeared.

The Dade County sheriff's office noted the finding of an abandoned automobile and returned it to Avis. They notified the Philadelphia police that a resident of that city had abandoned a car in a parking lot at Key Largo. Philadelphia notified Dade County that Chieppa had a criminal record, including one felony for which he had done time. And that was pretty much the end of that.

The disappearance of Filly O'Reilly was something else. I was asked to talk to a Philadelphia homicide detective. I sat down beside his desk, he smoked and drank coffee, I drank coffee, and we talked.

"The story is that she was your girl. That you lived together, in fact."

"She lived in my apartment. I didn't live there. I came there once in a while. Not an unusual arrangement, hmm?"

"Her name was not Filly O'Reilly. It was Filomena

Florio. As a juvenile she did some time in the Detention Home. The boys in Vice think she may have been a hooker, but small-time and not enough to worry about. Anyway . . . when did you see her last?"

I sighed. "I saw her at the Homestead airport. We'd flown down there in my company plane, planning to spend a couple of days fishing out of Key Largo, where I have a boat leased. On the way down she talked about how I was sixty-one years old and she was only twenty-three and how we didn't suit each other so much any-more."

"Cliché," said the detective dryly.

"Right. I was halfway relieved, to tell you the truth. I'd started to wonder how I was going to break it off with her. Anyway, she said her boyfriend was waiting for her and she was going with him. That was a shock, but I accepted it. I asked her who this boyfriend was and how he knew she'd be at the Homestead airport that evening. She said she'd called him. She said she was in love with him."

"Who was the boyfriend? Did she name him?"

"No. But I saw him. That is, I had a glimpse of him. While I was renting a car, I saw her through the window with this guy. I was shocked. I'd suppose she'd be off with some kind of big, handsome beach boy. This guy was—well, he looked something like Fredo, Michael's brother in *The Godfather*."

This was true. Lou Chieppa did look something like Fredo—that is, like the talented actor who had played Fredo.

The detective frowned. "I'd like to know where they went," he said.

Which was the end of the intervention of the law in the disappearance of Lou Chieppa and Filomena Florio. Actually, they didn't much give a damn. You can get yourself in that kind of circumstance: where nobody gives a damn what happens to you.

But I did give a damn about why somebody had put a hit man on me.

Something hung in the back of my mind and nagged me. She'd come to me complaining that Sal was hurting her with his enormous cock. He never denied he'd had her; in fact, he said he'd paid her. So Filly—Filomena—had started out seeing Sal, then switched to me. Why?

I asked my store managers. Louise, at the store on Walnut Street, had hired Filly.

"She came from Don Napolitano. You know, the one they called Ice Cream. I think she was his girl, to tell you the truth. When he was killed, she was left without protection. Mr. Nero saw her and decided he wanted her. I mean . . . Mr. Cooper, she was something else again, wasn't she? She's missing. Does that mean she's . . . dead? Did she get herself into something *too deep?*"

"I wouldn't know," I said. "What about Chieppa?"

She snickered. " 'Don Cheap.' He came around. Listen, Filly wouldn't look at him. What would a beautiful, sexy girl want with the likes of him?"

"Didn't he get to be a pretty big boy lately?" I asked. It was a shot in the dark. I had no idea if Chieppa had become a big boy. Maybe the woman knew.

"Well . . . he tried to float the story that he was the hitter who whacked out Don Enrico—revenge for the killing of Don Napolitano. But nobody believed it. He'd have been a dead man overnight if Don Enrico's family had believed it. They satisfied themselves for his big talk by having the crap beat out of him. It's just possible, though, that Chieppa did have something to do with the death of Don Enrico. The Napolitano Boiardos gave him a little business. For example, the girls who work here are paying him ten bucks a week."

"I thought I put a stop to that."

"You did. But Don Cheap was a bully. What's more, he was here, and you were in New York."

"Why didn't you tell me?"

"Same reason. He was here, and you were in New York. Hey man . . ."

I did a quick mental calculation. I had maybe forty employees that Chieppa could have collected "dues" from. Four hundred a week. Sixteen hundred a month. He wouldn't have tried to kill me for that. No. Something more had to be involved.

I don't believe in private detectives. In fact, I despise them as a breed. But I hired one in Philadelphia, a woman named Morgana Brock. What I wanted her to do was check some entries in public records. She did, and we met for lunch.

"Filomena Florio . . ." she said. "Also known as Filly, with various last names."

"O'Reilly," I said.

Morgana Brock smoked as heavily as anyone I had ever seen, even the Frenchmen I'd known in years long past. While I was having a couple of drinks, she smoked four cigarettes. Naturally she reeked of smoke.

"O'Reilly," she agreed. "She had a telephone listed as Filly O'Reilly. I don't know what your interest in her is, so I don't know if you'll care to know that she was in and out of juvenile detention centers from the time she was twelve. She grew up in the slammer, you might say."

"Why?"

"The first time it was just for being incorrigible. Truancy and so on. Then, when she was just short of fourteen she pulled a switchblade and cut a guy, nearly killed him. So back she went."

"So what did she do?"

"She got married."

"Who to?"

"It's on record. Filomena Florio, retail clerk, to Louis Chieppa, insurance salesman."

"Chieppa . . ." I said, trying to seem calm.

"Insurance!" she sneered. "He was a button man of the Napolitano Boiardos."

"What kind of record did *he* have?"

"Well, she married him when she was eighteen. It couldn't have been much of a marriage. I get the sense they didn't acknowledge it. She rented a place in the name O'Reilly, listed herself in the phone book as O'Reilly, and so on. As long as she looked single, they could run various scams, blackmail and the like, and in a pinch sell her as a hooker. Then about a year ago he went to jail for a year—felonious assault. He was a knife man."

So. Since he put a knife to my throat, he'd spent a year in jail, likely for doing the same thing to somebody else.

"With Chieppa in jail what'd she live on?"

"She was married to a soldier for Don Napolitano. They take care of their own, no matter how small the guy. For a price. I can't imagine what the price may have been."

I could. I talked it over with Sal and this time with Buddy.

"The Philadelphia families are nuts," said Buddy. "There's no restraint down there."

"But, hey, what did I do to them that would make them want to kill me?"

"I wondered about that," said Sal. "Until Thursday. Thursday I think I got a clue."

"Which is?"

"I've been makin' some calls, tryin' to find out. Thursday I talked to a Teamsters guy in Newark, one of the old Provenzano crowd. There's been a sort of runnin' feud between them and the Napolitano branch of the Boiardos ever since we started haulin' our merchandise with Jersey trucks. There's a lot of bad feelin' in the Napolitano crowd."

"Enough to—?"

"It wouldn't take much," Buddy interrupted. "Not with that bunch."

I sighed and shook my head. "While her husband was in jail, she lived off me. But—"

"So why'd she want to kill her meal ticket?" Sal asked. "My guess would be that Chieppa talked the Napolitanos into givin' him a big contract on you. A big contract. Retirement. And it would have been without her. That broad would never have settled in a little house in Fort Lauderdoodle and contented herself with walking her dog and playing bingo."

"So why'd she throw herself in with the sharks to try to save Don Cheap?"

Sal grinned. "You knew her. She was one of those broads whose emotions get in the way of their judgment sometimes. Ten seconds in the water, and I bet she wished she was back on the boat. Then the first shark grabbed her."

"So now?"

"Who knows. They know you whacked out their hitter—plus his wife. One of two things. If there's a next time, you won't get it from a sleazeball with a knife; you'll get it from a big guy. Or, could be this is the end of it. How much are you worth to them, after all?"

Great! Something more to worry about.

41

LEN

When we formed the corporation my father was in his sixties. He showed no sign of slowing down, certainly none of retiring. I was not yet thirty. Vicky was in her forties, as was Melissa. Of all of us, I think I was the only one who was acutely conscious of our ages. When you are thirteen or fourteen, someone seventeen or eighteen is awesomely older than you. When you are twenty-two a person of thirty is a *little* older than you. After, say, thirty-five, you feel contemporary with anyone within twenty years of you, either way.

As I approached thirty I was happily aware that I was involved in a devoted and passionate affair with a woman eighteen years my elder. Her son, Anthony, had accepted me and visited us often. He was only ten years younger than I was and treated me like a brother—certainly not like a stepfather.

Vicky showed no sign of growing bored, and certainly she was the most exciting woman I had ever known.

She tried almost everything Cheeks sold. I remember one outfit in particular. It was fire-engine red lambskin. Bras that exposed nipples had been a staple of the business for a long time. Now we sold what were called shelf bras, that is to say, underwire bras that shoved the breasts up and out while leaving them entirely exposed. Panties with slit crotches were common by the eighties, but the red panties that went with this outfit had no crotch at all and left the entire pubic area exposed. A silver chain decorated with ornaments hung from the waistband, then disappeared between the labia, emerging from the anus where more ornaments appeared, then attached to the waistband at the rear. The sheer red stockings were held up by a red lambskin garter belt decorated with loops of silver chain. Her shoes matched. It was a Larkin design, and so far as erotica was concerned, he had outdone himself.

In fact, he was outdoing himself a bit much, of late. I guess erotic imagination has its limits. The distinction between erotic and grotesque is subtle.

Knowing the red outfit was one of my favorites, Vicky wore it around the apartment many evenings. She loved giving me access to her anytime and anywhere.

Well, what was sauce for the goose . . . By now we stocked erotic items for men, not just the thong briefs but blatantly lascivious straps in soft black leather that bound the male parts and either forced them to fill a tight pouch or simply to stand up, thrust forward, bare and displayed. Vicky liked those things. I wore things like that for her—rings or straps around the penis, leather cages for the cock and balls, and so on. My father had long ago banned the Arab strap, because he thought it could cause a dangerous interruption of blood flow, but they were available, and I had one. I wore it, never more than half an hour at a time. It did interfere with circulation, and the organ hardened and swelled unnaturally. We took it off before entry.

Two years after we began to live together, Vicky and I were still as horny about each other as we had been that first night.

So—

I came home one evening about seven. Vicky had been at my father's office part of the afternoon, where she was playing an ever-bigger role in the management of the company. She had changed and was wearing a simple white-lace teddy, not one of our radically daring models. It exposed her hips and butt but otherwise was mostly modest.

She poured me a Scotch and soda as usual, and poured for herself something unusual: a glass of white wine.

"Sit down, lover," she said. "I have to tell you something."

I heard something ominous in her voice. I accepted my drink and sat on the couch. She sat in a chair opposite me, on the other side of the heavy glass coffee table.

"I have some news for you," she said. She drew a breath. "To be blunt . . . I am pregnant."

She was forty-six years old. I knew she took the Pill. I had seen her take it, many times. How could she be pregnant? And . . . was a pregnancy safe for a woman her age?

I had never said I loved her, and she had never told me she loved me.

I just sat there with my mouth open, stunned. I should have said, "How very wonderful!" or "I couldn't be happier."

"We don't have to have it," she said quietly, solemnly. "I'm not that good a Catholic."

I shook my head. "You know my wife and I—what we did. I told you. I don't want to do that again, Vicky. If it won't harm you . . . I want to have it."

"We're an odd pair to be having a baby," she said.

I stood up, went behind her chair, embraced her, and kissed her neck. "There's something I've never said to you," I whispered in her ear. Tears were running down my cheeks. "At first I was afraid to, for fear it might . . . spoil things. Then the failure got to be a habit. But I hope you know. I hope you've known—"

"Yes," she whispered. "And I love you, too."

"Then that settles it, doesn't it? I love you, and you love me, and we've made a baby. The decision is up to you. But my choice is to go ahead and have it."

Vicky nodded. "If it's okay," she said. "I mean healthy. If the tests show it's okay."

"Vicky," I said, "if you and I are going to be mommy and daddy, I think we better get married."

My father couldn't believe it. "I threw her at you—or maybe I threw you at her—to get your mind off Tinkerbell. But . . . Christ, Lenny! Didn't Vicky use the Pill?"

"A woman can take the Pill only so many years, and she'd taken it a *great* many. Then her periods—well, they became irregular. I mean, for a while she didn't have any. So she stopped taking it. Then they came again, and she started taking it again. So—"

"Well I think you're lucky. She's a whole lot older than you, but she's one hell of a woman."

We were married by a justice of the peace. I don't have to say why. The ceremony was held on the terrace of a country club in Westchester County, witnessed by a hundred invited guests and all the people in the swimming pool.

Vicky was married in a rose-colored dress, since this was not her first wedding. I wore black tie, as did my father and Vicky's son. Melissa was bridesmaid and wore yellow.

The presence of the Friends of Friends could not be denied. Twenty times I was clasped in an enthusiastic *abbraccio* by men I had never met. A score of other times it was a painfully tight handshake, with a fervent *"Mazel tov."* The Jews and Italians embraced each other and traded greetings and jokes as if they had been best friends all their lives.

Everyone was relieved, I think, by the simplicity of the ceremony. We declared our love, and that was it.

The Jews adopted the Italian custom of putting an envelope in the bride's purse, a copious silk bag she carried for the purpose. After the reception and dinner and joyous dancing, Vicky and I retired to our bridal suite in a Scarsdale hotel. We poured the envelopes out on the bed. To my utter astonishment, we counted $58,000 in cash. No glassware. No silver. No toasters. Money.

Our little daughter was born squalling-healthy. A new set of envelopes appeared, containing enough money to pay for the girl's college education—after it had lain in an investment account for eighteen years.

We discussed her name. Vicky's maternal grandmother had been Filomena, and she favored that name. For some reason I will never fathom, that produced a hard emotional negative from my father. He all but begged Vicky to name the little girl something else. Vicky's mother was Katerina. We settled on Catherine. Catherine Cooper.

Though we had other resources, we used the $58,000 as a down payment on a house in Greenwich, Connecticut. If it had been understood that I was a Jew and Vicky was Italian we would have been limited to one or two neighborhoods. As it was, nobody knew it, and we bought a house in the Riverside neighborhood, between the railroad tracks and the beaches of Long Island Sound. Catherine Cooper would grow up on a WASP street, apparently a WASP herself.

My father glanced at the tall old trees, at the manicured lawns, at the saltbox houses and the Saabs and Volvos in the driveways. He shook his head. "Shit," he muttered.

42

Four years out of law school, I was made a partner at Gottsman, Scheck & Shapiro. A man who had been there seven years and was passed over left the firm. Others resented me. But I was a rainmaker.

I was elected to the board of directors of Interboro Fruit. Anthony Lucchese didn't like that, but Vicky spoke to him as she spoke to everybody, in direct terms. "You expect a gift. Well, you're going to get it, so don't sulk if it doesn't come as soon as you'd like. It was your father's business. Now it's *my* business. You're in line to inherit it. But graduate from college first. I want an M.B.A. in administration."

Nothing else that I did in business was as interesting as my small role with Cheeks. It was not just the line of merchandise, which God knew was interesting, but I was watching—now participating in—the growth of a major new business that would soon explode into a billion-dollar enterprise.

The number of stores grew. By late in 1991 there were a hundred eighteen stores and national coverage. The line had broadened immensely. I didn't like it, and my father didn't like it, but the line of sado-masochistic merchandise we offered became a big profit center, as Sal had insisted it would.

Besides handcuffs and leg irons and thumb cuffs and toe cuffs, blindfolds and gags, cock rings and spreader bars, we sold an assortment of whips, including riding crops and cat-o'-nine-tails.

The cat-o'-nine-tails was especially popular. Since it was not a single-strand whip, it did not usually cut the way a whip was all too likely to do. Users could develop a skill for using it, causing just enough pain to be sensual without risking injury. The flat strands landed across the naked buttocks or across the shoulders, spreading the impact over six inches or more of flesh, causing pain and raising welts, yet not cutting the skin, drawing blood, or making scars. Though some men took whippings, most of the victims were women, and they were more likely to show bruises on their wrists from tugging on their cuffs than they were to show welts.

Personally, I couldn't imagine buying and using cats or whips or crops. Vicky liked to be chained, but she would not have submitted to flogging—and I would not have flogged her. But—the world has all kinds of people. I tried not to be judgmental.

"You're naive, kid," Sal told me. "It's a kinky world, like it or not. Hey, you wanta see this kind of stuff in use? I can take you and show you."

He did. One night he took me to an establishment in Brooklyn. It was an ordinary-looking bar on the ground floor, though occupied by more gays and transvestites than was ordinary. He spoke to the bartender, who called out the manager. Sal handed the man a couple of bills, and he led us along a hallway to a door that looked like the door to a supplies closet but was the entrance to the cellar under the bar.

It *was* a cellar: damp and dark, with brick floors and walls. It was divided into six or seven medium-size rooms. The manager took us to one of those rooms.

A naked man hung by his wrists from the ceiling. He

could have stood, actually, but his knees had buckled, and so he hung. His ankles were chained together. He was gagged with a rubber ball strapped in his mouth. Short, narrow straps were buckled around his cock. A dog chain some eight feet long was clipped to one of those straps.

He was being "disciplined" by a dominatrix who wore a motorcycle cap with white bill and a pair of knee-high boots, and that was all. She held the chain, and as we walked in she gave a yank on it. The guy grunted deep in his throat.

"Stand up!" she barked. "Stand up, you bastard."

He straightened his knees and stood.

She handed the chain to a man standing with his back to the wall. This guy didn't work there. He was a spectator, the same as I was. There were maybe ten of us, men and women.

"Don't pull too hard. We don't want to pull it off."

The man gave it a tentative pull, just enough to elicit a moan.

The dominatrix picked up a cat-o'-nine-tails. "Want a whack?" she asked.

"Uhmm-huhmm," the guy muttered through the rubber ball. He seemed to be begging for it.

She didn't pretend. She spread her legs, brought the cat back across her shoulder, and gave the man a backhand lash across his butt. The sound of the impact of leather on flesh was sickening. A choking scream was stifled by the rubber ball.

"Want some more?"

He was crying, but he grunted an affirmative and nodded his head. She obliged him.

Well . . . the same kind of thing was going on in two other rooms. Spectators watched in dumb fascination. Whatever *I* might think of what I was seeing, these people were turned on by it; and I knew some of them were wondering if they could take it, or if they should volunteer.

A mannish-looking redheaded girl was being flogged

by another woman. Her back and butt were criss-crossed with red welts.

"Lovers," the manager said. "They take turns. Next week Wilma will be doing the flogging, and Carla will be taking it." I could believe it. Carla's back and butt showed white scars.

As we left, a lovely blond girl was being led in handcuffs toward one of the rooms.

"A lot of those people watching will get ideas from what they're seeing," Sal told me. "They'll go home and make a lot of sore butts."

In fact, we got a letter about how people used the cat.

Dear Sirs,

I thought you might like to read a story about how my husband and I use our cat-o'-nine-tails. Weekends we watch a lot of TV football. He likes it more than I do, and we've found a great way to make sure it's not boring for me.

What we do is bet on one of the Saturday college games, one of the Sunday pro games, and the Monday night pro game. We pick our teams. Whenever my team scores, my husband has to give me five dollars for every point scored. A field goal costs him $15, and a touchdown with extra point costs him $35. I'm building one hell of a Christmas fund.

But I have to take a whack from the cat for every point his team scores. For a field goal I have to take 3 across the shoulders. For a touchdown with extra point I get seven across my bottom. This makes the games a hell of a lot more interesting. You can imagine me rooting for my team's defense!

Notre Dame didn't score at all Saturday, so I got off with nothing. But on Monday night he had the Vikes, and they scored 42! With the 17 whacks I'd taken Sunday afternoon, I didn't sit down comfortably until about Thursday.

We like your handcuffs too, and I wear them during the games.

I don't know what we'll do after the football season is over. Basketball scores are too high. Baseball we can work out.

Sincerely,
Matty L.

It was my suggestion that we publish a catalog and mail it widely. Frederick's of Hollywood did. Victoria's Secret did. So did a few other merchants of erotic merchandise, some of them sleazy. They knew what they were doing, though, even the sleazeballs. Their catalogs were printed on slick paper, and the finest color reproduction was used.

We didn't list everything. In point of fact, we couldn't have. We selected about two dozen of our best items, had them photographed on handsome models by professional photographers, and listed them in the catalog. We flew models to Paris and London and to beaches in the Caribbean. We spared little expense on this catalog. It was erotic and classy and won widespread attention.

For the best example, we offered a black fishnet teddy trimmed with black satin, with attached garters, to be worn with lace-top fishnet stockings. We pictured it with black panties, but obviously they were optional. Black, patent-leather, stiletto-heel shoes completed the outfit. We used two models to show this set. They were twins, and one seemed to be looking out from a mirror—except that she was reaching out and beginning to embrace her sister.

In the month after the catalog was mailed, we sold 35,786 of the teddies and almost as many of the stockings. Just 10,449 of the customers who ordered the teddy also ordered the panties. The shoes sold for $149, and we sold just 8,337 pairs.

Other merchandise offered in the catalog also sold well. Catalog selling was a whole new line of business.

From that point on, I received a salary as a director— $40,000 per annum for my part-time participation.

My partner share of the firm's income drew me $54,000 from Gottsman, Scheck & Shapiro.

If I had been taken in by Hale & Dorr, I wouldn't have been doing that well.

Roger Middleton, our director from Allied Chemical Bank, lived in Greenwich as Vicky and I did—though in what was called Back Country, a far spiffier neighborhood than ours in Riverside.

He and his wife invited Vicky and me to dinner. Catherine was by now old enough to be left with a baby-sitter, so we accepted the invitation gratefully and showed up at seven on a Saturday evening at an Edwardian stone house that would have been called a mansion anywhere else but Greenwich.

We sat down on the stone-paved terrace for cocktails, and after a little discussion about the weather and so on, Roger remarked, "Well, the three of us make almost a quorum of the Gazelle board of directors."

His wife, Ariana—a tall, slender, blond woman with prominent teeth—was unable to conceal her skepticism over inviting into her home an upwardly mobile New York Jew whose family business was intimate undergarments and a woman who was as connected as a person could get.

Roger quickly made it plain that he had not invited us simply to be social. He had something on his mind.

"How much attention have you given," he asked, "to our suppliers? I mean, are you aware of who *makes* our merchandise?"

"We've got a very wide variety of suppliers," I said. "Most of our merchandise is, in fact, made for us on special orders."

"Much of it by Charlie Han," said Roger. "Or by friends of his."

I nodded. "And you are going to tell me he's a sweatshop operator. Actually, Charlie owns no shops at all anymore. He takes contracts for merchandise and subcontracts to others."

"Yes, and those subcontractors subcontract to still others. They try to build a barrier of insulation between the sweatshops and the ultimate seller of the goods. But that barrier is being broken. New York State inspectors and federal inspectors are tracing the line from sweatshop to seller."

Ariana joined the conversation. I was to learn that she was an anti-sweatshop activist. She was on a crusade and had influenced Roger to join her. "They violate every law on the books," she said. "Wages and hours, sanitary conditions, immigration . . . The only way to enforce the laws effectively is to trace the merchandise up the line to the ultimate retailer. And that's the tack that's going to be taken."

"Are you saying we're liable to criminal prosecution?"

"It's possible," said Roger. "Of course we can always defend on the rationale that we didn't know about working conditions at the manufacturing end."

"Okay."

"But how much bad publicity can we take? The news media will savage us. They don't much like our line of business anyway."

He was right. Before long Kathie Lee Gifford would be savaged, and her line was not erotic lingerie and S-M devices.

"I'll take the matter up with my father," I said.

You think I'm dumb?" my father asked irritably when I raised the subject. We were having dinner in Vicky's and my house in Greenwich. Our Connecticut address had not ceased to annoy him. I knew by then how he had vetoed a prep school for me, and he thought our home in the Riverside section of Greenwich was no suitable place for his son, much less for Vittoria Castellano Lucchese Cooper. (One evening when we were grilling steaks over charcoal on the patio—this was an enterprise he scorned, since he believed that Peter Luger's Steak House was the only place where you could get a steak really cooked right— he took note of the friendly wave of a neighbor and asked, "Y'think he'll wave hello when he finds out who you are?")

"You've never seen a sweatshop, have you? Well, I have, but I can't take you to see one because we don't have anything to do with them anymore. New York wages-and-hours laws? New York sanitary laws? New York fire laws? U.S. immigration laws? None of that has anything to do with us. Hey. The handcuffs and stuff like that are made in this country, in little factories that meet every requirement of those laws you're talking about. Hell, police departments buy the same things from the same shops, and so do the FBI and federal marshals. I figured out the dangers in dealing with sweatshops a long time ago. Hey, Melissa, pull off your panties and hand them here."

The ever-complaisant Melissa reached beneath the table, pulled off her G-string panties, and handed them to my father.

He stared at the label, then handed them to me. The label read:

CHEEKS
Made in U.S.A.
Exclusively for Cheeks

" 'Made in U.S.A.,' " he said. "Now, where in the U.S.A. you figure?"

I shook my head. I knew he was driving at something significant, but I couldn't imagine what.

"Okay. Made on the Island of Saipan, part of the Commonwealth of the Northern Marianas . . . a United States protectorate. That's way-the-hell out in the Pacific, and I don't know what kind of conditions their workers work under—except this, except that I know they work under the laws of the Commonwealth. What's more, the U.S. granted their legislature the right to make their own immigration laws, so their workers don't need green cards. They sell stuff cheap, and there's no import tax."

"It's stretching things a little to say this stuff is made in the U.S.A.," Vicky said wryly as she squinted at the label.

"Folks like that good ol' 'Made in U.S.A.' label," my father said, smiling slyly. "Hey, Vicky, if you don't mind, let's see what label you're wearing."

Vicky glanced at me. Since she could pull down her panties under the table, she did and handed them to me. That label read:

CHEEKS
Made in Hong Kong
Exclusively for Cheeks

My father glanced at the label. "See? We don't deal in sweatshop merchandise. Everything we import is perfectly legal under the laws of its place of origin."

"Legal, maybe," I said. "But when word gets out that girls and women work twelve hours a day, seven days a week, for thirty cents an hour—which sometimes isn't even paid—and live in filthy barracks under armed guard, like prisoners in a reformatory, the publicity may be ruinous."

"Son, you worry too much," he said.

Three weeks after that evening, our bedside telephone rang after two in the morning.

I picked it up, and at first I couldn't imagine who was on the line. All I could hear was uncontrolled sobbing. A voice tried to break through, and I realized it was my father.

I couldn't understand his words at first. Then I did. *"Melissa is dead!"*

I drove to New York. Vicky would follow after she arranged for a baby-sitter.

He had wakened to go to the bathroom and had returned to bed to discover that Melissa was not breathing. She had suffered a sudden, massive brain hemorrhage.

It was almost as if he had suffered it himself. My father would never again be the same.

43

It was Vicky who conceived the idea of our flying out to Saipan, then down to Hong Kong, to see if sweatshop conditions were as bad as Ariana Middleton said they were—so bad as to risk our becoming involved in a damaging scandal. Actually, what she had in mind was that my father should spend two or three weeks away from home, to help him recover from the loss of Melissa. Traveling to such an outlandishly remote place as Saipan, then to so exotic a place as Hong Kong, would claim all his attention for a while.

He and I were alone together for more time than we had ever been since my mother died, and I learned more about my father than I had ever known before.

He told me how his Uncle Harry had stolen his girl-friend Kitty Benson and married her. He told me how Harry had stolen the money from his parents' life-insurance policies. He told me about rebuilding Jeeps in Paris.

I asked him about my mother.

"Well . . . you have to understand it was tough times in Europe. Even after *I* got to Paris, after the war had moved on north, I saw girls scrounging in garbage cans for scraps of food. I mean regular girls, trying to go to school and so on. Your Aunt Thérèse had let a Kraut soldier feed her and had suffered painful consequences. Your mother made her living the best way she could. Yes, she danced nude. The first time I ever saw her she was naked and gorgeous, and I thought she was the most beautiful girl I'd ever seen. But there was no funny business on the side. We shared an apartment. At first that was just because it was the only way we could afford such nice digs. Then—well, you know."

During the flight I told him that Vicky was pregnant again. "You've got to stop that," he said to me rather gruffly. "She's too old for it. You'll kill her."

"I offered to have a vasectomy," I said. "She wouldn't hear of it, said I was too young. But she had her tubes tied."

"You listen to what she says. She's got good sense. I knew when I introduced you to her that she'd be good for you."

"I'll always be grateful that you introduced me to her."

"Okay. So don't mess around. It was all right to mess around with Tinkerbell, but don't you do it with Vicky."

"I never have."

"I messed around on Melissa once. I regret it more than anything that's ever happened to me except your mother's death."

The travel was a burden on me, let alone on my father. Too many hours in the air, even if we did go first class. We spent one night in Tokyo, which was no great privilege, and then flew down to Saipan.

Sweatshop conditions there were worse than Ariana Middleton had described. Or so we assumed, since we were denied access to the shops where goods that would have our label sewn in were manufactured. The shops were surrounded by barbed wire, as were the barracks where the workers lived—young women, many from the Philippines, others from wherever work was scarce. Sweatshops. In New York, temperatures usually did not rise much above eighty. On Saipan they rose as high as a hundred ten and sometimes higher.

But we stayed in a luxurious modern hotel, comfortably air-conditioned, and took a late-afternoon dip in a pool shaded by palms and other tropical vegetation. We could have strolled on a white-sand beach.

I was conscious of the island's history, all but invisible now. It had been a League of Nations mandate, assigned to Japan. The Japanese had fortified it heavily. United States forces had blasted it from the air and from the sea, had come ashore, and had killed the tens of thousands of Japanese in its bunkers. I remembered TV documentaries showing flame throwers filling bunkers with fire, then seeing burning Japanese running out. I could not remember the numbers but knew that very many young Americans had died taking Saipan.

After the war, the United States had governed it as a United Nations trusteeship. In 1986 a Commonwealth of the Northern Marianas was formed. Saipan and Tinian—from where the Bomb was flown to Hiroshima—were parts of this commonwealth. It elected its own governor and legislature, but it was a United States protectorate. That was what gave it the special status that allowed it to produce goods in slave-labor conditions and ship them to the States without restriction.

We were guests for dinner with George Alexander, president of a company called Alexander Products. He was the same man Charlie Han had mentioned in his testimony when he was on trial for labor-law violations. Charlie had testified he didn't know where Alexander was, and maybe he didn't. Anyway, *we* now knew where he was.

George Alexander was a cue-ball bald man and appeared for dinner in a linen blue blazer, white shirt, and rep tie. For him, Saipan was an exile. He lived well there, making big money. It was a haven for George Alexander.

It had been he, that afternoon, who had refused to allow us to see his working people at work. "They're excitable," he had said. "A visitor slows them down for an hour."

We had been sitting in his spartan office. An air conditioner had been laboring in a window, but it was still stifling hot, and we were sweating.

"Are the workshops air-conditioned?" I had asked.

He had smiled broadly. "These are *tropical* people," he had said. "Air-conditioning gives them colds, sinusitis, bronchitis, even pneumonia. They refuse to work in air-conditioncd rooms. They think there is something unnatural about air-conditioning."

"Why the barbed wire?" I had asked.

"Predators," he said. "Our workers are primitive young women, and every pilot or ship crewman can take advantage of them."

Over dinner he said something a little different. "I wasn't exactly honest with you when I said you couldn't see inside our shops. You see . . . it *is* hot in the shops. The girls don't want air-conditioning, but they do what they do on their home islands—which is that they strip down to the minimum. Men fly down here from Tokyo just to see the naked girls working in our shops. Needless to say, I do not put *our* girls on display. I guess some operators do, but Alexander does not."

Bullshitting my father was not a good idea. We were in Tokyo only one night before flying on to Hong Kong, but that was long enough for him to wire New York to cancel every contract with Alexander.

On the flight to Hong Kong he talked about Melissa.

"She was just the finest kind of girl you could imagine. I swear to you, as God is my witness, that I never touched her while your mother was alive. That's a tribute to your mother, not to me. You know by now how things get. I mean, domestic. I should have married her. We loved each other. Why do the women I love die so young?"

He told me a lot more about his days in Paris. He made me understand why Buddy was so good a friend.

"Every man would like to think there's somebody he could count on if everything went to shit. Buddy and I don't have much in common, except some life experiences I wouldn't trade for anything, but I know if the shit hit the fan Buddy would be there for me. And I'd be there for him. It's been an odd friendship, some ways. Buddy just showed up one day when I was still very young, and he befriended me instantly. I've often wondered why. My good luck, as far as I'm concerned."

We landed at Hong Kong's adventurous airport, Kai Tak, coming in on an approach so low over the city that, as they used to say, you could look in apartment windows and see what TV shows people were watching. That is an exaggeration. But you could see if they were watching TV or not.

We checked into the plush Mandarin Oriental Hotel.

I wish I could have spent more time in Hong Kong on that visit. I have never seen a more fascinating city. It was at that time still a British colony, but it was emphatically a Chinese city. If we define a building over fifty stories as a high-rise, there were at least two in Hong Kong for every one in Manhattan. The harbor was one of the busiest in the world, crowded with cruise ships, container ships, and tankers, among which the little Star Ferries hurried back and forth between Hong Kong and Kowloon. The streets, subtropical and hot, were jammed with traffic. The population exceeded six million people, the vast, vast majority of them busy, well-dressed Chinese, jostling each other as they hurried purposefully up and down steep and narrow streets and along broad boulevards as well. No one knew really how many people lived there because the so-called I.I.s, illegal immigrants, were an uncountable additional element of the population. One had a sense that anything was for sale there, *anything*, in a community more cosmopolitan than any other I have ever seen.

But that was the impression of a mere three days in Hong Kong.

My father was not so impressed. "Goddamned anthill," he grumbled. He did not understand that the city had one of the most active stock exchanges in Asia, some of the biggest banks in the world, and that half the world's billionaires lived there. He did not understand, either, that Cheeks, though an important customer to a few makers of clothing, was small-time in Hong Kong business terms.

Our contact was Henry Wu, owner of a shop that made some of our most exotic merchandise. Everything from Wu was of meticulously high quality—and cost twice what we had imported from Saipan. We met him for lunch at Luk Yu Tea Shop, a dim sum restaurant. Dim sum were little dumplings filled with all kinds of things: shrimp, vegetables, chicken, fish, and so on. It was a typical Hong Kong lunch.

Though my father and I did not guess it at the time, Wu was honoring us to meet us there. I began to understand it as I observed the businessmen at nearby tables. So far as my father was concerned, we might as well have been eating at McDonald's. But Luk Yu had stayed open during the Japanese occupation and had been, for seventy years and more, a distinguished Hong Kong restaurant.

"You are anxious to know the conditions in which our goods are made," Wu said when we—that is, my father and I—were struggling to conquer slippery dim sum with chopsticks. "We will visit some shops tomorrow."

The next morning he took us in his car for a tour of Hong Kong. They drive on the left there, in the British fashion—which took a little getting used to. We had lunch in a café on the Peak, the highest point on the island. We spent the afternoon visiting three workshops.

Hong Kong sweatshops were nothing like the barbed-wire camps on Saipan. They were certainly not luxurious, and they would not have begun to meet U.S. federal or state standards, but the young women who worked in them were not slaves.

"Any of these girls can quit her job at any time if she doesn't like it," said Wu.

"As a practical matter—" I started to say.

"As a practical matter, she has to earn a living, but there are many shops, and she can try others."

"Looks pretty rough to me," my father said. We were looking at a room where twenty or so young women worked at sewing machines. The windows were open, and oscillating fans blew air across the workbenches, but the temperature had to be in the high eighties.

"They come here from the Philippines, typically," said Wu. "A girl works five or six years and then goes home. She may come back after a few months, for another five or six years. Anyway, she talks about the working conditions and the wages in Hong Kong, and her sisters and friends come here looking for this kind of work. So, they must not think it too bad."

"Don't they want to get married?" my father asked.

Henry Wu nodded. "They come here at age seventeen, typically, work five or six years, then maybe another five or six years, and go home to marry before they are thirty—holding a dowry a young man has been glad to wait for. They are paid in Hong Kong dollars, one of the world's most stable currencies, and they deposit their savings in Hong Kong banks."

"But when they go home—"

"They leave their money here, where the banks can be trusted absolutely."

"Then how do they get their money out?"

Wu smiled. "Bank-machine cards. ATM cards. They work the same as they do in the States. Internationally. These are the nineties. We've had ATM cards for years."

My father thought he had been subtle and had not shown his growing impatience with Chinese food and chopsticks. Apparently he had not succeeded in concealing his wish for Western-style food eaten with silverware, since that evening Henry Wu took us to an excellent Austrian restaurant called Mozart Stub'n, all but hidden on an out-of-the-way street in the part of Hong Kong called Mid-Levels. There we dined on asparagus for an opener, followed by green salad, then beef and potatoes with turnips—cooked so you could eat them, as my father put it to me later—followed by a rich chocolate torte and coffee.

We drank two bottles of an excellent Austrian red wine, then generous splashes of Courvoisier with our coffee.

"You don't run things the way they do in Saipan," my father said to Henry Wu as we contemplated our brandy.

"That's a very different thing," said Wu.

"I've canceled our contracts with Alexander on Saipan. I'm looking for someone to take them up."

"I can't match Saipan prices," said Wu frankly.

"We can negotiate," said my father brusquely.

"You don't want to risk the wretched publicity that's going to come out of Saipan."

My father ignored the comment. "I'm going to have to put someone out here for a time to talk about designs and quality, shipments, and so on."

Henry Wu nodded toward me. My father looked at me quizzically.

"I wish I could," I said. "But there's no way."

44

JERRY

I hired Charlie Han and sent him to Hong Kong. It was a great choice. As a New York Chinatown Chinese, he spoke the Cantonese that was spoken in Hong Kong and southern China, not the Mandarin that was spoken in Beijing. He knew the garment business and did his job well. On the other hand, as I'd had to expect, word came back before long that he was establishing a business of his own. Next the word came that he had married a young Hong Kong Chinese girl and had become a father. Charlie was a professional hustler.

I couldn't leave him out there on his own, with no supervision, so I leased a furnished apartment in Mid-Levels. We used it as a headquarters. I would go out and live in it for a week. Len would go. After Vicky had her second child—a rambunctious boy they named Jerry—she went out, too. Hong Kong became a sort of second home for us, each visit an adventure.

None of us ever learned a damned word of Chinese. It made Len think of Sue Ellen and remember the struggle she had gone through to learn the language of a quarter of the world's population. He tried to learn a few words at least, as did Vicky. I never tried.

Something very strange—I got so I could read some of the Chinese characters, even when I could not understand the words. I learned the character for "exit," for example, and could identify it without looking at the English word below it.

I learned to do something I had done in New York decades ago and had never done in recent years: ride the subway. The Hong Kong underground was so clean and efficient that I chose it often, even over the cheap little taxis whose drivers often refused a tip.

I should not exaggerate my Hong Kong experience. Len came to spend a great deal more time there than I did.

An odd thing happened. When I returned from Hong Kong, a letter from Lyon was waiting for me. It was from Giselle's sister, Thérèse.

> *Dear Jerry,*
> *You will my bad English excuse as always. I am think it is bad for us no seeing each other no time. Giselle would have wished. I not see little Len since he was small boy. I no family here no more. Could you come and bring boy? Please? Write to say.*
> *Thérèse*

I did not write. I put through a telephone call to her.

"Thérèse . . . Len is a married man with two children. Right now he's in Hong Kong on business. I'd like for you to meet his wife and children. But I don't see how I can bring them all to France. It has big problems."

"No? Sorree, Jerree. I had hope . . ."

"I've got a better idea. Let me fly you here, Thérèse. Trip to the States, first class, at my expense. I'd like to see you again. Len would like to. Plan on staying a month at least. I'm alone, too. You can live in my apartment with me."

"You would do this for me?"

I arranged for her a first-class ticket to Kennedy. When I finally recognized her coming out, I was amazed. Some Frenchwomen age badly, growing fat and mustachioed. Giselle, of course, had never done that. Well . . . neither had her sister.

Thérèse had lines on her face, especially around her eyes, and the flesh under her chin was loose. She was sixty-five years old that year, two years younger than I was. But she was slender and walked with a spring in her step; and, wearing a rose print silk minidress, she had a figure many women would have died for. She was blond—not naturally so, I knew—and had had her hair styled quite short. She had a flair for makeup, knowing what was enough and what was not quite enough. Coming toward me, carrying a small, simple case and letting a porter push a cart with the rest of her luggage, Thérèse was a vision of a self-confident, mature woman.

We kissed as we met there in the airport. I supposed some of the kids who saw us smiled, even laughed at us old people, but that kid rekindled a passion I had felt for Thérèse long ago. We had spent an erotic night together, years before I married Giselle.

"*Zheree* . . ." she whispered.

"Thérèse. It is so very good to see you!"

The second night in my apartment we slept together. We had wonderful sex together. Thérèse had a flair for it. I was ready to think it was a Frenchwoman's special flair, but I don't think so anymore; I think she shared with Giselle simply a healthy *woman's* flair. Maybe being French subdued some inhibitions.

My wife's sister. I don't think Giselle would have objected. To the contrary. She had set me up to spend a night with her kid sister, who had all but fucked me out of my mind—back in France, in the old days.

Thérèse had not been entirely straightforward with me. I needed only a few days to figure out that she did not intend to return to France, unless she had to. She had brought with her everything she very much cared about.

One night in the bedroom she opened an old, cracked leather photo album and showed me some faded, browning photographs.

"You know about zis thing," she said. The pictures were of a brick-paved street in an apparently middle-class neighborhood. A *boulangerie* and a *boucherie* were visible; also, in one picture, the doorway of a church where two priests stood laughing. I had walked on such French streets a thousand times. But in these pictures a heckling mob herded five crying, cringing, stark naked girls, heads shaved, down the middle of the street. "Iss me," she said, laying her finger on one image. "I am *ninezeen* year old. Zey take *sousands* of picture."

If ever a girl looked utterly miserable, in whatever circumstance, Thérèse looked agonized in those pictures. I could not understand why she had preserved them all these years.

"You have heard of zis thing, no? You know what I have done and what they have done to me?"

I took her hands in mine. "I have heard of it, Thérèse. The war. Many of us did odd things. A lot of time has passed. I did things I'm not proud of. We all do."

"You heard," she murmured. "For all zese years I have live where everybody knows about zis."

"And nearly everybody has forgiven," I suggested.

"Uhh . . . zey say. I not know."

We talked a lot and reached a decision that she would stay in New York. Not only that. When Len came home from Hong Kong, we confronted him with our decision that we would marry.

I was going to marry his mother's sister. I didn't ask Len if he liked it. I suspected he did not. I liked it, and Thérèse liked it, and that was all that counted.

Thérèse and I left on a wedding trip. We flew Cathay Pacific to Hong Kong, settled into my apartment there, and made Hong Kong our base for visits to Bangkok, Singapore, and Beijing.

I did not turn our wedding trip into a business trip.

Except in Hong Kong, where we lived in our apartment, we stayed in the best hotels. I had a sense that this might be my last great romantic fling, and Thérèse had the same sense for herself. We wanted to savor and cherish every moment.

We did not carry cameras. Our eyes were our cameras, our memories our film.

Thérèse was the only woman I ever knew who had utterly no interest in Cheeks merchandise. She was a direct, earthy Frenchwoman, and when the time came to be intimate she simply stripped and that was that. The time to be intimate might begin at six and go on till midnight, and she might be naked all that time; but naked was the way to think about love, work up to love, and make love—not wearing some odd, impractical garment.

I could not complain, even if the erotica she scorned were my business and my living.

"Ah, Zherree, you want I should wear zees, I wear zees, but ees more beauty zan zee *skeen?*"

She called my cock "beauty." "He is very beauty. He look good, feel good, taste good."

She told me about the German lieutenant who got her in trouble. "He want marry me," she said. "He say he send for me as soon as war is over. We live in Germany, he say. On day when I was shamed I didn't know he already dead. Shot by Résistance sniper in streets of Paris. Zis I learn only in 1946. His family invite me to come, live with them. I could not."

She knew more about me than I had imagined. Giselle had told her. "She lucky girl," Thérèse said of Giselle. "She dance *tout nu,* but she no fuck with Boches, not never. Never enough hungry. Fortune always smile on Giselle."

We stayed in the Far East for a month, then went home to find that my son had created a problem.

* * *

By now our gross sales, stores and catalogs, exceeded five billion dollars a year. Something like 60 percent of our merchandise was imported, a little of it from France, still, but most of it from Asia, chiefly Hong Kong.

As if anticipating my visits to Bangkok and Singapore—and skimming off a little for himself, I am sure—Charlie Han had arranged for some of the goods labeled "Made in Hong Kong" to be manufactured actually in some other places. The old Chinese city of Canton, now called by its real name, Guangzhou, was a center for the manufacture of knock-offs. Name a famous brand, and likely you could buy a replica made in Guangzhou. The Chinese factories in Guangzhou were especially good at making vinyl and latex clothing. Black vinyl miniskirts were a specialty, and were seen on girls astride motorcycles all over the world. Latex clothes were a fetishist line, not just for us but for others in our business, and most of them were made in Guangzhou and sent all over the world with labels saying they were made in Hong Kong.

Our merchandise entered the United States across the docks supposedly regulated by the New York Port Authority. Other merchandise landed at Kennedy.

Returning from my wedding trip, I learned that my son had executed contracts moving most of our imports into container shipping.

I had seen the ships moving out of Hong Kong. I had seen them arriving in New York. Huge, squarish ships loaded with hundreds of sealed containers.

Sealed containers. That was the point. Since time began the longshoremen and others had pilfered a certain amount of merchandise off every shipment arriving in the port. It was a tradition. With sealed containers—

"*No, by God!*" Len was a fanatic about it. "The time is past! The time is past when every fuckin' dockworker can dip his hands into our shipments and help himself to what he wants. Business isn't being done that way anymore."

We sat over dinner in Thérèse's and my apartment on

Third Avenue. Things were more like they had been when Giselle was alive: *good* wines, good food. Thérèse knows the difference. We were four: Vicky and Thérèse, Len and I.

My son was taller than I was, lean and muscular, with dark-brown hair and intent blue eyes. His hair was thin. He was going to show male-pattern baldness by his thirties. He was personable and self-confident. He also had a very clear vision of what he wanted his world to be. I was proud of him. I was proud of the part I had played in making him what he was. He was the best thing I ever did.

"What way is it different, Len?" I asked. "What's changed?"

"Letting ourselves be ripped off by—"

"Longshoremen who pilfer a little out of the shipments," I said. "How many television sets do they take out of a hundred arriving from Japan? I can tell you— one. Doesn't a Toyota disappear off the dock occasionally? How many fur coats disappear? How many cases of wine? Len! It's the way business is done!"

"Not anymore," he said stubbornly. "It's changing. The prosecutors are moving against this kind of stuff."

"Oh. Against the longshoremen who rip us off for less than half of one percent. What do you think we pay to inspectors to overlook all kinds of things? What do you think we pay assessors to undervalue our merchandise? What do we pay cops? Fire inspectors? And so on. How many bottles of booze do we give away every year? My Uncle Harry, a cheap grifter if ever there was one, used to give a box of cigars and a bushel of apples to every cop in his precinct at Christmas."

"We're not cheap grifters," said Len. "We don't have to do business that way. We're *big* now, Dad. We don't have to—"

I don't remember that he had ever called me Dad before. It caught at me. But I had—for the moment—to continue the argument. "We don't, huh?" I said. "We're too big to make payoffs? Len, we don't own any congressmen. Maybe we should. A company our size ought to own a few. Some companies ought to depreciate senators and representatives on their tax returns—they're assets, and they own them."

"Hey! This kind of cynicism—You're living in the past."

"Okay," I said. "Let's put bribery out of the discussion. Let's look at regular daily business. Every time you pay an insurance premium you're paying off a scam artist. I don't see any difference between paying our friends the longshoremen a pittance to see that our merchandise makes it across the docks safe and paying an insurance company more than a pittance for guaranteeing the same. Given a choice, I'll take the longshoremen. Then we pay the Teamsters to see to safe delivery at our stores. And we pay the goddamned insurers for the same thing. I can walk down to the docks and say to the longshoremen guy, 'Hey, I got a little package comin' through. See it gets through, okay?' And he says, 'Okay, Jerry, you got it.' At the same time your fuckin' pious insurance guy will screw me. And, son, business will continue this way. It's not a thing of the past."

"You bringing in narcotics?" Len asked me.

"You think that, fuck you!"

"I didn't mean that. I'm sorry."

Our two women looked at us in dead silence. They sensed that something was happening, something more than just an angry argument. Father and son . . .

45

It was tough talk, I suppose. But, goddamn him, during my wedding trip he had made a major decision about my business without consulting me. He could have reached me by phone, but he was so goddamned certain of himself that he didn't think it necessary.

From that day something became certain: Either Len was going to be a lawyer or he was going to be my heir at Cheeks and take over the business as I, inevitably, would have to give it up. The flesh is heir to a thousand ills, of which life is one. Anyway, there wasn't room in the business for both of us.

Sal was furious. "We've had cooperation from the long-shoremen from day one," he growled at Len. "Now you tell me we're gonna cut 'em off. No way, little man. No way."

"It's *done,* Sal," Len said, his blue eyes turning to ice.

"Then *un*done it. A man doesn't screw his friends."

"Friends don't steal from each other," said Len.

"One hand washes the other," said Sal.

"And picks the other's pocket while doing it?"

For a moment I thought my seventy-year-old partner was going to take a punch at my thirty-year-old son. And

I realized Len would have decked him if he'd tried it.

I suppose I should have realized that my son was my son. What else should I have expected?

How should I define myself? I'm the kid of a royal fucking. I loved my parents, but I came from *nothing*. I shoved my way into every opportunity I could find, and I made the best of it. I got lucky in the end and took my larcenous, heartless Uncle Harry for two million. I turned the tables. Still, who can guess what other ways Harry fucked me, that I didn't even know?

With only one or two exceptions, I suppose I've never done anything I'm really ashamed of. And I've done only one or two things that I've regretted. Like the way I fell for Filly and cheated on Melissa.

But, Christ, am I going to let my son take over from me, just like that?

He had a powerful ally in Vittoria Castellano Lucchese Cooper. To start with, she was his fuck-off money. He could walk away from his law firm or walk away from me. With Vicky he had a comfortable living available to him. And he had connections—connections independent of me, independent of his law firm, and independent of Sal.

I understood that he had not fucked the longshoremen without Vicky's advice and approval.

"It's not the same anymore," she said to me quietly one night over an after-dinner cognac and coffee. Len was still at his law office, deeply involved in the immense amount of paperwork necessary to register a new issue of corporate securities. Thérèse listened but could not understand the talk.

"Nobody is afraid anymore," Vicky went on. "I mean, not in a big way. It's just street-corner stuff now. The day has passed when Meyer Lansky could say 'We're as big as United States Steel.' Oh, billions go through the rackets, but it's a few thousand here, a few thousand there, selling coke and crack. The sellers use the stuff, too, and are not usually victims of their own product. Only the small boys are. The day of the really big boys is over. Where would you find an Arnold Rothstein now? A Lucky Luciano? A Carlo Gambino?"

"Gotti?" I suggested.

Vicky sniffed. "Don't kid yourself."

"Why?"

I knew she was aware of my attention on her sleek legs, crossed under a Cheeks black vinyl miniskirt. She wore things like that at home but never on the streets of Greenwich.

"It all depended on the *omertà*. Where would you find today a man who'd die before he'd tell the secrets? They testify and go into the witness protection program. They write books! The *omertà* meant trust. When nobody trusts anybody, there is no honored society, no men of respect."

"The longshoremen . . ."

"The longshoremen can strike. And they will, too, against container shipping. But where do they stand? They'll be saying, 'We're striking for the right to steal off the docks.' What kind of sympathy is that going to get?"

"And . . . you so advised Len."

"Len has to function in the real world. And the new real world is different from the old real world."

"Sal?"

"Sal's an antique. He always reminded me of Bugsy Siegel. He's an artifact of a gone world."

"Am I?"

She frowned at me. "No, Jerry, you're not. Unless you choose to be."

She was right about container shipping. There were strikes, but the longshoremen and Teamsters lacked an appealing case.

Residence in Greenwich carried with it access to beaches on Long Island Sound. Thérèse and I could go to the beach as guests. Neither of us could swim, but Thérèse loved the beach and the gentle surf that the Sound offered.

We made a domestic scene. Little Catherine would toddle in the edge of the surf, thinking she was chasing seagulls. My grandson, Jerry, was still an infant. Vicky pretty much stayed on the blanket with the baby. Thérèse wandered along the beach, staying close to Catherine. Vicky and Thérèse wore our international-orange swimsuits that had seemed so scandalous when they first exposed women's hips and butts on the beaches and at pools—a cut that was now so common. Those suits had been the sensation of our business at the beginning. When we went to the Greenwich beaches, our wives weren't the only women on the beach so outfitted. That damned swimsuit was our impact on the world.

Len and I would go walking. He had discovered a tiny rocky promontory that was submerged at high tide and was left with clear tidal pools when the tide was out. Saw grass grew thick on the whole area; it, too, was submerged twice a day by the tide. Len enjoyed looking at the tiny shrimps and crabs that lived in the tidal pools, protected there against fish large enough to eat them—though not protected against gulls and nasty little boys with nets.

We talked.

I said to him one day, "You were right about the unions and container shipping. We don't lose merchandise to pilfering anymore. But did you ever think of the other side of that?"

"What other side?"

"In the old days, thousands of men went down to the waterfront every morning and got day-jobs wrestling crates across the docks by the sheer force of their muscles. Now, the containers are moved by machinery. What do you suppose happened to all those men? What happened to them and their families?"

My son looked at me as though I were insane. "Have you developed a social conscience?" he asked, almost scornfully; and I recognized then that he shared the genes that had produced me—the genes, indeed, that had produced Uncle Harry.

My father was a small-timer, and he always would have been, kept that way by Harry if not by his own limitations. Harry was a grifter, never big; he never could have been; he didn't have the guts or the brains. That I had built a billion-dollar business had been—luck? I couldn't think of myself as cold, unfeeling ruthless. Luck had to have had something to do with it.

The kid had had luck, the luck to be born to parents who loved him—though I'd had that luck, too—and who had the resources to get him a first-class education. But I could see now that he was also a hard, self-focused man.

Fool!" Buddy said when I talked to him about it. "You've always been *shrewd,* man. You've always seen where the main chance was. Me, I couldn't see it. But you did. It's smarts that got you where you are. So don't be surprised if the kid's got smarts and is ruthless enough to use 'em."

"The kid's as cold as a whore's tit," Sal said to me. "They always are, when everything's been handed to them on a plate. He's a spoiled brat, Jerry. He never had to work for anything, never had to take a chance. He'll never cut some asshole's throat and dump him to the sharks. 'Cause he hasn't got guts, either."

"He's a different sort of guy from what we are, Sal," I said. "I've talked with Vicky about the different way things are. Maybe it's a better way. Guys with smarts, guys with education—"

Sal shrugged. "Yeah. Educated greed."

46

I was seventy years old. I didn't feel seventy. I'd quit smoking a long time ago. I drank, but not all that much. I'd never had a physical. I didn't want to know what a doctor might find.

Maybe it was time to start taking it a little easier, though.

Len pushed me. "Look," he said. "You've got no second-level management. There's just you and then employees. Personal, hands-on management is great for small business. It doesn't work for a billion-dollar business like Cheeks."

"We've got lawyers and accountants, designers and—"

He nodded impatiently. "And artists. And store managers—"

"And regional managers," I added.

"Uh-huh. Suppose you have a heart attack tomorrow. Who runs the business while you're in the hospital?"

There was no point in arguing with him. He was right, of course. And he anticipated what I was going to say. It was inevitable. "You do, I guess."

"Until you're out of the hospital. And then?"

I had to make the concession. "I can't ask you to leave

your law practice and come into the business anything like full-time . . . unless I'm willing to . . . to give you control."

"And I can't afford to do it," he said bluntly. "You're the head man. You could change your mind any time and shove me out in the cold."

"You think I'd do that?"

"No, I don't think you would. But you *could*. Did you ever put your entire life in the hands of one man? No matter how much I trust you, I'd still be putting myself in the hands of one man."

"We'll talk about it some other time," I said.

We reorganized. I stepped down as president of Gazelle, Incorporated, and took the title chairman of the board of directors and chief executive officer. Len became president and chief operating officer. Sal continued to be a vice president, though with no specific duties, as it had always been. Roger Middleton left his bank and became vice president of finance. Len contracted with a headhunter and hired away from another company a man named Richard Pincus to be vice president of the mail-order division; Len also persuaded the lawyer he most admired, Hugh Scheck, to leave their firm and become general counsel. Since the loss of Len and Hugh all but ruined Gottsman, Scheck & Shapiro, Len retained the firm as our outside lawyers, which turned out to be a good deal for all concerned.

Len was a shrewd and sometimes ruthless executive. I remember an incident that happened only a few months after he became president:

Roger Middleton had persuaded Len to contract with his wife, Ariana, as a consultant on sweatshops. I suspect Vicky had something to do with it, too, since the two women had become friends in Greenwich. Len put her on with small compensation.

"Look," he said to me. "If we get some kind of shit

about buying sweatshop merchandise, we can say, 'Hey, we've got a known anti-sweatshop activist looking into things like that for us. Does any other company retain an outside expert to check this kind of stuff?' "

But Ariana didn't take long to become a nuisance. For one thing, she wanted an expense-paid trip to the Far East to look into shop conditions. I was in Len's office when he confronted her.

I should say that Len laid stress on having an imposing office. From his several visits to Hong Kong he had become interested in feng shui, the Chinese art of situating buildings and arranging furniture to gain the most restful and pleasing effects, plus taking the best effects of *chi,* the mysterious Chinese life force I cannot begin to define.

Anyway, in his office, nothing sat parallel to the walls. His desk was at an angle. He kept a big saltwater aquarium filled with colorful fish that glided around in the clear water. In a much smaller freshwater tank he had two piranhas. Oddly, two small catfish prowled the bottom of that tank, eating debris. The piranhas never attacked those little fellows. One of them was missing a fin it had lost when it tried. The water being pumped through the filters splashed and gurgled. He had a profusion of plants. Two parakeets chattered away in a huge wicker cage in one corner of the room. The office was comfortable for him and weird for me but, I imagine, formidable for others.

He had before him Ariana's memorandum asking for a trip to the Far East.

"Why should we send you to Saipan?" he asked. "We do no business with Saipan. We haven't since my father and I went there and saw the kind of conditions you deplore. Why should we send you to Hong Kong? My father and I go there from time to time and inspect those shops ourselves."

"Some of the merchandise labeled 'Hong Kong' actually originates in Bangkok, Singapore, and cities on the Chinese mainland. What are the conditions in shops in those places?"

"Thread is spun in shops around the world," said Len. "Fabric is woven. Vinyl is brewed. Leather is tanned and dyed. Buttons are manufactured. Steel is made. Handcuffs are forged. And so on. Are we to look into working conditions in every place where some component of our products is made? *Be practical, Ariana!"*

"People are enslaved!" she shrieked.

"Not . . . by . . . us," he said coldly. "Where we've found deplorable conditions, we've withdrawn our business, in New York and in Asia. And . . . and now, Ariana, I have another appointment." He tore up her letter and tossed it in the trash. He smiled and locked his blue eyes on hers. "Keep up the good work. Find out what you can. I know you can learn a whole lot without going out to the Pacific at the company's expense. Keep me informed. I do read your memos."

He stood. The interview was over.

After I was, in effect, retired from the business, I bought a home in Fort Lauderdale, on a canal, and Thérèse and I went down for the winter. I really had enjoyed fishing, and I took up surf casting. One night I had a chilling nightmare that I reeled in the corpse of Filly. But I did not give up fishing.

Len was on the telephone to me almost daily. He replaced eighteen store managers and three regional managers. He bought four stores that competed with us, at least in a sense, turned two of them into Cheeks stores, and closed the other two. He began to talk about going public with a stock issue—a subject on which I had to defer to him, since I knew little about it.

Len had become single-focused. He lived and breathed the business. He had developed an incredible discipline— which he had not inherited from me.

In January I went up to New York for a few days to attend the annual meetings of the stockholders and directors of Gazelle, Incorporated. It was nothing very fancy, since I owned 5,500 of the ten thousand shares of stock, Sal owned 2,500, Len and Vicky owned one thousand and one thousand were retained by the company as treasury shares. We sat down at a table in a small conference room. Roger Middleton, Richard Pincus, and Hugh Scheck were also present.

Len could vote 3,500 shares, actually, since before I went to Florida I had given him my proxy to vote 2,500 of my shares—so Sal could not outvote him in a stockholders' meeting, in case one had to be held suddenly or in case one had to be held with me in a hospital. Though I was present at the January meeting, I did not revoke the proxy. If Len was going to run the company, let him run the company.

As soon as the formalities of a stockholders' meeting were finished, Len nominated a slate of directors. There had always been five directors: he and I, Vicky, Sal, and Roger. He nominated a slate of seven, adding Pincus and Scheck. The slate was elected.

We adjourned the stockholders' meeting and convened a meeting of the board of directors.

Len nominated a slate of officers. He omitted nominating Sal as a vice president.

"What is this?" Sal asked angrily. "You squeezin' me out, son?"

Len shook his head. "Sal, you've never functioned as an officer of this company—"

"I was a *partner*."

"When it was a partnership, which it hasn't been since 1989. You rarely take part in anything. You rarely even come to the offices. What difference does it make? You'll still get your dividends."

"But my name won't be on the fuckin' door!"

"Neither will mine," said Len calmly. "Nobody's name is on the fuckin' door."

Sal turned to me. "Proxy or no fuckin' proxy, you can vote three thousand shares, and I can vote twenty-five hundred. You goin' along with this?"

"Sal . . ." Len said with the air of a man whose patience endures but is being tried. "Stockholders elect directors. Directors elect officers. We've already elected the directors. If they want you to continue as a vice president, they'll elect you."

"Fat fuckin' chance," Sal grunted, glancing at the directors seated around the table. Then he glared at me. "Thanks, *partner*."

Son of a bitch! I'd been had by my own son. I had not realized that the majority stockholder in a corporation might lose the power to elect its officers.

I could have called for a special stockholders' meeting a little later. But I didn't.

Late that night Sal was hauled to the Columbia-Presbyterian Hospital in an emergency-squad ambulance. By the time I heard of it and arrived the next morning, he was going. It wasn't a heart attack. It was a stroke.

I sat down beside his bed. That was when he told me he was the man who had pulled the trigger on Jimmy Hoffa. That's when he told me that whole story, in a weak voice but with an apparently lucid mind.

"Len's fucked me," he whispered. "Maybe you let him."

"I didn't mean to fuck you, partner," I said quietly. "You were right about one thing, wrong about another. Len's as cold as a whore's tit. But he's got guts."

I wasn't sure Sal was conscious and heard me, but he said, "Wait'n see."

"We've always been very different guys, Sal."

"Not so different. They will say kaddish for me. I hope you can be there."

I was there. He was lowered into a simple earth grave, in a simple pine box, and the mourners did our best to follow and join in the words of the kaddish, the Jewish prayer for the dead.

* * *

By now I was not sure if I could take control of my company back from my son. Well . . . of course I could have, but it would have involved a bitter confrontation, not just with Len but with Vicky.

She and I sat down over a steak at Peter Luger's one day when Len was in a meeting with the lawyers.

"There's no point in a bitter fight, Jerry," she said. "You'd win, but you'd lose."

"Meaning?"

"Oh, you can take back control of the business. There's no question about that. And then what? You know Len. You know he won't sit in an office and draw a salary and not run things. Not anymore. If you take back control, he'll leave the company. And he won't go back to his law firm, because its best men now work for the company."

"So, he'll—?"

"He'll come with me at Interboro Fruit."

"And be bitter," I said.

She nodded.

"He'll hate me."

"No, he'll never hate you. But he will be bitter."

"Meaning I won't see him and you as much, meaning I won't see the grandkids."

"Meaning you'll have won but you'll have lost," she said.

"I've already done something he won't like," I told her. "I bought Sal's stock from his sons. Len bid for them, but I bid higher. Tell him he'll get them in my will. Maybe he'll get them sooner."

So Len stayed where he was. I didn't try to put him down.

He and Hugh explained to me their plan to take our shares public. The more they explained it, the more I didn't understand it. They wanted to raise capital. I understood that. Why? Because they had plans for Gazelle, Incorporated, to buy new businesses. They had targets. Some of them, as I pointed out, were in no business even vaguely related to ours. Among the businesses they were thinking of buying was the foundry that stamped out our handcuffs, along with a hundred totally unrelated products such as a respected brand of kitchen knives. They had eyes on a chain of health-food stores—most of whose merchandise was, in my judgment, nothing but scams. I couldn't believe that they were also looking at a small, Midwestern commuter airline.

Well, why not? I had tried to sell French spring water.

I felt control slipping away from me. It was damn tough. I'm not the kind of guy who gives up on things. But I supposed I could let my son have his head, so long as he used good judgment.

Then suddenly I learned he wasn't using good judgment.

Her name was Susan Gillis. She was a thirty-four-year-old public-relations expert who had worked for us for a while and then had been brought into the company by Len, who said he valued her skills.

She had skills, I have no doubt. But they weren't the skills he admitted to admiring.

She had smoothly styled blond hair. Her eyes were dark green with flecks of brown. Her lips were sensual. Her understated makeup enhanced her beauty. She wore knit dresses, short and tight, clinging to a voluptuous figure. Damn her. She was an uncomfortable reminder of Filly. It looked as if Len and I had similar tastes in women.

I had only to observe the significant glances that passed between them to know what was going on. What was more, I wasn't the only one who could see it.

I made myself comfortable in a chair facing his desk and accepted a cup of coffee. Then I asked him, "What's between you and Ms. Gillis?"

"Look," Len said. He loved to begin conversations by saying "look," as if he were about to explain something to someone he was not sure could understand it. "When your chief business is Cheeks stores—"

"Our *only* business," I corrected him.

"When your business is selling our lines, you need to build *respectability*. I mean . . . on Wall Street, we are only *tolerated*."

"They like our money."

"Okay. But to build a diversified business, you need a better image. That's what Susan is for. I send her to meetings of bankers, brokers, and so on. She is our image. And I like the image she's helping us build."

"You're fuckin' her, Len."

His eyes turned hard and cold. "That's none of your business."

"You're fuckin' her."

"Dad . . . yeah, okay, I've been with her once or twice. Just for fun."

"I was married to your mother for eighteen years. During that time I never once had 'fun' with another woman."

"We're of different generations," he said, as if that closed the conversation.

"You've been married to Vicky for three years. She's the mother of your children. Of course . . . she's fifty years old. Doesn't she take care of you anymore?"

"It's not that."

"What's gonna happen when she finds out? You think she's not gonna find out?"

"You going to tell her?"

"I won't have to."

"What'll she do, put out a contract on me?"

I threw my coffee cup across the room. It left a trail of coffee across his white carpet, and shards of cup scattered at the base of the wall where it hit. "Sal said something to me about you," I growled at Len. "I deeply resented it at the time, but he was right. He said you were a spoiled brat who'd been given everything and never had to work or take a risk for anything. He also said you were colder than a whore's tit. It doesn't even occur to you, does it, how much this is gonna hurt Vicky? I know she came on to you hard when she met you, but she married you and has been as good a wife as a man could ask for, and—"

"You think you can run my life the way you've always run the business—hands-on personal management."

"Until you're man enough to run it yourself," I said coldly.

He was silent for a moment, then asked, "What do you expect me to do?"

"Go out there and tell Ms. Gillis that she's fired. Tell her the chief executive officer ordered you to fire her."

"I can't do that!"

"Then the chief executive officer gives you another order. Clean out your desk and be out of here in an hour."

"You can't do that."

"I own eighty percent of the stock in this company. If I can't get you out of here in an hour, I sure as hell can get you out a little later. You might use corporation law to frustrate me for a little while, but not for long."

Len was tough. I had seen that when he faced down the fag proctor-instructor at Lodge. The man had been a bully, but Len literally destroyed him. I remembered that now. I should have judged that correctly at the time—that there is no honor in beating up cripples.

Len conceded nothing. "If you turn me out of the company, how will either one of us explain *that* to Vicky?"

"I'll leave that to you," I said.

"But Susan . . . I *can't*. Jesus Christ!"

I was adamant.

"If we fire her, she might sue for sexual harassment."

"Let's hear what Hugh has to say about that. He's our general counsel."

Hugh Scheck lumbered in, walking with his two canes, and dropped on a couch. Len described the situation very briefly. It was apparent to me that Hugh already knew about Miss Gillis

"There is a perfectly simple solution," said Hugh, fixing a quizzical eye on the trail of spilled coffee and the shattered cup. "We get rid of the young woman by promoting her. You fired your regional manager in San Francisco.

Send Ms. Gillis out there as his replacement. She's capable. She can handle it."

And so it was done.

Len remained as the company's chief operating officer. But he understood which side his bread was buttered on. I figured by the time I had to stop interfering he would have matured; he would be ready to run the business on his own.

Thérèse and I had dinner with Vicky and Len that evening. A heavy snow was falling in New York, and I was glad we had two tickets for Fort Lauderdale on a flight leaving before noon the next day.

Len was glum, but I was in a jolly mood. When we had our before-dinner drinks in hand, I raised my glass and proposed a toast. "To the business that's gonna grow beyond any dream I ever had. To my son, who's gonna lead that growth. And—" I paused and laughed. "To my Uncle Harry! Thank you, Uncle Harry, for teaching your nephew to be a fuck*er* and not a fuck*ee!*"

The three others frowned. Vicky and Thérèse had no idea what I meant. Len did, sort of. Vicky would insist that he explain, and he'd have to use what was in his genes to put a gloss on what I'd said. It was a good test.

I knew he could do it. He'd better use what was in his genes, because he was going to face other problems damned soon.

47

LEN

As more and more of our manufacturing shifted to the Far East, I spent more and more time in Hong Kong. Our apartment there was in Mid-Levels, a name that refers to the mountainous nature of Hong Kong. The waterfront districts of the city are called Sheung Wan, Admiralty, Central, Wan Chair, and Causeway Bay. Upward there is Mid-Levels, and far above is the Peak. The Peak is the home of the beyond-luxurious estates of Hong Kong's many billionaires.

Our apartment was in a building on Arbuthnot Street, about a hundred yards up the street from a grim, gray stone building called Victoria Prison. A little more down the slope one came to Hollywood Road. A short walk on that brought one to an interesting feature of Hong Kong: a mile-long escalator that carries people up and down from the upper ends of Mid-Levels to the waterfront.

The apartment was on the twenty-third floor of a thirty-story building. It was nicely appointed, with parquet floors and modern appliances. Real estate is grotesquely expensive per square foot in Hong Kong, so what was really a luxury apartment had only one bathroom. The building had just two apartments on each floor, and when the apartment across the hall became available, we took it too.

That gave us room for something we very much needed: a maid and nanny. The girl we hired was, naturally, a Filipino. She spoke fluent Spanish, reasonably good English, and a bit of Chinese. We gave her a room in the second apartment and generally left the doors open between the two, though we locked them at night and when all of us were away, since the elevator did stop in the foyer between the apartments. The children played happily back and forth between the apartments.

I converted the living room of the second apartment into an office.

We also had enough space for Thérèse and my father to live with us when they came out.

Our quarters were idiosyncratic but comfortable. We spent four months of the year in Hong Kong at first, then more.

We tried to avoid the summer months, when the heat and humidity were oppressive. We had to remember that this was a subtropical city, with a climate not unlike Miami's.

Naturally, I spent much time with Charlie Han. He was our man in Hong Kong, to begin with, but he was also my entry into Hong Kong business.

Speaking Chinese was not the point. Every businessman in Hong Kong spoke perfect English. Their secretaries spoke English. The clerks in stores spoke English. The only language inconvenience I ever had was with cab drivers. Sometimes Charlie would scribble where I wanted to go in Chinese characters, and I would show his note to the driver.

Though my son Jerry, whom we called J. J., was not yet three years old, Vicky decided he should learn Chinese. The earlier a child begins to learn a language, the easier it is for him. Thérèse thought he should learn French, but Vicky pointed out that for every one person who could speak French, fifty could speak Chinese. English and Chinese, she said, were the languages of the future and would be essential in business.

I won't go into the next big question: whether J. J. should be introduced to Cantonese or Mandarin. Vicky decided that, too. It was to be Mandarin Chinese, which eighty or ninety percent of the Chinese spoke.

Vicky began to absorb herself in Chinese culture— something unhappily reminiscent to me of Sue Ellen.

"We've got to see something of that country, Len."

"We'll go on a tour sometime," I said.

"Sometime soon."

"Sometime soon."

I had business in China. With Charlie Han along to be my interpreter, I made my first venture onto the Mainland by boarding a train at Kowloon Station and traveling about forty minutes through the New Territories and across the border to Shenzhen.

That city was astonishing. In the course of no more than five years it had grown from a town of a few thousand people to a city of three and a half million. This was the result of Deng Xiaoping's creation of the New Economic Zone, a free-enterprise and free-trade zone in Guangzhou Province. Capitalism flourished there as it flourished nowhere else in the world—for the time being.

Shenzhen was a city of high-rise buildings and luxury hotels, plus of course gridlock traffic made more difficult by tens of thousands of motorbikes and bicycles weaving through the lines of cars and trucks.

We had come there to meet a businessman by the name of Bai Fuyuan, and we did meet him in the dining room of our hotel. The Guangdong Hotel is as luxurious as the Mandarin Oriental in Hong Kong, which means as luxurious as *any* hotel in the States or Europe.

Bai Fuyuan was a rather ordinary-looking Chinese man, with a great mole on his cheek à la Chairman Mao. I guessed his age as fifty, though I had difficulty judging the ages of Chinese people. He wore an impeccably tailored, tropical-weight, double-breasted white suit, with a maroon paisley handkerchief in his breast pocket.

He ordered champagne, and champagne is all we had to drink throughout the dinner. The very finest French champagne, Dom Perignon Rose. Bottle after bottle. Bai was paying, and we drank it like water.

"You have a highly successful merchandising operation in the States," he said. "It is so successful that you have a large amount of accumulated capital and are looking for investment opportunities."

He then proceeded to review our financial position. A Wall Street investment banker could not have known more about us than Bai Fuyuan knew. He knew our gross sales, our net profit, the details of our balance sheet, the names and some of the characters of our officers and directors. He knew where we were most successful—the Northeast—and where we were least—the Southwest. He guessed why:

"The Cowboy girls . . . how do you call them? You have just made a deal to outfit Cowboy cheerleaders. A very good move." I was astonished. No one was supposed to know about that deal, which we had just made. "The Cheeks merchandise is not suitable for wearing under tight blue jeans. Incidentally, I would be interested in hearing from you an offer to sell me, say, a thousand dozen pairs of skintight blue denim jeans. I think I have a market for them. If you have not a good, economical source, then let us talk about a deal whereby we make the jeans here and sew in the Cheeks label. The label is not unknown here, you know."

Charlie Han spoke. "I understand there are Cheeks knockoffs for sale in Shanghai."

"You should be flattered," said Bai. "Only the best is knocked off for the Chinese market. Gucci, Hèrmes, Versace . . . Hart, Schaffner & Marx . . . Rolex. The government tries to control that. It is not easy."

"I imagine there is little market for Cheeks merchandise in China," I said.

"Ah! Forgive me, but you are wrong. We are a nation

of a billion and a quarter people. There are Chinese living in the hinterlands who still live as Pearl Buck described. There are men and women here and there who still wear Mao suits—though have you seen any on the streets of Shenzhen? Ours is a confusingly complex country. But I can tell you there are scores of millions of Chinese who make a market for Cheeks lingerie. Look at the girls on the streets! What are they wearing? Black vinyl miniskirts, Izod shirts. What do you think they want to wear under? There is a market here for your line."

I had to admit I had not seen a Mao suit since I arrived in China—though that had been only hours ago. I had not seen oppressed people trudging to their jobs. I had seen girls with helmets on their heads, clinging to the young men at the handlebars of motorcycles. This was young China. Somewhere, I suppose, there were girls wading in the rice paddies. Not here.

"You were thinking about investment, Mr. Bai," said Charlie Han.

"Yes. *Investment,*" said Bai. "In the old days, the days of Mao Tse-tung, we used to hear on the radio the endless repetition of a . . . I suppose we could call it a mantra. It went, 'A handful of Party persons in power, taking the capitalist road . . .' They were criminals, as Mao would have had it. But today, Little Bottle—"

Little Bottle was the meaning of Xiaoping.

"—has turned us all into capitalists. I can offer you investments, gentlemen. For example, you considered investing in a little feeder airline serving three or four states in the American Midwest. Suppose I offer the chance to invest in a regional airline that will serve Guangzhou Province, with service to Hong Kong and Beijing?"

"We know nothing about how airlines are licensed and controlled in China," I said.

Bai Fuyuan smiled. "Everything in China is licensed and controlled by . . . how say? . . . dollars."

"Meaning?"

"Capitalism is a new idea for us—new, that is, since

1949. We run by no rules. The only rule is: make money! We have no labor rights, no women's rights, no worries about pollution rules. . . . We make money the way your robber barons did a century ago. Today, China is the best investment opportunity anyone ever dreamed of."

"Difficulties in getting your profits out?" I asked.

"Well . . . some controls. Like all others, they can be avoided. It is usually a matter of some money placed correctly."

"An airline," said Charlie Han. "That impresses me as a very big commitment for a company just ready to dip its toes. What else can you offer, Mr. Bai?"

Bai shrugged. "I own a company that copies American videotapes. Our government and yours has agreed that will not happen." He shrugged. "If I don't, somebody else will."

"I'm not quite ready," I said, "to get into that kind of business."

"Or CD disks?"

"Or CD disks."

"We weave wool and manufacture lovely sweaters. They are without labels. You can put in whatever label you like. I can sell you as many as you wish, quality assured."

I glanced at Charlie. He nodded, almost imperceptibly.

"It is something we can consider," I said.

"The label must, however, read, 'Made in Hong Kong.' There are certain, shall we say, prejudices to overcome. To Americans, 'Made in China' means made in Taiwan."

"Which means made in China," said Charlie. He was a diplomat.

Bai smiled and nodded. "There will be some small problems in getting the unlabeled sweaters from here to Hong Kong. We can overcome those. And we can negotiate a mutually agreeable price."

* * *

After dinner and half a dozen bottles of Dom Perignon among the three of us, Bai suggested a visit to a nightclub. We went to a very expensive club, designed to separate suckers from as much cash as possible. The lighting, the décor, the furnishings, the food, the drink, the personnel: all were superb and conspicuously costly. That club compared to the Lido in Paris for elaborately staged shows. Businessmen—a few Europeans and Americans, but mostly Japanese—sat on couches with hostesses cuddling up to them, drank champagne and tea, and ate hors d'oeuvres, mostly fruit, from platters placed on low tables. Though most of the hostesses were Chinese, a few were Australians and even Brits. Blondes were especially prized.

Though I didn't ask for her, I found myself attended by a lovely Eurasian girl in a microskirt and halter. The other men were also attended to by Chinese beauties. We sat on a pair of facing, leather-upholstered couches, with a knee-high table between.

"You American, yes?"

"I am American, yes."

"My father American. GI. You believe?"

"Sure. Why not?"

"Many do not. Many . . . well, you know. Where in America you from?"

"New York."

"Ah, New York! Is the most American place!"

She wasn't there to make conversation. She never said her name. She let her skirt hike back until I could see her panties. They were not from Cheeks.

Bai explained the whole deal. She could leave the club with me and go with me to a hot-sheet hotel, or even to the Guangzhou Hotel, if I paid the club a fee to release her for the evening and then paid her whatever we might negotiate. I would also have to pay the floor woman in the hotel a fee for allowing me to bring a girl to my room.

"What a hell of a way to make a living," I muttered to Charlie.

He was not concerned. He had already made a deal with his girl, who was, oddly, a natural blonde, an Australian.

"It's the way the world goes, Len," he said. "You may as well take advantage of it. If you don't, somebody else will. You can't change anything."

What kind of guy am I? I don't know. Here was a pretty little girl available to me for not a lot of money. Did I handle it the way I did because of loyalty to Vicky? I'd like to think so.

I paid the club's fee for taking out one of its girls. I took her out on the street, where I hailed a cab. Before she got in, I pushed into her hands a thousand Hong Kong dollars—say a hundred and thirty American—and I got in alone and closed the door.

I looked back as the cab pulled away. The girl turned and went immediately back into the club.

48

From Shenzhen we went on to Guangzhou, the old Chinese port city Europeans called Canton.

Charlie Han had hired a car with driver to take us there. We drove along a superhighway as modern as any I had ever seen in the States. The signs were in English as well as Chinese. From the car as we drove we could see Chinese villages that looked like Pearl Buck villages, except for one thing: Over the roofs of what we would have called hovels stood television antennas, the kind that used to rise from the roofs of American homes before we got cable. God knows how people lived inside those structures, but they did watch television.

I wondered what kind of television they received. I knew that in Hong Kong we received Hong Kong stations, Chinese stations, and cable services such as CNN and the BBC. I learned later that those flimsy antennae above those flimsy hovels received only Mainland China stations. Why not the others? "The others send out too much false news," a man explained to me.

Well . . . I am sure the Chinese of Guangzhou Province worried little, if at all, about the news they received on their television. I'd watched their stations in Hong Kong and had seen what the kind of programs they saw: a diet of colorful drama and opera—incomprehensible to me—that must have been immensely adventuresome and satisfying to the peasants living in those drab villages. Charlie Han pointed out to me that those very same peasants in their hundreds of millions were a market for western-style clothes—the sweaters we were talking about to Bai, if not the scanties we sold as Cheeks clothes.

"China is a great and wholly confusing market," he said. "Hey, Len. In the back country they *sell girls.* I mean they sell them, as brides. They display them with placards around their necks, naming their prices. Girls dressed in Western clothes fetch the best prices. A girl put on sale hopes to be able to stand in the market in a black skirt and a white blouse, European style. She gets a better price, and a husband who will respect her more for what he paid for her, if she looks like she came from San Francisco or New York—which of course none of them did. It's a great market for black skirts and white blouses."

"I don't want any part of it," I said. I must confess I would have liked to see one of those markets, but seeing was as much as I wanted of it.

"Me neither. I'm trying to say something to you about Chinese reality."

Guangzhou, not Shenzhen, was a typical Chinese city. I have seen Los Angeles smog. I never before saw anything of the like before I saw Guangzhou. It was apparent from ten or twenty miles out. It hung above the city like a low cloud, and when you got into the city it limited visibility. You had difficulty seeing tall buildings a mile or more away.

I remember an imposing television broadcasting antenna on a tall hill. The big clock on the railroad station. Traffic, traffic, traffic. Homeless living under overpasses. Guangzhou was a magnet for rural Chinese, who flocked there to work. The government had essentially given up trying to regulate people's movements within the country; the Chinese pretty much went where they wanted, and coastal cities were where they wanted to go.

And—as at Shenzhen—endless strings of motorcycles and motorbikes, most of them with helmeted, miniskirted girls riding behind helmeted young men, white panties often showing. Vinyl microskirts. Izod shirts—knockoffs or not.

Then sweaty laborers in vest undershirts and straw hats. Jobs being done by sweat labor that in the States would have been done by machines. Little, steel muscled men. Grim. You wondered where they went when the workday was over. What kind of lives did these slim and wiry guys live? I guessed they were the source of China's out-of-control population growth.

Our hotel was as fine as the one in Shenzhen, and in fact had the same name: Guangdong, the name of the province. Guangzhou knew how to take care of the foreign businessman. I learned to drink ginseng tea. A carafe of hot water, not ice water, waited for me in my room when I returned at night, with assorted tea bags, including ginseng. To this day I would rather have a cup of ginseng tea at bedtime than a cup of coffee.

But we were not there to study China or to enjoy hotels. In the lobby of the hotel the first evening we met another businessman, this one by the name of Zhang Feng: a small, muscular man at least twenty years younger than Bai Fuyuan, meaning he was much over thirty. He had been educated in the States, he said, at Oberlin College, in Ohio. His English, though perfect, tended to sound Midwestern. He smoked heavily.

We would have dinner together. Guangzhou, Charlie had suggested to me, was a place to sample authentic and exotic Chinese cuisine. I confessed a curiosity about something, and Zhang took us to a restaurant where I could satisfy that curiosity by eating a snake.

The restaurant was busy and rather noisy. On the way in I had noticed cages of chickens, tanks of fish, and great plastic tubs, like kiddie wading pools, containing shrimp and crabs. To the Chinese—the Hong Kong Chinese, too—fresh means *alive* when you order the meal. If it's already dead, it's not fresh.

We sat down at a round table with a large pot in the center. Our waitress, a pretty little girl in blue blazer, white blouse, and blue microskirt, squatted to turn the valve on a propane tank under the table and lighted a fire that would shortly have a gallon or so of water boiling briskly in the pot.

When I said I was interested in a snake, she beckoned me to come outside. There, in cages I had not noticed before, was an assortment of squirming snakes. I could not have chosen an individual snake; my choice was simply of one of three sizes displayed in the three cages. I chose a medium-sized one. The girl spoke to the attendant, and he reached in and grabbed a snake some three feet long. I suppose it was not venomous, but it might have been.

As we returned to our table we came upon Charlie and Zhang Feng looking at the fish in an aquarium. Zhang pointed at one: a big, dull-colored fellow. An attendant dipped a net in the tank and captured it. It would be another part of our meal.

Bottles of beer, white wine, and mineral water were on our table when we sat down again. The Chinese do not favor hard liquor.

"I understand you are seeking investments," Zhang said.

"Not aggressively," I said. "But we are looking around."

"Let me suggest one," said Zhang. "In Houston there is the remnant of a technology company called Sphere Corporation. It assembled a desktop computer it called the Sphere. Unfortunately, it also decided to write its own operating software, also called Sphere. It rejected everything Microsoft, including, of course, DOS and Windows. It wrote its own spreadsheet program, its own word-processing program, and so on. Its software was rather ingenious, but it was incompatible with everyone else's. Well . . . In the course of time it shared the fate of so many little start-up companies in the computer field. Today you can hardly find a Sphere computer—though many who once used them have fond memories of them, and the name is worthy."

"So you want—"

The conversation was interrupted by the delivery to the table of plates of vegetables and meats. The drill was that you picked up bits of vegetable and meat with your chopsticks and loaded the little wire basket provided each diner. The basket, the size of two tablespoons maybe, was on a handle, and you used it to dip your food in the boiling water. It would be ready to eat in half a minute or so, and then you took it to your plate, where you would add your choice of the sauces that had also been brought, and eat. I watched Zhang and Charlie to see how it was done.

Zhang and Charlie called it "hot pot." They identified some of the meats for me: squid, octopus, hare, beef, pork. The vegetables were more difficult to identify. They were Chinese. I did boil some mushrooms. I recognized those. The others were kinds of cabbage and the like, and root vegetables such as radishes, each with a distinct delicious flavor. They dumped whole plates of vegetables and meats into the pot, and soon we were boiling our food in a savory soup. From time to time the waitress added water from a teapot.

Everything was eaten without salt, of course.

"I want the Sphere name," said Zhang, returning to our business conversation.

"You are going to make computers?"

"Nothing so glamorous. Nothing so consuming of capital. Nothing in so competitive a field. What I want to export to the States and elsewhere is a variety of microprocessors. Microprocessors are the future. You know very well that your automobile engine is governed by microprocessors. They receive information from sensors and adjust the engine accordingly, for heat and humidity and a dozen other things, including altitude. All manner of things will be governed that way in a few years: air conditioners, furnaces, every type of appliance."

The snake was brought to the table. The head and tail had been cut off, and it had been slit end to end and gutted; then it had been washed out with rice wine, cut in three-inch pieces, and deep-fried. The pieces were drenched in a sauce. The platter of snake was put in the center of the table to be shared by the three of us.

Some people say eating a snake is something like eating chicken. I would say it is more like pork spare ribs. You have to use your teeth to separate the meat from the ribs and spine, and the meat you get is lean and a little tough and has a perfectly agreeable flavor. There is nothing nauseating about eating snake. If you did not know what it was, you would eat it without hesitation.

"Sphere still has a very positive reputation in the States," Zhang went on. "Many people who once used the Sphere computer remember it very fondly."

"I know people who deeply regret the demise of some old names that used to be important," I said. "Talk to someone who used to drive a Studebaker or Packard."

Zhang nodded. "So what does all this have to do with you? What I want is a license to use the Sphere name and the Sphere logo. I am looking for a respected American company to buy a controlling interest in Sphere. I will supply money to buy the stock, most of it anyway. You would have a minimal investment in it. You will recover your investment from my licensing fees."

"Why don't you buy it yourself?"

Zhang smiled. "Texans don't like to sell their stock to Chinese investors. It goes against the grain, so to speak."

I nodded. "So to speak."

"Something more," he said. "I will ask you to represent our product to American buyers. The Chinese involvement can be minimized. You will be able to label our products 'Made in U.S.A.' Sphere has the capacity to attach components to circuit boards. That the components come from China need not be emphasized. Do you see?"

I did. But at the moment I was seeing something else. The gas in our propane tank had run out, and our fire had gone out. Our waitress brought a new tank and hunkered down to replace old tank with new. As she squatted beside my chair her microskirt crept up and up. She was wearing no underwear, and soon she was hiding nothing at all. For a full two minutes she stayed there, intent on unscrewing and screwing the hoses. She was showing everything she wanted to.

"There are details to be worked out, but I wonder if this proposition has any interest for you," said Zhang. "If not, I have other ideas to present that may have more appeal."

"I reserve judgment on the Sphere idea," I said. "Tell me about your other ideas."

"We can manufacture Cheeks merchandise in China," he said smoothly. "We can do it to your quality standards. I know, however, the difficulties you might have with American law, at least with the American news media, if it should get around that you were selling products made according to *our* standards of labor relations. So? Suppose I were to suggest to you that we manufacture Cheeks products in China for sale only in China?"

"You can do that without my approval," I said. "It's being done to hundreds of American companies."

"Yes," he said. "I could. But there is a great enthusiasm in this country for authentic American goods. Our people know knockoffs from real."

"So what is the proposition?"

"We manufacture here, according to your designs and standards. The merchandise goes out to sea as if it were being exported. But the ship goes only from Guangzhou to Shanghai, say. It enters the port of Shanghai with papers saying the garments were made in the States. Then—"

"But what have *I* got to do with this? You can do it

without me. Chinese companies do, all the time."

"Except . . ." he said with a new smile. "Except that you, sir, and maybe your father, make appearances in our stores, bringing American models, and you endorse this merchandise as if it had all been made in the States."

"Which makes me a shill," I said. "And my father. I don't think he'd go for it."

"He's gone for a number of things in his day," said Zhang. "Do you want to refuse for him?"

"What's in it for us?" I asked.

"We can negotiate," said Zhang. "Obviously you are going to get a percentage off every sale of every item. Let me assure you right now, I can sell twenty million pairs of crotchless panties in one year. *Twenty million!* That's only one pair for every thirty women in China. Mr. Cooper, I can sell more than that. Look at those girls riding on the backs of motorbikes. How they'd love to be wearing Cheeks panties instead of Sears ones! We've got a hell of a market here. What would you want? Five percent? Six? Seven?"

"Ten," I said.

Zhang grinned. "We can negotiate."

"Frankly," I told him, "I am more interested in your microprocessors than I am in this. There is too much politics involved in it."

Zhang nodded. "Let us, then, focus on technology."

The fish he had chosen in the tank came now. I'd had more than I wanted to eat, but the tender white meat of that fish was irresistible. I was glad I'd tried the snake, but the fish was superior.

When we had finished, Zhang leaned across the table toward me. "Mei-ling let you see her pussy a little while ago. Would you like her for dessert?"

Maybe I was a fool to decline, but I did. Charlie took her. She spent the night in his room.

It was afternoon in Fort Lauderdale. I spent an hour on the telephone with my father.

49

JERRY

Maybe I shouldn't have sent the kid out to the Far East. Maybe he wasn't old enough. Maybe he wasn't mature enough.

On the other hand, hell, what had I been doing when I was his age—that is, in his very early thirties? Trying to sell Plescassier Water—better said, trying to establish a United States franchise for it. Still being screwed by Uncle Harry but already arranging the great final fucking of that old bastard.

Anyway, Len went over to China and called me to tell me all this stuff about propositions he was getting. I might have just said, "Use your own judgment, son," except for one thing he told me. *Christ Jesus, he ate a snake!* What the fuck had happened to lox and bagels with cream cheese?

Well, what is it they say about the Chinese? That they're the Jews of the Orient? We hadn't educated enough Jewishness into Len. His mother's idea. I'm a Jew. Len understands that and understands he's a Jew. But . . .

Well, what am I talking about? It's a new world. I suppose it's got something to do with being treated like Jews over many, many centuries. We had to get cautious. We had to use our brains. That's what it means to me: being careful, being shrewd. Not getting blindsided. Oh, it happens! We get screwed, like anybody. But maybe it's a little tougher to screw us than it is to screw most other people, because we've got centuries of caution in our genes.

Thérèse was fishing off our dock, in the canal.

"I think we better make a run out to Hong Kong," I told her.

"I am not so much like the place," she said.

"I got an idea Len needs help."

"Len . . . how we fly? What airline?"

We flew to New York and caught a Cathay Pacific flight. Len was back in Hong Kong and met us at the airport.

Though the two apartments we leased had two kitchens, Vicky rarely cooked dinner and rarely asked the maid to. Instead, they ate out almost every evening, leaving the children with Maria, the faithful Filipino maid and nanny.

That night Len introduced Thérèse and me to a hot-pot restaurant in Kowloon. He did not order a snake or anything of the kind—though I could not help being curious about some of the things that were served to us.

"I talked to Roger Middleton and Hugh Scheck about Sphere," I told Len. "I talked to them from Florida, and during our layover at Kennedy, Roger came out and briefed us. There'll be some more info, E-mail or fax, tomorrow. It's an interesting company. You're way beyond me when you talk about acquisitions. You know that. And you're certainly way beyond me when you talk about computers. But Roger and Hugh don't think the idea is impossible. They think it may just be possible to acquire control of Sphere. They think Sphere's people might actually welcome it. They've been looking for an infusion of capital."

"It's not so much the acquisition as it is what Zhang Feng wants to do with it that bothers me," Len said.

"You mean, just use the name and logo. Well . . . I'd have to give that a lot of thought, too."

"The problem we have in China," Len said, "is that these new millionaires operate like our own old-time robber barons. There's no regulation in China. Put it another way. There's no such thing as business ethics."

"Roger and Hugh said pretty much the same thing," I told him. "It's a different world, they say."

"Could it be as bad as what you encountered with the Boiardos in Philadelphia?" Vicky asked ingenuously. "Do they blow each other to pieces, cut each other down with lupos?"

She might have punched me. "How much do you know about that, Vicky?" I asked.

"I know about Don Enrico and Don Napolitano," she said.

"And . . . ?"

She shook her head. Whether that meant she didn't know about Filly and Chieppa or she did know and didn't choose to talk about it, I could not guess.

"What are you talking about?" Len asked.

Vicky answered. "A long time ago your father had some trouble in Philadelphia. It was a long time ago, and it's all over. It's not worth talking about."

I decided to change the subject. "The other idea . . . our letting them manufacture our line in China and sew in our labels. I could buy it if we had quality control."

"They'd find ways around that," Len said.

"So what do we do, turn down all these guys? I thought the Far East was supposed to be our future."

Len had been thinking. "I figure the Sphere idea may have some merit. Suppose we let Zhang Feng put in some money to help us acquire it. We cooperate on letting him import components into the States to install on circuit boards made by Sphere. Sphere can sell the miniprocessors as 'Made in U.S.A.' because nothing in 'Made in U.S.A.' says components don't come from somewhere else."

"I see one big problem," I told him. "You and I don't know from computers. Either we find a guy at Sphere we can trust absolutely, or we gotta hire somebody."

"If we are going to diversify, we'll have to build a staff that can help us with our new businesses," he said. He'd been thinking about it, plainly.

The chief thing on my mind that night was how much Vicky knew about Filly and Don Cheap. I had to find a way to have a private word with her.

I couldn't that night, but in the morning Len took Thérèse up Hollywood Road where there were antiques stores and art shops. Vicky would have gone with them but was sensitive enough to realize that I wanted to talk with her.

"So," I said. We sat over tea and slices of fruit in the living room of the first apartment, the one Len had not converted into an office with computers and fax. "You know the story of Don Enrico and Don Napolitano."

"You supposed I wouldn't?"

Vicky was dressed that morning in odd leggings—black-and-white checkered—with a yellow golf shirt. There were times when I was sorry I had set her up with my son and not with myself—though that would have been impossible at the time. Anyway, she was the best thing I ever did for him.

"What do you know about the rest of it?"

"They meant to kill you, and they underestimated you. That was a smooth performance, Jerry. I don't know how you did it, exactly. Neither does anybody else. But Chieppa and his gorgeous little chippy disappeared. Gone. A lot of people would have liked to know how you did it. The cops didn't give a damn, frankly, but I have an idea they would never have figured it out even if they had given a damn."

"You knew about this when I introduced you to my son."

"Everybody knew about it. I mean, everybody who

knows anything. You got a whole new level of respect after that. Don't tell me you didn't notice."

"Len . . . ?"

"No, my dear friend. He has no idea. And he will *never* hear anything from me. It's strange. What does he think?"

"I hope he hasn't *stopped* thinking. He's out in the fuckin' world, Vicky. I can't protect him always."

She stood and walked to the window. From the apartment we could see the Bank of China building and much of central Hong Kong, plus some of the harbor. "Challenging damned place to become independent," she said.

Len and Thérèse came back from Hollywood Road carrying purchases. Len had introduced her to an art form called netsuke: a tiny Japanese carving of bone or ivory once used as a sort of button on a man's sash. Each netsuke was a highly realistic figure of a man, woman, or animal. The little people were engaged in daily activities: business, trades, farming, cooking. Some of them were completely realistic portrayals of men and women copulating or enjoying oral sex.

Thérèse had been fascinated with the netsuke and had bought four of them, two of which were lascivious.

Len wanted me to meet Bai Fuyuan and Zhang Feng, but I did not want to go over to China. Not just yet, anyway. So Zhang Feng came to Hong Kong.

He wanted to talk about Sphere. Neither Vicky nor Thérèse were much interested in the details of that, so they decided not to go with Len and me as we accompanied Zhang Feng to dinner.

It was an odd evening. Zhang had rented a boat, with crew, and we went out to Lamma Island, south of Hong Kong and a mile or two out in the ocean. Lamma Island is a sort of shopping mall for seafood, featuring restaurants and markets all offering fresh fish.

By now I would have welcomed a steak with french fries, but still had to concede that the meal was delicious. We had platters of fish that had been selected from big glass tanks as we came in. I didn't know what all of it was: prawns, shrimp, clams, mussels—everything called by Chinese names, of course. We were favored with an exotic delicacy I quickly learned to appreciate: shark's-fin soup. Other bits of meats and spices came in little morsels of boiled egg white, and I ate them without asking what they might be.

"The acquisition of Sphere will involve one obstacle," Zhang said. "Mr. Tom Malloy. He is like Steve Jobs and Stephen Wozniak. He created Sphere, company and computer; and he is most reluctant to surrender even a particle of control. He has rejected important opportunities."

"I have a question for you, Mr. Zhang," I said. "If we agree it is a good idea to acquire Sphere as you have suggested, what part of the necessary capital do *you* propose to contribute?"

We smiled. He had anticipated the question. I learned soon enough that Zhang anticipated most questions and came to meetings prepared with answers.

He took up on his chopsticks a morsel of deep-fried fish. "This is calamari," he said. "The junior Mrs. Cooper would be an afficionado of this Mediterranean speciality, I am sure, and could tell us if this is good. I am thinking it will take some seventy or eighty million dollars to acquire control of Sphere. My own contribution cannot exceed, let us say, twenty million. We will have to negotiate detailed contracts to define our several obligations to the business."

Len interrupted. "When we spoke before you suggested you would put up *most* of the money necessary to take control of Sphere."

Zhang smiled and shrugged. "We can negotiate," he said, as if so saying were enough to dismiss the subject.

We did agree over that dinner to the general outline of a deal. Gazelle, Incorporated would acquire a controlling interest in Sphere. The acquired company would give up the computer business and devote its technological resources—which remained formidable—to the design and manufacture of microprocessors. The microprocessors would be assembled in Texas and marketed by Americans. The components on the boards would come chiefly from China, from companies controlled by Zhang.

"Boats," said Zhang sadly, "must go out more and more miles to fish. The coastal waters of Southeast Asia are becoming more and more polluted. It is a tragedy. This fish we are eating"— he gestured toward the big son of a bitch on a platter before us —"may very well have been taken in the waters of Vietnam."

Back in the apartments, we found that the fax had been printing away. We were lucky the machine had not run out of paper.

Part of what had come in from Roger Middleton in New York read:

> *Zhang Feng is a billionaire, a beneficiary of the economic policies of Deng Xiaoping. He was once a colonel in the People's Liberation Army. Although he appears for the moment to be financially sound, having money on deposit in Hong Kong especially but also in Tokyo, San Francisco, London, and Zurich, it must be remembered that a radical change in government could result in worse than his immediate bankruptcy.*
>
> *Do not forget that the Handover of Hong Kong to the government of the PRC is only a few years away. Deposits in Hong Kong banks promise to be sound after that change, but they will not necessarily be so. For this reason, all financial arrangements must be on the basis of immediate fund transfers to our accounts.*

Tom Malloy is, above all else, a colossal egomaniac. Plus a certifiable genius. The latter probably entitles him to the former.

He will fight anything likely to cost him any control of Sphere, even to the point of destroying the company before allowing it to slip out of his hands.

He can afford to do pretty much anything he wants to. Sphere has made him a millionaire many times over. If the whole thing went down the tubes tomorrow, he would land on his feet.

We continue to investigate every aspect and will keep you informed. Suggest you plan on returning to the States soon.

I liked the final suggestion. Thérèse and I flew back a few days later, and Len and his family returned a week later. They brought with them their Filipino maid and nanny, Maria, having arranged after some difficulty to secure her entry into the States.

50

There was nothing to do but go down to Texas and meet this Mr. Tom Malloy.

I have to confess I had never before been in Texas, and neither had Len or Vicky, nor, of course, Thérèse.

We went with different ideas in mind about what we were going to encounter.

Thérèse went expecting to see cowboys and Indians. She was disappointed when we did not spend an evening at a rodeo. She was impressed, though, with the size of everything, and with the conspicuous presence of *money*.

Vicky went with an antecedent hostility. She couldn't think of anything positive she had ever heard of Texas, even though we were doing business with the Cowboy cheerleaders. As a sports fan, she *detested* the Cowboys. For one reason, she found the notion of a "Fellowship of Christian Athletes" nauseating. I can remember her asking, "What could those Baptist assholes know about Christianity?" She didn't like people out-defining other people. And she didn't like the state where John F. Kennedy had been murdered.

Len? Well, he had known Texans at Amherst and Yale. They weren't necessarily such bad fellows, he said. And what made Texans Texans wasn't necessarily bad. Remember Lyndon Johnson.

As for myself, I didn't see how it could be much worse than California, so I went with an open mind.

We flew down on the Lear jet. For people who had seen Hong Kong and lived there, Houston wasn't much. On the other hand, there was nothing wrong with it. I suppose the people who lived there lived rather pleasantly.

We had two suites on the same floor in the Hyatt Regency Hotel. There were other hotels in Houston, maybe more distinguished, but none were more comfortable and convenient, and the Regency suited us fine.

We saw no cowboy hats. We saw no cowboy boots. A waitress in the bar explained, "Mistah Coopah . . . whut y'awl must understand ee-is, there are no *Texans* in *Houston!*"

Well . . . I don't know how you define a Texan, but I guess Tom Malloy was one. He had no education, essentially. He had about as much as I had. In fact, I suspect Tom had experienced his own version of Uncle Harry. And he had taken the bull by the horns, I guessed, and wrestled it to the ground. He had been, among other things, a wildcatter—meaning an entrepreneur who had drilled for oil where oil was not supposed to be, and had found it.

His wife was with him. *She* was the Texan of the pair.

His most memorable characteristic was his obsessive intellectual curiosity. That was what had made him as a man. Instead of turning his energies to reassembling Jeeps—in effect, stealing them, as I had done—and then to selling fraud designer water, Tom Malloy had worried his way through the mathematics and other theories that were the foundation of computer science. I suppose the best thing about him was that he saw the *potential* in computers, as he had seen the potential in land that was supposed to have no oil under it, and from that had made opportunity.

I remember the first one I ever saw. I thought it was wonderful, but I couldn't think of a single useful thing it could do. Did I *need* a machine to—?

Over dinner in the Regency that first night, sitting behind glass that afforded us a view of the lobby two or three floors below, I listened to Tom Malloy describe his commitment to a thing that, when he committed to it, was entirely new, with an uncertain future.

"The thing about it that struck me from the start was that it was so *beautiful,* so *elegant.* The mathematics that made it work was elegant. That had been there all along, of course, but we had to wait until the 'seventies, then 'eighties, to have the technology. Look at it this way. No matter how skilled a carpenter you are, you can't build a wooden television set. No matter what fine wood you can get, you can't make a wooden picture tube."

"You have to have transistors," said Len. "And resistors and capacitors and—"

"Yes, and now chips that have all those components on chips the size of a postage stamp. They did build 'em with tubes, but those were in no way practical for most applications. Too big, too sensitive, too unreliable. . . . We had to have transistors. And circuit boards."

Malloy was in his forties. He was six-feet-five, I estimate, but even so was not the kind of man who would attract attention. His dark hair was cut short and was accented by the beginning of gray. He was handsome, with chiseled features. He read the menu with a pair of half-glasses which he returned to his pocket as soon as he was through reading.

He was dressed more conservatively than either Len or I, in a charcoal-gray three-button suit with narrow lapels, a white shirt, and a regimental tie. When we had met him in the lobby he had been wearing an oilman's champagne-colored Stetson, which was now in the checkroom. I guess we'd expected a beige suit with fancy stitching.

He didn't look like a techie whiz, either. I did detect a certain excess of enthusiasm when he talked about Sphere, the company and the computer.

The wife was . . . Len put it that she could have been a cheerleader. I didn't know from cheerleaders, but when the facts were disclosed, it turned out that she had been a cheerleader for the Houston Oilers. She was Tom's second wife and was maybe fifteen years younger than he, and she was his trophy. Some guys bought Porsches and some Ferraris, some bought boats, and some leased Lear jets. Tom Malloy had married an Oilers cheerleader.

Her hair had been stripped—not bleached, *stripped*. She did not have telltale dark eyebrows because she had almost no eyebrows at all. She did not wear a beehive— she was not that unstylish—but she had a lot of hair, artificially curled. She wore shiny pink lipstick. Her figure was perfect. You could guess that she worked out at a gym regularly. Her white minidress fit like it had been spray-painted on her.

Her name was Becky.

"Hong Kong!" she said. "Oh, I'd love to go there! I suppose a person ought to see it before it's handed over to the Mainland Chinese. I have friends who despised Tokyo but loved Hong Kong. How very different is Cantonese from Mandarin?"

Malloy wanted to talk about his computer.

"It was the *best*, Cooper, I swear the Sphere was the best, for its time. We were, in fact, ahead of our time. We went to five-and-a-half-inch floppies when everybody else was still using those great big awkward ones. We began to offer a mouse when everybody else was still keyboarding everything."

"What went wrong?" Len asked bluntly.

"Nothing went wrong. The Sphere is still the best—or could be, if we had the capital to add some refinements and market it."

"What kind of refinements?" I asked. I wanted him to open up on this subject because I planned to hire an expert to determine whether or not his ideas were still sound.

"Voice recognition," he said. "There are recognition programs, but they are primitive. Imagine sitting down at your computer and talking to it. Imagine saying 'Power on . . . boot . . . word processor,' and it turns itself on, boots, and sets up the word processor. Imagine saying, 'Letter format,' and it sets up the word processor to take a letter. Then you dictate the letter, and your words appear on the screen as you talk. When you're finished you might want to make a correction or two with the keyboard. Then you say, 'Save letter in Acme file and print. Print envelope.' It does it all. You might have to fold the letter and stuff it in the envelope, but the computer has printed the postage on the envelope, which is ready to go."

"How about a laptop?" Len asked.

"We have one. But I think the big future is with the multifunction, easy-to-use desktop computer. Given a choice between a computer that can do all the things I just mentioned, plus hundreds of other jobs, with full automation, and one you can carry around in your briefcase, more users will want the functions."

"You're going to run Windows?" Len asked.

"I'm afraid we are."

I changed the subject. "Have you ever been in a Cheeks store, Mr. Malloy?"

"You bet. When you fellows proposed to come to Houston and talk, I went to the Cheeks store in the Galleria and took a look. Bought Becky a nightie, too. Better than that, I asked my bank to give me a rundown on you. Hope you won't think that's pushy, Mr. Cooper."

"Not at all. You can bet we've done a study of you. And . . . let's make it Jerry and Len, also Vicky and ThERèse."

"Sure. Tom and Becky."

"The nightie is great," said Becky. "I'm going over to the Galleria and look into *that* store for myself."

"I hope you won't mind my asking this question so soon," said Tom, "but why does a company in your line of business want to acquire a company in *my* line?"

Len answered. "You just said yourself that one of your problems is marketing. We are a marketing company. Sure, we have great designs, but the secret of Gazelle, Incorporated is marketing."

I took it up. "One of your problems, Tom, is that people don't *know* about Sphere. People who do, people who used to run Spheres, swear by you, but there aren't enough of them."

My God, what was I saying? We had no intention whatever of selling his Sphere computer. We were going to turn Sphere, Incorporated into an assembler of microprocessors, which would not be sold to the public but to a limited number of manufacturers who would incorporate them in their products.

And what the hell was I thinking? I hardly knew what a microprocessor was.

"I've told Tom," said Becky, "that we ought to look at how Dell, for example, works. They send out beautiful catalogs. Tom has tended to believe that was beneath Sphere's dignity."

"The key to almost every business is marketing," Len said—surprising me; I had not supposed he had such insights.

We had ordered oysters on the half shell to begin our dinner, and their delivery interrupted the talk. The table was silent for a moment as we took oysters and began to eat them.

When talk resumed—

"It would be a departure for you, though, wouldn't it?" Tom asked. "I mean, the two lines of business don't seem to match."

"They don't have to match," said Len. "Mead was a paper company. Paper! A smokestack industry if ever there was one. Then they went into the computer business and eventually sold off that business for one-point-five billion dollars, cash. The point is, we've got investment capital, and you need investment capital."

Tom frowned over an oyster. Someone said it was a brave man who first ate an oyster. Giselle had taught me how to eat them: with lemon juice and French bread with butter, and white wine. A sauce of ketchup and horseradish was an abomination, she had insisted. None of that was on the table.

"You'll want control," said Tom.

"Enough to guide the company into a new line of business," Len said.

"And what is that?"

Len explained what Zhang Feng had in mind.

"Assemble Chinese components onto circuit boards! Gentlemen, there is no way Sphere is going to do that."

"Sphere will run quality-control checks on the components," Len said, "and assure itself the components are good. It's a coming line of business."

"I'm inclined to say no to this," said Tom.

"You may not have the luxury," I told him. "You've got a lot of debt out. If we buy up enough of that, we will take control of Sphere, Incorporated whether you like it or not."

I could have sworn I saw a glitter of triumph in Becky's eyes.

"And what happens to Sphere Four?" Tom asked dolefully.

"We'll look into it. Maybe—"

Was I saying that maybe even Gazelle was going into the computer business?

51

LEN

Zhang Feng had gotten us interested in a business about which my father knew nothing and I knew very little more. It would be essential for us to bring aboard a computer guru.

But where to find one?

Middleton put out inquiries. So did Scheck.

Computer types did not flock to the offices of a company known for selling women's underwear. How would *that* look on their precious résumés?

Each one who came in was flawed. One was a drinker. One smoked—which is a no-no around computers, not to mention around our offices. References and letters of recommendation are useless. Who would give as a reference or solicit a letter from anyone except someone who was going to endorse the candidate in glowing terms?

I interviewed one candidate who had never in his entire life associated with anyone or with any enterprise that was not identified with his religion. He had gone to religious schools and worked for religious institutions, was a member of religious organizations, was married in his faith, and was making certain that his children were being educated in that faith. I will not say what faith it was; that doesn't make any difference. He was too parochial for Gazelle.

I interviewed a young man who, in spite of his doctorate in mathematics from an American university, could not speak English. He had been passed through the public schools and made his way to his Ph.D. without being able to read or speak English.

I interviewed candidates who came in with chips on their shoulders and literally defied me not to hire them. If they didn't get the job, they would know what I was: sexist, racist, anti-this, or anti-that.

Hiring is not an easy process, particularly when you want someone in whom you can place your confidence.

Eventually she showed up: Elizabeth McAllister.

Elizabeth was an unfortunate young woman in an important respect. It shouldn't have made so damned much difference, but it did—Elizabeth was an unattractive girl. And she knew it. She was painfully aware of it.

It would have been difficult to define what was wrong with her. Actually, nothing was. Her problem simply was that there was too much of her. She was not obese, but she was big, and she was gawky. *Horsy* is the word people used. A young man in the office told his wife, "You don't have to worry about my sleeping with Liz. What you have to worry about is that she will step on my foot."

Her dishwater-blond hair was coarse and frizzy. Her features were regular but oversized. Her big face was round and flushed.

She tried to compensate with effervescence. Liz was enthusiastic. When she heard something she agreed with, she bubbled over it. She actually broke into little dances in the office.

She was intelligent. She was articulate. She had a doctorate in computer science from the University of Michigan. She should have easily found employment in a responsible position, but she hadn't; she came to us from a decidedly minor position in a big company.

"What do you think of Sphere computers?" I asked her during her interview.

"They're obsolete," she said simply.

"Why?"

"Because they ran out of development money, I imagine. The company made a big mistake. They insisted their computer must run their own proprietary operating system, which meant it could not run any off-the-shelf software."

This was exactly what we had been told in Guangzhou and again in Hong Kong, by Zhang Feng.

"Who wanted a system that could not run Visi-Calc or WordStar?" she asked. "Or wants one that can't run Windows today? Or Word or WordPerfect or Quicken? A lot of people swore by Sphere. I played with one in the lab. It was a good machine. But it's practically worthless today. Practically? It *is* worthless."

"What would it cost to upgrade it?" I asked.

"A lot more than it would be worth," she said. "There's too much competition out there, already established with good names. Dell. Hewlett-Packard. Micron. Gateway. Not to mention IBM and Compaq."

"Well . . . just suppose."

"You couldn't do it without Tom Malloy," she said. "And I'm not sure you could do it with him. He could be a major impediment."

"Why?"

"He might insist on keeping the major features of the old Sphere. You might have a difficult time weaning him off his original ideas."

"But you also say we couldn't do it without him."

"Mr. Cooper, computer manufacturing today is mostly just a matter of buying components and assembling them. The components come from Intel, Texas Instruments, and so on."

"Are you saying we could assemble a computer and put the Sphere name on it?"

Her chin rose. Her big blue eyes opened wider. "Is that what you're thinking of doing?"

"Well . . . something like that. Maybe. What is the Sphere name worth?"

"It stands for innovation and quality," she said without hesitation. "Tom Malloy would campaign against you fiercely if you tried to change that."

She had said pretty much what we had deduced. I had to believe she knew her business. I had Middleton and Scheck interview her. I called my father in Florida. I offered her a job.

I soon learned more about Liz. She was starved for affection. She wanted a man, sure, but she wanted respect from women; she wanted people to like her. She was often misunderstood. Too often men took her affability for an invitation.

She called people "honey" and "darling." From others it might have been taken in a different way, but from her it was just an element of her personality.

I let her teach me about some computer programs, and she would stand behind me as I sat at the keyboard and say things like, "C'mon now, honey babe. You've done it before, remember? Like last time, sweet." She would lean forward to point at something on the screen, and I would feel her big, soft breasts pressing against my neck and shoulder. I don't know if she was unconscious of that or did it purposefully. Outwardly, she was happy, exuberant even. I would understand in time that she was starved for affection.

Anyway, we made it plain to her what we intended to do with Sphere if we acquired it. She expressed enthusiasm for the idea.

She went to Texas to have a look at Sphere and came back with a report.

"All that's keeping the Sphere company afloat right now is their laser printer."

"Their what?"

"Laser printer. It prints your computer output: your text, your spreadsheets, your graphs, your pictures. The Sphere prints fast and with extremely good quality. What's more, it's in a reasonable price range for that kind of equipment. Malloy was smart enough to make his printer compatible with just about anything. It can print from any computer, even the Apple line. The hardware of it is mostly outside stuff, but the software that runs it is strictly Malloy and company."

" 'And company?' "

"A few of their key people have remained loyal to Tom Malloy and are still there. There's a rumor afloat that a New York company with more money than good sense is about to bail Sphere out and make it a comer again."

"Meaning . . . ?"

"Meaning *us,* of course!" She laughed. "The very rumor of us is what's holding some of those people. They dream of returning to the glory days."

She gave us a written report, which Scheck and Middleton pronounced "competent" and "thorough."

One day I called her into my office.

"Sit down, Liz. I want to talk with you."

She sat down a bit apprehensively, as if she suspected I had called her in to notify her she was being terminated.

"You haven't been with us long," I said to her. "But you've become a valued person for us. You've got some rough edges, though. I'm going to ask you to avoid calling people 'dear' and 'darling.' You understand why?"

She nodded. I sensed that she was holding back tears.

"Well . . . I've had some new business cards engraved for you. Have a look."

I handed her a card from a box of them on my desk. It read:

ELIZABETH T. MCALLISTER
VICE PRESIDENT, TECHNOLOGY OPERATIONS
GAZELLE, INCORPORATED

I had expected she would be demonstrative. I couldn't have guessed how much.

She began to cry. She dropped on her knees before me and seized my legs in her arms.

"Oh, Len! Len! I love you, Len! I simply love you!"

Leaving me to wonder exactly what that meant.

While Liz was in Houston I received two large packages from Bai Fuyuan in Shenzhen. One contained finely woven wool sweaters in a variety of styles and colors. The other contained knockoffs of some of the most popular Cheeks styles of panties, bras, garter belts, and teddies, most of them in black.

I also received a letter from Bai—Federal Express.

Dear Mr. Cooper,

I have dispatched to you two cartons containing goods for your examination and, I hope, approval. They are examples of the sort of thing we might be able to work in partnership to manufacture and sell, both in China and in the United States.

I should very much welcome the opportunity to sit down with you to discuss this merchandise and explore the terms on which mutually profitable and mutually agreeable arrangements might be made.

I could come to the States, but I am wondering if we might not better meet in Hong Kong, where your Mr. Chan can join in our conversations.

I would hope, too, that your father might see fit to come.

Most sincerely,
Bai Fuyuan

I ordered the Lear and flew to Florida, taking the packages and the letter with me.

"It's good-enough merchandise," my father said.

We sat on the lanai—a word my father considered affected and so despised. Just outside its screens was a small swimming pool, where my father and Therèse both swam regularly. Beyond that was a canal, where yachts passed by in an almost regular procession. The pool and yard were surrounded by a strong chain-link fence that was anchored to the ground by steel stakes every foot or eighteen inches of its length. The fence was there because alligators had been known to lunge out of the canal and seize small dogs or cats, or to take up residence in swimming pools.

"He suggests you meet him in Hong Kong with Charlie Han. What I'd do is write him back and tell him to send Charlie the same samples he's sent us. Charlie he knows sewn merchandise. This stuff may have defects we don't see."

"Notice the labels," I said. Each item had a sewn-in label—MADE IN HONG KONG. "None of this stuff ever saw Hong Kong. It was made in China."

"And he wants to put in Cheeks labels?"

"Exactly."

"Well . . . if the merchandise is of high quality—and I mean we inspect every shipment, in China or on its way here—I suppose it could be a deal. If we have things manufactured for us in Hong Kong, why not in China? It's a matter of politics."

"It's a matter of quality," I said.

"All right. And quality. And we have to work out a way to be sure Ariana Middleton doesn't find out what we are doing. I rather imagine we can trust Roger not to tell her."

"This is going to mean another trip to Hong Kong," I said.

"You could be doing worse. You could be making business trips to Cleveland."

"Somebody is going to have to keep an eye on Houston," I said.

"You won't be going to Hong Kong for a while. Let's try to acquire Sphere before you leave. Or drop it."

52

Zhang Feng had said in Guangzhou that Tom Malloy would resist any effort to acquire Sphere that did not involve an absolute commitment that the company would continue to make and sell the Sphere computer. We had not told him that this was no part of our plans. Liz had reported that he would rear back and fight if he suspected we were going to scrap his wonderful machine.

As I had told him, we could do what we wanted whether he liked it or not. Sphere, Incorporated, and Malloy personally, owed a lot of money. We could buy up the paper and call the loans. Much of the debt had been secured by pledging Sphere stock as security, and by calling the loans we could acquire the pledged stock that secured them. We would own controlling interest and could elect our own directors, who would in turn elect our officers. We could simply force Malloy out.

Maybe it was a brutal way of doing business, but it was not uncommon.

Liz also cautioned us, though, that if Malloy left, his people would very likely leave, too.

"Something you must understand, Len," she said to me. "The chief asset of a technology-based company is its people. The chief asset is *brains*. Otherwise, you've got a lot of desks and chairs, plus some bins of components, and probably a small inventory of machines. Absent the people, the brains, the company is nothing. It's nothing like a smokestack industry, where the mill, the machinery, the trucks, and so on loom large on the balance sheet."

"The laser printer . . . ?"

"Great today. Obsolete tomorrow. I might put it another way—a big asset of a technology company is its *future*. They have got to have a vision of the future and keep working toward it." She grinned. "Some speech, huh, sweetie?"

I nodded. "Okay. What about the value of the name?"

"I'm not sure there will be any name without Malloy. And what if he travels around bad-mouthing the new management of his company? He could do that."

"That would hurt?"

"You wouldn't find any benefit in it."

I began to wonder if we should not back away from Sphere. The only one we'd be disappointing would be Zhang.

Plus Liz. I had to think of her. What good was a vice president of technology operations if we backed away from going into technology? And she was being honest. She could have put a more positive spin on the idea of acquiring Sphere, to save the new position she cherished so much.

There was no point in asking my father what to do. He knew nothing about technology.

I decided I had to have a second opinion. With the help of Hugh Scheck I identified a reputable professor at MIT and went up to meet with him.

His name was William Cable, professor of applied mathematics. We met at Boston's Logan Airport, where I arrived in the company Lear. He was a tall man, I judged about forty, with a pink face and a pink pate, which his sandy hair was rapidly abandoning. He wore round, gold-rimmed eyeglasses and a never-failing little smile.

I had arranged for a limo to take us wherever we wanted to go. I had supposed his office, but he suggested a seafood restaurant on the harbor. The driver knew where it was. In the car we exchanged pleasantries for a minute or so, and then I moved directly to the point. "Professor, I have come up from New York to pick your brains. I don't expect you to allow me to do that free of charge. Would a fee of one thousand dollars for this first meeting be satisfactory?"

He was all restraint. I think he would gladly have accepted a hundred, but he concealed his surprise perfectly. He nodded. "Yes. That will be entirely satisfactory."

I pulled from my jacket pocket an inexpensive but real leather black billfold. "For the time being, we can deal in cash," I said. There were ten one-hundred-dollar bills in the billfold.

He looked at them but didn't count them. He put the billfold in his own pocket and folded his hands in his lap. I knew he wouldn't report the thousand as taxable income. I'd have been disappointed in him if I learned he had.

"There is one more thing," I told him. "I should like for our conversation to be entirely confidential, including the fact that we met at all. You will see from our conversation that I am not involved in anything illegal or unethical. You will also see why I want it to be confidential."

He nodded and said nothing.

"My father, over the past forty years, has built a multibillion dollar corporation. Gazelle, Incorporated owns and operates the Cheeks stores and its catalog sales. Have you heard of us?"

His smile broadened. "I know about Cheeks shops. I've been your customer a few times over the years."

"Good. We are in the fortunate position of holding a lot of cash, which we need to invest. We also need to diversify. It has been suggested to us that we acquire Sphere, Incorporated, of Houston. I understand they make a fine laser printer but that their computer has become obsolete. What can you tell me?"

"Have you ever seen a Sphere computer?" he asked me.

"No, I never have. People talk about them in glowing terms, but I have never seen one."

"I'll show you one, later. A great many experiments were conducted in the early years of the technology. Many of the ideas weren't bad. But they failed for a variety of reasons, often for want of adequate financing. I could re-cite a litany of names: intelligently designed computers that failed."

"Sphere?" I asked.

"Well . . . looking at them from the outside, a computer is a computer: a beige box with a screen and keyboard. The Sphere was not sphere-shaped exactly, but it was rounded. It was not beige but made mostly of dark green transparent plastic, and you could see the parts inside: the circuit boards, transformer, rectifier, and so on. You could see the disks spinning. You could see the read heads mov-ing across the disks. Of course, that was the only visible movement in the computer. For the rest it was just invis-ible electrons speeding over the circuits and through the components. I don't know. Somehow it was exciting to think you could see the thing working.

"It's what we can't see that is really elegant," he said. "The circuit design. The redundancies."

"Redundancies?"

"If something fails, usually there is something behind it, ready to pick up the work and prevent a crash and loss of data."

"Why did the company fail? Why is the Sphere obso-lete?"

The professor looked out across the harbor, at white gulls soaring on the wind, at fishing boats going and com-ing, trailed by hopeful birds.

"Two reasons," he said. "Lack of capital and Tom Mal-loy's stubbornness."

"If we acquire the company," I said, "our plan is to use

its expertise to assemble microprocessors, chiefly using components we'll import from China."

"Where you can get them cheap, but—you hope—with acceptable quality."

"Exactly."

"And you'll put the Sphere name on the microprocessors," he added. "Not a bad idea. The wave of the future. The possibilities are endless. You get up in the morning in a bedroom at seventy-two degrees, bathe, dress, and go downstairs. The microprocessor senses that you have left the room and lets the temperature in the bedroom drift down to sixty. You go down to a kitchen where overnight the temperature has been as low as fifty, but when you walk in it is seventy-two. That's based on time, not that you've come into the room. You glance at the refrigerator door and see a printed inventory of what's inside. You decide to have eggs, and when you take the two out, the inventory goes down from eight to six. Your cooktop knows how you like your eggs and gives the right amount of heat for the right amount of time. When you are about ready to leave, you press a button that starts your car, to let it warm up. A sensor in the garage detects that an engine is running and opens the garage door to let out exhaust fumes. And so on. And that's just your house."

"Tom Malloy wants to build Sphere Four," I said.

Professor Cable nodded. "First he'll have to make his peace with Microsoft—which won't be all that difficult to do; the antitrust division would never allow Microsoft to refuse to license to him. But he'll have to give up his old dream of a proprietary operating system, no matter how good it might be. The investment in cash may not be formidable for you. But the commitment to marketing may be. You are experts at that. But selling computers will be a very different thing from selling ladies' undergarments."

"Have you ever heard of Elizabeth McAllister?" I asked.

"No."

"Well, you may. She is going to be our vice president, technology operations, and she may be calling on you. If she does, you have never talked to me. She may ask you to agree to a permanent consulting relationship with us, in which case it will really be me asking. Here is my card with my home phone number. If you need to talk with me for any reason, call that number. Also, here is my number in Hong Kong. We may be doing some more business."

"You want me to second-guess your young woman," he said. He was no simple academic but was a shrewd and perceptive man. I wished I could have hired him but knew I couldn't.

"This meeting has been very helpful to me, Professor. What you have told me confirms what my Chinese associate in Guangzhou says and what Liz McAllister says. Unless it's all just conventional wisdom, I think I'm hearing three knowledgeable people agreeing on basic points."

Now I called my father—when I could tell him I had three independent analyses that agreed.

"They sing from the same sheet, hey? Maybe that's because they're all members of the same fraternity."

I flew to Houston, this time leaving Vicky behind. She'd had enough of Houston and quite enough of Tom and Becky Malloy.

Liz did go with me, though, on the Lear. I had decided that her declaration that she loved me was as innocent as most of the things she said that were subject to misinterpretation. She said "I love you" almost—not quite—as casually as I might say "Good morning." We sipped champagne on the flight and talked business. We could see nothing from the windows but the tops of clouds.

After we had shared a bottle of champagne, her "I love you" took on a slightly different meaning than I had given it. "Anytime, Len," she whispered. "I don't expect you to want it . . . but anytime. No obligation attached."

"I'll remember that, Liz. But I won't be asking you."

I don't know what Malloy had in mind; maybe to overwhelm us with Texas hospitality. In any case, we found that he had our schedule worked out for us for our first evening in Houston. First we would take a dip in his pool, then eat some barbecue on his patio, and finally we were going to a rodeo.

"I bet you've never seen a rodeo," he said with enthusiasm so apparently genuine it was hard to believe it was not. "The best one is in Vegas, these days: the National Finals. Used to be Forth Worth. But you're gonna love this one."

But first we went swimming. Not having anticipated this at all, neither Liz nor I had brought swimsuits. No matter. The Malloys kept a supply on hand, all sizes.

Wearing a bikini was not good judgment for Liz, but that was all they had for women, not even one of our Cheeks oranges. She came out to the pool in as modest a bikini as they had. It didn't cover enough—which the Malloys pretended, at least, not to notice. She was a sport, though—a game young woman I had to admire. She swam strongly. And she could dive. Even when she had to pull up the bikini top after a graceful dive knocked it down around her belly, she was not conspicuously daunted.

We hadn't brought clothes suitable for a rodeo either. But the Malloys entertained people from all over the world and took them to rodeos. As with swimsuits, they had an assortment of clothes for rodeos. For me it was a pair of tight blue jeans, a lemon-yellow shirt with pearl buttons, a cowboy hat, and boots. For poor Liz it was a white satin blouse with a fringed suede vest, a cowboy hat, a pair of Guess jeans, and white lizard Mercedes boots.

The rodeo was a lot more fun than I had expected. We watched men ride bucking broncos, rope calves, and— what was most interesting to me—ride bulls. Among the women performers one of the most interesting was barrel racing, which required proficiency and courage. The performers were well known to the crowd, just as fans know baseball and football players, and they were judged by their skill and endurance.

Rodeo events were not for the faint of heart. Liz was sickened when she saw one bull rider thrown and trampled, suffering a broken arm before the rodeo clowns could distract the bull. The stench of manure bothered her sinuses. She confessed to me later that she found the crowd more interesting than the performers.

When we returned to the Hyatt Regency, she and I sat down for a final drink in the lobby bar.

"You deserve a bonus for tonight, Liz," I said to her.

"I can't remember ever being so goddamned humiliated," she said quietly.

"When in Rome, do as the Romans do," I said. "You'd have got stares if you had done anything differently."

When we went upstairs, we hugged and kissed lightly at her door. She smiled, opened with her key, and disappeared inside.

The next morning we sat down with Tom Malloy in his office. I opened the discussion by telling him what exactly Gazelle, Inc. planned for Sphere.

"We've been assured by some very capable people that microprocessors are going to become more and more important and that there will be a growing market for them. Sphere, Incorporated is very well situated to take advantage of that opportunity. You have expertise and a name. Sphere could become a major factor in microprocessing."

"We already make microprocessors," said Malloy. "What do you think makes the Sphere computer work?"

"I understand. It's another reason why your company is so well positioned to move in the areas my company is interested in."

"Components from China," said Malloy. "Do you want to name your Chinese partner?"

"We have no partnership with anyone in China. If we can move on this deal, our supplier will be Zhang Feng."

"I might have known," said Malloy. "Guangdong Micro-Technology—GMT."

"What do you know of Zhang and his company?"

"He's a young man who's made himself very rich very quickly, partly by theft, partly by *guanxi*."

"What's *guanxi*?" I asked.

"It's the grease that makes anything in China run well— that is, anything that does run well. It means 'pull,' or influence, often with bribery."

"I take it you don't much like him."

"He tried to sell us components. They didn't test well."

"I would expect you to test very thoroughly every single item that comes from Zhang," I said. "We won't accept and we won't pay for anything that doesn't pass."

"Am I expected to put GMT components in Sphere Four?"

"We haven't committed to fund Sphere four."

"Well, do commit. If you don't, I'll leave the company the minute you take over."

"We won't commit," I said, "until you come up with a business plan. We'll want the design and all the specifications for Sphere Four. We'll want a complete estimate of what it will cost to develop and build it, based on two assumptions: one, that you use GMT components, and two, that you don't."

"How soon do you want this?"

"I have to fly out to Hong Kong for a week or two. I'd like to see it when I come back. In the meantime, you can work with Liz."

Malloy smiled. " 'Vice President, Technology Operations.' She's the only computer scientist you have, isn't she?"

"I have others on a consulting basis."

"Obviously it will do me no good to try to convince you what an extraordinary machine Sphere Four will be. Okay, then. I will try to convince Liz."

"Convince her in writing," I said. "Convince her with documents I can show to others. And, incidentally . . . while we're on the subject, let me see what your plans are to prevent your laser printer from becoming obsolete. Let me have cost figures on that."

"I see I'm going to have to deal with bean counters," he said grudgingly.

I nodded. "Three separate people who don't know each other have described you to me as a genius but also as a stubborn and unrealistic egomaniac. Gazelle is ready, just about, to give you a major new infusion of capital. You had better get used to the idea that you won't be able to make major policy by the snap of your finger, just because *you* think it's a good idea. My father ran Gazelle that way when it was a small business. Even he can't do it that way anymore."

53

I flew back to Hong Kong, this time alone. Vicky and the kids stayed at home.

Vicky offered to send Maria with me, to take care of things in the apartments, but I said no. Maria was more important with the children. We had been assured that her Chinese was not accented, and she spoke it to little J. J. and Catherine. It was Cantonese, not Mandarin, but we were assured also that for the kids to learn a little Cantonese would help them when they studied Mandarin in earnest.

Anyway, we had contracted with a company to send personnel into the apartments twice a week, to dust and make certain all was in order. When I knew I was going out there, I called them, and they assigned a fulltime maid for the duration of my stay. When I arrived, the refrigerator and bar were stocked, the air conditioners were running, and the *South China Morning Post* lay on my dining table.

I had E-mail waiting: a message from Zhang Feng saying he would fly to Hong Kong at my convenience. I had a fax from Charlie Han, saying Bai Fuyuan would come down from Shenzhen on whatever date we suggested.

I had dinner with Charlie my first night in town. We ate in an excellent—and I mean *excellent*—Italian restaurant called Tutta Luna, which served Italian cuisine that would have met Vicky's approval. It was within walking distance of the apartments.

"What do you think of the merchandise Bai Fuyuan sent?" I asked Charlie.

"It's like a letter of recommendation, Len," he said. "If it wasn't first-class stuff he wouldn't have sent it to us. The question will be: Can he keep it up? Or will he? Does he intend to?"

"So what deal does he want?"

"He wants to manufacture Cheeks merchandise in China. He wants to sell much of it in China, but he wants to export much of it to the States, where it will enter the stock of Cheeks stores. He is willing to submit to our most rigorous standards of quality control, to allow our inspectors to look at every item individually."

"And of course he can manufacture cheap."

"Yes. Very cheap."

"And sell for—?"

"American prices. The profit will be immense."

"Are his Chinese customers going to be so stupid as to believe they are buying something that was manufactured outside China? That stretches credibility a little, doesn't it?"

"There is a way of making them believe it," said Charlie. "He sews the goods in Shenzhen, takes them to Guangzhou by truck, and loads the crates on Chinese ships. The crates bear stenciled signs saying the port of origin is Hong Kong or maybe even New York. No one cares about that. The shipping documents sealed to the crates say the port of origin is Guangzhou. In the port of Shanghai the crates are unloaded. The shipping documents, now unsealed, say the crates were put aboard the ship in Guangzhou. That makes the merchandise coastal trade. Legally, it has never been out of China, so it is not subject to tariffs. The inspectors tear off the documents, which are all *they* are interested in, and clear the crates to leave the ship. The merchandise arrives in warehouses here and there, in crates saying it came from Hong Kong or the States, and the labels sewn in the garments say they are Cheeks items, made in the U.S.A. or in Hong Kong."

"It's almost exactly what Zhang Feng wants to do," I said.

Charlie smiled. "They may very well be partners."

"It's a little too transparent, it seems to me," I objected.

"Well, there's a certain amount of *guanxi* involved."

"Okay. What about the merchandise he wants to send to the States?" I asked.

"The stuff comes from Shenzhen by truck. British inspectors look at the merchandise—and will until the Handover, after which the inspectors will be Hong Kong Chinese, whom we may expect will be a little more lax. It bears labels saying the articles were made in China and identifying a maker. In warehouses here the labels are changed to ones reading, like, 'Made in Hong Kong exclusively for Cheeks.' Coming in, the merchandise is valued as stuff manufactured in China, so it's quite cheap. Going out, it is Hong Kong merchandise, already worth three times as much. In the States you sell it for your regular prices."

"Will he also want us to shill for him in China?" I asked. "That's what Zhang wants."

"He will want you and your father to make one or two well-publicized tours of China, appearing in stores and on television, saying how happy you are that Cheeks merchandise is now available in China."

"And our way will be smoothed by *guanxi,*" I said sarcastically.

"Well . . . you will be endorsing merchandise made from Cheeks designs, to Cheeks standards, inspected by Cheeks inspectors. So, what's the problem?"

"There's a problem," I said. "It's called Jerry Cooper."

"And you will make a lot of money," said Charlie Han. For him that was the clinching argument.

* * *

Two days later Bai Fuyuan arrived from Shenzhen. He took a suite in the Kimberly Hotel in Kowloon and asked me and Charlie to have lunch with him and let him show us some more merchandise.

Kowloon is not my favorite part of Hong Kong. It is not, of course, on Hong Kong island but is across the harbor on the mainland. American tourists obsessed with the idea that Hong Kong is a shoppers' paradise go to Kowloon to be ripped off on Nathan Road.

The hotel, even so, was first class. Bai had a spacious suite—unfortunately overlooking, for the time being, an enormous scaffolding made of bamboo, on which workmen swarmed as they erected a twenty-story building. I had observed this before: that the Chinese put up bamboo scaffolding that looked flimsy but was, I was assured, as strong as scaffolding made of steel.

Bai wore again a white double-breasted suit, as he had the first time I met him. He welcomed us effusively and gestured toward a long table where an elaborate buffet luncheon had been spread for us. Three delicately beautiful Chinese girls stood behind the table. They poured and handed us flutes of champagne.

"The little girls speak very little or no English, I am afraid," Bai said to us. "Just point at anything that pleases you, and they will serve your plates."

The food was a curious mixture of Chinese and Western. There was caviar and foie gras but also little cups of shark's-fin soup and egg-white medallions flavored with birds' nest and crabmeat. I recognized these dishes. Others I did not.

We sat on two couches facing low tables, on which the girls placed our loaded plates.

"Enjoy, enjoy," said Bai. "While we eat, the girls will model some items for us."

He gestured, and two of the girls hurried away into a bedroom, leaving one to continue serving us.

After a moment one of the girls came out. She was wearing crotchless panties—it was our bestselling example of that item—and a bra with holes to show her little brown nipples. She was not a professional model, but she knew how to show off her body.

Bai spoke to her in Chinese, and she slipped out of the bra and panties and handed them to me, leaving herself standing quite naked.

"Can you see," Bai asked, "that these garments have been sewn to the very same standard you habitually use?"

I examined the items perfunctorily, then handed them to Charlie, who examined them critically. The girl stood there patiently, showing not the least sign of discomfort. Charlie handed the things back to her, and she walked to the bedroom.

This was repeated maybe twenty times. A girl would come out and model something, then she would take it off and offer it to be inspected, while she stood naked. We looked at panties, bras, nighties, teddies, G-strings. The girls also demonstrated Bai's ability to make fetishist items of leather and rubber. Looking at some of those items being modeled, I was actually sorry that every item was a knockoff on something offered in the Cheeks catalog.

"You see?" Bai said finally. "I am prepared to offer exact replicas of the things you sell, made to your standards of quality. But available for a fraction of what you pay."

Cued, I suppose, one of the girls came from the bedroom wearing an innovative design for a bra, consisting only of satin bands that stretched tightly under the breasts to lift them and thrust them forward—plus a G-string with a wide slit.

This girl's nipples had been pierced, and she wore little platinum rings in them.

"This you sell for thirty dollars," said Bai. "I can deliver you this item for four dollars."

Finally a model came from the bedroom wearing a garment I had never seen before, something we didn't sell in Cheeks shops. I don't know what to call it: a teddy, I suppose. Anyway, it was fabricated of small aluminum rings woven together after the fashion of medieval chain mail. Obviously it covered nothing. I supposed, too, it had to be quite uncomfortable; for example, the girl's butt would be marked with little ring indentations if she sat down. She, too, had pierced nipples, and platinum rings set with green stones hung from them.

"I suggest you stock this item," said Bai. "I can offer them to you for twelve dollars apiece."

"Very interesting," I said noncommittally.

Bai dismissed the model with a curt gesture. "So," he said. "Do you think we can do business?"

"On the basis of the quality of your merchandise, I see no reason why not," I said. "On the basis of your prices, that looks doable, too. The only element of the thing that troubles me is the . . . irregular ways we will have to operate to disguise the origin of the goods. Also, I am not sure I can persuade my father to visit China to promote them."

"Let us, then, set to work to resolve these minor problems," said Bai.

And that was where we left it.

Zhang Feng liked to take people for boat rides. It was a way to get his business associates isolated with him. This time—it was on a Sunday—he took Charlie and me aboard a chartered yacht much bigger than the one that had taken us to Lamma Island. Our destination was Lantau Island, an island larger than Hong Kong Island and even more mountainous.

The trip out took about an hour, from Hong Kong Central to Silver Mine Bay. The yacht was luxurious and carried for the day a buffet lunch comparable to the one Bai Fuyuan had spread for us in the Kimberley Hotel. Three girls in colorful microskirted, skintight dresses poured champagne for us.

The trip across the water was pleasant. A bracing wind blew, and the yacht plowed through three-foot seas. One of the girls began to show signs of motion sickness, and I went to her and explained to her how to avoid it.

"Stand up. Don't sit. Now flex your knees a little, opposite to the movement of the boat. When you're sitting, your whole body moves with every motion of the boat. When you stand and use your knees, you will move less than half as much, if at all."

She tried it and found it relieved her queasiness. From that moment she attached herself to me. Her name was Chang Li, and she was a diminutive, perfectly formed Chinese girl who spoke a bit of English. Her little dress was silk, emerald green, and fit like her skin. It was obvious she wore nothing under it. My eyes could trace the dent of her navel and the cleft of her behind.

We docked at Silver Mine Bay and went ashore to find a Mercedes limousine with driver waiting for us. Li sat close beside me.

Zhang wanted us to see the Po Lin monastery, high on a mountain on Lantau Island. It featured the world's largest outdoor sitting statue of Buddha, cast in bronze and one hundred ten feet tall. The statue was visible for miles. We could have left the car and climbed the stairs to its base, but we elected to view it from the limo.

We returned to the yacht, which eased out and began a leisurely circuit of the island, in generally smooth waters. Hong Kong's immense new airport was under construction on the north side of Lantau Island.

We sat on couches in the aft cabin. Li sat close to me. Zhang wanted to talk business.

"I am confident," I told him, "that we are going to acquire control of Sphere. We are going to have the problem you anticipated."

"Malloy," said Zhang.

"He wants to continue to build the Sphere computer.

That is to say, he wants to *resume* building it: a new version."

"That could be useful, if you are willing to invest the money."

"How so?"

"It will be Sphere Corporation's *signature* product, its *façade*, as we might say. If Sphere is once more known as the maker of a superior computer, that should facilitate sales of the Sphere microprocessors. And . . . the use of GMT components will enable you to manufacture the new computer at a price that will attract the market."

I smiled. "So we will need more GMT components. To incorporate in the computers."

Zhang returned my smile and nodded.

"Quality is the key," I said.

He nodded again. "Quality is the key."

The crew of the yacht laid out a dinner on a big table that was lifted from the floor in the main cabin. We sat down to a meal of Chinese delicacies—Li beside me as always.

"Would you like," Zhang asked, "to see Macau? It is an hour or so from here. The activity there will just be beginning. I can introduce you to the finest casinos."

"I love the casinos," said Charlie Han. This was something I had observed in the Chinese. They loved to gamble—from mah jong, on which some of them risked huge sums, to horse races, to cockroaches placed in a circle, the bet being on which one would leave the circle first.

"We can sleep on the boat. And have breakfast. It has accommodations."

I understood from that moment that "accommodations" was going to include Li in my bed. I had cheated on Vicky only once and very briefly, with Susan. But maybe this small, affectionate Chinese girl . . . whom I'd never see again.

I remember little about Macau. The casinos just didn't appeal to me. And, in anticipation of what was going to happen, my attention was fixed on Li. I decided I wanted her. I wanted her very much.

While the others were gambling, I quietly suggested to Li that we return to the boat. We were holding hands, and she squeezed my hand and nodded.

Our cabin was small but lavish. It had a bed and one upholstered chair, a telephone, television, and its own head, with shower. I suggested to Li that we shower together. She undressed immediately, and I held her and felt her smooth skin. She unzipped me and pulled out my cock, then pushed down my pants. We couldn't undress fast enough. My socks were still on my feet when I led her into the shower.

Under the stream of hot water, I knelt and introduced my tongue into her. It quickly found her tiny clit. She gasped, and I felt it harden. She urged me to stand, and when I did she seized my cock and pushed it into herself.

She was exquisite. I mean she was exquisite in her little body as well as in her ardor. She made love with me as though we were two kids just learning.

"Word in Chinese is *dew*," she said, "which means fuck. We fuck good, Len. We fuck very good."

I had to realize she had fucked many times before. Innocent as she looked and acted, she was a hooker.

I was glad, when I reflected on that. She was being paid for what she was doing. I would give her some more money. And we were establishing no relationship whatever. I would remember her. Maybe she would remember me for a while. For the money, I imagine, and for the fact that I had not been abusive. I was racist enough to wonder what Chinese men did to her.

When we left the boat, I hugged and kissed her. I hoped I would never see her again, but I was not going to be that lucky.

54

JERRY

Our neighbors had been right in telling us that alligators would climb the bank from the canal, nose up to our fence, and then slip back down to the water. Our neighbors to one side had no fence, and an occasional 'gator would reach the street and even enter our driveway. I was tempted to run one over with the car, but I was also told that wildlife fanatics would demand my prosecution.

On the other hand, Thérèse had cultivated the friendship of two or three great white herons. She bought chicken necks for them and tossed those out for the herons to feed on. They made no mess. They found the chicken necks on the grass by the pool and gulped them in one swallow. They flew away, did their business somewhere else, and returned—as if they knew better than to dirty the lawns of their benefactors. On the other hand, when they did not find their chicken necks when they thought they should have them they would peck on our glass doors and make a hell of a noise.

This is the kind of thing that held my attention in my retirement in Florida. Do I have to say I was bored? Well, I was, and no amount of fishing or bridge playing—which

Thérèse had gotten me into with a few neighbors—made me less bored.

Len came home from his latest trip to Hong Kong and flew down to meet with me. We sat on the lanai and watched Thérèse's herons—whom she had named Jake, Pierre, and Lizzie, God knew why—while we talked.

"The problem is, as I see it," I told him, "we are venturing into two situations where we don't know much and where we can take one hell of a beating."

"In the one," he said, "we are expanding into a field, technology, where we don't know much; and in the other we are expanding in a field where we know everything, but we will be doing it by joining a partner who wants to lie, cheat, and steal."

"In an area of the world where we are even more ignorant than we are in the area of technology," I said.

"We can repair our ignorance of technology," he said. "And of China, too."

"This Liz you've hired and that professor who is consulting can help us with that," I said. "Charlie Han knows something of the ways of China. But does he know enough?"

" 'In ways that are mean and tricks that are vain, the heathen Chinee are peculiar,' " Len recited from Bret Harte.

"Whatever that means," I said. I didn't know the quotation. I never did get much education.

"The Chinese will play by their own rules, some of which they will make up as they go along," said Len. "We have to count on that, whether we're dealing with Zhang or Bai."

"Well . . ."

"On the other hand," he said, "we can import computer chips with Chinese prices, inspect them thoroughly, test them, and install them on Sphere microprocessor boards, which Sphere can then sell at a price reflecting what we paid for the chips. It makes us highly competitive."

"That's Zhang's point, isn't it? So, what about Malloy's damned computer?"

"Zhang Feng thinks we should do it. Full of Chinese components, it will sell at an attractive price. If it's as good as he thinks Malloy is capable of making it, it will be a good front for our microprocessor business."

I was dubious. "On this one, I'm going to say it depends on how much money we have to put in it. You said that Zhang once said he'd put up the majority of it. Then he said twenty million—"

"Let's think of another point," said Len. "If we put up a majority of the dollars, we control Sphere. If Zhang puts up more than we do, *he* controls Sphere."

"Not necessarily," I said. "If Zhang puts up fifty million, he lends it to us, and we buy the stock. A fifty-million-dollar loan is not going to buy him any position in Gazelle."

Len smiled. "As Zhang always says, we can negotiate."

After Len went to bed in the guest room, I sat alone on the lanai, drinking a glass of red wine and pondering.

The night when Uncle Harry and Aunt Lila came to my family's apartment to tell me my father and mother had been killed, I was broke. That is, I would be shortly, because Harry and my girlfriend, whom he later married, would fuck me out of the few dollars I might have had from my father's life insurance, and some proceeds from his numbers running. I wasn't broke, but I was stupid and soon *was* broke.

I went to work for a pittance and had nothing but a pittance until things got worse—I was drafted. I might have died in combat but for my perforated eardrum that got me classified One-B: noncombatant. In the army I used my skills as a hustler, so that when the war ended I had a stash of money, a beautiful, loving girlfriend, and prospects. I got the North American franchise for Plescassier water, and Uncle Harry tried to fuck me out of that. With the help of guys like Frank Costello and Meyer Lansky I fucked Harry royally, to the tune of two million dollars.

The two million funded the Cheeks shops. From then on I was in the ladies' undergarments business, as Buddy scornfully put it sometimes; and by now I had so much money I could afford to risk, say, fifty million dollars on microprocessor chips. If I lost it all, it wouldn't break me, or even come near it.

But it was a very strange turn of fate. From selling sexy scanties I was going into a high-tech industry I knew nothing about. If Giselle had been alive she would have reminded me that when I went into lingerie I had known nothing about that, either. Or about marketing, which had proved to be the key. I'd had to learn.

Well . . . maybe I wasn't too old to learn something about this new field. Low-tech to high-tech!

I should have been more comfortable with the Bai Fuyuan proposition. There was nothing high-tech about that.

In the morning, Len and I talked about it.

"It troubles me," Len said, "that Bai Fuyuan and Zhang Feng offered almost identical propositions on manufacturing Cheeks goods in China and sneaking them out and back in again as Hong Kong goods."

"I did what you suggested on the telephone," I told him. "I had Middleton find out everything he could about Bai and Zhang, focusing on the possibility that they are some way associated. They could find no evidence of it—though God knows the Chinese could find ways to conceal that."

"I think there's another possibility," said Len.

"Which is?"

"That this way of doing business is so common that many operators do it. They are offering the same kind of deal because many rascals do it, and it is an accepted way of working."

"So what happens to the round-eyes who gets caught?" I asked.

"We'll have to shield ourselves."

"I suppose that can be worked out."

"Let's be clear about something more," Len said. "You've been in business for a long time and were around when things were done differently. Was it ever, in your observation, a common practice for businessmen to offer girls to sell their deals? I mean, offer girls' tails to soften up the guy on the other side of negotiations?"

I shook my head. "I have known it to happen. I couldn't say it was ever common." I frowned and tried to remember. "Yes, I've known it to happen. If you think that's because I'm so much older than you and was around when things were different, forget it. If anything, it's more likely today than it was in the 1950s."

"Well . . . Zhang Feng will set you up with a girl."

"You didn't . . . ?" I asked.

"No," Len said simply.

"I didn't think you were that dumb."

"The other real problem is," said Len, "are you willing to go to China and shill for Bai's merchandise?"

I shrugged. "What the hell?"

We decided to go to Houston again. Thérèse had been disappointed with it and was not interested in going this time. Vicky felt she should not leave the kids with Maria any more than was necessary and told Len go on without her. Both women had met Liz McAllister by then and were not concerned about their husbands traveling with her without their wives.

This guy Tom Malloy was something else again. And so was his wife, the one-time Oilers cheerleader. Hell, for that matter so was Texas something else again, and so was Houston, even if "there *are* no *Texans* in Houston."

The Malloys insisted we must be their guests in their suburban home, and so we wound up in three separate guest bedrooms—Malloy having, not very subtly, determined that neither Len nor I would want to share a bed with Liz. ("I mean, fellas, she's one *helluva* woman, ain't she? I got a sister about her size.")

Warned by Len, Liz and I brought along swimsuits and the kind of clothes we would need if we were badgered into going to a rodeo—everything but the hats, which we were willing to let the Malloys provide.

Even if it was a business meeting, the Malloys wanted to hold it around the pool, where we would sit sipping bourbon poured over chipped ice.

Len had taken Liz to a Cheeks shop in Manhattan and had her fitted into one of our international-orange swimsuits. There was nothing that girl could have done to conceal her bulk—and, dammit, I wouldn't have wanted her to; she was handsome in her way and should not have been made to feel she was flawed. The suit uncovered her hips and butt and stretched tight over other parts and left her looking . . . well, large, but with a grace in the way she carried herself.

Malloy had by now offered a business plan for building Sphere IV and bringing it to market. With American components strictly, it could not be sold for less than $2,895, bare. With GMT parts from China it could go on the market at $1,695, bare. With more RAM, whatever the hell that might be, and greater speed in its CPU, again whatever the hell that might be, it could come up to $2,895, but would then have what the computer community liked to call "blinding speed."

Malloy talked to Liz about "modems" and about "monitors" and about "CD ROM drives," which terms my son seemed to understand. I became more painfully conscious that a whole new world existed of which I was ignorant.

"Do you want to fly out to Hong Kong and go over to Guangzhou and see how he manufactures chips?" Len asked.

"Do you want to know what you're going to find?" Malloy asked. "Tell 'em, Liz."

"Guangdong Micro-Technology will be an office," she said. "Likely in an office that does a hundred other kinds of business. The chips come in from twenty or more little shops where people labor over designs to make the tiny CPUs. Zhang Feng has them under contract. He supplies a design from some genius designer who is paid little. The shop does the work. I've never been to China, but I understand this is how it works. It's a cottage industry, so to speak."

"A cottage industry in so sophisticated . . . ?"

"Once a design is made, making the chip is a matter of very tedious labor," she said.

"Americans," said Malloy, "automate the making of chips. But automation costs money. When you have, as they have in China, an endless supply of labor, you have much less need to automate."

"Well," I said. "Tell me the downside of this. If their chips pass muster, why not use them?"

"Why not?" said Malloy. "The only thing that bothers me is that we may become *dependent* on these Chinese chips. What if Zhang Feng doubles his price a year from now?"

"Easy enough, I think," said Len. "If Zhang doubles his price, we buy from someone else. I'd bet Bai Fuyuan can supply the same. If not he, someone else. Once we enter the market, we'll get proposals from all sides."

"Quality, quality, quality, darling," said Liz. "Everything must be tested, tested, tested. I'd raise our estimated price on machines with Chinese components to include the cost of quality control."

Len told me I was lucky the Malloys didn't insist on dragging us off to a rodeo. Instead, as the sun set, guests began to arrive, and we were to be subjected to a Texas-style pool party, with barbecue.

I'm going to say something first about the barbecue. I'm not entirely sure how they did it. An immense piece

of beef—a whole side—was put in a pit where wood
smoldered and generated heat. The meat cooked slowly
for a very long time; it was cooking all the time we sat
at the pool talking business, at least. It was ready when
we were ready, and I have never eaten anything better—
though it makes a Jewish boy from Brooklyn blush to
admit it. The Chinese should learn to do Texas barbecue.
And to make the sauce.

It was served on handsome plastic plates from Neiman
Marcus, with baked beans, corn on the cob, and all the
potato salad or coleslaw you could pile on. With frosted
schooners of ice-cold beer. It was lucky we were in swimsuits and by the pool, because our monogrammed napkins
were sometimes defeated by our dribbling, and we could
best clean ourselves with a plunge in the pool.

The guests were Texans, even if there were supposed
to be none in Houston. It was amazing to see how many
men had found football cheerleaders for wives. Malloy
was not alone in that, though he was fortunate in having
found one with brains. They walked around in their
skimpy bikinis and open-toed-high-heeled shoes, cowgirl
hats, and gaudy gold jewelry.

Well, not all. I didn't see a woman who would have
been taken for a matron back East. But some bikini-clad
women had about them a certain hard-bitten charisma,
suggesting that money didn't buy you out of every disappointment.

Texas is a hardscrabble place, and the bar girl who had
said there were no Texans in Houston had been wrong,
but had known what she was talking about.

A man with too much beer in him came on to Liz. I
watched him pat her on the fanny and talk quietly to her.
Unhappily, she was flattered by the attention and tolerated
him. Starved for attention, she let him fondle her. And
then . . . I don't know what he said, though it was easy to
guess; she stiffened and said something definite to him.
He slinked away.

I kept an eye on Liz after that. The big, gawky girl was

out of place and visibly uncomfortable. She wandered around the pool, finding it difficult to join in conversations.

I took a little concern in the amount of beer Liz was drinking. I tried to get Len's attention but couldn't without being noticeable. Finally I went to her side.

"Liz, how ya doin'?"

" 'Kay, Jerry. Thanks for asking."

"Are you as bored as I am?" I asked her.

"Probably worse," she answered.

Gently, I took her beer mug from her hands and set it aside on a table. She looked at me quizzically but said nothing. I guided her away from the party crowd, to a white-painted wrought-iron bench at the edge of the light and beyond the reach of the talk. We sat down and were silent for a few minutes, just watching the party, where by now people had begun to push each other into the pool.

Liz began to glance at me—to glance, in fact, back and forth between me and the party. And finally she broke our silence.

"Jerry," she asked solemnly, "would you like a nice blow job?"

I was stunned and for too long a moment was unable to answer.

"I mean it," she said quietly. "I'd enjoy going down on you. I really would enjoy it."

I drew a deep breath. "Is it a good idea, Liz?" was all I could think of to say.

"It's a damned good idea. I do it very well, I've been told."

"I'm surprised that you do it at all."

"Huh! If you're me and you don't want to be lonely, you do it. The word got around at the university— Michigan—that Liz McAllister would suck cocks. I had dates after that. Of course, that's all they wanted." She sighed, deeply, audibly. "I just didn't want to be lonely," she whispered tearfully.

"You want to come with me to my room?"

"Yes . . ."

"And sleep with me?"

"Yes."

"Okay. But you don't have to give me a blow job. You aren't going to be alone tonight, but you don't have to do . . . anything."

We went to my room and to my bed. There, slipped under my door, I found a telegram. It was from Hugh Scheck.

FORGIVE THE QUAINT METHOD OF COMMUNICATION. HAVE BEEN UNABLE TO REACH YOU BY PHONE OR FAX. I KNEW YOU WOULD WANT TO KNOW ASAP THAT BUDDY HAS BEEN SHOT. HE IS IN LINCOLN HOSPITAL IN CRITICAL CONDITION AND IS ASKING FOR YOU.

Hugh met me at LaGuardia, and by the time we reached the hospital he had briefed me on what had happened. Buddy was the victim of a drive-by shooting. The police thought it was not a random shooting but was meant to kill him specifically.

As we rode in a cab to the hospital, I suppose Hugh found me oddly silent. I was thinking about Buddy, specifically about the day I met him. I was working in Uncle Harry's store, and Buddy wandered in as if by chance. He made small talk, and quickly I realized that this street-smart guy was offering friendship. I couldn't imagine why. Two guys couldn't have been more different. But at that time in my life I was happy to have anyone offer friendship.

We reached the hospital. The doctors just shook their heads, but they let me in to see him.

I had to remember that Buddy was five to seven years older than I was and so was in his late seventies. He lay there attached to tubes and was a terrible reminder of how the human body can be reduced from everything to nothing in one cruel moment.

I spoke his name.

He opened his eyes and looked at me.

"I'm told it's gonna be okay," I lied.

"B'lieve *that* y'believe in the tooth fairy," he muttered. He sighed. It was a rattle. "But I been layin' here, half dreaming, and my mind goes back to Paris. Those were good days, weren't they? Giselle . . . and Thérèse . . . and Ulla. You fucked Giselle's little sister and wound up married to her. Those were good days."

"Every day I ever spent with you was a good day, Buddy," I whispered tearfully. "You saved my life, you know. When Chieppa and Filly tried to kill me, I used what you taught me: how to cut with a razor. How many times did you make me practice that move?"

"You were a good kid, but you weren't smart. I tried to make you smart."

"Why? Why did you want to do that for me, Buddy?"

"I gotta tell ya somethin'. I'm glad you got here in time."

I sobbed. "Nobody ever had a better friend, Buddy . . ."

"Not so good as you think. That's what I gotta tell ya."

"Buddy . . ."

"Your father and mother were killed on the Jersey Pike," he whispered hoarsely. He shook his head faintly. "No accident. They were forced off the road by a truck. It was a hit."

"You mean they were murdered?" I asked, shocked.

"Yeah . . . They were murdered. *By me.* I was drivin' the truck. I'd been paid good. I rammed that truck against their back bumper and made your father drive faster. Then I pulled out and nudged him off the road, through the guardrail and into the water. I'd picked the spot."

"Buddy!"

"Then I heard about you and came to meet you, and saw what I'd done. You were . . . so goddamned innocent. And bein' fucked every which way. That's why I tried to be your friend—to save you from that son of a bitch!"

"You mean the man who hired you to kill my parents was—"

"Right. He lied, he cheated, he stole. Hell, he even married your girl, Kitty, after he knew she'd got her claws on all your money."

"Uncle Harry?!"

Buddy nodded weakly. "Uncle Harry. . . . Well . . . A long time later . . . Uncle Harry hated you and was still plotting to have your ass. I fixed it so Harry wouldn't have anybody's ass anymore. That move I made you learn."

"*Buddy!* My God, Buddy!"

He closed his eyes. "I'm sorry, Jerry. About your father and mother. I'm so goddamned sorry! I'm even sorry I kept the secret all these years. I should have told you. The secret has been a brick in my stomach for fifty years."

I sat with him until the end, thinking of all the days and all the years. He said nothing more. In an hour he was gone.

55

LEN

We acquired controlling interest in Sphere, Incorporated. Zhang Feng put up $25 million in the form of a loan to Gazelle, Incorporated. Gazelle bought up Sphere's debt and took its hypothecated stock for a total of $75 million—meaning of course, that we put in $50 million. Though Gazelle owed Zhang $25 million, he acquired none of the Sphere stock. Gazelle had total control of Sphere.

Zhang asked for two seats on the board of directors, so his representatives would be present at meetings and could keep him fully informed. This presented no problem. There were nine directors: Tom Malloy, Jerry Cooper, Len Cooper, Vicky Cooper, Roger Middleton, Hugh Scheck, and . . . My father surprised me. He suggested Liz McAllister be elected to the board. I agreed, and she was elected. Zhang's two directors were Vincent Lowe, a vice president at Marine Midland Bank, and Professor Du Jin of Columbia University.

My father was elected the chairman of the board. I was elected the chief executive officer. Malloy was elected president and chief operating officer.

All of this meant, of course, that Tom Malloy lost control of Sphere, absolutely. He would run it as we prescribed.

On the other hand, it meant Sphere's entire debt was retired, and it was in a position to borrow again to finance the new things it was going to do. Texas banks were happy to lend money to the newly and surprisingly solvent Sphere, Incorporated, and we let the Texas banks do the financing. Except that one significant loan came from the Bank of Hong Kong and Shanghai.

Professor William Cable became a permanent consultant to Sphere. With Liz McAllister, he examined every element of the designs Malloy came up with.

I found myself affected by Tom Malloy's enthusiasm about Sphere IV. We would earn more revenue from our microprocessors, at least initially, but Sphere IV might in time become another Cheeks. If for no other reason, it would be a handsome stylishly ultra-sleek computer, not a beige box.

I was thirty-six years old. My father was seventy-four. Vicky was fifty-four. We had a seven-year-old daughter, Catherine, and a five-year-old son, J. J. Anthony Lucchese was twenty-six, had his MBA, and was installed as heir apparent at Interboro Fruit.

Anthony was an intelligent businessman and began to suggest to Vicky that Interboro should begin to diversify. Diversification was a buzz word in business now. He wondered if Interboro should not buy into Sphere. Vicky said no, for the moment anyway.

My children were a joy. With Maria's assistance and Vicky's encouragement, both of them could say simple things in Chinese. That made it easier for us to contemplate returning to Hong Kong. On the other hand, it was difficult to contemplate a peripatetic life, living in New York eight months of the year and Hong Kong four. Catherine had to go to school.

Our options were limited. I would go out to Hong Kong

and stay as long as I needed to, leaving my family behind, or we would all go to Hong Kong and would have to stay there long enough for Catherine to complete a school year.

The Handover had occurred by now. Charlie Han and others assured me that life in Hong Kong was little changed, that the Beijing government had not imposed tyranny and showed no sign of intending to.

The decision was business-driven. We needed someone on the ground in the Far East if we were to do there the things to which we were committed and which we planned.

So we decided. We would move into our apartments in Hong Kong and stay there nine or ten months.

Charlie was right. The place had not changed much. The principal change I noted at first was that the new airport was open and was as efficient as any airport in the world. Downtown, we noted chiefly the absence of the Union Jack. The flags of China and Hong Kong flew. The police were the same men and women who had been police before. The difference was that they no longer wore crowns for insignia but badges of red, with stars.

Hong Kong remained one of the best-run cities in the world, with quiet, expeditious subways, fast-running traffic, a telephone system par excellence, modern new buildings dominating everything, air-conditioning overcoming the subtropical heat . . . I had come to like the place, in spite of the fact that I could speak only a few words of Chinese.

We enrolled Catherine in a school in Kowloon that was run by Jesuits. They quietly accepted the fact that she was of Jewish heritage and said they would not try to influence her to become Christian. At her age she could not travel on the subway alone, so I leased a Toyota and hired a driver.

So . . . the first problem was to deal with Bai Fuyuan.

* * *

He asked me to come to Shenzhen this time. I went, with Charlie Han. The train trip from Kowloon Station was easier this time—easier in that we made a much quicker exit from Shenzhen Station. I had to wonder if the Chinese government had not made the passport ordeal at Shenzhen more difficult when Hong Kong was a British colony than it was now that Hong Kong was a province of China.

We met Bai Fuyuan in an exclusive club. Once again he was wearing a white suit, as he had the first time I met him. We were served champagne and slices of fruit by stark-naked little girls. I began to suspect that he had been in touch with Zhang Feng and knew that I had succumbed to the charms of Chang Li.

But now he wanted to talk business. We moved slowly toward an agreement. I wanted to start with the merchandise that would go to America.

"I must ask you, Mr. Bai, hasn't the new relationship between China and Hong Kong made our arrangements more difficult?"

"To the contrary, Mr. Cooper. And, incidentally, there is no longer any reason to speak about differences between Hong Kong and China. It is all China now. The Brits could be stiff-necked. We Chinese know how to do business."

"*Guanxi,*" I suggested.

"*Guanxi,*" he agreed with a modest smile. "In the States there used to be a cliché, I believe. 'One hand washes the other.' So . . . the whole point is, how can we make a mutually satisfactory profit?"

"You spoke once of selling us microchips," I said.

Bai turned down the corners of his mouth and shrugged. "I can do better business selling you sewn merchandise. I know that business better, as do you."

I wondered if this didn't mean he knew Zhang Feng had gotten the microchip contracts. I wondered if the two of them did not work together. I also had to wonder if we were in the grip of two Chinese bandits.

"Have you considered the suit made with the aluminum links?" he asked.

He pointed a finger, said something in Chinese, and one of the girls trotted off toward another room. I knew she would return momentarily wearing the teddy made of aluminum chain mail.

"I think it would have a limited market, owing to the fact that it has to be uncomfortable to wear."

"But, Mr. Cooper. Is it not uncomfortable to wear the handcuffs, leg irons, and other restraint articles that you sell?"

"You have a point," I admitted.

When the girl returned she was wearing the aluminum-ring teddy. I had to admit it was erotic.

"I gave you a price of twelve dollars," said Bai. "On reflection, I think I would have to ask fourteen. I believe you can sell it for thirty or forty dollars, maybe more. You might invest in, say, a hundred dozen. I wager you will sell them in four months."

"Sell me a hundred dozen at your original price of twelve dollars, and if I sell them in four months or so and re-order, I will take them at fourteen."

Bai smiled broadly. "You might be . . . Chinese," he said. "You might be . . . Chinese."

"That raises another point," I said. "If I am going to do business in China, I must learn something of the language. Shall I learn Cantonese or Mandarin? My children are learning Mandarin."

"Let me urge you to learn Cantonese," he said. "It is not the language of government. It is much the language of business. Then . . . in time you can learn Putonghua as well."

Putonghua was the official name of Mandarin Chinese, the official language of China.

He smiled again. "Do you like our little Xin there? I can offer her to you as an instructor in Cantonese. She can instruct in the Glorious Positions as well."

"My wife, who is with me in Hong Kong now and will be in Hong Kong as long as I will, might object to little Xin."

He nodded. "Then, sir, can we talk about your father and you appearing in China to endorse our merchandise?"

The first show for the endorsement of merchandise was held in Guangzhou, in what was called the Friendship Store.

My father did not come out to the Far East for that show. I went, accompanied by Vicky.

Vicky and I were treated as royalty. We were delivered to the store in a Mercedes limousine and escorted immediately to a lounge, where we were treated to champagne and caviar.

We went with a high degree of skepticism. Although I had seen Guangzhou and stayed there in a luxury hotel, I could not imagine the opulence of the Friendship Store. Though a great many of its customers were obviously foreign, the great majority were Chinese. To all appearances, anyone could enter and shop there.

Floors that were not marble were parquet. People moved up and down on quiet, slow-moving escalators. The lighting was subdued and colored to display merchandise at its best advantage. The merchandise was mostly western—Gucci, Bruno Magli, Hèrmes, Versace, Rolex. . . . Girls in blue blazers and gray skirts hovered over customers and offered service. Each girl spoke perfect English, more often American-accented than British English. Others—sometimes the same ones—spoke Japanese. The only suggestion that this was China was in the photo identification badges they all wore.

Bai, obviously, was proud of the Friendship Store. He was like a child with a good report card.

"This kind of merchandising is growing in China," he said. "We have stores like this in Beijing, Shanghai, Shenzhen, Chongquing, and many other cities. The young people shop here. They have money to spend and are good customers."

He took us to a large room furnished chiefly with couches and low tables. A cast-bronze sign by the door said:

CHEEKS
Intimate apparel

It said the same in Chinese characters, also.

On the side of the room opposite the door stood a platform some two feet above the floor, carpeted and brilliantly lighted by spots in a track overhead. It was the stage for the models.

Two television cameras in the far corners of the room were ready to tape the show.

Men and women sat on the couches, sipped champagne or tea, and nibbled on slices of fruit. Most of them were Chinese, though a few looked Japanese, and there were half a dozen westerners in the room, one or two of them American.

Bai escorted Vicky and me and Charlie Han to a couch near the stage. He handed Vicky and me two sets of small earphones, which were attached to boxes small enough for me to stick mine in my outside jacket pocket. We would hear a translation of what would be said in Chinese, Bai explained. He pointed to what he called a projector high above the stage and explained that it would transmit sound to our receiver boxes by means of infrared light. He told me to take the box out of my pocket and let it lie on my lap, where its sensor would receive the signal.

Bai Fuyuan opened the style show. He introduced the deputy governor of Guangdong province, then the mayor of Guangzhou, then Vicky, then Charlie Han, and finally me.

The lights in the room dimmed to brownish-yellow, leaving only the stage brightly lighted.

The first model to appear wore one of our international-orange swimsuits: a Cheeks signature item. Bai so described it. He said it was seen on beaches and at pools everywhere in America and Europe.

The next model showed a sheer black catsuit stitched with floral lace. After that came a teddy of similar material, to which garters were attached to hold up the model's dark stockings. Then a series of bra-and-panty sets.

I was curious to know how far Bai would go. During an initial show at home we did not show everything we sold.

Bai Fuyuan did. He showed bras with holes to display the nipples. He showed panties with slit crotches. Two of his models were shaved and showed their inner parts when they modeled slit panties.

Then he had his models show items we never showed but only sold in private rooms in our shops—fetishist items: handcuffs, leg irons, leather collars fastened with padlocks, rubber-ball gags . . .

The people on the couches nodded solemnly, whispered comments to each other, and tittered.

Bai's commentary came through my headphones in English, loud and clear. I heard him say, "Before we show you our final item, I want to introduce an honored guest to say a few words. We are able to sell Cheeks merchandise in China by the courtesy of the officers and directors of Gazelle, Incorporated, which owns the Cheeks line. May I present Mr. Len Cooper, the president of Gazelle."

Bai had earlier presented me a text and suggested I use it. I didn't. I simply acknowledged the presence of the two dignitaries, thanked the audience for coming, and said how very glad we were to be able to offer our merchandise to Chinese customers. I said I hoped they would always be pleased with anything they bought from us and invited them to return anything they found defective, for a full refund.

Bai winced at that last. He had anticipated no such thing.

And now the finale of his style show. "You all remember pretty little Ling," he said. "She modeled several items for you. As did Lufeng. They will now demonstrate the value of one more item we will make available."

Ling, a tiny Chinese girl who could not have been older than seventeen, stark naked, blindfolded and gagged, was led to the stage by Lufeng, herself naked but for a tiny white G-string and a white nippleless bra. She carried a cat-o'-nine-tails. A heavy black leather collar was padlocked around Ling's neck. A strap from that collar ran down her back to leather cuffs that were locked around her wrists, pinning her hands together and behind her. Her nipples were pinched by clamps, with a chain running between them. Lufeng wore the nipple clamps, too.

Lufeng gave Ling a firm slap on the rear, and the little girl bent forward. Lufeng swung the cat. It swished audibly through the air and smacked Ling's hinder cheeks with a sickening jolt. The little girl grunted through the rubber ball of her gag.

Lufeng swung again. Ling moaned.

"It is sufficient," said Bai. "You see the point. Some love to receive the blows. Ling does, believe it or not. Some would rather give them. Lufeng would. This kind of merchandise will be available to our more adventurous customers."

The six models all came out then and showed themselves to the assembly, all of them absolutely naked. Little Ling received a round of applause.

Vicky allowed herself to be escorted through a round of dinners and cocktail parties and a second show, this one in Shenzhen. She smiled on cue, said nothing, and accepted gifts that included earrings of the finest dark green jade. She accepted and wore a cheongsam: an exquisite dress made of emerald-green silk embroidered with gold and silver thread. It fit like water poured over her body. Its collar reached her ears. The skirt reached below her knees, but it was slit almost to her hip. She was spectacular in it.

After one of these events, when we had been home ten minutes, Vicky spoke.

"I haven't said a fuckin' word. Every word we spoke in those hotel rooms was recorded. But I don't think they've got *this* place bugged, so I can tell you what I think."

"What do you think, honey?" I asked.

"I think you can't do business with those people. I think sooner or later the shit's gonna hit the fan."

"Like . . . ? Meaning . . . ?"

"You ever bang one of those models?" she asked.

I shook my head emphatically.

"I can live with that. I'm your wife, I'm the mother of your kids, and so long as you don't get it in your head to leave home for some Chinese whore I can understand your fucking one now and then. But I'll bet you something. If you ever did, you're on videotape. Those guys are not stupid. Nothing happens without a purpose. 'Let's go to the videotape!' "

"Maybe I'm naive," I conceded.

"I doubt that," said Vicky grimly. "But they don't supply you with whores for nothing. These Chinese bastards don't do *anything* for nothing. But they've got a big surprise coming when they show a tape like that to me."

"Vicky—"

She kissed me. "When they do, I'm gonna say, 'Too fuckin' bad. Don't show me this shit. I don't care.' "

I shook my head. "They wouldn't."

"Hey, Len. You think you know everything? Okay. Maybe you oughta be wiser. I'm gonna tell you something you don't know. Your father made his bones some years back. Not too long ago, either—maybe ten years ago. Before you and I met. A guy and a gal tried to kill him. They sleep with the fishes. That's a silly cliché nobody really uses. But that pair do. They tried to kill your dad, and they got eaten by sharks. Or . . . apparently they did. They disappeared in Florida and were never seen or heard from again."

I can't say how shocked I was. I knew Vicky wouldn't lie about such a thing. I also knew she had sources of information.

"I've just proved something to you, my darling," she said. "You can't rely on promises."

"From whatever source," I said bitterly.

"Okay. The world is the world, Len. What I'm telling you right now is that you can't rely on those Chinese operators. Cover your ass, Len. Cover your ass, because they're gonna cover theirs, for damned sure, and they'll take the first opportunity to steal you blind."

"You telling me to back out?"

"No, I'm not telling you to back out. I'm telling you not to trust them."

"You're telling me not to trust anybody, not even you. Isn't that what you're telling me?

"Trust me? Well . . . *I've told you.* I've trusted you. I do trust you, lover."

"What do you mean by that?"

"I promised your father I would never tell what I've just told you." She shrugged. "I lied to him. I didn't know I was lying to him when I said that, but . . . Don't tell your father what I said to you about Florida. Okay? Don't ever mention that to him."

"All right," I said.

I suppose I was as depressed that night as I have ever been—ever, anyway, since I was given the news of the death of my mother. When we were in bed, Vicky did that thing for me that she alone could do; she sucked my entire scrotum and testicles into her mouth and held them there, licking and warming them, until I could think of nothing else but what she was doing. She was eighteen years older than I was, and I suppose Chang Li was eighteen years younger, but Vicky was the artist Li would never be.

56

Tom Malloy and Liz McAllister pronounced themselves satisfied with the chips coming to us from China. Guangdong Micro-Technology, GMT, proved capable of producing chips that consistently met every test. The tests were beyond my comprehension but not beyond my understanding that *they worked,* which was what counted, so far as I was concerned.

Malloy designed the Sphere IV and put it out for beta testing. He took it to national trade shows and let the computer types play with it. It got good notices in the trade journals. There was a half-breathless anticipation for it, something like what there had been for Windows 95 before it shipped.

All I knew was, it was a handsome machine. And, more important, it ran Windows, not just a Malloy proprietary operating system. That would make all the difference.

The merchandise from Bai Fuyuan was generally good. Charlie Han inspected it in Hong Kong before it was shipped to the States. He rejected an occasional batch of items, but on the whole the lingerie was put together well from high-quality fabrics. Charlie Han knew fabrics, and he knew stitching. We were lucky to have him.

The only real problem we had was with colors. For some odd reason, Bai's people could not exactly match our colors. That is, he could not match the colors used by our Hong Kong makers.

Okay . . .

We were doing business as we had planned. The legalities of some parts of it were mysterious, but we relied on Hong Kong solicitors to steer us. The merchandise was made in China and shipped to Guangzhou or Hong Kong without labels. In those two cities labels were sewn in saying the merchandise was made in Hong Kong, some of it in the United States. Shipments to the States—merchandise with Hong Kong labels—went out as air cargo. When it arrived in the States, import tariffs were paid. Shipments from Guangzhou went up the coast and were delivered at various Chinese ports, chiefly Shanghai. The labels on the merchandise said it had been made in Hong Kong. The shipping documents said it had been made in China and was being shipped only in coastal trade.

I asked my father to come out to Hong Kong. I wanted him to see the Friendship Store in Guangzhou, and Bai wanted him to be present for the opening of our two shops in Beijing. He insisted that an appearance by Jerry Cooper was important.

One reason why he did not want to come was that Therèse did not want to. She had settled into a comfortable life in Florida, fishing, playing bridge, and feeding her herons; and it was true that the flight out and back was an ordeal, even for younger people, even if they did travel in the first-class section.

Reluctantly, my father agreed to make the trip alone. He sounded weary on the telephone, and I was tempted to tell him to forget it, that he was entitled to his relaxation.

Imagine my surprise when I met him at the new airport and found him not alone. Liz was with him.

"She wants to see how Zhang makes chips," he explained. "So, it occurred to me that she could come with me and ease some of the burden of travel."

My father was full of surprises for me always. He casually announced that Liz would not be going to a hotel but would share his room in the second apartment.

She had brought with her a Sphere IV. She hooked it up in my apartment office and shortly had it doing impressive things. I'd learned a lot about computers before leading our company into making the commitment it had made, but Liz was a computer guru and could make the machine do things I didn't know any machine could do.

"Look, honey," she said to me, leaning over me and brushing me with her oversized breasts. "This one is set up with both Microsoft Word *and* Corel WordPerfect."

I knew that was important. Loyalists for both programs wanted to see documents formatted for their choice between these major word processors. To do that, the Sphere had to have a lot of RAM: a lot of memory, plus a capacious hard drive. What was more, this computer ran at six hundred megahertz, which was about as fast as any desktop could then run—what the advertising copywriters liked to call "blinding speed." Of course, I knew that today's blinding speed would be a crawl tomorrow.

My father watched quizzically, without total interest, as Liz demonstrated the Sphere and then turned it over to me. He didn't pretend to know what we were talking about. He had pronounced himself too far along in life to learn a whole new science.

He was no innocent, though. At the end of his second day in Hong Kong he took me aside in my apartment office and asked me a pointed question.

"How much are we paying Charlie Han?"

"A hundred twenty thousand," I said. "Plus perks."

"Do his perks include that Mercedes? That's one hell of a luxury car."

"No. We've known all along that he was doing some business on the side."

"All I want to know is, is he competing with us? Or worse, is he cheating on us? You know, he could be putting his imprimatur on merchandise that does not in fact meet standards."

I nodded. "Are we getting complaints? Are the customers back home . . . ?"

"No. Well . . . it would take time. But no. We've had no complaints about the merchandise. But I can walk into a store and tell immediately what was made in Hong Kong and what in China. It's good stuff. It's correctly sewn. But the colors are all a little off."

"I've noticed that," I said.

"I wonder," said my father, "if Bai Fuyuan doesn't have some reason for that. I mean, he can walk into any store, anywhere, and know what part of the stock came from him."

"I tend to trust Charlie Han," I said.

"I've got good reason to trust him," said my father. "He committed perjury for me, one time."

"But it's a slippery business. I lose sleep over it."

Liz went over to Guangzhou to meet Zhang Feng and see his shops. Charlie sent along a young Chinese woman to be Liz's interpreter.

Bai Fuyuan wanted us to be in Beijing for the opening of the first Cheeks shop there. Liz very much wanted to see Beijing and said she would pay her own expenses to go there. So it was arranged that she would fly from Guangzhou to Beijing and meet us there. I knew, of course, that my father would take care of her expenses.

She already had her visa for visiting China. We had to obtain ours and so had to go to the Chinese travel agency, be photographed, and fill out our applications. Two days later we returned to pick up our passports with the visas stamped inside.

Before we left for Beijing, Zhang Feng appeared in Hong Kong and offered us a boat ride. We agreed to go. The boat would circle Hong Kong Island and stop for a fish dinner on Lamma Island. We would have a good time, he promised.

Zhang was conspicuously taken aback when he discovered that my wife was with me. He had brought along three little girls. He had planned that we should have a good time.

At least he had the sensitivity not to bring Chang Li.

Or maybe she was not available.

"I had supposed," I said to Zhang, "you would stay in Guangzhou and escort Liz McAllister to your shops."

"This I did for two days," he said. "Your young woman asks many questions."

"Good," I said. "That's her job."

"She is a very intelligent young woman."

He did not offer a run to Macau or an overnight stay on the boat. We were at home before midnight.

I wish, though, that I had known who owned the boat we were on that evening.

We flew from Hong Kong to Beijing—my father, Vicky, and I, with Charlie Han—and landed on an airport that did little credit to the People's Republic. We were treated courteously and efficiently and moved to our waiting limousine with no trouble, but the airport terminal was shabby. Someone told me later that they are building a new one. I hope so.

The drive to our hotel was uninteresting, on an expressway that might have been seen in Los Angeles except the Chinese characters on the signs—which were also in English.

Our hotel was the Sheraton Great Wall. It was even more opulent than the hotels in Shenzhen and Guangdong.

Even so, it told me something about China: There was a serious unemployment problem there. The hotel was overstaffed. We would observe that one little girl did nothing all day but run a dry mop over the marble floors of the lobby. Twenty minutes after she had mopped a given area, she would be back to do it again. You could not press an up or down button to call an elevator. A young man in blue blazer would do that for you. You could not press the button for your floor. He would step in and do that for you. On your floor you could not take an ice bucket to the ice machine. You hardly got out your door before someone in blue blazer would appear to take it for you.

Liz was there, luxuriating. She moved into my father's room, rather than him moving into hers. The hotel staff noticed. When they returned to their room at night, *two* servings of hot water and *two* sets of tea bags would be waiting.

Liz introduced my father to ginseng tea. He acquired the taste, as I had.

The first Beijing store would be in the Sheraton Great Wall hotel, in a mall just off the lobby. It was far more open than any Cheeks store in the States. People strolling along the marble-floored corridor would have a full view of the merchandise, the clerks, and the customers. In fact, there was no door, no windows; the store was open to the mall, and it would be open twenty-four hours a day.

The store was already open and doing business, even though we were there for its official opening.

I suppose I have to admit that we remained coy about our inventory. We still kept what we thought of as bolder items—especially fetishist things—halfway concealed. The Chinese were realistic. If a pair of panties was attractive and might sell, they displayed it, no matter that it had no crotch at all. Mannequins stood about in leather handcuffs and leg restraints, some of them clothed in fetishist rubber and vinyl. Westerners gawked. The Chinese were interested or not interested and regarded our merchandise as they would any other.

The first night in Beijing Bai Fuyuan took us to dinner

in a club that featured Chinese opera. The performance on the stage was highly stylized—I thought stiff. The performers wore makeup so heavy that you could not tell when one came on stage if it was an actor you had seen before or a different one. They sang, much of it falsetto. They gesticulated wildly. The dancing was athletic, involving leaps. For us it was all but impossible to follow the story lines, even though the programs summarized them in English.

It was a memorable experience. I wouldn't want to see much more of it, but I was glad I had seen this much.

My father was bored.

Over dinner he presented Liz a gift. When she opened the box and found a black sheer-and-satin teddy, she blushed deeply. It had been custom made to fit her, in Hong Kong, on the order of Charlie Han. I tried, but I frankly could not imagine how she would look wearing it.

The next day we attended the formal opening of the shop, which was held not in the shop but in a meeting room in the hotel. It was much like the show I had attended in Guangzhou. My father spoke briefly and said the same sort of thing I had said in Guangzhou. That night he saw himself on Beijing television, speaking Chinese.

The next day we set out in limousines to drive north of Beijing to the Great Wall of China, stopping along the way for a visit to the famous Ming tombs.

"There's something funny going on here," my father said as we rolled out of Beijing.

He and I, Vicky and Liz, sat in the backseat of the car. In front was a chauffeur and an interpreter. A glass separated the front and back seats. I was not sure the interpreter and chauffeur could not hear. I gestured that that might be the case, and my father nodded.

He went on. "The stuff Bai sends to the States is a shade off our colors. What he's selling in Beijing is an exact match of the original color. What's he got in mind?"

I suggested an answer. "He could prove that what we're

selling in the States, labeled 'Made in Hong Kong,' was in fact made in China, since the color is wrong."

"Which gets him what?" my father asked.

"It's not all odd colors," Vicky said. "I noticed a few items in the shop that are exact duplicates of our items."

"I'd like to know why that is," my father said.

"Well, let me ask Liz a question," I said. "What about Zhang Feng's chips? Do they follow Malloy's designs absolutely? Or are there little differences?"

"There are little differences," she said. "Nonperformance differences. Zhang's chips do precisely what Tom designed them to do, without question. But there are small differences in layout. An expert can tell how Zhang's chips differ. To be perfectly frank with you, some of Zhang's differences improve performance—which he would use to explain if you asked him why he deviated from the Malloy design."

"He would say he improved on it," my father commented.

She nodded. "He would say he improved on it."

"Okay," I said. "Bai Fuyuang could say his all-but-imperceptible deviations from our color standards *improve* our merchandise, make it more attractive."

"Then," asked my father, "why is some of the merchandise in his Beijing store dyed to our exact specifications?"

"Easy," said Vicky. "He's selling some merchandise he's not manufacturing in China."

"Meaning . . . ?"

"Meaning he's ripping us off somewhere, some way."

We had to pause to think about that. The implications were too complex to be considered in a minute's thought.

What can I say about the Great Wall of China? What can I say that hasn't been said? Just this—that you don't climb the Great Wall; you climb *on* it. There are places where it has been restored to make climbing possible for the average man or woman. Where we went, you were lifted to the Wall on a modern cable car. From the station at the top you could climb and walk a half mile or so in either direction. I'm glad I did it. I am not glad my father tried. He was too old for it, and even with help he could not do it.

That experience made me more aware than I had been before of my father's age. I knew he was beyond the age when he could do anything and everything, but seeing him struggle, flushed in the face, on those irregular stone steps made me acutely aware of his vulnerability.

And, I suppose, of my own.

57

JERRY

I did not tell Thérèse that I fooled around with Liz. I am not sure she would have found that particularly distressing. What counted for Thérèse was that we had a pleasant home in a pleasant place where she could indulge in her pleasant activities and never be challenged. What is more, she had an identity. Maybe for the first time in five decades she was not the girl who had been stripped, had her head shaved, and had been marched naked through the streets of Lyon. She was Mrs. Jerry Cooper, a gentle, intelligent, amusing Frenchwoman, married to an odd American who sold scanties. To our neighbors in Fort Lauderdale we were a little eccentric and the more interesting for it.

Did I love Thérèse? Absolutely. She was a comfort and a companion, and I knew I was lucky to have her.

Liz had nothing to do with that, and Liz understood. Big and gawky though Liz might be, she was smart as hell. She needed respect and got it, but she needed affection also, and men could take advantage of her. I determined I wouldn't. So it wouldn't be that way, I made sure we understood each other, from the beginning. I would enjoy her. I hoped she would enjoy me. But she was never to imagine I was in love with her, and she was not to allow herself to fall in love with me. That was how it had to be.

Liz was one hundred percent at liberty to involve herself with another man, anytime. I had one reservation, which I did not mention to her. She was not to give herself to my son, Len. And I think she had thought about it.

Her reaction to being given a sheer black teddy, sized for her big body, was endearing. She wore it that night in our hotel room in Beijing and every night after that until I gave her other things. Back in Hong Kong I asked Charlie Han to have panties—including crotchless ones—and bras made up for her. It amused Charlie, I am sure, to have a strip panel made up for Liz.

What in the world would she do with it? Charlie must have smiled and wondered.

Len described Liz with the word Rubenesque. I didn't know what that meant. I even had to ask him how to spell it. He showed me some pictures in an art book, to illustrate. So okay, she was Rubenesque, but I would rather have had her than some stringbean model—or, for that matter, any little Chinese girl I saw. Liz McAllister was a *woman*, all woman, every pound of her.

Len used another word. He said her hooters were enormous. I guess they were. I liked her big, shiny-pink nipples. She had an ample tummy with a deep, dark navel, a fleshy butt, and chubby arms and legs. She had a forest of pubic hair. It took some convincing to get her to show all these things. But when she did, and when I praised them, it made her ingenuously happy.

It was easy to make Liz happy.

She gave sloppy head, bobbing up and down energetically, with enthusiasm, and slavering, and watching her do it was almost as good as feeling it.

And she could talk about anything. She had the education I had never had myself but had seen to it that Len had. If Len had told her she was Rubenesque, she would have known exactly what he meant.

Hell. Liz was a fun girl. I was going to be in Hong Kong another ten days after we returned from Beijing. She was supposed to go back to Houston. I decided to keep her with me. Apart from everything else, she would be company on that long, long flight.

Len pressed Charlie Han on the question of why Bai Fuyuan could not match our colors precisely, and also on the question of why some of the merchandise in the Beijing store did match.

"I've been worrying about that," Charlie said.

We were at dinner at Mozart Stub'n, the Viennese restaurant I looked on as a refuge from Chinese cuisine. Vicky and Liz were with us. The place was within walking distance from our apartment building, and we had become known there.

"If he can make some items with exactly matching colors, why can't he make others?" I asked.

"It's not a matter of some items and other items," said Vicky. "It was different examples of the same items. I looked very closely. The same panty or teddy was piled up with those slightly nonmatching colors."

"Which means . . . ?" I asked.

"Which means," she said, "that not all his merchandise comes from his establishments in China. He's somehow getting his hands on some of *our* merchandise."

"I think he's not matching the colors because he doesn't want to match them," said Len. "He's got some reason for wanting to be able to distinguish what he makes for the Cheeks label from what is made here and elsewhere."

"I wish we could prove that," I said.

"Why bother?" Charlie asked. "The line is making a nice profit, so . . ."

"I'm going to talk with Henry Wu," said Len. "I want to know if the dyes he uses for us are unique."

"I wouldn't want Bai to think he can pull a fast one on

us," I said. "He had better understand who he is dealing with."

The next day we received an invitation to dinner from a man I had never met and Len had never met. His name was Yasheng Lin, and he was identified to us by Charlie Han as a Hong Kong billionaire.

I should have done more homework on Hong Kong billionaires. I had supposed that the world's real money men lived in the States chiefly, with a few in the U.K. maybe some in Germany, and a few in France—with, I should add, some in Japan.

I'd had no idea who lived on the Peak.

A Mercedes limousine picked us up at our apartments and set off on a climbing route that would take us to the highest elevations of Hong Kong.

We arrived at a compound. Like everyone else, I suppose, I had seen the *Godfather* movies and carried in my mind an image of the Coreleone compound. The Yasheng compound was the same, for real.

A wall surrounded it. We entered through a gate ostensibly guarded by a turbaned Sikh but in fact guarded by ominous little Gurkhas hovering in the shadows.

Inside the compound we faced an Edwardian mansion. But the compound also contained at least half a dozen homes on a private street inside the walls. Just inside the gate was a garage that housed three Rolls cars and three more Mercedes. To its left was a broad swimming pool faced by cabanas.

"I wanted you to see," Charlie Han said before we left the car, "how Hong Kong billionaires live." Then he added ominously, "The Honorable Yasheng Lin could buy Gazelle, Incorporated out of pocket change."

I glanced at Len. He stared at me. What had led Charlie Han to make that statement?

As we entered the mansion, the word *taipan* came to mind. This, surely, had been the home of some rich and powerful British trader. I wondered how long it had been owned by a Chinese.

Inside the ponderous iron-bound oak front door we waited in a cavernous foyer. Lighted glass showcases covered all the stone walls, displaying a varied collection of things someone thought worth collecting and displaying. Some of the items were Western in origin, and others were Chinese.

Charlie pointed out a set of cups. "Wine cups," he said. "Solid gold." He explained why each cup had in the center a stem capped with a gold ball. "The ball would hit your nose if you tried to tip the cup all the way back and drink all the wine at once. You would have to *sip* the wine. It was a way of keeping people from getting drunk."

Another case displayed a set of trophies won in yacht races. This confirmed my suspicion that the house had been British.

Still another case contained antique knives and pistols, also an apparently genuine steel chastity belt.

Most fascinating was an enameled crown, turquoise-colored, set with precious and semiprecious jewels, topped with a gold fringe of dragons. Ropes of pearls hung from the heads of the outermost dragons and would have fallen over the wearer's shoulders.

"Yasheng Lin," Charlie said under his breath as a door opened and a small Chinese gentleman came toward us.

"Good evening, Mr. and Mrs. Cooper, Mr. Cooper Senior, and Miss McAllister. Welcome. It is good to see you again, Charlie. Come with me."

Yasheng Lin was, I suppose, sixty to sixty-five years old. His face was what I would call Oriental, with slanting dark eyes and a shiny, faintly yellow complexion. He wore a dark blue double-breasted suit and a white silk shirt.

By gesture he directed us to an adjoining room where we found a bar and a buffet of hors d'oeuvres.

When I was in Paris, Giselle had taken me out to see the Palace of Versailles. This room was like the rooms in that palace: gleaming parquet floors, walls covered in pale yellow silk, graceful antique French furniture . . .

Two little Chinese girls served us. They might have been twins. Each wore a form-fitting knee-length cheongsam with skirts slit to their hips, showing and then concealing their sleek legs as they walked. These were made of silk, one green and one red, and they were embroidered with gold and silver thread. One girl brought us little plates and offered hors d'oeuvres from a tray. The other took our orders for drinks. I asked for a Scotch and soda.

"Well . . . Misters Cooper. You have learned to like Hong Kong, have you not?"

"I have," I said. "Very much. I'm impressed just now with the dresses your young women are wearing. I was thinking that maybe we should sell dresses like those in our shops in the States."

"Cheongsams," said Yasheng. "Yes. I have visited your shops. You could perhaps have them made up in sheer fabrics."

"I think they would sell made just as they are. They are very attractive."

"Well . . . perhaps they would be a—how shall I say?— a little pricey for the retail trade."

"You can't buy those in stores," said Charlie. "Mr. Yasheng has them made. If I had one made up like that— that quality silk, that embroidery—I'd have to charge you . . . say, two thousand dollars for it. I mean American dollars."

"You saw the one given to me in Shenzhen," said Vicky. "How much is it worth?"

Charlie Han turned down the corners of his mouth. "More than that," he said quietly.

Vicky frowned. "I suppose it's rude of me to ask the price of a gift," she said.

"Anyway, they are pretty, are they not?" Yasheng asked.

"Beautiful," said Vicky.

A servant—another little girl in a cheongsam—came into the room and spoke to Yasheng.

He rose. "A friend of ours has come. I will welcome him." He went out to the foyer and in a moment returned with a smiling and bowing Bai Fuyuan.

I began to wonder if this evening was not for some purpose other than to show us how a Hong Kong billionaire lived.

Bai greeted us all with great—I thought exaggerated—cordiality. He accepted champagne and sat down. He was wearing the white suit that seemed to be his trademark.

The conversation quickly turned to business. "You understand, I believe," said Bai Fuyuan, "that the honorable Mr. Yasheng is an investor in our enterprise."

"We didn't know that," Len told him curtly.

"Yes. To manufacture such a variety of goods in such quantities and to open the kind of stores you have seen requires a substantial injection of capital. Mr. Yasheng has provided."

"That would not be a loan, I imagine," my son said. "Mr. Yasheng owns your company."

"Quite so," said Yasheng. "I should say, however that the relationship is more subtle than that."

"Then we are dealing with you, sir," I said to Yasheng. "And not with Mr. Bai."

"No. You continue to deal with him. He will represent me in everything."

"I suppose the merchandise goes to Shanghai in your ships," said Len.

"And sometimes is flown to the States in my airplanes," said Yasheng. "Yasheng companies have invested in many enterprises."

So. The man was a taipan. I tried to remember what I had read about them. They exercised enormous economic power. With complete autonomy. This one might be one of the few left. Powerful though they were, there was little room in the world for their kind anymore.

"Then in a sense, at least," said Len, "we are partners."

He was speaking to Yasheng. "Do you know the meaning of the term 'ripped off,' Mr. Yasheng?"

"I do indeed."

"In some sense we are being ripped off, probably in a minor way. Mr. Bai manufactures Cheeks merchandise to Cheeks specifications. He does it very well. It would be difficult to distinguish a garment made in China from one made in Hong Kong or in the States. Except for one thing. The colors don't exactly match. Now—"

"This is true?" Yasheng asked Bai.

"It is true. The differences are subtle, but we have had difficulty matching the dyes. Black is black, of course, but—"

"The dyes are standard," Len interrupted. "The colors vary, not by chance, but for some reason. We are not complaining about that, not yet anyway, but there is something else."

"And what is that, Mr. Cooper?" Yasheng asked grimly.

"When we went to the store in Beijing we noticed that some of the merchandise in the showcases was Mr. Bai's colors and some was ours. In other words, not everything being sold in Beijing originated in China. Some of it came from somewhere else—Hong Kong, I imagine. Someone is selling—"

"Stolen goods," Yasheng interjected ominously.

"That thought had occurred to us," said Len, though it had occurred to him alone, not to me.

"Why do the colors vary?" Yasheng asked Bai.

Bai hesitated for a moment, then said, "So the inspectors can see that what we are selling in China is in fact made in China. That makes a great difference—"

"In the payoffs," said Yasheng.

Bai nodded.

I was surprised that they did not lapse into Chinese and leave us out of the conversation. Charlie glanced back and forth between Yasheng and Bai, looking apprehensive—in fact, miserable.

"Very well," said Yasheng. "Then what is the origin of the merchandise *not* made in China?"

"I don't know," said Bai. "The merchandise is examined well before it reaches the stores. The inspectors are satisfied, adjustments are made, and we stock the stores."

"Somebody is paying for the non-Chinese merchandise," said Yasheng. "Who is buying it?"

"I will make it my business to find out," said Bai. "I have no doubt I can do so."

"Do that."

We went in to dinner shortly. I cannot tell you what I ate. I didn't know. I didn't want to know. I have been told that birds'-nest soup has nothing to do with twigs and straw but comes from birds' saliva. I don't know. I don't want to know. Nothing we were fed was nauseating. The flavors were subtle. Bai and Charlie oohed and aahed over some of the dishes and pronounced them exquisite. I ate whatever it was that was exquisite. I complimented Yasheng and said the meal was wonderful.

No one said anything in the car as we descended from the Peak to Arbuthnot Street. We sat down in the living room of the first apartment—Len and I, Vicky and Liz. From the windows we could see the lighted tower of the Bank of China Building, lights that were so bright through our windows that we needed not switch on night lights to go to the bathrooms. We poured nightcaps and sat sipping them. We turned on the TV and without sound glanced from time to time at the Chinese television programs coming in from Guangzhou. Oddly, perhaps, the new government had not squelched the broadcasting from the BCC or CNN, but we did not want to watch or hear the news just then.

"I have an odd feeling," said Len. He was leaning back so far on his sofa that his head touched the wall. "Tonight. . . . Tonight the shit hit the fan."

I nodded. "There's been something wrong all the time."

"Someplace in all this there's larceny," Len said. "There has to be."

"We knew that and risked it," I said.

"I'm not sure we're the victims," Len said.

"We weren't invited up to the Peak just to see how a Hong Kong billionaire lives," I said. "Charlie was *told* to deliver us up there. And Christ, Jesus, when Meyer Lansky said his crowd was bigger than United States Steel, he couldn't have imagined—Yasheng has got to be *enormously* wealthy."

"I was appraising," said Liz. "I don't know the value of things, much, but I'll tell you, the wealth up there is *tremendous.*"

"Be a hell of a town to do business in," said Vicky.

"Under the Brits," Len said, "the maximum income-tax rate was sixteen percent. And it's not in Beijing's interest to raise it."

"So what do *we* do?" I asked.

"Sleep on it," said Liz.

So we did. Only I didn't sleep much.

That night Liz did not wear her teddy but stripped to the crotchless panties, nipple-baring bra, black garter belt, and dark stockings she had been wearing all evening. She knew that was more erotic than nudity. If she had been a smaller, more handsome girl, she could have been a showgirl. She had the instincts for it.

She also knew I was distressed and knew how to relieve.

Afterward we felt a want for one final brandy, and she put on a robe and went to get the bottle and snifters. Returning, she threw aside the robe and poured small drinks. We fluffed up the pillows and sat with our backs to the head of the bed, sipping placidly. I fondled her gently, and she fondled me.

"Forgive me," she said, "if I venture to meddle in something that's really none of my business; but I can't help but believe I know who's ripping off whom."

"Your opinion will be as good as mine," I said.

"Okay. It's Charlie Han."

"Charlie has been a damned good friend of mine since . . . well, since before you were born, Liz."

"I'm sorry, Jerry. But think about it. He rips off some of the merchandise he's having made for you here. Instead of sending it to the States, he sends it to China. He sells it there, probably for not much after he makes what were this evening called 'adjustments,' and pockets a profit. He's a hustler. I think I know the type."

"So am I. I ought to know the type."

"So you think he's not?"

"No, he is. You're right. But it's really hard for me to believe that Charlie Han is stealing from *me*."

"He's your agent. He counts the merchandise."

"Liz, really . . . don't ask me to believe this. Or . . . don't ask me to believe it until I see the proof."

"Well. Okay, I've said too much already."

She reached behind her back and unhooked the bra and then the garter belt. She was going to sleep nude. We always did.

As she slipped her stockings down, she whispered to me. "I can't tell you how grateful I am that you've brought me out here. It's the experience of a lifetime."

"I need hardly say that the pleasure has been mine."

"I dread going home. I won't see you anymore."

"We'll arrange it so we see each other," I told her. "We'll arrange it."

58

LEN

We breakfasted together the next morning. It was a Sunday, so Catherine did not have to be driven to school, and Maria had the day off, as all Filipino maids did that one day of each week. We decided that this would be a good day to take Catherine and J. J. for a drive to the south side of the island, where we would see Repulse Bay and have lunch in a restaurant in Stanley. Because the Toyota could not carry all of us, someone had to do something different. Liz volunteered for that. She said she wanted to see the famous shopping street Nathan Road in Kowloon. My father said he would go with Liz.

That is how we spent Sunday. Our driver suggested after lunch that we might like to see something of the New Territories. He drove us through a tunnel to Kowloon and from there out into the country. We went, in fact, within a mile of the border. We were close enough to the border to see the towers of Shenzhen. Though Hong Kong was now part of China, the border remained heavily guarded to prevent unwanted immigration. At one point we encountered a roadblock, and a Chinese soldier courteously but firmly ordered a U-turn.

When we got home Catherine wanted to know where

Grandpa was. We told her he was taking a nap. Where was Miss McAllister? She was taking a nap, too.

On Monday morning Vicky went with the driver to take Catherine to school. Maria took J. J. for a walk and Chinese lesson. As they walked, she would point out things and call them by their Chinese names. My father, and Liz, and I remained in the apartment. We had some E-mail and three faxes to scan and answer.

About 9:30 a call came up from the reception desk. An Inspector Kung Yuk-kam of the Hong Kong Police wanted to see us. I met him as he stepped off the elevator. My father was just behind me. Knowing that a police inspector had come to see us, he was as anxious as I was to know why.

"You are, I imagine, Mr. Leonard Cooper," he said politely. "And this gentleman would be Mr. Jerry Cooper."

"Yes. What can we do for you, Inspector?"

"I'm afraid I have some distressing news for you, Mr. Cooper."

I was gripped with cold alarm and nearly fell to the floor. I supposed the news was about Vicky and Catherine, probably about an accident with the car.

"You had in your employ, I believe, a man named Han Wong, more often called Charlie Han."

I stared blankly, not yet comprehending that he had said we'd *had* in our employ a man named Charlie Han.

"Am I wrong?"

"Uh . . . no. Charlie Han works for our company."

Inspector Kung nodded. "The distressing news is that Han Wong is dead. Worse than that, he was murdered."

"Murdered . . . ?" I said blandly. I had not yet recovered from the shock of believing, if only for a moment, that something terrible had happened to Vicky and Catherine.

"Yes. May I come in?" he asked, pointing to the open door of the apartment where I was keeping an office.

"Certainly," I said. I began to assemble my wits again. "Yes. Do come in."

Now it was my father who was numb and speechless.

I gestured toward the couch, and Inspector Kung sat down. He was a man in his fifties, as I judged. He was bald, though his hair on the sides of his head was thick and black and his eyebrows were heavy. He had a faintly daunting mien, I thought, with piercing black eyes that stared at the whole world accusingly.

"How was he killed?" my father muttered.

"With a knife. His body was found floating in the harbor this morning, just off Wan Chai."

Liz winced and covered her mouth with her hand, as if she were going to vomit.

"Have you any idea who did it or why?" I asked.

I asked, though I had a pretty good idea who killed Charlie Han. You don't steal from a man like the billionaire who had entertained us for dinner Saturday night. I remembered how Charlie had been absolutely trembling when we left the mansion. I was sorry now that I had raised the subject of somebody ripping somebody off. It had been Charlie, and he had been killed for it.

In another sense it would have been difficult to feel sorry for Charlie Han. He had assumed we were too stupid to see what he was doing.

Inspector Kung began to explain why he had as yet no idea who had killed Charlie or why. "He was engaged in many things. Gambling, smuggling, prostitution . . . maybe narcotics. Any one of his businesses could have brought him ill fortune."

"Charlie was an operator," my father said sorrowfully.

"If you knew, or suspected, he was engaged in all these things, why didn't you deport him?" I asked. "I thought Hong Kong is intolerant of petty criminals."

"Deport him? He was a citizen of Hong Kong. He was born here. He carried a Hong Kong passport. He lived in the States for many years, with what I believe you call a green card, but he was a citizen here."

"He spoke the language," my father said.

"Exactly what was your business relationship with him?" the inspector asked.

My father looked at me and nodded.

"Do you know what business we are in?" I asked.

"I do."

"Ten or more years ago we began to import a large part of our merchandise from Saipan, Hong Kong, Singapore, and so on. Seven or eight years ago my father and I visited Saipan and found our goods were being manufactured by slave labor. We took all our business away from there, and most of it was transferred to Hong Kong. We felt we needed an agent here, someone who knew our line of merchandise very well and spoke Cantonese fluently. My father had known Charlie Han for many years, and he seemed the perfect man. We hired him and sent him to Hong Kong. He was to contract with sewing shops, to provide and explain our specifications, and to inspect what they made to be certain it met our standards. He has been doing that . . . until now."

"What did you know of his other enterprises?"

"Only that he had some other enterprises. He lived too well for what we paid him."

"When and where did you see him last?"

"Saturday night, at the home of Yasheng Lin on the Peak. We had dinner there."

"Yasheng Lin invited *Han Wong* to dinner in his mansion?" the inspector asked incredulously.

"Yes. Also present was Mr. Bai Fuyuan, from Shenzhen."

"You have entered into an arrangement to allow Bai Fuyuan to manufacture goods for you. This begins to make sense. You understand, I suppose, that Bai Fuyuan is the Shenzhen agent for Yasheng. And—unless I am seriously mistaken—there are certain arrangements for goods manufactured in Guangdong Province to be exported to the United States as goods from Hong Kong."

"Got us," my father muttered.

Inspector Fung laughed. "Don't worry about that, Mr. Cooper. My concern is homicide. Even if I were worried about misrepresenting the origin of exported merchandise, I wouldn't touch this one. Yasheng Lin is a multi-billionaire."

I grinned. "And the People's Republic . . . ?"

"Is very happy to have him invest in Chinese industries."

"His *guanxi* is . . . ?"

"Limitless."

"Then," said my father glumly, "we probably never *will* find out who killed Charlie."

"I am assuming it is the result of some other of his enterprises," said Inspector Fung. "A man like Yasheng Lin is rarely so crude. Oh, never that crude. Come, think of it. A dark, foggy night on the waterfront. A knife. A body falling from the quay into the water of Victoria Harbor. It is a dramatic scene from Clavell, is it not? The killer might be Three-Fingers Somebody."

"Well, it happened," my father said.

Liz stood and sighed. "Would you like a cup of tea, Inspector?" she asked.

"That is very kind of you, Miss McAllister."

She went into the adjoining kitchen to make the tea herself, instead of calling on Maria to do it. She poured water from a two-liter green bottle into the teapot. I guess I haven't mentioned that in Hong Kong you don't drink the tap water. You don't even brush your teeth with it. In one of the world's most civilized cities, everyone but the bag ladies drinks bottled water.

"May I ask why you came to see us this morning?" I asked the detective.

"Routine," he said. "You are the dead man's employer."

"I understand he left a wife and children," said my father.

"Not really," said Inspector Kung. "He had a string of

girls, and sometimes he took his own pleasure with them. I don't believe there were any children."

"Which explains why we never saw any," I said.

The inspector glanced at Liz in the kitchen, as if he were about to say something too indelicate for a woman to hear. "He worked a string of the most attractive young women you could imagine," he said.

"Why didn't you stop him?" my father asked.

Inspector Kung smiled. "To stop prostitution in Hong Kong would require an army. Wouldn't it in New York? We discourage open displays of it, but—well . . . Han Wong did most of his business aboard his boats, which carried his girls beyond our waters."

"Boats?" I asked.

"He did not deal in street hookers. His girls were delightfully beautiful and were offered only to high-paying clients—typically to businessmen wanting to impress and influence other businessmen. He owned three yachts—party boats. He chartered them for very high prices, often for runs to Macau, where his clients gambled before returning to the boat and the delights of the girls."

Yes. I knew what he meant.

"You have never used his services of that nature?" the inspector asked.

"No," I said. "I am not sure we could afford it."

The detective sat and sipped the tea Liz brought him, as did the rest of us. It was an awkward time.

"May I respectfully suggest to you," said Inspector Kung, "that you have become involved in a rather complex business, with ramifications you do not understand. Han Wong was not a faithful agent for you. But you can employ honest agents in this city. May I suggest you retain a solicitor? Let him help you. You can navigate these waters. To great profit. But you must avoid the shoals."

After Inspector Kung left I spoke earnestly to my father. "I think we are in waters that are far too deep for us. I think we should pull out of Hong Kong and go home. I don't want to live here. I want to give up this apartment and go back to Greenwich."

My father stood, stared for a minute at Liz, and began to pace the floor.

"The hell with that," he said. "The goddamned Chinks are not going to run *me* out of town. No, sir."

"Which of us will wind up floating in the harbor?" I asked.

"Yasheng Lin. He's the goddamned key. I wouldn't be surprised if he also owns Zhang Feng. Multibillionaire! He's got tentacles everywhere."

"He can buy and sell us out of pocket change," I said.

"No, he can't. Us, yes. Sure. But we represent something he hasn't got. Just like Malloy. *We know what the fuck we're doing.* So does Malloy. So does Zhang Feng, maybe. If Yasheng destroys us, he destroys the business, because he can't run it without us. I've spent too many goddamned years in this business not to have learned something. We meet our competitors. We know our business. Could a bunch of Chink amateurs do it? Let 'em try it. Money ain't everything."

Then I got a phone call I had never thought I'd get.

"Is Chang Li. You remember me, Len?" She was the girl on the boat to Macau.

"Of course I remember you."

"Would like to speak with you. No ominous. No mean to blackmail you. Nothing like that. Would like to speak."

"Where and when?" I asked curtly.

"I live now in Miramar Hotel, Kowloon. Could you come? I do you no harm."

Late in the afternoon I knocked on her door.

My God! That beautiful little girl was as bald as a cue ball! Her head was shaved.

"This," she said immediately, touching her naked scalp. "This Charlie. When he make a girl *his* girl, he do this.

It supposed to make a girl wrong for any other man. He not want *his* girl to see other man."

She led me into her modest suite. She had a small parlor, a bedroom, a tiny kitchen, and of course a bathroom.

"Charlie, he do," she said, meaning that Charlie had provided the suite.

She poured us two drinks of good Scotch without asking if I wanted one.

"When you and I . . ." I said.

"Not then. When Charlie see I please you, then he decide I please him."

"You would please any man, Li," I said simply. "I can't imagine a man you would not please. If I were not married—"

"I live here. You visit me as you wish."

"No. It can't be. My wife is the mother of my children, and she is very smart."

"Ah. You lucky man."

I sipped the Scotch she had poured for me. "Why did you want to see me?" I asked.

"Charlie dead. You know why, maybe you can help me, small way."

"Why is he dead, Li?"

"Charlie stealing from you. Didn't you know?"

"We trusted him,"

At last the solemn little girl smiled. "He make whore of me. Didn't you know?"

"No."

"Yes. Charlie make whore. He buy me from my family and make me whore." She nodded. "It is done in China, in Hong Kong. I lucky maybe. He didn't sell me in marriage."

"Marriage?"

"I am from Quinghai Province. Girls sold there. I put on display, wearing sign that says my price. Auction. All kind man bid. Man work for Charlie hear I speak English. He bid me. Sneak me into Hong Kong. No buy me Charlie, I maybe marry to factory worker in Beijing, Shanghai, by now have babies, many."

"So you felt some loyalty to Charlie."

"Yes. Much better be whore for Charlie than—But they kill him, yes?"

"Who killed him?"

"He steal from you. Not much. Just a little, the same he steal from everyone he in business with. He steal a little and send into China to be sell in your shops."

"Who bought what he sold?"

"Bai Fuyuan. He dead too, you know."

"I didn't know."

"Yes. Why kill Charlie and not Bai? No percentage in that."

"What do you want me to do for you?" I asked.

"Tell Yasheng Lin I am good girl, no help Charlie steal. Tell Yasheng Lin I like be his girl."

"You mean . . . ?"

"Be whore for Yasheng Lin. Was good whore for Charlie. *You* know. Be good whore for Yasheng Lin."

"Do you need money?" I asked. "I mean, right now."

"Charlie leave me good," she said. "I live in hotel. I can live till hair grow out." The little girl ran her hand over her naked scalp. "Is much embarrass, yes?" she asked quietly.

59

Bai Fuyuan was dead. I do not conceal the fact that I was scared. Scared? Hell, I was terrified.

Given my choice, I would have done exactly what I'd said to my father I would do: abandon the apartments in Hong Kong, pull out of the Far East, and go home. We were deep in things we didn't know how to handle. I was a stranger, and afraid in a world I never made.

Not the old man. So far as he was concerned the world anywhere was not much different from what he'd learned on the mean streets, where you fought dirty, took your lumps, and gave lumps in return. He had made his bones, Vicky had told me. If I had heard that from anyone but Vicky I wouldn't have believed it.

My father was not about to be run out of Hong Kong. The first thing he did was to call and ask Hugh Scheck to identify a solicitor to represent us. Hugh E-mailed back in a few hours with the name of Sir Arthur Xu. I telephoned to make an appointment with him, and the next day we sat in his office.

Sir Arthur was not intimidated by the name Yasheng Lin. What was more, he was not in the least surprised by the brutal murder of Charlie Han.

The solicitor was a lifelong resident of Hong Kong, a graduate of a Jesuit school in Kowloon and of Columbia University, and received his law training at Gray's Inn, London. His office was much like the one occupied by Charles Laughton in *Witness for the Prosecution*. He dressed like Laughton in that film—in somber black with a heavy gold watch chain drooped across his waistcoat. He was, nevertheless, absolutely Chinese, with straight black hair showing a touch of gray only above his ears, slanted eyes, and a dusty-gold complexion.

"Yasheng Lin will not hurt you," he said. "If he meant to do that, he would have done it by now. What good would it do him, anyway? I can't imagine you were surprised to learn that Charlie Han was stealing from you."

"What about Bai Fuyuan?" my father asked. "Why in the world was *he* killed?"

"Yasheng had a clever thing going. *He* leased the space and bought the appointments for the Cheeks shops in China. *He* bought the merchandise—allowing Bai a percentage. Bai was his . . . traveling salesman, as you might say. But Bai and Han were greedy men. Han stole merchandise from you. It cost him nothing, except maybe some small bribes to men on the loading platforms. Bai bought it from him for a small amount—small, but profitable for Han because he'd paid nothing for it. Then Bai put it in the shops and charged Yasheng the same price as he got for other merchandise. Bai was making more than Han."

"How can you know so much about this?" I asked.

Sir Arthur shrugged. "You called me *yesterday,* did you not? I made a few inquiries."

I had noticed this about the Hong Kong Chinese. When in New York you asked for legal advice, asked for a bid, asked for information, you could expect, *perhaps,* to receive a response in ten days or two weeks. In Hong Kong you expected it before the end of the day, and usually got it.

"How did Bai Fuyuan die?" my father asked.

"When he learned of the death of Han, he took poison. Unnecessarily, I think."

"What should we do about this business?" I asked. "Frankly, I am thinking of pulling out."

"I suppose you could do that," said Sir Arthur. "Are you making any money?"

"Yes."

"And you have a good deal invested in a presence in Hong Kong. Two expensive apartments . . . You have made a commitment to doing business in this part of the world. You know the potential here. You know the future lies here."

"I guess we're not accustomed to the idea that our business associates will be stabbed and dumped in the harbor," I said.

Sir Arthur smiled tolerantly. "Hong Kong has a population approaching . . . oh, six and a half million people. How many people are murdered in New York per million, per year? Or in Boston or Philadelphia? Or Washington? This sort of thing is rare. But Charlie Han took unusual risks."

"In falsely labeling goods?" I asked.

"No. That is common. In stealing from Yasheng."

"It is common . . ." my father repeated.

"You should have secured the services of a Hong Kong solicitor from the outset. There are ways to shield yourself from the consequences of such misdemeanors. Actually, Han had you reasonably well protected. It was *he* who was violating the law. Of course, he was your employee . . ."

"Let me change the subject," I said. "You seem to know a great deal about us. What do you know about our business relationship with Zhang Feng?"

"I know who Zhang Feng is. More than that—*your* relationship, I know nothing."

"Can we trust him?"

"So far as you can trust any man. Zhang is one of the new breed of Chinese capitalists made possible by Deng

Xiaoping. It is my impression that Zhang would not go so far as to mislabel goods. On the other hand, he is sharp. If you have a contract with him, I would be sure it is nailed down at all four corners."

I left my chair and went to stare down at the street. Hong Kong was a strange mixture of great high-rise office buildings and old stone buildings from the colonial days. Sir Arthur kept his office in one of the old buildings, not far from the law courts.

"To what extent can we trust Yasheng Lin?" I asked.

"To the same extent you can trust Bill Gates," said Sir Arthur. "He will not lie, cheat, or steal. On the other hand, he will take whatever advantage there is to be taken. He is voracious. He is the fourth generation of his family to own and build businesses in Hong Kong. He is an empire builder."

"He *has* an empire," I said.

Sir Arthur smiled. "Are you a student of history, Mr. Cooper? Can you name me an empire builder who was ever satisfied with his empire and did not want a bigger one? Napoleon? Rockefeller?"

"Well, then . . . did he have Charlie Han murdered?" my father asked.

"Directly . . . no. He simply put out the word that Charlie Han was no longer under his protection. That is all it would have needed. Han was hated by many."

"And in twenty-four hours . . . ?"

Sir Arthur nodded.

"It's too damn melodramatic," my father said. "A dark and foggy night on the Hong Kong waterfront—"

"They don't kill with guns here," said the solicitor. "Guns are not allowed here, so they kill with knives, sometimes with machetes. It can be brutal, but it doesn't happen nearly as commonly as murder happens in some American cities."

"As I told you on the telephone," I said, "we will probably need to employ a new agent. Have you anyone to suggest?"

"Tentatively, yes, I do," said Sir Arthur. "You need someone familiar with the sewing trades, someone who can inspect merchandise for quality. I have in mind a young woman. Her name is Xiang Yi, often called Lily Xiang."

We met Lily Xiang in the dingy office of a small sewing company on Yee Woo Street in Wan Chai, not far from the waterfront and not far from where Charlie Han was killed. She was manager of the company and knew fabrics and the cutting and sewing trades very well. She had been with the company four years and was reasonably well content with her job, but she would be receptive to an offer of a better job.

She was a plump woman with coarse black hair unstylishly bobbed just below her ears, round, dark-rimmed eyeglasses, and a cigarette constantly in a corner of her mouth. She wore a pair of gray sweat pants and a white T-shirt.

Sir Arthur had arranged the meeting, so Lily knew why we were there.

"I know the Cheeks line," she said brusquely, almost immediately, having taken no time for amenities. "Maybe you don't know this, but we make certain items for you."

She picked up a pair of sheer white panties decorated with glistening rhinestones and showed them to us. They sold well in the States. The next item she showed us—a black lace bra with generous cutouts to show the nipples—did not sell nearly as well, but we had no complaint about how it was made.

"We do items made with sheer fabrics," she said. "Panties, nightgowns, teddies, negligées, and so on. We don't do things that require elastic fabrics or vinyl. I like to think we make *feminine* things. You know: loose and soft and provocative. The kind of stuff that flatters a woman, for herself and for her man."

"Which doesn't describe our whole line," I said.

"No," she said without hesitation. "It doesn't. I wear Cheeks things myself, but you show a good many items I wouldn't want to put on."

"What will you wear if you come to work for us?" my father asked bluntly.

"Well . . . not what you see me in here," she replied. She slapped at her pants. "Work clothes. What do you want me to wear?"

"I want you to represent our company," my father said.

"Understood."

"We will ask you to confine your smoking to private times and places," I said.

"Can do."

"How much are you being paid here?" I asked.

"A hundred eighty thousand," she said.

I looked at my father. "She means Hong Kong dollars," I told him. "Meaning, she is being paid . . . a little more than twenty-three thousand U.S."

"We'll double it," my father said blandly. "I want you to start tomorrow. Your first job is to locate an office. Bring the lease to us. Find an office big enough for you and a secretary. Like you, the office will represent our company."

We were not as careless as this might sound. Sir Arthur Xu had briefed us thoroughly on Lily Xiang.

When we returned to the apartments on Arbuthnot Street, we found we had a visitor. Zhang Feng had come to Hong Kong. When we arrived he was sitting at the Sphere IV.

He was a little nervous, since Vicky had told him emphatically that he could not smoke in our apartments. In fact, as Vicky had told me, he had stepped outside on our balcony to smoke, but being twenty-three floors above the street with only a waist-high barrier between him and a plunge, he had given up his smoke and retreated indoors.

I had wondered if he were associated with Bai Fuyuan. Apparently he was not. He said he didn't know Bai was dead. But he knew Charlie Han was dead and how he got that way, and he was troubled.

He tried to speak to me apart from the others. My father and Vicky decided there was some reason for that, and invited Liz to go across to the other apartment while Zhang and I talked in the office.

"Chang Li called me," Zhang said.

"I saw her," I told him. "Charlie shaved her head."

"She wants help," he said.

"That shouldn't be too difficult to arrange," I said. "Between us we should be able to come up with something."

"Such as?"

"The night we went to Macau, that was Charlie's boat, wasn't it? And Chang Li was working for Charlie."

"That was Charlie's business, partly: to provide entertainment. That girl is one of the finest he ever had."

"So he married her, as we might put it," I said. "He shaved her head so she wouldn't be attractive to other men."

"Charlie Han was a fool," said Zhang. "It only makes her *more* attractive. A prominent actress here in Hong Kong shaved her head . . . and got better roles than she'd ever had before. There is something intriguing about—"

"She wants to work for Yasheng Lin," I said.

"Every girl wants to work for Yasheng Lin. But he is not in the business of hiring girls like her."

"You are, apparently," I said. "You hired her with Charlie's boat, to entertain me."

"We have done good business together, haven't we?" he asked. "Mr. Malloy's Sphere Four is impressive. I understand it is doing well in the States."

"It has just been introduced. So far it is doing all right."

Zhang walked to the window and stared toward the Bank of China Building. A tropical rain had begun to fall. In fact, a typhoon was in the forecast.

"You wonder if I am owned by Yasheng Lin," he said.

"The question has occurred to us."

"I am not. He doesn't own *everything*. He owned Charlie Han and Bai Fuyuan. If he chose to raid you, he could probably own you—your Far Eastern operations, in any case. He controls more assets than many nations do." Zhang shrugged. "On the other hand, it is more difficult for him to exert his influence inside China."

"He is not the only Hong Kong billionaire," I suggested.

"He is not even the largest."

"So . . ."

"Anyway. My reason for coming to see you," said Zhang. "Mr. Malloy has contacted a Taiwanese supplier and is talking to him about buying certain electronic components from him. It must not happen. This could destroy *our* relationship. My government will tolerate a great deal, but not that. You must choose between a relationship with China and one with Taiwan."

"That choice has already been made," I said.

"Then rein in Malloy, please."

We did. I discussed it with my father after Zhang left, then called Tom Malloy in Houston and gave him the only direct order he had so far received from us.

"Okay. You're the boss, pardner," Malloy said. "But there *is* a problem."

"Which is?"

"We got a congressman here in Texas that's got a strong opinion about doing business with China. He figures we oughta do business with the non-Communist Chinese."

"You tell the congressman that I guarantee him one hundred thousand dollars support for his next campaign—provided he shuts his mouth on this deal."

"You're talking his language, pardner."

"Liz will be with you in a few days. Is there anything you want to tell me that she's going to report?"

"I figger everything's going damn well. Sphere Four is pickin' up steam."

"Would it if we didn't have chips at Zhang Feng's prices?"

"You make your point very persuasively."

"And our microprocessors?"

"Sometime next year two percent of all the cars sold in America will have engines controlled by our microprocessors."

"Kee-rist!" I said to my father after I hung up the telephone. "In five years we may be a high-technology company!"

By now the rain was pouring hard. We could barely see the bright lights on the Bank of China Building. He stood at the window and watched. I could guess what he was thinking: It was all so alien, all so much beyond his experience.

"Don't be too confident," he said. "We're also getting to be a company completely dependent on Hong Kong and China. That's chancy, Len. That's damn chancy."

The storm kept us in the apartments, where we didn't have much in the way of fancy dinner. We ate frozen things that night: pizzas and lasagna.

The kids were a bit afraid. Catherine looked out at the wind-driven rain and wondered. "Could it get so bad it could break through our windows?"

"Sissy! Sissy!" mocked J. J, though his own eyes were wide and wondering as he heard the wind whip rain against the glass sliders of the living room.

It was not Greenwich, Connecticut, for damn sure—though I had been there when a hurricane glanced off the town.

After the kids were long asleep and Vicky and I were in bed, aware that the worst of the monsoon had passed and that it was moderating, she talked about what my father had said.

"This place isn't us, Len," she said. "It can never be us. I have to wonder, the way your father does, if we aren't getting too dependent on it. I mean, what the hell are we doing? Catherine is learning two dialects of Chinese!"

"You want her to learn Spanish?" I asked.

"I want her to be an American."

"I'd much rather," I said, "she would be a Chinese-speaking American than a Spanish-speaking American."

That was all I had to say.

That night Vicky did her special thing for me. I felt her warm lips slowly sucking my entire scrotum into her mouth. We lay together that way for some time, she using her tongue to massage me gently, until I thought I might explode. Abruptly she moved to the tip of my cock and used her tongue on that, more vigorously. Finally she slipped down until she had the whole thing in her mouth and sucked hard on it. I *did* explode!

60

JERRY

I called Thérèse. I can remember when placing a call from one side of Paris to another was dicey, when calling Los Angeles from New York was a matter of calling an operator, giving her the number, and answering a ring half an hour later when she'd gotten the call through. They called that "long distance." By the mid-nineties, calling Fort Lauderdale from Hong Kong was a matter of punching in the numbers. Within five seconds the phone rang. Thérèse answered, and I told her I would be home in a few days.

She told me someone had run over the alligator on the street. It had risked crossing one too many times, and a driver who didn't give a damn had run over it and killed it. I can't pretend that I cared, though I had come to think of the creature as something of a neighborhood pet and realized I would miss it, sort of. I had never imagined it would bite me, and since I didn't have a dog or cat . . .

"Honey babe, I miss you," I said. "I wish you were out here, in Hong Kong."

That was a lie. Liz was with me.

"I not want to travel so far much, anymore," Thérèse said. "Hong Kong long way."

She told me about a bridge game she had played, then about the herons and their chicken necks. Friends had invited her to go on their boat for a cruise to Miami.

Thérèse would be all right. I would, in fact, see her soon. The truth was, we would fuck: we seventy-some-years-old citizens. We would do it, and we would like it. Once. Then again sometime. Not too often. Not nearly as often as I would have liked.

Okay. Liz was a sloppy cocksucker. She left me wet with her spit as she ran to the bathroom to rinse out her mouth.

But, God, I would have missed her if I hadn't had her! I had become too much involved with her.

Watching her run to the bathroom, fat butt bouncing, was a special small pleasure.

I could keep her. Sure. Yes, I could. But for how long? I had to think about that.

Then there was Len. The boy was—Christ! I should have been proud of him. And I was.

But there was something. He wasn't what I was. He wasn't what Buddy was. And maybe he was right, too. He wasn't reckless. He planned carefully and was not reckless.

Had I been, though? I guess not.

But I wasn't about to be run out of Hong Kong. By God, I wasn't going to be! Son of a bitch, I wasn't *going* to be!

Any more than I'd been run out of Philadelphia.

This girl we'd hired. Lily. She was damned smart. I couldn't believe what she told us one day within a week after we hired her:

"We're missing something," she said. "There's a marketing ploy that's not in use. I don't know how you *can* use it, but I want you two gentlemen to be aware of it. Maybe you can find a way to sell merchandise with it."

At this point it was no more sweat pants and T-shirts.

No more cigarettes dangling out of her mouth. She was wearing a dark blue miniskirted cheongsam. We sat over lunch in Luk Yu Tea Shop, the famous dim sum restaurant. As she wielded chopsticks with confidence and pretended not to notice that Len and I wielded ours more awkwardly, she talked business.

"I don't know how you advertise this," she said, "but do you have any idea why many girls wear crotchless panties under tight jeans? Hey! Crotchless panties under tight jeans!"

We shook our heads.

"Tight jeans," she said. "Bare pussies. Can you guys, being men, imagine how that feels? Rough, tight denim rubbing your private parts, every step you take. Hey! Girls *come!*"

"Why not no panties at all?" Len asked.

"Rear-end hygiene, Lennie. C'mon!"

I understood what she meant. So did Len. But she had asked the right question. How did we advertise it? I couldn't think of a way, and I doubted Len could, either.

By that day Lily had visited all of our suppliers and was satisfied that no one was ripping us off more than was conscionable. She had rejected one small batch of merchandise. Charlie, she said, had been letting some stuff through that was not up to standards—not much, just a little, presumably in return for a percentage.

"He couldn't help himself," she said. "I know the type. He considered that day lost when he didn't manage to cheat somebody. He must have been an endearing man," she added slyly.

Len took me to Kowloon Tong that evening, leaving behind a suspicious Vicky and Liz. We sat down in a courtyard open to the sky, where we had what the Kowloon proprietors imagined was a French-style dinner—snails, borscht, sole, and wine—in the company of a shyly beautiful little Chinese girl.

Len introduced her as Li, Mrs. Charlie Han. She was delicately lovely, with appealing almond eyes. But she had a dramatic characteristic, too. She had only a spare bristle of hair on her recently shaved head. I was supposed to imagine that I had been brought here to meet Charlie's widow, but I was not fool enough to buy that. It was obvious to me that Len had had her. It would have been obvious to Vicky, too, and I resolved that the two should never meet.

Well, what was I supposed to expect? I mean, Vicky was as fine a woman as any man was ever married to, but—Okay. So long as this did not get out of hand. Which obviously it had if he thought it necessary to introduce her to me.

"I want to do something for Li," he said solemnly. "I want you to do something for her. She was *sold* to Charlie. She'd been put on an open-air market and sold!"

"I can imagine."

"No, you can't. No. It's not so simple. Charlie supported her. He left her some money. But she needs a new connection. I am hoping we can provide something."

"What do you do, Li?" I asked her.

"I am whore," the little girl said with calming simplicity, obviously not in the slightest embarrassed.

I glanced at Len. "I am not sure we can hire any girls for that," I said.

"She wants to work for Yasheng Lin," my son said to me. "I doubt we have enough clout with him to arrange that. I am wondering if Lily could use her as a model."

"With no hair?" I asked.

"It grow out!" the little girl protested.

"It might make her the most famous model in Hong Kong," said Len. "She could travel for us. We could show her in China and even in the States."

I was emphatic. "And you keep hands off. She's not to be your plaything, my son."

"I'll keep hands off. You have my word."

"Li," I said to her, "how would you like to be a model and not a whore?"

"No whore?" she whispered.

Len answered her. "You do whore, we won't want you anymore. You wear the clothes we make, show them to people. And you will have to keep your head shaved."

She put her fingers to her head. "Embarrass this," she said quietly. "Many embarrass . . ."

"But it may make you famous and rich," I said.

Well . . . getting ahead of things, it did.

I'd had a lot of experience in my life. Experience taught me that the best way to confront a problem was to *confront* it. So I called Sir Arthur Xu and asked him if the best way to deal with Yasheng Lin was not to meet with Yasheng Lin and openly negotiate.

"Yasheng Lin," he answered, "likes straightforward dealing. Yes. Straightforward dealing."

So we went a second time to the imposing compound of the Hong Kong billionaire: Len, Vicky, Liz, and I, with Sir Arthur Xu and Lily Xiang.

We gathered on a stone terrace outside the mansion where we had a view of Hong Kong, the harbor, and Kowloon. We sat on white-painted cast-iron furniture. Torches provided the light. A fountain splashed. Girls in chenogsams served hors d'oeuvres and drinks.

Vicky wore the cheongsam given her by Bai Fuyuan. It was, I thought, a gesture of defiance. Lily's dark blue brocaded cheongsam was not a gesture, and she was not uncomfortable about the slit in her skirt that sometimes exposed her leg all the way to her hip. She was a Chinese woman, comfortable in Chinese wear. Liz wore a white lace minidress that did not flatter her.

Yasheng Lin greeted us as a gracious host. He was dressed as before in a double-breasted suit, this one black, a white silk shirt, and a regimental necktie.

I meant to avoid the topic of the death of Charlie Han, but he raised it immediately.

"I hear that your Hong Kong agent has been killed," he said. "Unfortunate."

He said it as if it were a matter of no consequence that he had heard about as a piece of business news, as if he had read a brief account of it in a newspaper.

"We have been very fortunate," I said, "in that we have been able to employ Miss Lily Xiang as our new agent."

"Yes. I know Xiang Yi by reputation. She is an excellent choice." He nodded at Lily. "My congratulations. I am confident that you will serve the Coopers well."

"I mean to," she said evenly.

We talked about the typhoon, then, and the recovery of the Asian economies.

After a while I turned to business. "You know, Mr. Yasheng, our company has committed itself pretty fully to doing business in China and Asia. Companies in this area have become the major suppliers for important elements of our businesses. I am not ready to say we are dependent on Southeast Asia, but we are deeply involved in it. Which I like, frankly. Also, I like the way you do business in this part of the world."

"Except the fact that Han Wong was stealing from you," said Yasheng with a faint smile.

"And from you, too, sir, if you don't mind my mentioning it," said Len.

Yasheng nodded. His smile widened. "I wonder if Charlie didn't learn that way of doing business in the States."

I don't know what Len meant to say, but I spoke before he could. "I suppose that's possible," I said. "Charlie Han lived in the States for many years."

"Bai Fuyuan was stealing, too," said Yasheng.

"Our other chief associate in this area is Zhang Feng, of Guangzhou. What can you tell us about him, if anything? Would you suspect he is stealing?"

"Zhang Feng is one of a new breed of billionaires made

possible by the policies of the late Deng Xiaoping. If he is delivering goods to specification at acceptable prices, what do you care if he has small deals going on the side? Han Wong was crudely stealing from your shipments. That is another matter entirely."

"And in so doing was also stealing from you," I said.

Yasheng closed his eyes and nodded again.

Sir Arthur Xu's face was rigid. He was not accustomed to doing business this way. Straightforward, he had said. This was more than straightforward. I had in effect suggested that Yasheng Lin bore some responsibility for the death of Charlie Han.

But it didn't appear to bother Yasheng.

I went on. "Mr. Yasheng, you are one of the wealthiest men in Hong Kong, perhaps one of the wealthiest men in the world."

Yasheng shook his head, simulating modesty.

"I has occurred to me," I said, "that you might want to *acquire* my businesses. You seem to acquire most of the businesses you—"

This was too much for Sir Arthur. "Oh, no," he interjected. "Mr. Yasheng is involved in real estate, chiefly, and—"

"And shipping," Yasheng interrupted. "Involving my group of companies in merchandising, as Bai Fuyuan recommended, was something of a departure for us. It did seem like a good investment. And I think it will be."

"Let us work together to *see* that it will be," I suggested.

"Nothing would please me more."

"I have no doubt, Mr. Yasheng, that you are a shrewd and careful investor. I'd like to offer some ideas as to why it would not be a good idea for you to acquire my company."

Yasheng raised a peremptory finger and ordered my drink refreshed. A girl rushed to my side with a new Scotch and soda. Others of the little girls hurried to the rest of the guests.

"In the first place," I said, "our stock is closely held, and we have no great outstanding debt. We are not interested in selling."

Yasheng nodded.

"Even so, a man with your resources could probably find a way to drive us out of business."

"If I wanted to. But why would I *want* to do that?"

"Which is my point entirely," I said. "I am sure you have much valuable knowledge and expertise in many subjects, but I also doubt you have much in the fields of ladies' intimate wear or the technology of computer chips."

Again, Yasheng nodded and did not speak.

I went on. "You just said that you thought selling Cheeks goods in China would be a good investment for you. You had a knowledgeable man working for you: Bai Fuyuan. Unfortunately, Charlie Han was stealing from us, and Bai knew it and was helping him. What is more, their defalcations were increasing and would have increased still more."

"That is true," said Yasheng Lin.

"I have a suggestion. I suggest we work in partnership, directly, and not through a man like Bai. We need to be represented by an honest manager. I suggest Lily Xiang. The work she will be doing for Gazelle in Hong Kong will not require her services full-time, any more than they required Charlie's. I suggest we make her our joint representative, with power to hire the help she will need."

"That is an interesting proposition, which I will take into consideration," said Yasheng.

I sipped my Scotch and waited to see if Yasheng wanted to say anything more. Then I went on: "Also, in our subsidiary Sphere Corporation we have acquired expertise in advanced technology. I acknowledge that I know next to nothing about it. In the beginning I knew nothing about the manufacture and sale of intimate underwear. In almost forty years I have learned a great deal about it. Learning a new line of business takes *time*, Mr.

Yasheng. If you are interested in advanced technology, I'd like to suggest we consider a relationship between your companies and mine in that field also."

"That, too, we can discuss," he said.

61

LEN

We returned to the apartments on Arbuthnot Road and shortly went to bed. Around two in the morning we were awakened by Liz's hysterical shrieks. An emergency squad hurried my father to Matilda Hospital, a private hospital on the Peak, and perhaps the finest in Hong Kong. The doctors there decided he had suffered a stroke.

Therèse arrived in two days. She moved into his room in the apartments. Liz had moved to the Kimberley Hotel in Kowloon, from where she departed in a few days for New York.

Five weeks later a chartered jet carried my father to Miami International Airport. He was able to travel by limousine to Fort Lauderdale.

That was the end of my father so far as the business is concerned. I call him every few days to report to him the developments in our businesses, but he is less and less interested. He is partially paralyzed and does not travel. He will never return to Hong Kong. He spends his time fishing, studying the alligators in the canal, and watching the birds come to eat Therèse's chicken necks. He spotted a manatee in the canal, which was for him a big enough event to require a call to Hong Kong.

And he writes. He spends hours every day writing his chapters of these memoirs. His memory is perfect.

We did enter into a form of partnership with Yasheng Lin. It is a complex deal, put together by Sir Arthur Xu, Hugh Scheck, and a firm of San Francisco lawyers specializing in business arrangements in Southeast Asian countries.

It is working smoothly. Our businesses are expanding. The name Yasheng gives us entry into places where we would not otherwise find a ready welcome.

Tom Malloy was right about the Sphere IV. It is steadily growing in market share. It goes against the conventional wisdom in the computer world, which is obsessed with miniaturization. Millions of people still want to work at what some computer gurus scornfully call desktops.

My personal attention is focused chiefly on the expansion of Cheeks into Asia. Bai Fuyuan was right when he said the Chinese would buy many millions of our items. We had expanded about as far as we could in the States. The Europeans have not been terribly receptive to what we sell. But we have a burgeoning market in China and Japan, plus a prosperous market in Malaysia, Thailand, Burma, and Singapore.

Lily Xiang has proved a fortunate choice for us. She supervises our Hong Kong manufacturing operations and manages our expansion into China. We have a different manager for Japan, and others, locals, in the other countries.

Vicky and I, with our children, spend eight or nine months of the year in Hong Kong. The kids are being educated there, and we can't run them back and forth between Hong Kong schools and Connecticut schools, so we make Arbuthnot Road our home most of the time. Of course, I have to make frequent trips to New York.

Sir Arthur arranged for us to have permanent-resident status in Hong Kong, a necessity. We carry United States passports but can live full-time in Hong Kong.

Poor Liz saw my father for the last time when she visited him at Matilda Hospital. She lives in Houston now. My father can't go there, and she can't go to Fort Lauderdale. She has thrown herself into her work, but I also understand she has taken to drinking a bit more and has developed something of a reputation for being indiscriminate about men. I see her whenever I go to Houston, which is not often. She offered herself to me. I turned her down as gently as I could.

Little Chang Lin has, of course, become an internationally famous model. She worked for us for a while, and then was picked up by a New York modeling agency. She models for us occasionally but much more often for designers. She has kept her head shaved, and sometimes she sticks flower decals on her head to give the appearance that she has had her scalp tattooed.

She is very grateful to me. And she is a problem. I can't resist her, and Vicky has found out about her. I have been with her only three times since the night we went to Macau—once in Hong Kong, twice in New York. Vicky is resentful, but she has not made a horrible fuss about it. She would if she thought Li threatened our marriage, I am sure. But Li absolutely does not. She is an appealing novelty, and Vicky thinks of her that way.

Finally, what goes around comes around. One October morning shortly after Vicky left to deliver the kids to school, an outing that always took an hour and a half, the telephone rang, and I had a call from the reception office on the ground floor.

"A Mrs. Sue Ellen Cooper is here to see you, Sir."

I told him to send her up, and shortly there arrived at my door my ex-wife, whom I had not seen in ten years.

"You haven't changed, Len," she said as she stepped into my office, took my hand, and offered her cheek for a kiss.

"You haven't either," I said.

She hadn't, either. She was still defined by her oversized boobs; almost forty years old, she was still taut of figure and was still the somewhat vacuous blond I had married.

She was direct. "I've come to ask you a favor," she said immediately.

I pointed to the couch and asked, "Which is?"

"I came out here looking for a job. My father sent me. The only really unusual qualification I have is that I am still fluent in Chinese. My father has given me references to two American companies with offices in Beijing, but I decided to come here first. I spent some time in Beijing, you know, and found it a pretty depressing place."

"You speak Mandarin," I said.

"So I've been forcefully reminded since I arrived in Hong Kong. Coming here, I tried to tell the cab driver where I wanted to go, in Chinese. I wound up having to tell him in English."

"You can learn Cantonese," I said.

She sighed loudly. "Could you give me a drink, Len? I'm in deep shit. I'm living at home with my parents, who despise me. I can't do anything right. I can't get or keep a job. I'm too good for the jobs and I can get and not good enough for the ones I want."

I stepped into the kitchen and poured her a Scotch. "What's with Mollie?" I asked.

"I haven't seen her in five years."

"I don't know what you'd do in Hong Kong," I told her. "It's not an easy place to get a job. Besides, you'd have to get a work permit, and they restrict those to people who have skills not readily available here."

She swallowed her Scotch and used the back of her left hand to wipe tears from her eyes. "I was hoping you could help me," she whispered. "I understand you're running an expanding business from Hong Kong."

The last thing I wanted was to have Sue Ellen in Hong Kong. I shook my head. "You see all the office I have here. We have another one downtown, but there are only three people working there. We have branch offices and stores on the Mainland—"

"Lenny . . ." she wept. To my amazement she dropped on her knees in front of me and yanked up her polo shirt, exposing her breasts. "Isn't this how a woman is supposed to beg?" she whispered hoarsely. "On her knees, with bared breasts?" I stared at her. She wasn't wearing rings in her nipples. In fact, I couldn't see the holes. Apparently she had stopped wearing rings, and the holes had closed. "Help me, Lenny! I'm begging you."

"Mollie taught you to give a first-class blow job," I said coldly. I am an evil man. I confess.

Sue Ellen's eyes widened. "Sure. Sure, Lenny. Why not?"

She did it, just as Mollie had taught her, just as she had done for me a hundred times. And when she was finished, she wiped her mouth and said, "Anytime you want it. And I'll be invisible. Your wife won't know I'm in Hong Kong."

"No, because you won't be. I'm going to send you to a woman called Lily Xiang. She does our hiring for the Mainland. If we have a job for you, that's where it will be."

When Sue Ellen had left, I called Lily and explained who was coming to see her. I told her she didn't have to hire Sue Ellen, that it was up to her. Of course I knew she would. I didn't have to tell her that I wanted my ex-wife out of Hong Kong and as far away as possible.

Tianjin, once called Tientsin, is a river port not far from Beijing. It is a city of more than six million people, the third-largest city in China, and we had two Cheeks stores there. It is the site of a university, has museums and art galleries, and Lily thought Sue Ellen would be happy there. She appointed her her own deputy, so to speak, and assigned her the duty of making frequent trips to Beijing to look in on our three stores there. Also, she was to visit container ships as they arrived from Hong Kong carrying our goods. It was a responsible job, and Lily proposed we pay well.

So . . . I am an evil man, but I did something good for Sue Ellen, too.

I am not ashamed of myself.

The world's best-selling novelist returns
with a high stakes game of moral ambiguity,
love, betrayal, and dangerous consequences in

NEVER
ENOUGH

1

SATURDAY EVENING, APRIL 20, 1974

Four of them were together that Saturday evening: Dave Shea, Cole Jennings, Bill Morris, and Tony DeFelice. It was a warm spring evening, and teenagers from Wyckoff, New Jersey were doing what teenagers everywhere in America were doing: hanging out.

They and their peers groused constantly about what teenagers always grouse about: that there is "nothing to do." They had hung out on the streets of Wyckoff and Ridgefield, sometimes sitting on the fenders of other people's cars. They were conscious—sometimes resentfully conscious, usually just amused—that they were not welcome on the streets of the several small towns they frequented. Teenagers generally were not. They were not thought of as menacing, only annoying and nuisances.

Apart from sitting on cars, apart from sometimes obstructing sidewalks, they were often boisterous and loud, capering around, slapping at each other, shooting punches that were not meant to land. The police often ordered them to move on. Only rarely was any action taken against them, and that usually was just notifying their parents.

With an exception—

When they were tanked up with beer, they could make themselves a real problem. Occasionally, only occasionally, one or more of them was arrested and held until his parents could come and take him home.

These four—Shea, Jennings, Morris, and DeFelice—had minor reputations as more than common exuberant troublemakers.

—Dave Shea was a handsome young man, tall and muscular, a football player. He was charismatic. Every girl's dream was to date Dave Shea. He was his school's quarterback two years, during which years his team lost only one game. In his senior year the team went undefeated. Besides that, he was an outstanding scholar. He was inducted into National Honor Society in his junior year. His special subjects were mathematics, chemistry, and physics. As of April he had accepted a football scholarship at Rutgers University. Without the scholarship he would have been unable to go to college. But he had the scholarship, and his future seemed assured.

He had, though, a dark side. It wasn't the beer. The unhappy fact was that Dave would *cheat*. He did it on the football field, where he had an exceptional talent for knowing when officials weren't looking and then clipping, and for face-mask violations, even for punching an opposing player on the nose. In close contact with a defensive lineman, he might growl "Nigger!" and precipitate a furious assault that got a star defense man ejected from the game, while Dave stood gaping and shaking his head and ostensibly wondering what had caused the foul. In the chemistry lab he knew what results were expected from a problem in qualitative analysis and pretended to have achieved that result, when he really hadn't. He was in fact a good player and a good student, but he had his little tricks to make himself look even better.

"You're good enough, Shea." In the manner of teenagers, they called each other by their last names. "Why . . . ?"

"Look, Jennings. Your family will send you to college,

no matter what. You're smart, too, but you don't need a scholarship. I *do*. I have to be, by god, good enough to . . . "

"Gotcha. But you *are* good enough!"

"Yeah? Well, don't begrudge me a little insurance on it. The son of a wholesale grocery salesman who drives around the country begging for little orders . . . Hey! Like Willy Loman. Like in *Death of a Salesman*. They add up their nickels every month, hopin' there's enough to make the payment on the car. I don't want to live like that, Jennings!"

He didn't want to live without sex either. Hung like a horse, he first shoved his big penis into a girl when he was thirteen years old.

She was seventeen.

"Jesus Christ! The guys said you're . . . Hey, I can't take all that, Shea."

"Bet ya can. Why would I have it if a girl can't take it?"

"Well . . . Hey! God almighty! Hey! I wouldn't have believe it!"

Eventually, Amy, who also declared she couldn't possibly, but did. And complained it hurt.

You gotta be a football hero to get along with the beautiful girls. Okay, he was a football hero. It was no disadvantage to be known for being a stud.

—Cole Jennings played basketball and was good at it. He was tall, six-feet-six, and had an indefinable agility on the polished floor that brought him recognition as a valuable player. His blond hair fell over his forehead as he dribbled toward the basket, dodging this way and that, avoiding the players trying to guard him, until at the last moment he passed the ball to a teammate close to the goal and charged in to take the rebound if the shot missed. He made most of his points by capturing rebounds and jamming the ball through the basket.

He, too, was an excellent student. One of them, Dave or Cole, would be valedictorian of their high school class.

As Dave had suggested, Cole did not need a scholarship, athletic or academic, to go to college. His father was senior partner in a major realty firm. His family could and would pay his tuition at any school he wanted to attend.

From the time he was old enough to drive, Cole had his own car. That night he was driving his graduation present, already given him though graduation was six weeks away. It was a black Pontiac TransAm. That his parents had given such a car to an eighteen-year-old boy spoke something about their indulgence and their judgment.

Cole was a responsible young man, and though he could burn rubber he didn't. He was in fact sober and thoughtful, compared to Dave.

Dave was immensely jealous of Cole's sporty new car. He never even got to drive his father's old Chevy. That car was too important to making a living for his father to allow his son to drive it.

—Bill Morris played both football and basketball, though he was not the star that Dave and Cole were. He spent most of his time on the bench. Even so, he "went out" for sports and was considered a jock. All of these four were. He was not the scholar his two friends were, either; and his parents had been squirreling away money for years, in anticipation of his college tuition. Bill would not win a scholarship.

He was a solid young man, not heavy enough for football and not tall enough for basketball. On the basketball floor he wore plastic-rimmed eyeglasses held in place by a rubber strap behind his head. On the football field he wore no glasses and relied on a slightly blurry vision of the developing play. Since he was a guard and all but invariably was blocked after he did or did not block *his* man, it made little difference. He was dark-haired, and oddly was already showing, on his forehead, the initial evidence of baldness.

—Of the four, many would have called Tony DeFelice the most interesting. They were all jocks, but Tony was

a jock in a very different sense. He was a Golden Gloves
boxer.

He was a welterweight, knife-thin, with muscles as hard
as the steel of a knife. Many were afraid of him, but he
had been trained to restrain himself and never use his
boxing skills outside the ring. His ambition was to turn
professional.

He was an extremely intense young man, with hard
eyes. People who knew him well were aware that he had
a ready sense of humor and found amusement in all manner of things and people.

His family owned a score of packer trucks and collected
trash and garbage over a wide area of Bergen County.
They were said to be "connected." It was not true. They
were a family of shrewd, hard-working Italian immigrants,
who had hauled first in a single mule-drawn wagon and
had gradually worked their way up to the considerable
business they now owned.

On this April night it was the same old thing: nothing to
do. The four boys had bought six-packs of beer and drunk
twenty bottles among them. The remaining four bottles
were on the floor of the backseat of Cole's car. A little
after ten Cole drove into the parking lot of Pizza Palace
on the edge of Wyckoff.

The Palace might more realistically have been called
the shack. It had only four small tables. Customers were
expected to take delivery of their pizzas, ordered earlier,
and drive them home. The boys ordered two pizzas and
returned to the car to wait the twenty minutes until their
pizzas would be ready. They opened their last four bottles
of beer and talked about whether or not they should drive
off during the twenty minutes and buy another six-pack
or two.

They had sat there, drinking their last beers and talking
aimlessly when Jim Amos came alongside the car.

"Well, if it ain't Slaw," he said in a beer-slurred voice.

Slaw was a nickname sometimes fastened on Cole. He didn't like it, but he didn't make an issue of it.

Amos was twenty-four years old and had served four years in the United States Navy. He was known in the town and area as a drunk and a bully. He would walk up to a smaller and younger boy on the street and ask him what was the finest service in the United States armed forces. The boy might not know that Amos had been in the navy and might say United States Marines or something else. If he didn't say navy, Amos might deck him.

Or he might say, "You're wrong, and I'll let you buy me a few drinks to make up for it."

In any case, Jim Amos was a swaggering bully. He'd been beaten up two or three times, for having taken a swing at the wrong young man; but that had not discouraged him, and he remained a blustering punk.

Tonight he was feeling aggressive.

"Slaw and his Three Musketeers. Nice car," he said as he hopped up on the fender and sat.

Dave came out of the passenger side, fast, and rushed around the car. "Get your ass down from there, Amos," he yelled.

"Y' gonna make me?"

"I'm gonna make you."

Cole was out of the car now, followed by Bill and Tony from the backseat.

"Oh. All four of you. Fine. Suits me. Who's first?"

Dave grabbed Amos by the legs and threw him off the fender, onto the gravel of the parking lot. Amos was drunk, but he was quick and strong. He scrambled up and charged Dave, throwing a shoulder against his chest and knocking him back against the car, where he was vulnerable to the punch to the chin that Amos threw.

Amos set himself to throw more punches to Dave's face and down one of his opponents. But Cole grabbed him from behind and wrestled him away. He punched him hard on the kidneys.

Amos broke out of Cole's grip, turned, and punched

him in the stomach. Cole doubled over and vomited beer.

Bill stunned Amos with a hard punch to the ear.

Dave was furiously angry. As Amos momentarily dis-
oriented, Dave shot a hard fist against his nose, which
collapsed in a spray of blood. Amos shook his head and
moaned. His knees began to buckle. He was finished.

But Dave's anger was not assuaged. He stepped up to
the staggering Amos and put every ounce of his weight
and strength into a crushing blow to Amos's jaw. Amos
dropped backward to the gravel. His head hit with a sickening crunch.

The police arrived a moment later. One of the officers
knelt beside Amos and examined him.

"This man is dead."

The families gathered at the Bergen County Jail.

The Sheas were frightened. Dave's mother was weep-
ing, and his father's lips trembled. "That poor boy! That
poor boy!" Mrs. Shea kept murmuring through her tears.
She meant Jim Amos.

The Jennings family was grimly composed. Stuart Jennings was prepared to confront trouble and had summoned
his lawyer.

The Morrises seemed not to comprehend what was going on. Their faces were blank, as though they were in
shock, which in fact they were.

Anthony DeFelice glowered. He was not connected, but
sometimes it was shrewd to allow some people to imagine
he was.

Witnesses from Pizza Palace assembled to give state-
ments. None of the witnesses was quite sure what had
happened, except that all agreed Tony DeFelice had not
hit Amos.

From that point, all was confusion.

"Those three there, they all hit him. I seen 'em," an old
man with a three-day stubble of white whiskers declared.

"It was self-defense," Dave asserted angrily.

"Three of you? Self-defense against *one feller*?"

A fat girl spoke. "Jim Amos was a drunken bully. He was always starting fights."

"We know that," said the chief of police. He was a muscular, middle-aged man in a suntan uniform. "On the other hand . . . Well—"

"He's dead," said the old man. "An' three of 'em were beaten' up on 'im."

"Which one of you swung the punch that broke his neck?" asked the chief of police.

"Uh . . . Just a moment," said a white-haired man with a flushed face. "I'm going to advise these boys not to answer that question. Or any others, until they've had a chance to consult with counsel."

The white-haired man was Lloyd Paul Strecker. He was attorney for the Jenningses and had arrived at the police station before they did. He had a formidable reputation in Bergen County, not just for being a tough lawyer but for his political connections.

An assistant district attorney arrived. Her name was Lela Goldish, and she was about thirty years old, an attractive young woman, though with broad hips and a priminent butt. She was also hyper, moved in jerks and spoke in clipped sentences.

"What've we got here?" she asked.

The chief of police gave her a brief statement.

"Manslaughter," she said. "Maybe involuntary manslaughter. Sure as hell not murder."

"Okay," said Strecker. "I think these boys should be given a chance to confer among themselves. They are all involved. They should sing from the same sheet."

No one disagreed. Dave, Cole, Bill, and Tony went into a little conference room to talk.

Dave put his elbows on the table and his face in his hands. "Well . . . " he said. "It's the end for me. Manslaughter charge. There goes my scholarship. There goes my friggin' life. If I don't go to the slammer, anyway Rutgers won't want me. It's the end!" He sobbed.

"You didn't have to hit him that last time," said Cole. "We had him. He was finished."

"I was . . . mad," Dave sobbed. "The *son of a bitch* . . . "

"We're the witnesses," said Tony calmly. "Whatever we say happened, happened. Self-defense."

"They won't buy that," Dave muttered. "Four of us . . . "

"Only the guy that shot the last punch," said Bill Morris. "He was out. The guy that—"

"Yeah, sure," said Dave. "*I* killed him."

"Jesus, man," said Cole. "I guess it's gonna go tough for you. I don't think you'll get a big sentence, but—"

"But goombye scholarship, goombye chances, goombye future," Dave sobbed. "I'll wind up like my old man."

"We oughta talk to the lawyer," said Tony.

They asked Strecker to come in.

"Here's where it stands," he told them immediately. "We can make it voluntary manslaughter. The man who threw the last punch can plead guilty to that. He'll get probation."

"But he'll have a felony record," said Dave despondently.

"Well . . . Actually, that can be expunged from the records in a few years. It won't prevent a man from getting into law school, for example—because the record won't exist."

"But right now—" Dave muttered disconsolately.

"For a while it will be an impediment," said Strecker.

"An impediment that—"

"Can ruin his whole life," said Cole sadly.

"I see where this is going," said the lawyer. "I'm going to leave you boys to talk together."

With the lawyer out of the room, the four boys sat silent for a full minute. Then—

"I'm the one with the most to lose," said Dave. "You guys are going to college because your families can pay for it. Mine can't. My scholarship is the only way I'm going to get a college education. The only goddam way."

"What you're saying," said Tony, "is that one of *us* should confess he shot the last punch."

Dave closed his eyes and nodded. "I'm the only one whose life is on the line."

"I'll go this far," said Tony coldly. "If one of these guys wants to take it, I won't screw it up. I won't tell the truth."

Dave looked at Cole. "You've got the *least* to lose. You're going to whatever university you choose, because your family will pay for it. You've got a first-class lawyer. Your family and your lawyer have got political connections. You can come out of this smelling like roses. *I* come out smelling like shit."

Cole drew a deep breath. "Except for you, Tony, we all hit him. All of us. Dave couldn't have—Well, he couldn't have if Bill and I hadn't done what we did. I mean, I figure we *share* the responsibility. And—Dave's right. He's got the most to lose. I've got the least." He stood and opened the door. "Mr. Strecker—

The lawyer listened gravely to what Cole told him. He shook his head. "Alright. I don't buy it, but if that's what you want to do. I know what you have in mind."

The newspapers were angry—

TEENS BEAT NAVY VET TO DEATH!

Rampaging Wyckoff teenagers, drunk on beer, beat a navy veteran to death in the parking lot of Pizza Palace Saturday night.

What began as a Saturday-night rumble, arising from the fact that the veteran sat on the fender of a car belonging to Cole Jennings, 18, resulted, after a savage beating, in the death of James Amos, 24, a veteran of four years service in the United States Navy.

Cole Jennings has entered a guilty plea to involuntary manslaughter. His companions, David Shea,

William Morris, and Anthony DeFelice, have not been charged.

James Amos, Senior, father of the slain young man, says that his son had an exemplary record in the Navy and had never been in any kind of trouble at home.

"Half the town believes that," said Bill Morris.

"And the other half knows what a prick Amos was," said Dave.

"Anyway . . . it's all settled," said Cole. "Three years probation, after which the record will be erased. I'm accepted at Princeton. And—" He turned to Dave. "Your scholarship is intact, and you'll be going to Rutgers. All's well that ends well, huh?"

Dave nodded. "All's well that ends well."